GEEK VERSUS GEEK

36 heated debates on *Trek* vs. *Wars*,
Marvel vs. DC, Alien vs. Predator,
and so much more

From the pages of *Geek Speak Magazine*

EDITED BY RACHEL HYLAND

Cover art by Mark Gonyea

Overlord Publishing
overlordpublishing.com

Copyright Declaration

Overlord Publishing. As was foretold.

ISBN: 978-1-925770-05-6

1 2 3 4 5 6 7 8 9 10

For Kai, a formidable opponent indeed.

CONTENTS

FOREWORD
TO ERR IS HUMAN, TO ARGUE, DIVINE

People like to argue, and if your first instinct was to argue with me about that fact, well, you've sort of proven my point. Arguing, provided there are no real stakes, is fun. That's why we fight (hopefully good-naturedly) over whether Bradbury is better than Jones (he isn't, although he is excellent), whether the sonnet is superior to the sestina (depends on what you need it for, but generally, yes, it is), and whether dogs are better than cats.

Arguing is an important means of building a community. Yes, it can lead to gatekeeping and exclusionism, both of which we can hopefully agree are bad things, but those little debates—can Captain America defeat Cyclops in fair combat? What would happen if Matilda met Eleven? Who's better, Batman or Superman?—keep us unified in our engagement with the things we love. Sure, we may be fighting about them, but we're fighting passionately, as people who share a common ground.

Sometimes arguing is what lets us solidify or reconsider our positions. Sure, I may not change your mind, and you may not change mine, but by discussing my opinion and listening to yours, I can find my way to a deeper understanding of the conflict as a whole. It's good. It's healthy. And—again—it's fun. We need more fun.

The world is full of big, important arguments with real consequences for real people. Arguments that can harm far more than they can heal: arguments where the cost of losing is concrete and sometimes more than people can handle. But this just makes it more important for us to occasionally argue X-Men vs. Teen Titans, alligators vs. crocodiles, Snow White vs. the Snow Queen, and all the other little, delightful, eventually inconsequential minutia of the fannish heart. It's not wasting time. It's recharging our batteries and finding our way back to equilibrium.

In this volume you will find a variety of arguments, only a few of which have the potential to carry consequences. Most are, as I've already said, simply a matter of kicking back, strapping on the verbal boxing gloves, and having fun. We need more fun.

If you disagree, well. We can always argue about it.

Seanan McGuire
December, 2017

INTRODUCTION

We all know the joy of a really good argument. You have an opinion, you know your stuff, and you let loose all of your thousand-dollar-words and collected wisdom on an unsuspecting enemy who is firmly opposed to all you hold dear. It's fun! Especially when it happens to be about some obscure (often very obscure) point of pop culture. Here, a collection of thirty-six just such arguments, all of which are passionately argued from almost diametrically opposite viewpoints, mostly in a collegial spirit, but no less furiously for all that.

Many of these are debates of their time – for example, it would be difficult for William Cashin to so stridently make a case for DC movies over Marvel movies as of this current writing as he did in 2010, though doubtless he'd give it a red-hot go; and the appearance of disgraced comedian Louis C. K. in anecdote here would doubtless have been presented with a trigger warning, or simply excised completely, were it written today – but the fervor with which they are put forth is simply timeless. Across seven years, the crack staff of *Geek Speak Magazine* – along with a few very welcome guests – faced off on such burning subjects as the classic status of *2001: A Space Odyssey*, the feasibility of international copyright and *Buffy the Vampire Slayer*'s highly controversial sixth season. You know. The important stuff.

These are discussions that are, in many ways, highly personal – how many people care about Christopher Paolini's dragon-laden YA series *The Inheritance Cycle* enough to rail against it? – but at the same time, are entirely universal. Because we've all had a conviction that we've held dear in the face of intractable resistance, and we've all wished we had the wherewithal to make our case in full, without fear, favor, nor feverish interruption.

True, even these exponents of the craft may not have actually "won" any of these tussles, but they have most definitely been heard.

And sometimes, that is enough.

– Rachel Hyland, Editor-in-Chief
Geek Speak Magazine (2010 – 2017)

2001: A SPACE ODYSSEY
A TERRIBLE, TERRIBLE MOVIE
by Rachel Hyland

The first time I watched this film, I was twelve years old, deep in the grips of the *Star Trek*-ian love that would soon lead me to embrace the Space Opera subgenre as a beloved playground. I had long been a lover of Fantasy, both in literature and on film, but serious sci-fi was a brave new world little explored by the nascent geek I then was. Sure, childhood favorites like *The Last Starfighter* and *Flight of the Navigator* — and, of course, *Star Wars* – had kept me riveted for multiple viewings, and repeats of old TV shows like *Doctor Who* and the original *Battlestar Galactica* continued to broaden my understanding of the genre, but it was with this initial viewing of *2001* that I made a discovery I could not until then have imagined: science fiction can be boring.

(I hated it.)

I watched it again at sixteen, at the suggestion of a pretentious boyfriend who was sure that it was terribly hip and cool of us, as if anyone could be said to have been hip and cool in the 90s, which none of us were, except perhaps for Luke Perry.

(Still hated it.)

I watched it again at twenty, compelled to do so by a film school-attending friend who wouldn't shut up about the compelling allegory of child growing to adulthood or some such, and okay, sure, I got it. I just didn't care.

(Still hated it.)

My most recent brush with this try-try-again lunacy, before today, was a couple of years ago when a revival theater was playing *2001* in a late-night screening, and I went along under protest, but assured by all that I would surely appreciate the grandeur and beauty of this idiocy if only I could see it in its intended form. Liars!

(Still hated it.)

Which brings us to my latest viewing, which I endured with much the same grace as a truculent teenager receiving a lecture on proper bedroom cleanliness. I groaned. Rolled my eyes. Occasionally flung pillows and stamped my foot furiously, more at myself than anything for deciding to take on this nonsense. I spent an hour and a half so, so bored I spent the time jointly watching the movie, searching eBay for vintage Trixie Belden books and playing *Words with Friends*—after about half an hour I decided to get up and bake some muffins, all the while still watching, still suffering. Then came the part with Dave (Keir Dullea) and Frank (Gary Lockwood), and the malfunctioning HAL 9000 computer against which they were forced to plot, and I got all interested in the movie for about three minutes... until suddenly I was confronted again with an inexplicably extended black screen, a sound analogous with an orchestra tuning up, and then a bunch of heavy breathing that seemed to last an eternity. I got interested in the movie one more time after that. One. Only the death of HAL, quite heartbreaking in his childlike humanity, managed to rouse me from my apathy for a moment... but even that was utterly spoiled by needless, grating reiteration. "I'm afraid... My mind is going... I'm afraid... My mind is going... I'm afraid..." GEEZ, STOP WHINING, HAL!

My inescapable conclusion: *2001: A Space Odyssey* is a terrible, TERRIBLE film.

But let me go back to the beginning, so that we might further explore why.

From the very outset, this movie makes it clear that this is not going to be some jaw-dropping thrill-ride. The first chapter, helpfully entitled "The Dawn of Man", is just tedious, all lengthy silences, drawn-out establishing shots, inordinately long transitions and cacophonous ape-like creatures being attacked by predators, puzzling over the presence of what is, essentially, a big rock, and then going all Ape Fight Club once they learn to use bones as tools/weapons. Indeed, that whole part of the movie is probably the most irritating quarter hour of any sci-fi film ever, and in this I am including the bit in *Contact* when Jodie Foster is communing with the aliens and you just want to smack her upside the head and demand that she stop staring meaningfully at the camera and just *say something already*. Indeed, in this I am including all of *Contact*. I mean, dude, at least give us a David Attenborough narration: "The Dawn of Man rises over the savannah..."

Then, miraculously, Man has dawned and now we're in space, and there are space executives videoconferencing with precious, if dim, young moppets and engaging in banal chitchat that is way more portentous than they make it seem. There are odd happenings at a distant outpost and a secret discovery on the moon and lots of 60s fashion, including one woman's hat that makes her look like the little toadstool from *Mario Kart*.

"18 Months Later" and the first manned mission to Jupiter is put in jeopardy by the shenanigans of the onboard artificial intelligence, the aforementioned HAL 9000, who has serious reservations about their objective and who takes self-preservation to aggressively homicidal heights. But it turns out that HAL's conflict could well have arisen from his awareness that the trip to Jupiter's purpose was not mere exploration, but to discover what might be the origin or design of the "40-million-year-old monolith" that is hanging out there, and is apparently in communication with its brethren on the moon. HAL is shut down, and the only surviving crewmember, Dave (you know, the "I'm sorry, Dave. I'm afraid I can't do that" Dave), ends up being reborn as a giant space baby after a bizarrely quiet stay at a place that looks like Versailles crossed with the White Lodge from *Twin Peaks*—thanks once again to those meddlesome alien rocks.

(I still hated it.)

Oh, in its time, I can see where this movie's effects would have made it something of a revelation, and there can be no denying that the set design is remarkable, clean and timeless while simultaneously sinister and futuristic. Released a year before Apollo 11's lander successfully made it to the moon, and long before IBM's Big Blue took on a chess Grand Master and won, this must have come at audiences as wondrous and prescient, and certainly the effects are so well done as to hold up almost impeccably even now. But mere innovation does not great entertainment make; otherwise *The Phantom Menace*, that pinnacle of ground-breaking CGI awesomeness, would be held in far greater esteem. Director Stanley Kubrick was clearly in love with his ship models and his camera angles and his costume designs, so he spends a lot of time lovingly dwelling upon even the most inane of their functions; when gravity is reversed aboard ship, it does so SLOWLY, when Dave's capsule spins around, it does so SLOWLY, and Heaven forbid we should miss a scintillating second of his drawn-out EVA to check on an allegedly malfunctioning ship part.

Everything.

Just.

Takes.

So.

Long.

Also, the repetitive nature of much of the film's sound effects is annoying, in that "shut the hell up!" kind of way one might react to a neighbor's car alarm endlessly protesting in the dead of night. There's ape screeching, heavy breathing, beeping, whirring, and then SILENCE, unnecessarily long and signifying nothing. And for all the dialogue the movie interjects in between all of this, it might as well be the script for a 30-second commercial. For all that *The Artist* was acclaimed as the first major silent movie of the modern era (aside, of course, from Mel Brooks's *Silent Movie*), I would contend that *2001* pretty much belongs in that category, as well.

In many ways, *2001* is just an extended, slightly *avant garde* film clip for assorted classical music offerings, from "Zarathustra" to "The Blue Danube" – there are some beautiful compositions in this film, which have sadly become so synonymous with it that many people believe they were actually composed *for* it. But in reflecting on the soundtrack, I think I have finally figured out why I find the film not only dull but entirely distasteful, and also why it has always, without fail, left me with a pounding headache. The discordance! The dissonance! An entirely inhumane need to

10

inflict upon us a score as ugly as the works by assorted Strausses are mellifluous and inspiring. As though the screeching and the beeping and the breathing weren't bad enough, there are these long "musical" interludes in which the notes are constantly at odds; it's upsetting, fingernails-on-a-chalkboard irksome, like an argument carried out by instruments all fighting over which can make the most irritating noise. Indeed, much of the last fifteen minutes of the movie is just an iridescent Laser Floyd-esque extravaganza accompanied by the sound of a middle school band room on the first day of practice. And someone in there plays the theremin. Badly.

There is a whole other level upon which I object to this movie, too. *Of course* there is! If it was just that it was slow and dull and discordant and… I mentioned, dull, right?... then I would not have watched it again after that first disastrous viewing, and that would have been that. But *2001* has somehow garnered for itself a place of cinematic greatness – it ranked at #15 on the AFI Top 100 in 2007 – and is constantly held up by cinephiles as something rare and wonderful, a treasure that transcends its vulgar sci-fi roots to become a masterpiece of clever parable. Now, I have a big problem with the idea, often perpetuated by mainstream movie critics, that if a science fiction movie is capital-G Good then it must therefore not actually be science fiction. We saw this happen, most recently, with *Inception* – it was sci-fi, but it was *more than* sci-fi, because it was thought-provoking and intelligent and witty and paradigm-shifting, featuring gorgeous set pieces and a stunning virtual world—as though science fiction is not inherently all these things, and more.

But a movie can be all of these things and not Good, too. *2001* is an unabashedly sci-fi flick, but it is a *bad* sci-fi flick, and not remotely in a fun way; it's a genius notion executed horribly, as my enjoyment of the book Arthur C. Clarke later penned of his and Kubrick's screenplay must surely prove.

True, I must admit that for me, the film version of *2001* was probably my first inkling that in science fiction could be found philosophy and metaphor and alternative history as much as there could all the spaceships and robots and rayguns, and I will concede it remarkable that this point was made so effectively as far back as 1968. However, *Planet of the Apes* also came out in 1968, and does that job far more ably; I just happened to see *2001* first.

So, yeah. I've given it as much of the benefit of the doubt as I can here, but still… I hate it.

And once again it has left me with the most dreadful headache.

2001: A SPACE ODYSSEY
STILL A CLASSIC
by Chris Nagy

"Are you not entertained?"
— *Maximus Decimus Meridius*

Apparently, my esteemed colleague's answer to that is, no, she was not. I pose the question: "So what?" Like Commodus, I will put it to the masses: Are we discussing whether *2001: A Space Odyssey* was entertaining, or whether it was good?

I posit that those are not really the same thing. Are there movies you will watch over and over, but deep down, you know are really bad? Of course there are. We all have those. If I had to pick my "desert island" movie, it would be *Raiders of the Lost Ark*. But is that the best movie I have ever seen? Not by a longshot.

It appears that my opponent's principal arguments are that *2k1:ASO* is a) slow and b) noisy, to which I respond: Well, a) yes, and b) yes. But is that such a bad thing? That depends. I'm afraid that this is going to rapidly deteriorate into the age old "cinema as art" vs. "cinema as entertainment" discussion, so let's just consider both, starting with art. Is *2001* entertaining? I certainly thought so – more on that in a minute. Is *2001* capital-G good? I claim that it is.

The first sign of a good movie: does it remain in my thoughts for more than a few hours after I see it? This is one of a handful of films that I continue to try to interpret. It is far more than just a simple allegory about maturity. I won't subject my audience (today, anyway) to an extended essay on representation of man's place in the universe. Clearly, Kubrick dug Nietzsche. But the layers of symbolism, encompassing philosophy, religion, evolution, and psychology, separate this film from almost anything else in the genre.

The unfortunate thing about my opponent's reference to "vulgar sci-fi roots" is that there is a modicum of truth to that description. I completely agree with the assessment that being a very good film and being a sci-fi film are not automatically mutually exclusive. It just appears that way because the truly thought-provoking picture in this genre is becoming increasingly rare. We seem to be overwhelmed with CGI-fest thrill rides, superhero movies written barely above the level of the comic books upon which they are based, and Michael Bay beating me over the head with the simple and the obvious. Most sci-fi films go to great lengths to tell us the whole story, often in excessive detail via painfully contrived dialog. One of the great things about the masterpiece that is *2001* is that we, the viewers, are left to our own devices. That is the real beauty of this film: it is left open to vastly different interpretations.

Another thing that Kubrick did with this film, which was rare for the time and has become increasingly so, is strive for scientific accuracy. For example, many find the silence annoying, but guess what? Space is silent. Sound does not travel in a vacuum. We would never actually hear the Death Star explode, and a dude floating around in a space suit is going to hear his own breathing, and not a whole helluva lot else.

Additionally, this film was years ahead of its time in several areas. Despite my opponent's admission of their remarkableness, I feel the need to mention once again the visual effects and set design, which are spectacular. They hold up today, while films that are a quarter-century newer are beginning to appear dated. HAL might be the first use of a computer as a character, rather than a prop, with awareness, goals, and something approaching feelings. HAL begat WOPR, SKYNET, and Dr. Theopolis from *Buck Rogers in the 25th Century*. (Actually, Theopolis was more than just inspired by HAL; it was such an obvious ripoff that Kubrick and Clarke could've pulled Glen A. Larson off set, dragged him into the alley, and delivered a *Sons of Anarchy*-style beatdown, and no court in the land would've convicted.)

Along with being good, *2001* is hugely important. By my humble estimation, there were seven key turning points for science fiction entertainment in the 20th century, and this is among them. (One of these days, I will cough up the other six, but here is a quick spoiler: Lea Thompson is in zero of them). It is important because it created the genre of the big-budget sci-fi blockbuster. Prior to this film, sci-fi films were typically scratched together on a shoestring budget. Special effects were an afterthought. "Blockbuster" meant *Ben Hur*; DeMille and a cast of thousands. The idea of spending time and resources on science fiction was virtually unheard of. Without this film, Luke Skywalker stays on Tatooine and becomes a creepy, aging, lonely farmer; Neo takes the blue pill and returns to work the next morning; Ellen Ripley works as a forklift operator at an assembly plant in Indiana; and John Connor manages an IHOP right up until the moment he is vaporized by the nukes. None of the beloved films we cut our sci-fi teeth on ever happen without Kubrick and *2001*.

So finally, is it entertaining? While my opponent offered a resounding "no," I must counter with an emphatic "yes." Clearly this is going to be one of our "agree to disagree" situations. Admittedly, the cadence of the movie is not for everyone. But while some find it annoying, I see it as refreshing. I appreciate the opportunity to enjoy the cinematography, the set design, the almost anal-retentive attention to detail before being whisked onto the next scene. I appreciate the ability to consider a movie while I am watching it, rather than just stringing together a series of visceral reactions. The short version is this: I like the film for many of the reasons others, including my counterpart in this debate, dislike it. It is just so damned different. (I do agree that the intermission was a little strange.)

By the way, WTF is a theremin?

3D
BREEDS BAD MOVIES
by Jason Luna

3D movie technology is a rare example of something that has become worse since it was invented. While the appeal of 3D technology may be different for some, the simple technological effect isn't. What 3-Dimensional film does is project two images onto the screen. And once you put on your special glasses, the two images merge to become one. These two images create a sense of depth, and it almost looks like "The movie is right in front of you! You can almost touch it!"

That exclamation riddled statement describes the early era of 3D movies, which went hand in hand with the "low budget" craze of the mid-1950s. Movie masterminds of cheap cinema, like William Castle and Roger Corman, capitalized on the idea that technology with elaborate names, like "Smell-O-Vision," or you know, "movies in 3 Dimensions" would get people to come to the movie theater, as opposed to staying at home and watching their new television sets. One new invention counteracts another, or at least one could argue it that way.

And the idea failed. Miserably. People kept choosing their televisions. What saved the movies from TV's clutches?

Quality cinema! The lamestream media (so to speak) that produced the popular Hays Code dreck gave way to the greatest independent film era of the 20th Century. By the time Spielberg and Lucas got a ton of money to make *Jaws* and *Star Wars* in 1975 and 1977, respectively, the war with television was over, and so was any thought of 3D film (for a while).

The point I'm trying to make (other than I was a Film Studies major) is that 3D movie making was never based in making quality cinema, to facilitate some effect integral to storytelling. It's a novelty to make cash.

But to insert myself into this argument again, I enjoy the novelty of 3D movies. When a Terminator robot skull comes flying out of the screen towards your face during a visit to Universal Studios, Florida, you don't forget it. It's an underutilized technology, sure, but it could be used to make a fun, visually stunning romp at the movies.

But it's not, at least not anymore. Apparently what was good enough for *Honey, I Shrunk The Audience in 3D* and even *Beowulf 3D* is practically non-existent.

So what do you get out of watching a 3D movie these days?

Nothing. The movie doesn't do anything when you watch 3D these days.

And yes, I include *Avatar* in this, which I saw in 3D (and in IMAX). I thought it was okay, but it's still an inspirational action movie that happens to be 3D-itized. I couldn't see any great 3D visuals or anything.

The visual benefits of the new 3D film (often the bi-product of a technology called "Real 3D." Side note: I don't know if comparing your "movie glasses wearing" technology to reality holds up very well...) are practically non-existent.

When you watch a movie that is "also in 3D", even a great one, there is no clear difference. Studios will often take a "2D" movie and convert into 3D film. You can tell the difference in these movies as you watch, sort of.

For example, if you take your glasses off when you're watching a 3D movie nowadays (like all days), you'll see the movie has wavy lines. But when you put them back on, it's difficult to tell what you're gaining. My explanation of why the "3D option" is so popular these days is...

A placebo effect! Harsh, I know, but I think it's at least a plausible hypothesis. Not to construct too much of a straw man, but if someone tells you that you "have to see this movie in 3D!", it's probably because they liked the movie they saw in 3D. You should ask them for a report comparing *Avatar* in 3D, 2D, IMAX, and all combinations thereof.

The proof is really in the nature of the alternative. When a studio makes a 3D movie for you, they still release its 2D counterpart. On the one hand, it's kind of cool, I guess. The movie studio is giving you a choice. You can watch it in two different ways. 2D or 3D. And 3D will give you the glasses and the fuzzy screen.

But let me make that choice for you, if you don't mind the suggestion. You should watch 2D for one simple reason: it's cheaper. Going to a movie theater is expensive no matter what, so why pay more?

And the alternative method is a drag on cinematic innovation. No other technology gets to have it both ways like 3D does. As much as I don't like 3D (and find it more expensive than 2D, because, you know, it is), it should be able to sit on the marquee by itself.

Follow me here for another hypothesis, just for a second. Even IMAX doesn't allow for a consistent "double existence" for any movie, where two screens constantly have the same movie on it.

Think of all the glorious independent film activity that could happen if one movie had to fend for itself. It could practically be the 1970s independent era, "reborn!"

To conclude my argument, I want to discuss animated film. Pixar, for example. Those animators work hard. They produce these beautiful images that float across the screen. My point is, unlike a live action 3D movie (or at least slightly different from it), the unchanged image can actually be distorted by your choice.

You are paying the movie theater to put glasses on your face as you're watching some of the greatest hand-created art in cinematic history. The picture is right there in front of you; why pay extra for "special glasses" to help you see it?

3D
MAKES BAD MOVIES BETTER
by Rachel Hyland

There are a lot of reasons to despise the 3D craze that studios have thrust upon us unrelentingly these past few years. Increased ticket prices. Less readily-available indie films, as theaters are taken up with both 2D and 3D versions of the latest blockbuster. Delays in screening, as movies are post-converted prior to release. (Like Joss Whedon's *The Cabin in the Woods*, delayed for more than a year... and then the conversion never happened. Ludicrous.) At best, 3D is a gimmick we could do just as well without; at worst it is a cynical exercise in marketing and possibly hazardous to the health, as well.

Plus, no one looks good in those glasses. *No one*.

However, this is the "Pro 3D" side of the debate, so with all of that out of the way, let me state, firmly and for whatever record you happen to be keeping, that I love 3D movies. Oh, not every one of them. And not all the time. But as a concept, as a medium, as an experience – LOVE.

First, let's take a look at what 3D is. It's genius, is what; I'd almost go so far as to say sorcery, except that upon further investigation it is an effect that is thoroughly explainable by science and only *seems* like magic. Basically, our ability to sense three dimensions comes from our eyes being set ever so slightly apart in our faces, and thus picking up ever so slightly different angles on whatever we are looking at. Our brain processes these differences, blends the images together and, hey presto, depth perception! (Sorry, pirates, Mad-Eye Moody, Snake Plissken and Xander from *Buffy*, Season 7! No 3D for you.) This has been understood biologically since the early 1800s, but it took the creation of film to really bring the technology into being, and now filmmakers (or just the post-production team) do their damndest to mess with our minds with every new 3D movie they create. Just purely as an invention, as an incredible concept and a piece of impressive optical trickery, I think 3D is worthy of our praise.

But it is more than just merely in the abstract that I love it, but in the particulars as well.

Because you know what 3D does? It gets people to the theater. In a world in which VOD and streaming and downloading are increasingly becoming the norm, and wherein films are often released onto DVD and Blu-ray mere months after their cinematic debuts, 3D has made of movie-going an event once more. And now we have the phenomenon of rereleasing old films anew in 3D on the big screen, seeking to entice those of us who already paid once to see them to do so again, or giving anyone who missed the original run a chance to, as for example, "… go back to *Titanic*." And I love that, too, because I am a fan of revival showings – in *Rocky Horror* and *The Blues Brothers*, in *Star Trek* movie marathons and *Sing-a-Long Sound of Music* sessions, I've worn the wigs, thrown the toast, mouthed the lines and sung the songs – and to me a 3D reissue of a classic film is like visiting a revival cinema on heavy-duty hallucinogenic drugs, without the nasty side-effects. "Woah, dude, it's like the ship is *right there!*" So cool, and so worth the price of admission. (Yes, even to *The Phantom Menace*. True, the movie still sucked, but the podrace in 3D was kickass!)

My worthy opponent points out that the history of 3D cinema is riddled with B-movie dreck, and indeed, this is true. The 50s gave us 3D Westerns like *Jesse James Versus the Daltons*, 3D Sci-Fi fare like *It Came from Outer Space*, dull 3D Horror like *House of Wax* and 3D Monster flicks like *The Creature from the Black Lagoon*. But it wasn't all bad, even in those days: Hitchcock's *Dial M for Murder* saw a 3D release, and if anyone has a disrespectful word to say about Hitchcock 'round these parts, I invite them to take their leave.

But leaving inherent quality aside, what any nay-3D-sayer neglects to note is that 3D makes a bad movie better, raising even cinematic abominations like *Wrath of the Titans* into the realms of the remotely watchable, if only for the spectacle that 3D provides. Would I have gone to see *Wrath* in plain old 2D? Well, probably, because I am just that masochistic. But the fact that it was 3D, and therefore offered up the occasional moment of visceral thrill, made me less annoyed at myself for having done so. Similarly, when I was forced into seeing *Alvin and the Chipmunks 3: Chipwrecked* by a winsome young tween who played on my affection for her and thereby managed to overcome my natural reluctance to bestow hard-earned cash upon such theatrical torture, I was dismayed to learn that I would have to watch it without the benefit of 3D, it being one of the only kids' movies of late – and certainly, one of the only kids' movies with the number "3" in the title – to not be offered in the format. It made the whole *Chipwrecked* ordeal even worse than I'd thought it would be, I give you my word.

Do you know what the first 3D movie of what I believe we should call the Modern 3D Era was? (Not counting, of course, all of those 3D rides and showings you get at assorted theme parks throughout the world, nor IMAX documentaries.) It was *Spy Kids 3D*, back in 2003. There followed, in 2004, T*he Polar Express* and *The Adventures of Sharkboy and Lavagirl*, and let me tell you, not a one of those movies would have been made more tolerable by the removal of the gimmicky special effects coming out of the screen *right at us*. (!!!). Since then, of course, the highest grossing movie of all time, 2009's *Avatar*, showed film studios that even movies also aimed at grown-ups could benefit from a little mind-messing-with, and thus we have seen this recent upsurge in 3D showings of everything from comic book movies to concert spectaculars. This, to the apparent dismay of many – the majority of *Geek Speak*'s staff, for example, are violently opposed to the technology – and yet box office receipts make it clear that many people are going to see films in 3D format, and even more importantly, enjoying them. It's not just me.

So, are movies released in 3D for the pure artistry of it? No, of course not. I in no way dispute my honorable colleague when he suggests that 3D is "a novelty to make cash." My question is: what's wrong with that? Without cash, studios can't make more films, and I like that they make films… yes, even bad ones. I'll put up with a *Wrath of the Titans* if it means I can have an *Avatar*, or an *Immortals*, or a *Tintin*. And if I can have them in 3D, so much the better.

3D television, though – that I'm not quite as sold on. I mean, as ridiculous as we all look in those glasses in the movie theater, sitting there in the dark in our matching sets of shades, how much more so will we (or do we) look sitting on our own couches?

Next stop: 3D contacts!

© *Rachel Hyland, 2012*

ALIEN VS. PREDATOR
THE CASE FOR THE ALIEN
by William Cashin

It's one of those contentious issues that will probably never be solved. Like, was Deckard a replicant? Where would *FlashForward* have taken us? And why did f$#k$ng George Lucas think he could make Greedo shoot first?

The issue is this: pound for pound, who would win an Alien vs. Predator showdown? Sadly, we will never truly know. Why? Because every attempt to address this, in movies, novels, and even comics (anyone remember *Aliens versus Predator versus The Terminator*?) has been truly horrible. I couldn't even make it all the way through *Aliens vs. Predator: Requiem*, putting it in a distinguished handful of movies that, for me, remain unfinished (and half of which star Vin Diesel).

So, I'm going to ignore the *Alien vs. Predator* movies (right, like a Predator would ever slow down to help a lowly human survive an explosion!), and instead just consider the first two of each franchise. And on this basis, I have to award the championship belt to the Aliens.

The Movies

Don't get me wrong. I don't think any of the originals (*Alien, Aliens, Predator, Predator 2*) are truly excellent movies, although I do think they're very good. They all suffer, however, from the same ailment infecting all alien-related horror movies: the humans have to "win" in the end. Hah, like humans could hold a candle to either an Alien or a Predator. And yet, in countless movies of the genre now, the humans somehow get in the final punch, be it through a glorified bear trap in *Predator*, the cold, harsh reality of empty space in *Alien*, or sundry other unlikely scenarios. I have to say, I have for some time secretly desired for the "bad guy" to get one up on… well, us.

But not the Predator. The Predator annoys me. Perhaps it's his reliance on technology – let's face it, without the tech, the Predator is nothing – like the cloak, the laser sight (what is this, "Killing for "Beginners"?), and the pathetic self-destruct (more later). Or maybe it's all that sitting up in a tree/building, creepily watching the plot unfold but not actually doing anything. What can I say? I like a bad guy who, when he has the opportunity to rip your throat out, does. He doesn't over-analyze it. Think *The Birds*, or *Starship Troopers*. (Oh… come on, has anyone ever dared mention these two movies in the same breath?).

For me, this is a major failing of the Predator *oeuvre*. Admittedly, in both the *Alien* and *Predator* movies, the humans, who aren't ever squeaky-clean themselves (muscle men/women in *Predator* and *Aliens*, or scheming corporate/military research types in *Predator 2* and *Alien*), must somehow overcome their differences to take on, and eventually beat, the bad guy(s). As the audience, we're not stupid. We know who is going to eventually win, even if we sometimes don't want to believe it. But unlike in the *Alien* movies, you can easily see just where the Predator is going to go wrong. He's going to get goaded into something. Or he's going to get cocky and go hand to hand (has that ever come off? Ask Tommy Lee Jones how it worked out for him). In other words, the Predator is just as fallible as we are.

Meanwhile the Alien just goes for the kill. Mindless, relentless, no game plan, like a swarm of locusts. You don't really beat the Aliens – you just don't lose as badly as you could have.

The Creatures

It is the "personality" and "intelligence" of the Predator that costs him most dearly. First of all, let's get the big one out of the way: the self-destruct device. How pathetic. I don't get this one. If, as we are led to believe in *Predator 2*, they are a proud race only interested in the hunt, then what do you get out of blowing yourself up? Surely a better way to go out is to throw the proverbial kitchen/death-ray sink at your enemy and, if you do happen to still get knocked off, then either a) you're just not good enough, or b) your "prey" is actually pretty decent (and let's face it, Arnold is more than decent… though I'm not so sure about Danny). If the former, you deserve to die; if the latter, then eventually word is going to get back to the other Predators that there is "worthy" prey out there, and you can at least rest easy (which, being dead, is about all you're going to be doing) that you set the bar so high for others of your hunt-happy race. It's like getting the top score on a pinball game. Your last ball will fall through those flippers in the end, but that's still your name up on the board for all to see.

Would an Alien have this problem? Helllll no! Why? They are mindless killers. Emphasis on "mindless." Sure, occasionally they have to drag a few victims back to the hive to birth the next generation, but Aliens are pretty simple folk. They approach you with little stealth (you just don't see them) and prefer the head on charge. If you're lucky you might get to see their second set of teeth, but fairly quickly it's BOOM! You're dead. (Unless you're a cat.)

Would an Alien, upon noticing that its prey is pregnant (eg. Cantrall in *Predator 2*) retreat and not kill her? Not a chance. It might pause for a second to consider what little space she has left inside her to hold a baby Alien, but would probably still rip her in half anyway.

But for me, the one reason why the Aliens get the nod in this battle is not the acid blood, it's not that streamlined body perfect for climbing quickly through air vents, and it's not even that second set of teeth (cool though). The reason is the potential of Aliens *plural*. Now, you could maybe argue that one Predator would beat one Alien, and you might be right. But take a moment to admire the relentless skill on show by the Alien – or Xenomorphs, as they have come to be known in the extended universe – in *Aliens*. You take one down, there are ten others. You bring an army, they just see a bunch of baby Alien incubators.

Conclusion

One could say that the Predators' biggest weakness is that they are too much like humans. And we know how pathetic humans are. Aliens, on the other hand, you suspect will last much longer than mere Earthlings or even the Predator race. That there'll always be some humanoid population to stumble upon their eggs and, like a plague, the Aliens will tear through this new race quickly and efficiently. No mercy, no second thoughts, no fancy kills.

Meanwhile, some Predator somewhere will be still playing around with his self-destruct device. How sad.

© William Cashin, 2010

ALIEN VS. PREDATOR

The Case for the Predator

by Malcolm Matthews

The first *Alien vs. Predator* movie was, of course, garbage. And the second, *Alien vs. Predator: Requiem*, was an abomination. But the comparison itself is valid and thought-provoking and deserves to be laid to rest once and for all.

For my money, it's the Predator all the way.

The Movies

In the interest of time, I'll stick with the originals since *Aliens* was really good, but all the other sequels in both franchises were crap.

Alien is a classic, but it's also simply *Jaws in Space*. It's an excellent but one-dimensional film. It does what it does well. There is scary music in all the right places. People run around and scream. But it's clear which is the good guy and which is the bad guy. There's no question of who's going to come out on top. In *Predator*, though, you kind of find your loyalties and perceptions shifting as the movie progresses. In the end, it's a lot like *American Gladiators*: you can root for the contestant or for the hunter trying to rip the other guy's head off.

Alien belongs in the genre of Mutant Animals Attack! movies like *Deep Blue Sea, Tremors*, and *Eye of the Beast*: movies about scary super-creatures on a ravenous eating spree. *Predator* is more psychological. It's a tightly-constructed masterpiece that opens avenues of thought and lives on beyond the screen. There's an intelligence at work in both the alien and in the movie itself.

Take a good look at *Predator*. The first third of the movie is filled with muscles. It's all brawn and bawdy jokes. The military guys whip out their enormous phallic canons and mow down everything lush and green standing between them and their invisible adversary. In the second act, they get their comeuppance as they're picked off one by one, each death a bit more gruesome than the last. In the final act, the main muscle guy, stripped of his technology, goes native, paints his face, sets some traps, and turns the tables on the relentless hunter. We discover that the camouflaged Predator, whom we thought was the Natural Man, is actually the ultimate Techno Man. In spite of his reliance on technology, or perhaps because of that reliance, he is outmaneuvered, outsmarted, and ultimately defeated by the Natural Man. The moral of the story: be a natural human being, give up what you believed to be true, don't trust what you think you've seen, and if you want to win, you've got to give up what weighs you down.

The Creatures

As for the creatures themselves, it's the difference between Jason and Freddy Kreuger. Jason is a silent slasher, a stalker who's been tailor-made to fit our nightmares. Freddy, on the other hand, can talk. He's funny, tormented, and deadly, just like the rest of us. That makes him interesting.

Sure, the Alien is menacing. But in the end, it's just a mindless animal, while the Predator from McTiernan's film is a thinking creature, eerily human with its advanced technology, its insatiable desire to hunt and to collect trophies. It has a sense of humor. It mimics other creatures and the natural world around it even as it kills for kicks. In the end, it kills itself with its own nuclear bomb. Director Jean-Pierre Jeunet and writer Joss Whedon tried unsuccessfully to humanize the Aliens in *Alien: Resurrection*, which had the effect of a post-script: "Oh, by the way, these aren't mindless creatures at all. They have a complicated psychology and social structure..." In other words, Jeunet and Whedon tried to make the Alien more like the Predator.

Let's face it, the Predator is a more interesting alien than the Alien. The Alien has acid blood, a head like a melted bowling ball, and a little teeny second mouth that pops out like candy from a Pez dispenser. The Predator, on the other hand, has personality. You want to know about his background. What was he like as a baby Predator? What kind of training did it take to become such an effective hunter? Does he have a girlfriend? etc. The Alien is just a big ol', egg-laying bug. The Predator is a human offshoot, not an insect. He's fallible but inventive. He makes weapons to enhance his natural abilities. He hunts for sport, which is a lot more diabolical than sneaking through air vents picking off incontinent space colonists, unsuspecting miners, and gung-ho Marines. Everyone who would take a seven-foot tall armored alien Rastafarian trophy-hunter over a slime-soaked dung beetle any day raise your hand.

I thought so.

Conclusion

Predator asks the right question: "What the hell are you?" Dutch asks it of the Predator, and the Predator asks him right back. We humans need so spend less time trying to figure out everyone else and more time trying to figure out ourselves. In any other context, we're the predator.

In *Predator*, the Latin phrase applies: *de te fibula*. The story is about you.

Alien was invented. It's a movie. It happens for us.

Predator was cultivated. It's real. It happens to be us.

© *Malcolm Matthews, 2010*

BATMAN AND WONDER WOMAN
SUPER COUPLE
by Kim Sorensen

Valentine's Day is upon us, love is in the air, and so I thought it time to celebrate with a very special Geek vs. Geek about my favorite comic book pairing of all time: Batman and Wonder Woman. Throughout their incarnations (Wonder Woman was first introduced in 1941, Batman in 1939) the two have been teammates, friends, antagonists, and love interests. Many writers have explored – or a better term might be hinted at – their relationship across the DC Universe. Their relationship was also suggested on the *Justice League* and *Justice League Unlimited* cartoons that ran from 2001-2006.

In preparation for this debate I did some searching about the World's Greatest Detective and the Amazon Princess, and much like my fellow nerds at my local comic book store, the internet is just as divided about these two and their love lives. When it comes to Batman, there is of course a very pro Batman/Talia al Ghul fanbase arising out of the main DC *Batman* title. I respect their opinions and will acquiesce that those two have a deep connection. The two fell in love while Batman was trained by/working with Ras al Ghul. Batman and Talia have a child together, Damian Wayne, who, as the newest Robin, may have more issues than any other Boy Wonder save Jason Todd. I can understand Batman falling for Talia: she's intelligent, worldly, a master assassin, and a deep and complex character. However, she is also crazy, evil, a terrible mother, and not the best woman for Batman.

There is also, of course, another pairing for Batman that people love, and that is with Catwoman/Selina Kyle. In several incarnations there has been a relationship of some sort between Batman and Catwoman (such as in Burton's *Batman Returns*, in Nolan's abysmal – in my opinion – *The Dark Knight Rises*, and, of course, in the comics). In the Golden Age Batman comics, Batman and Catwoman fell in love, got married, and had a daughter who also became a superhero. Again, I get it, but this was the Golden Age, and characters weren't as deeply complex as they are now. When it comes to modern-day Batman, the pairing of Batman and Catwoman is completely senseless: a) Batman doesn't allow himself to have romantic relationships, and b) Batman would not fall for Catwoman. Bruce Wayne is a brilliant billionaire globe-trotting superhero. If he were going to fall in love it wouldn't be with some idiotic cat burglar whose greatest weapon is a slutty costume. Yes, I know it's not her fault; it is mostly men who are doing the art. But the only reason this relationship still exists or is hinted at now is because of its history.

Meanwhile, the internet, like the DC Universe, isn't quite sure what to do with the Amazing Amazon. There are some who think that she should be with Steve Trevor, her original love interest. In the Golden Age, Diana and Steve Trevor had a Lois Lane/Clark Kent relationship and eventually got married, had a daughter who became the superhero Fury and during the events of Crisis on Infinite Earths (when DC rebooted the universe) they were allowed to live on Mount Olympus. The next time Steve Trevor showed up in comics he was not Mr. Wonder Woman; as it should be. Their relationship is just too clichéd. All the writers did was copy Superman's love story with Lois Lane and swapped genders. It's not interesting.

There is also a very strong case for Superman/Wonder Woman. On the surface it makes sense. They are the two most powerful people in the DC Universe. Both are gorgeous. They are both outsiders: he's an alien, she's a mystical being from Paradise Island. The only thing wrong with this pairing is that it is too predictable. (Something Diana herself has said.) Clark and Diana are just friends and the only reason a relationship between the two of them exists in alternate stories (*Kingdom Come, The Dark Knight Strikes Again*) is because Lois Lane is dead. Clark Kent's soul mate is Lois Lane—even if you don't read comics you know that. Diana is not going to be with someone when she knows that they love someone else.

This brings us to the main point of this debate: Batman and Wonder Woman. I'll admit the last superhero one might expect to be a good match for Wonder Woman is the dark, grim and unlucky-in-love Batman, which is perhaps why Joe Kelly decided to explore such a relationship during his 2003-2004 run on *JLA*. During the storyline "The Obsidian Age," the Justice League journeyed into the ancient past in order to save a time-lost Aquaman. While there, Batman and Wonder Woman prepared to fight their enemies to the death and, before doing so, they surprised one another (and a lot of readers) by sharing a kiss. Once all the resurrection, time-travel, villain-fighting and day-saving was out the way, the two put off having to talk about their kiss for a while, with Batman being the more reluctant of the two, even standing Wonder Woman up on at least one occasion. (Which, yes, kind of dick move on his part.)

Eventually, in *JLA* #90, there was a resolution to the twosome's kiss during the *Obsidian Age* storyline. Wonder Woman put herself into Martian Manhunter's Martian Transconsciousness Articulator, a doohickey that plays out various possible futures in dream-like fashion for the user (it is a comic book). Some of these include her fighting crime alongside Batman in Gotham as Batwoman, her killing the Joker after he has killed Bruce—and perhaps one of the sweetest moments with Diana and a very, very old Bruce on Paradise Island right before his death. However, because writers love to tease and not give fans what they want the relationship never really started, even though it is clear that neither one of them is happy about it.

In 2003 Matt Wagner also showed his support for Batman/Wonder Woman in his mini-series *Batman/Superman/Wonder Woman: Trinity*. The three-issue run is a re-imagining of the big three coming together for the first time. It also includes a great moment when Batman sees Wonder Woman bathing on Themyscira and is apparently overwhelmed by her beauty so rushes to her and kisses her. Mind you, she then punches him, but it's awesome nonetheless.

The *Justice League* cartoon also hints at the feelings/tension between Diana and Bruce. In the episode "The Brave and the Bold" (S01E14/15) Diana is crushed under a missile and Bruce, looking distraught, begins to dig when all of a sudden Diana throws the missile off of her and is right as rain. She notices the dirt/mud on Batman's costume and kisses his cheek. In the episode "This Little Piggy" (S01E05) Wonder Woman is transformed into a pig by Circe (apparently her magic resistance doesn't exist in the cartoon) and Batman admits his feelings about Diana to Zatanna while requesting her help to change Diana back. He also sings to Circe in order to change her back – and that's good television. Batman and Wonder Woman also kissed in the episode "Starcrossed" (S02E51) while trying to hide their faces from Thanagarians. In an episode in which the Justice League were turned into children (yeah, it's a kids' cartoon) Wonder Woman constantly flirts with Batman and youngster Green Lantern, John Stewart, tells young Batman: "Your girlfriend sure is bossy."

After the events in JLA, the relationship between the two became pretty much non-existent in DC Canon, though it appeared in some alternate storylines. Then the 2009-2010 mega story *Blackest Night* was published, and Diana's love for Bruce was finally confirmed. In *Blackest Night: Wonder Woman* #2, Wonder Woman is possessed by an evil black lantern ring (it's complicated) and has killed: Cassie Sandsmark/Wonder Girl; her also-possessed sister Donna Troy; and is about to kill her mother when a batarang hits her in the face. She looks up and sees Batman who tells her to stop, but Black Lantern Wonder Woman attacks him. He grabs her by the throat and tells her that this is not her. Her inner voice stammers that this cannot be real, that Bruce is dead. The two then kiss while Diana's inner voice says "Bruce" and breaks the connection between Wonder Woman and the black lantern ring. Now, all of this was in a place that Aphrodite created so Diana didn't actually kill anyone, but it is such a beautifully sweet scene to see how evil Diana was, and how the only thing that could save her was her love for The Dark Knight.

There was also one issue of *The All-New Batman: The Brave and the Bold* in 2011 in which Batman and Wonder Woman have been hit by Eros's arrows and he asks her to marry him, and she says yes. Though it was a single issue and I don't really care for the campiness of the comic, it is still really sweet and quite funny. Especially when Robin doesn't understand why Bruce is getting married until he sees Diana in a wedding dress and quickly shuts his mouth. Of course, they don't get married, but it's such a cute little tease.

Batman and Wonder Woman are my favorite comic book relationship, even though they have never really gotten together in a canonical timeline. Their relationship is such an interesting study in contrasts. You have the ultimate human in Bruce Wayne, who is the very embodiment of the human spirit and potential. Then you have Wonder Woman who is a creature of myth and magic. It is interesting to see the man of science who has become, quite literally, a god-killer (he killed Darkseid) being paired with a woman created by the gods from clay. Batman is a warrior, more so than any other Wonder Woman love interest. Wonder Woman is the ultimate warrior. They work together because of how they are simultaneously similar and complete opposites. They work because of how well an immortal warrior with amazing powers can humanize the bravest and darkest human male in the DC universe. If only the writers would realize that.

Maybe the DCEU ones will?

© *Kimberly Sorensen, 2014*

BATMAN AND WONDER WOMAN
SUPER-CREEPY
By Rachel Hyland

When it comes to the cultural and spiritual divide that exists between the two major comic houses, one as epic as that of Capulet vs. Montague or York vs. Lancaster or even Stark vs. Lannister, I have often stated my allegiance to Marvel. I am so very definitely a Marvel girl that I almost automatically recoil from anything DC-related, and while there are some exceptions to this admittedly discriminatory rule – I love *Teen Titans* and the *Green Lantern* animated series, and have recently spent many a happy hour in the archives of Yale Stewart's clever DC-based webcomic *JL8* (it's *Tiny Titans*, but better) – by and large, if it bears the DC imprint, odds are that I probably couldn't care less.

Why, then, do I have any opinion at all on the concept of Batman and Wonder Woman as a couple? Sure, I watched the 70s *Wonder Woman* show in reruns when I was a kid – Lynda Carter's tiny waist simply defies science – and I dug the Burton *Batman*, but I really have as little vested interest in the romantic entanglements of these characters as I do in their *Super Friends* cohort Gleek's, and he's just a babbling blue space monkey. Really, when my learned colleague came at me with her yearning for a Batman and Wonder Woman happily ever after, my reaction should have been somewhere commensurate to the interest I take in gossip rag speculation regarding the love lives of minor European royalty, or sundry Kardashians. Which is exactly none.

But Kim said: "Hey, even though it's not exactly canon, you know who are a great couple? Batman and Wonder Woman!" (or words to that effect), and my automatic, almost violent, reaction was: "No. No they're not."

Let me tell you why.

It's not the Wonder Woman/Batman-ness of it all, I'll tell you that right now. As a non-partisan of either, I have no idea if perhaps Superman has a superior claim to Diana's affections or if it is only the feisty Selina Kyle who can and should light the Bat's dour fire, as apparently many *Justice League* fans believe—though I do think *The Dark Knight Rises* proved to us all that Catwoman is way too cool for that stodgy Bruce Wayne. No, it was the non-canon-ness of it all that had me immediately up in arms at the very suggestion of this cross-racial pairing. (DC Universe Amazons are a different race to humans, right? Or did the New 52 reboot retcon that?) Because non-canon makes me mad, people. MAD.

I think it started on that dark, desolate day during the internet's infancy, when I was painstakingly trawling my way around infant, text-based *Star Trek* sites via my neophyte search engine of choice, AltaVista, and a primordial web browser I have just now remembered the existence of, Netscape Navigator. (Wow, turns out both of those things still exist, though the former is now powered by Yahoo! How sad for them that I used Google to find that out.) One of these sites held an intriguing link to something called "Fan Fiction," which turned out to be stories based on both *The Original Series* and *The Next Generation*, and I figured, hey, I already read the franchise-sanctioned novels based on both series, why shouldn't I give these a whirl?

Oh. Dear. Such a mistake that was. I well remember my thoughts as I read one: "What?! What the hell is going on here? Kirk and Spock should not be doing *that!* Stop it, Kirk and Spock! My eyes, my eyes!" Yes, I had innocently stumbled onto my first example of slash fan fiction, and that is the kind of thing you just cannot unsee.

It's not that I have any problem with same-sex couplings. In fact, I encourage them. But even the most imaginative of fan fiction writers should, in my humble opinion, adhere to the boundaries set upon the characters by their creators and caretakers and not fly off on the most ridiculous of Alternate Universe tangents. I just feel like, when you're playing in someone else's playground, you should at least have the courtesy not to knock over the seesaw and break the chains on the swing-set. I mean, fine, suggest Angel (David Boreanaz) and Spike (James Marsters) crossed swords occasionally in their bad old days, or give *Lost Girl*'s bisexual Bo (Anna Silk) a tryst with the Dark Fae's seductive Morrigan (Emmanuelle Vaugier). Neither is unlikely. But don't force poor Bilbo into a sado-masochistic orgy with all his Dwarf companions, or make of poor Dean (Jensen Ackles) and Sam Winchester (Jared Padalecki) a Virginia Andrews novel. That's just wrong, man. Creepy and wrong.

Not that Batman and Wonder Woman is a same sex, against-preference thing, of course (though Wonder Woman's all-female birth society does make you wonder if maybe she and, say, Batgirl wouldn't be a more probable pairing, somewhere down the track), but you see what I mean. I have equal objections to stories that have Aragorn choosing Éowyn over Arwen, or give Castiel (Misha Collins) a romantic history with the Winchester boys' long-dead mom. And don't even get me started on crossover stories, the kind that see Harry Potter, devastated from the loss of Ginny in a tragic Floo Powder incident or some such, move to the US and hook up with Elena from *The Vampire Diaries*. Seriously, just stop it, people. Make up your own stuff.

Also, why bring upon yourself so much torment? Shipping a non-canon couple can only be considered a painful exercise in futility, as those who are certain Sam Witwicky (Shia LaBeouf) and his alien robot car Bumblebee are a match made in the AllSpark would no doubt tell you, if only they weren't—surely—currently under some form of psychiatric assessment.

My formidable opponent has since given us several examples across various media, seeking to prove that a Batman/Wonder Woman relationship might just possibly be sort of canon, and Lord knows I have clung to a hoped-for fictional coupling with perhaps even less to go on (hello, Jack and Sam of *Stargate SG-1*). And I am certainly not suggesting here that a love interest must have been planned, or even considered, from the beginning of the story to end up being awesome; indeed; there are times when a potential romance will catch even the creators off guard, like how Angel was supposed to die only a few episodes into *Buffy the Vampire Slayer* and how over on *Homeland* – if I may be allowed to step outside our usual purview for a moment – apparently only the intense chemistry of Claire Danes and Damien Lewis led to Carrie and Brody's obsessive, disturbing affair of the heart/terrorist mind game. But I think we should let the creators throw us those curve balls before we jump ahead to the end of the inning, and dammit, these characters have been around for upwards of eighty years and have hardly shared more than a chaste peck on the cheek when not under the alien influence of something or other in all that time. If, at this late stage, the DC Comics writers and artists find a way to get the World's Greatest Detective and the Amazing Amazon into some non-Alternate Universe snuggling, I'll be all for it, and if I then have latent questions about the wisdom of having an uncomplicated, earnest soul like Diana Prince as anti-hero, playboy Batman's significant other, I'll just remember how reluctant I was about Scott Summers and Emma Frost at first, and how great Team Marvel made that turn out. (Plus, Batman and Wonder Woman = his-and-her cool planes!)

Until that day, though, I hold fast to the opinion that Wonder Woman and Batman should remain nothing more than teammates and platonic, super-powered super friends.

Uh. Not that I care.

THE BIG BANG THEORY
ARE CATCHPHRASES STILL A THING?
by Matthew Layden

I tend to give things a fair chance. I think immediately hating something without seeing it for yourself is nonsense. So as I write this, I can honestly say that I have seen almost every episode of *The Big Bang Theory*. I can also honestly say that the show is an obnoxious look at a culture that the creators do not understand. I detest, hate, loathe, and despise *The Big Bang Theory*.

So where do I begin? There is so much to hate that it's hard to know, but I guess I can start where every episode basically does: with the concept and characters.

So here we have a show about four "geeks," each with a stereotypical personality: Sheldon (Jim Parsons), the know-it-all geek; Howard (Simon Helberg), the sex-obsessed geek; Raj (Kunal Nayyar), the geek who can't talk to girls; and then finally Leonard (Johnny Galecki), the so-called regular everyday geek. (And they all dress badly!) Leonard and Sheldon live together, get on each other's nerves, and do what the writers of this show think that all geeks do, which is play video games and perform science experiments. When Penny (Kaley Cuoco), an also stereotypical beautiful, dumb blonde, moves into the apartment across the hall from them, Leonard is instantly smitten and thus begins the clichéd will-they-won't-they relationship. Typical stuff you would expect from the multi-camera sitcom, which in itself is outdated and stale.

The so-called nerds on this show are ripe for mocking, yet they don't adhere to the social norms that the characters should be accustomed to. Every single one of these guys has attracted at least one girl that is way out of his league—yes, even Sheldon. I understand character arcs that would ultimately have them be less socially awkward around women, but give me something believable.

Mr. Chuck Lorre, the creator of this show, as well as the equally painful *Two and a Half Men*, *Mike & Molly* and *Dharma & Greg*, and his writers simply do not know the geek culture. They think that all they need to do is a simple Google search and they're good. It's painfully obvious when a joke is thrown in and you realize that no one knows what the joke is really about, but it is "geek centric" so it has to be funny, right? The characters, their set-ups and punch lines can be easily mapped out. Reference something that geeks love, from movies, to TV shows, comics, board games, video games, cosplay, etc. and then reference another one. Cue obnoxious laughter that goes on far too long (more on that later). Simply referencing *Star Wars* and *Star Trek* doesn't make a joke funny, or mean that you understand it. It's a cheap, uninspired and lazy laugh at something that people already recognize. Early on, the show actually offered up some smart and witty jokes, but they have long-since been replaced by the "go-to geek reference," and its often one that's been used before. (How many times has the poor quality of the movie *Daredevil* been played for laughs, for instance?) The only show that is worse at this is probably *Family Guy*, another show that is no longer funny. Want to watch a show that makes pop culture references funny? Watch *Community*.

The writers of this show seem to think that lazy, cheap and predictable humor is genius. Granted, *The Big Bang Theory* is popular, but popularity does not equal quality. The funniest shows on television over the past ten years or so have without a doubt been single camera series. Look to shows like *Arrested Development*, *It's Always Sunny in Philadelphia*, *Modern Family* and *The Office*; they changed the way comedy is done on television. *The Big Bang Theory* is stuck in the past. It wants to be a *Friends* or a *Seinfeld*, but I'm here to tell you it is far, FAR from either of those shows.

That obnoxious laugh track I mentioned earlier is one of the most irritating things about *The Big Bang Theory*, and it means that they can get away with things that a show without a laugh track can't. For one thing, they need far less dialogue; the show spends a chunk of its time simply waiting. Characters sit there in silence waiting for the forced laughter to come and go. Watch any one of the numerous videos online that take the laugh track OUT of the show and see how unfunny it actually is. We viewers know what is funny; we don't need prompting to laugh. Shows with a laugh track need the assistance. Being filmed in front of a live audience doesn't mean they don't add another layer of laughter on top to fill it out. They do and this show is guilty of that. A show can have a laugh track, but play out and be written without that style in mind. *How I Met Your Mother* is a perfect example of this; I didn't realize there was a laugh track until at least three seasons into the show.

Why do they still call it *The Big Bang Theory*, anyway? They should change the name to *The Sheldon Show*, since he has taken over completely. I get it, he's popular and Jim Parsons is actually quite good in the role, but overexposure is what kills characters that were once amusing. Sheldon has gone from funny (yes, he *was* funny) to tiresome. There are shows out there that embrace nerds and let the audience laugh with them, not AT them. Watch a little show called *Spaced* or *The IT Crowd*. Those shows get what it is like to be a geek. *The Big Bang Theory* does not.

Also, I really need to ask this...are catch phrases still a thing? BAZINGA.

Cue laughter.

33

"Bazinga!" is one of the worst catch phrases since Urkel's "Did I do that?" Again, I point to a show like *Community*, which has satirized the catchphrase, with the insanely stupid yet utterly hilarious use of "Pop-Pop." "Bazinga!" is overused and is an immediate cue for more laughter. When a joke falls flat, let's throw in a "Bazinga!" Again, all this points to lazy, uninspired writing.

The only thing that I find more irritating than this show are some of its fans, who come up with lame excuses for why I don't like it. "Oh, you don't get the humor, the jokes are too smart." So, because they are geeks and talk about science the jokes are all of a sudden smart? If I don't laugh, I don't get it? How obnoxious is that? Want a show that shoves "smart" down your throat, and is still funny? Watch *Frasier*.

I consider myself a true geek; a few of my friends are geeks as well. Does this show depict us correctly? Not a chance. As I mentioned before, it sidesteps real characters for stereotypical ones. It paints those of us in the geek community as those four core "losers." I urge, I plead, I sincerely hope that people will recognize the hollowness that is this show. *The Big Bang Theory* needs to die a quick death, but it probably won't, its ratings are way too high. So I guess I should be pleading with the vast majority of the viewers of this show: the non-geeks. So non-geeks out there, I'm talking to you. Stop watching this show. Choose something… anything else.

Community, for instance.

© *Matthew Layden, 2013*

THE BIG BANG THEORY
ARE WE ABOVE A LITTLE MOCKERY?
by Chris Nagy

Having digested my esteemed colleague's thoughts on *The Big Bang Theory*, I find myself in agreement with virtually every point made. However, I am left with a broader question:

So what?

To summarize, the case against *The Big Bang Theory* is that it is unrealistic, poorly written, with outdated production values and a complete misunderstanding (and implied disrespect) of the real geeks of the world. Of these points, I say true, arguable, true, and true. Of particular concern seems to be the perception of a blatant misrepresentation of the geek culture. Let's put it out there again: yes, this show is terribly, horribly unrealistic, perhaps even more so than my opponent has suggested. Out here in the real world, Sheldon is a friendless pariah who someday becomes the Unabomber. Howard spends his time and income in the "professional services" section of Craigslist. Raj is a raging alcoholic, as lonely + can't talk to women while sober = drunk 24/7. Leonard is bitter and alone. Penny acknowledges none of them. But, if you think the current show is unwatchable, try a few episodes of *The Real World: TBBT*. You will never turn on your TV again.

Recently, I have heard essentially the same complaint from a very different source. Among the few television shows I watch with any regularity is *Sons of Anarchy*. Having the opportunity to discuss the show with several patch-wearing bikers, I asked them about their view of it. Their immediate vitriol was surprising, and their primary argument was that the show was so misrepresentative of the culture they have strived to create that they found it personally insulting. Sound familiar? Their arguments are all completely correct, and yet they too seem to have missed an important point. These shows are not intended to be realistic representations of anyone, nor should they be. There is a generally universal understanding that television fiction is just that, and we should consider those who believe these shows are accurate representations of life in the same manner as we consider those who wear tin-foil hats. This is true whether you are a regular attendee of Comic-Con or Sturgis.

Fundamentally, most people do not watch television because it is realistic. They watch because it is not. None of us have everyday lives that are interesting enough to provide entertainment to a large group of viewers over six or seven seasons. Life is simultaneously more complex and less entertaining than that of any successful television character. As such, the creators might or might not recognize that they are not providing realistic representations, but I am certain they do not really care. Accuracy is never really the goal.

When viewed through the lens of "sitcom as simple entertainment, and nothing more," the other objections to this show become more palpable. *The Big Bang Theory* is intended not as anything resembling documentary, but rather as entertainment for the masses. As this, it is highly effective, being among the most watched and liked shows on television. But shows about geeks are written for everyone except geeks, just as shows about bikers are written for everyone except bikers. Are the creators of *The Big Bang Theory* making fun of me? Maybe. Am I worried about it? Of course not. As a culture, do we geeks really consider ourselves above a little mockery? I submit that cosplay, MMOGs, action figure collections, and Klingon language lessons are reasonable topics of humor, and our enjoyment in some or all of those interests should not and does not rely upon public understanding.

Once we get beyond that, these arguments boil down to taste. I agree that the show is done in an old (proven?) style. Yes, the laugh track can be annoying. But I personally find it to be cute and funny. And, while some are offended because they perceive themselves to be the butt of the joke, that is what I like most about this show. I regularly make math jokes, speak a (very) little bit of Klingon, and actually would stand in line for hours to see an extra twenty-one seconds of *Raiders of the Lost Ark*. Does that make me the subject of humor for others? Objectively, yes. I can live with that.

So, perhaps the geek culture should accept some minor slings and arrows, continue to enjoy what we do, and recognize that television is inherently unrealistic when it comes to us and every other group on the planet.

Except for *Lost*. That shit could really happen.

.

..

...

Bazinga.

BUFFY THE VAMPIRE SLAYER, SEASON 6
A COMPLETE MESS
by K. Burtt

There comes a time in every person's life where they realize that their favorite TV show isn't perfect. Having that realization and explaining some of the reasons behind it in a public forum are two completely different things, and yet here I am, about to do just that ("forced to do that" might be a better phrase to use, as I've been told certain photographs will be released if I do not cooperate and, well, that just wouldn't be pleasant. For everyone). Luckily (?) for me, doing so in this case is not actually as mental-scar-inducing as it might be otherwise, as the show in question is *Buffy*, and the lack-o'-perfection in question is Season 6.

I have often extolled the virtues of *Buffy* in general around these parts, and in doing so made mention of my dislike of Season 6. Before going into details about the reasons why, though, a confession must be made (*gasp*)... I haven't actually watched Season 6 in years, with the exception of the musical episode, "Once More With Feeling", of course. Why? Well, 'cause I didn't like it, obviously. But because of this, my forthcoming list of things that bugged me from the season is mostly coming from memory. I am not completely rigid in my opinions, though, and thus perhaps even I could be swayed by the eloquent and insightful comments by my opponent, at least enough to watch the season again (what, being forced to watch more *Buffy*? Horrors!). But confessions / disclaimers / escape-routes aside, here are some of the things that really bugged me about Season 6.

The Trio

Okay, time for confession #2. I am a geek. Yes, I realize that such a statement is incredibly earth-shattering to you, faithful readers, but it is true. As such, I can fully appreciate the humor the Trio provided. Quite the amusing (and somewhat endearing, perhaps) comic relief. What they weren't, though, were viable antagonists. Too much comic relief to really be taken as a serious threat. So the fact that they were around essentially the entire season as the only season-long-big-bad (besides the Scoobies themselves) just didn't work for me. I would have been fine with them creating/summoning/otherwise-being-the-cause-of an actual Big Bad halfway through the season, but lasting the entire season? Um, no. Plus, I never bought Jonathan (Danny Strong) being a bad guy. At all. Yes, I realize he attempted to redeem himself by the end of the season, but why was he being a bad guy to begin with? Just seemed out of character. So overall: geeky, *Buffy*-versions of the Three Stooges? Sure. A veritable Triumvirate of Terror? I think not.

Willow

Speaking of people acting out of character, one of the central plots for the entire season was Willow's addiction to magic. I didn't buy it. It's not that the concept was bad, per se – it was the execution (errr... the execution of the concept... not the actual execution performed by Willow herself later in the season). The way it was built up felt out of character considering Willow had started exploring magic use at the end of the second season. At no time between then and the sixth season has there been a hint of the idea that a) Willow had an addiction-prone personality, and b) magic was addictive (at least in the way it was portrayed here). How Willow turned dark and evil due to Tara's death... that I could buy. Corruption due to magic use? That fit. But addiction? Not so much.

Magic

Furthermore, most magic in previous seasons of *Buffy* seemed to require some amount of effort – a ritual, an incantation, something. So it also struck me as odd the extent in this season to which Willow (and Witch Amy) were throwing magic around randomly without much thought or effort. Seemed inconsistent.

Spike/Buffy

Returning to out-of-character theme, I also had issues with the... err... "relationship" between Spike and Buffy. Maybe I'm scarred and biased against it due to the fact that after several years I was finally able to convince my grandmother to watch the show (she's one cool lady) and the first episode she watches is "Smashed" in which Spike and Buffy... err... connect, and thus fervently wish that it had never happened. But still... Spike was a vampire, without a soul. He found out he could hurt Buffy. I think he would have killed her. I was okay with his Buffy-obsession that had been present throughout the past several seasons, but just couldn't believe this payoff being in character him. And neither with Buffy. I understand what they were going for with Buffy's dealing with returning from the dead and all the issues thereof, but I thought it felt forced by the writers to have Buffy and Spike hook up.

The Writing

Which brings me to the overall issue I think I had with the season: the writing wasn't up to *Buffy* standards. Maybe it was because the team was too ambitious with their plot ideas, particularly due to this being the first season on a new network. Maybe Joss was too distracted with both *Angel* and preparing for *Firefly* to make sure this season was up to par (really, this only had one Joss written/directed episode. One!). Whatever the reason, the season felt full of plot and character inconsistencies, without the quotable and clever writing (with exceptions, of course) to make up for it.

"Doublemeat Palace"

And "Doublemeat Palace"... really? Really. Terrible episode. No excuse for such an episode six seasons into a kickass show.

So, Season 6? Not a good season. Rather disappointing. Not without its merits or high points, to be sure, but certainly lacking the quality of *Buffy* of seasons past. When introducing the show to new watchers (which you are all doing even to this day, right?), don't start with this season. Particularly episode 9 "Smashed." Especially if your grandmother is around.

<Shudder>

BUFFY THE VAMPIRE SLAYER, SEASON 6
A COMPELLING METAPHOR
by Sara Paige

Last year while I was in school, I went through the first six seasons of *Buffy* with a friend whenever we needed to decompress. In a program that was 70% Type A male, it was nice to get a little female-oriented ass-kicking in when we could. When we got past Season 5 I warned my friend, who was new to Buffy, that Season 6 was the most universally hated season. As it turned out, we actually liked it quite a bit. Honestly, even when the season originally aired, I wondered why people didn't like it as much as I did. In the rewatching, I have come to see even more what Joss and company were trying to do.

The typical complaints about Season 6 (which my opponent brings up as well), are Willow's addiction story line, the crappy villains and the really dark place Buffy went to with Spike. But what I think I appreciated as others did not was the reality: sometimes everything just falls to pieces and you ask yourself: "Where am I going, and why am I in this hand basket?" It's what people don't like about those 60s movies where everyone dies at the end: there's no light. Buffy always had a light, funny side that was almost completely absent in this season. For me, that spoke to a time in my twenties where nothing was going right, and I lost who I was. It spoke to that dark part that's afraid nothing will ever get better.

Buffy sings out her suffering in "Once More With Feeling." Everyone can talk about the Trio and say how they were lame villains. They were! It's true! But they weren't the Big Bad of the season. Darth Rosenberg wasn't either. The Big Bad was Buffy being ripped from Heaven, Willow losing Tara and going off the deep end (twice!), Xander throwing away Anya because he was too immature, and Giles leaving. And like Season 4, all that mindless personal horror comes together in the end through metaphor. Willow can't handle how dark reality is, so does the only logical thing: she becomes the darkest thing on the planet. She becomes harsher than reality. Only love and self-sacrifice wakes them up to the fact that life doesn't have to only mean suffering.

Watching the episodes back to back gave me a new perspective. In terms of the Trio, we see an evolution. They begin as ineffective dorks who replay comic book fantasies. However, when Warren tries to rape Katrina and she calls all the men out, it becomes clear that Jonathan wakes up, Andrew is merely mindless, but I wouldn't walk down a dark alley with Warren if you paid me. He was scary in a very human way that we didn't often see on *Buffy*: totally without conscience, and for no reason. Five seasons of the Master and Glory and their like, and it was Warren, the ineffective geek, who gave me chills.

Spike and Buffy was absolutely a destructive relationship – literally and figuratively. And again, everything about it made sense to me. It encapsulated so many thoroughly toxic relationships I've seen. If Buffy had been raised from the dead and there had been no consequences, people would have complained. Buffy reacting to depression and anger in a way that young women do all the time? By getting into a poisonous sexual relationship with an asshole? People hate it. They hate it the same way people hate their smart, funny, adorable friend dating the creep that cheats on her. That it never makes sense is obvious, but that it also happens all the time is the truth. Joss Whedon and Marti Noxon were just taking a common reaction of depression and insecurity and creating a metaphor. The creep in real life is human. On Buffy, our friend really is screwing a monster. People complained about Noxon's handiwork in this: I thought it was pretty accurate to the consequences of Buffy's self-hatred.

I'll admit, Willow's addiction wasn't my favorite storyline. I would have preferred it to be about abuse of power, and it was for a time. Wiping Tara's memory, putting people in other dimensions, even altering the fabric of life and death were things that signaled Willow's power trip. Why the writers made Rack a dealer and Willow a drugged-out loser is a little confusing. Perhaps they had written themselves into a corner by making once sweet Willow a power-crazy douchebag? Better to make her an addict? (The large amounts of water she drank for two episodes was over the top. Does magic dehydrate you like a rum and diet?)

The one thing that does transcend the debate about whether she was an addict or an asshole is the common thread was that she was out of control. What speaks to me about her storyline is that sometimes you wake up from a situation and realize that you aren't the person you wanted to be. That maybe, you don't even like the person you've become. That was Willow in Season 6. The tragedy is that she tried to be a good person, but under pressure reverted back because she couldn't take life anymore.

Xander saves the world with talk of Kindergarten. As for the smaller stories of Xander and Anya, Giles, and Dawn, these mirror the horror of the main storylines. They all act out in the only way people do: by moving, by splitting or acting out to get attention. Anything to break through. That Xander saves the world is a reflection of what he'd been trying to do all season: inject reason and stop the hurting.

In any case, I hope that I have convinced you even a little bit that there are layers to this season that should be appreciated. Joss Whedon's vision was always to use the fantastical as a metaphor for the reality of life. This season reflects back to us the ugliness we see in ourselves: something we don't always want to see, but it is nevertheless what we occasionally need to confront.

© *Sara Paige, 2010*

CELEBRITY PRIVACY
JUST SIGN THE DAMN THING!
by Kate Nagy

In the midway of this our mortal life, I found myself in my lonely office, sipping Diet Coke and Googling "Jon Hamm's penis."

And I had to ask myself, "How did it ever come to this?"

A bit of background might be appropriate here. It seems that his Creator has seen fit to endow Jon Hamm, best known for his role as the manly Don Draper in *Mad Men*, with an apparatus that is the envy of all men everywhere. Indeed, it is whispered that neither boxers nor briefs are sufficient to contain his might. Photographic evidence exists (it's not hard to find). The modest Hamm finds this attention to his nethers to be somewhat perplexing; as he confided to Rolling Stone:

> *"...It is a little rude. It just speaks to a broader freedom that people feel like they have – a prurience...I'm wearing pants, for fuck's sake. Lay off. I mean, it's not like I'm a fucking lead miner. There are harder jobs in the world. But when people feel the freedom to create Tumblr accounts about my cock, I feel like that wasn't part of the deal ... But whatever. I guess it's better than being called out for the opposite."*

Somewhere, co-star Christina Hendricks – widely celebrated for her hourglass figure – is laughing mirthlessly. Also, given that at the time this quote was made, Season 6 of *Mad Men* was just about to premiere. I'd like to take a minute to acknowledge that Hamm's publicist is freakin' brilliant. "Oh, boo hoo hoo, everyone's talking about the UNPRECEDENTED SIZE OF MY WANG! It's so embarrassing! There are whole web sites dedicated to the MIND-BLOWING DIMENSIONS OF MY JUNK. I so wish that people would grow up and stop talking about the fact that I HAVE THE BIGGEST PENIS IN HOLLYWOOD, because it's so crass how people are commenting on MY ELEPHANTINE MEMBER all the time. – Oh yeah! Don't miss Mad Men, returning to AMC on April 7 at 9 p.m.! I implore you, during the press tour, DON'T ask me how I wrangle the ANACONDA IN MY PANTS, because, all appearances to the contrary, I DO value my privacy. AND MY GIANT SCHLONG."

Seriously, it's that publicist's world; we only live in it. What better way could there possibly be to promote the upcoming season premiere of a show about an unapologetic alpha male than by reminding the whole world that even the actor's dick swings longer, thicker, and stronger than anyone else's? Genius, I'm telling you.

At the end of the day, questions around the "how" and "why" of what I was doing on my computer that fatal evening are unimportant – suffice it to say that life as a *Geek Speak* editor is not all elegant soirees, witty banter, and exquisite vintages. A better question might be: what have we as a society come to, when a man's private parts can be used (successfully, I might add) as a marketing tool? What deeper sociological meaning can be drawn from the fact that an otherwise level-headed woman who searches the internet for evidence of the Hammer of Hamm will find it without any trouble at all? Isn't this a blatant invasion of Mr. Hamm's privacy? Does Hamm, as a public figure, have the same right to privacy that the rest of us do, for that matter? What is his duty to us – the fans who made him famous? What is our duty to him – the actor who so ably entertains us? What does it all mean?

Look, the world we live in is strange and often unpleasant. People e-mail one another photos of their genitalia and tweet their every fart. Facebook is a veritable wasteland of poop shots, wang shots, boob shots, barf shots, and rambling, drunken confessions. At the same time, reality TV has obliterated the line between the personal and the public. It's no wonder that "privacy" is but a word in the dictionary to a lot of people. (Blame the Kardashians. I do. It may not be accurate or fair, but they don't care and it makes me feel better.) Combine this let-it-all-hang-out culture with fans' natural interest in the artists who bring our favorite characters to life, and it's perhaps unfortunate but not surprising that some loyal fans are actually taken aback when their favorite star doesn't want to sign their buttocks in the frozen foods aisle at the Piggly Wiggly.

Most actors are gracious about the stream of autograph requests, overzealous photographers, and general importuning that flows their way. A few are not. I'm going to argue that Hamm – and other famous types – do have an expectation of privacy… but it's not the same expectation that you and I have. The famous artists we love have every right to lead their own private lives – but like it or not, autograph requests, photographs, and overeager fans are part of the package. They're part of the job. And if the actors don't like that aspect of the job, they're always free to go do something else.

Being an actor is not like being an accountant or a paralegal, and if you accept the perks that come with celebrity – the salaries in excess of $100K for a week of work, the swag bags at award shows, the free designer clothing – one must, as with any job, accept the downside. For an accountant, the downside may involve eyestrain and being stuck in an airless, windowless cubicle for 40+ hours per week. For an actor, it involves mingling with the little people from time to time, no matter how distasteful this may be.

Some actors are more open to interaction with their assorted publics than others. At one end of the spectrum are the Kardashians, Lohans, and

Real Housewives of the world, who personally notify *OK!* magazine pretty much every time they brush their teeth. A slightly less… pathological example is Tom Hiddleston, who has resolutely maintained a gracious and friendly composure in the face of a fanbase that could charitably be described as "batshit crazy." (Hiddleston is actually a lot nicer about some of his nuttier fans than I would be, and I can only wish him the best and hope that he has a competent security advisor on his personal staff.)

Others find a middle ground by taking to Twitter and parceling out their interactions with the Great Unwashed 140 characters at a time. And why not? Sending out the occasional Happy Birthday tweet to a fan makes the fan happy and helps enhance their project's reputation out in the world. And tweeting takes under a minute. It's a win-win for everyone involved, no?

At the opposite end of the spectrum, however, you have people like Tommy Lee Jones, whose chronic bad mood is so legendary that it was the object of considerable mirth at this year's Oscars, or *Once Upon a Time*'s Ginnifer Goodwin, who famously approaches the red carpet with all the verve of a condemned prisoner being led to the gallows. And I just want to shake her. "Ginnifer!" I want to cry. "You are being photographed at an event that most people would sell their firstborn to attend. Your frock, which was provided to you at no cost, is worth more than I take home in a month. Would it kill you to smile? I think it would not."

Fans can take things too far, of course. (Tom Hiddleston knows all about this.) Not for a minute am I suggesting otherwise. Specifically, this whole trend of people going on YouTube all "I live in small-town Oklahoma and my daddy is in Afghanistan and they just foreclosed on our farm and I tore my ACL, thereby shattering my dream of playing football in the NFL so I think Miss Mila Kunis needs to attend my senior prom with me" is pretty played. Actors leaving certain environments – a funeral, say, or their urologist's office – should be left strictly alone. Celebrities' kids are absolutely off limits. And assholes who take upskirt photographs fully deserve to be publicly castrated and forced to live out the remainder of their lives in a group house on 24-hour reality TV.

But it's also true that the stars who really want to keep things on the down low find a way. For example, evidently married couple Anna Paquin and Stephen Moyer of *True Blood* fame had twins last fall. We didn't hear about the birth until a month after the fact, and even today, I couldn't tell you the babies' names or even their genders. When Daniel Craig and Rachel Weisz got married, most people thought he and Satsuki Mitchell were still together, so hush-hush did Agent 007 keep his romantic life. And even as the tabloids were full of Sandra Bullock's divorce from that neo-Nazi motorcycle guy, she was out adopting an adorable little boy and not saying a word about it until months after the fact.

I get that it's tedious to – as Christina Hendricks often does – navigate interviews on the interesting subject of one's cleavage. It's annoying and probably a little scary to be ambushed by hug-seeking strangers in the allergy medicine aisle of the local pharmacy. And as an introvert myself, as I strongly suspect Ginnifer Goodwin to be, I can honestly say that if I were required, as a condition of my employment, to put on an uncomfortable gown and walk a gauntlet of screaming photographers, only to be critiqued the next day by the likes of Tom & Lorenzo and the Fug Girls on every aspect of my appearance, from makeup to pedicure, I wouldn't just scowl. I'd probably die.

I get it! But do you know what else is tedious? Spending hours up to one's elbows in cold, scummy water, struggling to keep the clean dishes flowing during the evening dinner rush. Scrubbing down a bathroom in which someone has just been violently ill. Baking in the sun while operating an unlicensed carnival ride that actually delivers a mild electrical shock whenever it's turned on. Those are all things I've done for considerably less pay and fewer perks, and even then I knew that as sucky as those jobs were, millions of people had it worse, and what's more? Ultimately, I was there because I was chose to be. So are the people whose faces grace the pages of People and Us.

Last spring, as I was reading my esteemed opponent's entertaining account of autograph hounds stalking their favorite stars at Oz Comic-Con, an anecdote shared by one Michael caught my attention:

> *"[Comedian] Louis C. K. said he hated people coming up to him and wanting a signature and wanting to get their photo taken with him when he was out and about. He refused to do that. However, what he would do was shake your hand, ask your name and have a conversation with you. And then afterwards, if you engaged with him, then he would sign and photograph or anything for free. But, here's the thing he got out of it. A lot of people, when he said 'no, I won't sign anything; no, I won't take a photo with you,' just walked away. They weren't interested in him for him, they were only interested in him as a celebrity."*

I was immediately struck by two thoughts.

First, dude comes off as a bit of a control freak. Do I think for one hot minute that he really cares about the people requesting his autograph in more than a general, existential sense? No, I do not. I do think that he's highly invested in controlling his interactions with his audience, and Teaching Them an Important Lesson about the Humanity of Celebrity, etc.

And second, "They weren't interested in him for him, they were only interested in him as a celebrity."

Like it or not, that's probably true. Accept it, Mr. C.K. Accept it, or find something different to do.

CELEBRITY PRIVACY
JUST LEAVE THEM ALONE!
by Rachel Hyland

I am not immune to the allure of celebrity. I understand the thrill that can come over one when suddenly in the orbit of someone you admire – especially if that someone is ridiculously attractive and/or inhabits a character you love on a show you adore. Whether at a convention or on the street, there is something so surreal about it: the moment of recognition and then the pounding of your heart, despite yourself, knowing you're breathing the very same air as Westley from *The Princess Bride*, or Spike from *Buffy the Vampire Slayer*, or William freaking Shatner. Even authors, directors and screenwriters can arouse the same level of breathless astonishment from those who know them on sight, as anyone who has also been in close proximity to George R. R. Martin, Steven Spielberg, or Aaron Sorkin can doubtless tell you.

But why is it we feel that it is then acceptable to approach these total strangers as they go about their lives and importune them for conversation, photographs, signatures, and (worst of all) hugs, just because we know them from TV, or wherever? Sure, a cordial "hello" is fine – that is no more than you'd say to anyone on the street, and seriously, people don't give each other enough such common courtesy any more. Even a "love your work" as you walk past probably wouldn't come amiss; most people like being told they're good at their jobs, even unsolicited and by random passersby. But expecting anyone to take time out of their lives to interact with you, to be working when they are on their own time, is frankly obscene.

My opponent in this debate referenced her inspiration for this Geek vs. Geek as a feature I penned earlier this year called "Smiles and Scribbles for Sale," in which I examine the weirdness that is attending fan conventions and paying celebrities to be nice to you. At the particular event I covered, one could get an autograph from the likes of *The Rocky Horror Picture Show*'s Patricia Quinn and *Stargate SG-1*'s Richard Dean Anderson for between $30 and $50—a cost thousands of fans were happy to pay across the course of a weekend. Photos with them, and their fellow celebrity guests, were also available for between $50 and $150 a pop, and the lines for these were really extraordinary, crowds of giddy fans waiting patiently to spend less than a minute with their all-too-human heroes before walking away, wreathed in smiles, exhilarated by their fully-paid brushes with fame.

My colleague was particularly struck by an anecdote about the comedian Louis C. K., who refuses all autograph and photo requests in public unless the person in question has a chat with him first. She thought it made Mr. C. K. seem controlling and ungracious – I, on the other hand, find the story utterly endearing, and think it makes him the opposite. It would be easy for him to just dash off a quick signature and send the demanding on their way; instead, he is willing to invest precious private minutes in their company and then also give them an autograph. Rather than shirking his Celebrity Responsibility, I actually think this means he's exceeding it. If, indeed, this story has any basis in truth, that is – for all I know Michael, my source for this, misremembered it or made it up entirely.

And it is actually another quote of this very same Michael's that really encapsulates my position on this whole approaching-celebrities thing:

> *"It makes me understand why they ask you to pay for these things at conventions. It's a fan experience with a character they got paid to play. You're treating them as their job, so why shouldn't they get a salary for it?"*

When you go up to a celebrity in public – be they an actor, a director, a writer, whatever – and expect them to put on a free show for your personal amusement, it's basically turning them into momentary indentured servants. It's "Dance, monkey! Dance!" with no regard to that person's right to refuse, because if they turn you down, or if they are perceived to be uncomfortable or unfriendly, then it is most likely they that will suffer for it as slighted fans take to social media (which can even end up being reported by the conventional media) and damn the famous people for daring to want to have lunch with their families uninterrupted, etc. It's not like they can log into their Twitter accounts and rant about you by name. Does this really seem fair?

My colleague says: "Being an actor is not like being an accountant or a paralegal, and if you accept the perks that come with celebrity – the salaries in excess of $100K for a week of work, the swag bags at award shows, the free designer clothing – one must, as with any job, accept the downside." She takes to task Ginnifer Goodwin and Tommy Lee Jones, among others, for disdaining, or even resenting, the natural consequence of being successful in their chosen field. But don't we all know doctors who gripe about being at parties and having people show them their suspicious moles—or, indeed, accountants who are frustrated that they are always expected to calculate the tip, and paralegals who resent having to dispense free legal advice? I mean, you wouldn't go up to a master bricklayer on a worksite and say you're so fond of his work that he simply must come over to your house and fix your front step, gratis. You wouldn't accost a taxi driver and tell him you're so impressed by his driving skill that he simply has to give you a ride to work, free of charge. You don't see a nanny playing tag with some kids in the park and decide she is so good at it that she needs to include yours in the game, too, while you sit back and read a magazine. Every day we make the conscious decision not to impose on others' time and skills – especially when they're not even casual acquaintances of ours. So why do we think it's okay to impose on an actor's? Their special skill in this world is convincing us that they are feeling something they are not; doesn't harassing them in their down-time, making them pretend they are absolutely delighted to meet random ol' us, feel a little like making someone work for free? After all, it's fine to contract the bricklayer, to hire the driver, to employ the nanny. If I worry that calling on one of my best friends, a surgeon, for free medical advice is a nuisance, then how much more of one is asking a total stranger to turn on their million-dollar charm for my fannish pleasure? When you approach an actor and get them to, essentially, perform for you – for nothing – you are basically just stealing their nice.

Now look, there may well be actors, writers, directors and the like who welcome the attention. If you happen upon that guy who played Crewman #2 in an episode of *Babylon 5* and you want to let him know you valued his work, then sure, he probably doesn't get it too often, go say hi. (But, obviously, back off if he seems unreceptive to your advances; it may be that convention appearances are now how he makes his living and you're stealing his nice, too.) But for those who don't get a minute's peace from either fans or paparazzi – think Robert Pattinson, at the height of the *Twilight* craze – shouldn't we all just let them be? Shouldn't we treat them as we would want to be treated, were our circumstances reversed? And surely none of us wants our garbage combed through by the curious. Right?

Speaking of the paparazzi, that is a whole other subject that I won't cover here, except that I don't quite understand how my opponent can advocate for the limited rights of the famous – leave them alone at the doctor's office, or at a funeral; absolutely lay off their kids – when it is clear that no such lines of decency exist for the determined autograph-hunter and money shot-seeker. The small way in which I protest this kind of hateful hounding of families out for a walk or new lovers on a date is to not (ever!) buy the magazines in which these photos are published. Though I will admit to occasionally flipping through them in the checkout aisle to read of Jennifer Aniston's latest romantic imbroglio or see Ryan Gosling half-naked on the beach. (I'm only human.)

Often we check out magazine stories about these A-through-D List people because we've been inducted into their lives, usually at their own buzz-building instigation, and so we want to know just what is (allegedly!) going on with them now. Or, y'know. They're really hot. But it is when that interest shifts from the page to real life that it becomes problematic, especially when it comes to the more cult-like stars. I would hazard a guess that most of us know nothing about their private lives at all – I'm unclear on whether most of my favorite genre actors are married, or gay, or have kids, or whatever – but in recognizing their faces, and in identifying them with characters that we do know, we somehow decide that they owe us reciprocal significance in a world utterly divorced from their onscreen pseudo-realities.

But that's not even the worst of it. Regardless of the reasoning behind this fetishizing of celebrity, the upshot is the same; when we insert ourselves into celebrity lives, when we make of them an Ideal, we give them power over us, because while we consider them important, to them we are – at best – mere irritants, and – at worst – pitiful sycophants. (Or vice versa.)

And frankly, I'd rather be the star of my own life story than play second fiddle to Jon Hamm's junk.

© Rachel Hyland, 2013

CHILDHOOD NOSTALGIA
SLEEPING DOGS, THOU SHALT LIE!
by Jason Murdoch

Let sleeping dogs lie.

That is all.

That's my point.

Here's the issue: I've recently gone back and re-watched a number of cartoon series that dare I say, went as far as to shape my very being. I mean, I am a true child of the 80's, and as such, Saturday morning TV practically raised me.

And when it wasn't Saturday morning TV, it was weekday afternoon TV.

Look at the list of pure awesomeness that was on around then: *ThunderCats, Transformers, He-Man, BraveStarr, SilverHawks, Ulysses 31* and so much more. And as far as afternoons went: *Teenage Mutant Ninja Turtles, Monkey Magic, Samurai Pizza Cats*... the list goes on.

Now I will defend these shows to the bitter end against anyone who would sully their good name. But a warning to those of a similar ilk who feel tempted to go back and re-visit these moments of radiant joy, these memories that make you all warm and fuzzy, and a little happy in the pants.

Don't.

Don't do it.

Nothing but disappointment awaits you. Heed my words and hang on to the glorious memories you have, hold the life lessons that the likes of Optimus Prime (the original one, not any one violated by technology and 3D graphics) imparted. But for the love of all that is holy, when you're browsing your local purveyor of digital versatile disks, and see Season 1 of *Centurions* sitting there on the shelf, walk on, dear friend. It is naught but a snake, tempting you with its apple.

Why? you may ask. You may even wonder what harm this could possibly bring.

Fine.

You asked for it.

Don't say I didn't warn you.

Get ready for some brutal truth.

First, you may not be aware, but every single episode of *Transformers* follows exactly the same formula:

"The Decepticons are stealing energon cubes"
"Autobots roll out"
Pew-pew!

"Megatron is getting away"
"Starscream!"

Now, let's look at *Inspector Gadget*:

"Bad guys are stealing stuff!"
"Go-Go Gadget something... woah... whoops... Oh no..."
"C'mon Brains, we'll go help Uncle Gadget!"
Bad guy gets foiled, Penny does all the work, Gadget gets praise.
"I'll get you next time Gadget"

Do I need to even mention *Scooby-Doo*?

Or *He-Man*? Cringer turns into Battlecat, Prince Adam turns into He-Man, Skeletor gets away, He-Man tells you to look both ways before crossing the street, or call your mother, or pick up litter.

And name one episode of *Voltron* where a bad dude doesn't get split open with a big ass sword at the end.

You can't, can you?

These are things that seem awesome when you were a kid. You didn't notice the formula, and if you did, it was AWESOME so you didn't care.

Growing up sucks. You notice this crap.

You notice the fact that every character across every series is exactly the same. You notice that the dialogue isn't particularly good, that the animation isn't particularly good, that the plot is nonexistent, and that the characters are two-dimensional.

Whilst you live in blissful ignorance of this, life is a happy place, full of rainbows and unicorns. Hold onto that. My main point is not that any of these shows are sub-epic. They were clearly the greatest entertainment ever invented. Hours of my life were spent absorbing them in detail. Would I change that? Not for a second.

I'm also not saying that TV has gotten any better since (my younger siblings were watching *Dragon Ball-Z* — that's just a dude on the screen with lines passing by him for half an hour). But all I'm saying is that it's a poor idea to go back and rewatch them. You won't enjoy it.

My counterpart will try and lead you to believe that rewatching these precious gems of your childhood will rekindle past joy, that it will provide you with some kind of escape back to the innocence of times gone by.

This is a fallacy.

You will want to revisit a simpler time, but there is no way you can avoid seeing the standard plots, the standard characters, the complete lack of violence. (I swear all my cartoon heroes kicked some serious ass, yet no one ever got hurt. Stupid G ratings...)

Unfortunately, brothers and sisters, like it or not, you have grown. Grown into cynical, angry, jaded readers of online magazines. You can't view the world through the eyes of your younger selves.

There are two possible results that can come of rewatching your old favorites:

1. They will transport you back to a happier time.
OR
2. You will inflict your years of "wisdom" onto them, you will peer too deeply into the rabbit hole, and try and make sense of what peers back.

Guess which option is more likely. It is not a happy place.

© Jason Murdoch, 2017

CHILDHOOD NOSTALGIA
AWAKE, SLEEPING DOGS! RUN! JUMP! FROLIC!
by Rachel Hyland

I have always enjoyed returning to familiar and favored fictional haunts. As a child, I reread every Enid Blyton book on my shelf until the bindings nearly gave out; I watched my preferred movies — *Pete's Dragon, Robin Hood, The Boy Who Could Fly*, and *Xanadu* — over and over and over, to the point of wearing out the fragile video tapes on which they then reposed; and I absorbed rerun after rerun of *Astro Boy, Danger Mouse*, and *She-Ra* with not only forbearance but delight. Isn't that how we all spent our time as kids? In finding cool stuff and then OD'ing on it until, almost out of nowhere, our one-time all-consuming obsession became nothing more than that thing we used to like.

This makes sense when you're growing up, of course. Your view of the world changes inexorably as you learn more about it, and yourself. Others shape your opinions as they deem things hot, or not, and you encounter a wider array of options that you'd ever dreamed possible once the magical lands of PG-13, M- and/or R-rated movies are opened up. All too soon, it seems, it comes time to put away childish things, and suddenly there is an expectation of maturity, of rectitude. You get caught watching *Rocky and Bullwinkle* at four in the morning and you receive funny looks. You sigh over a mint condition — ruinously expensive — Silver Age comic book, and you get told to act your age. You watch *Twilight: Eclipse* at the theater several times, and you have your sanity called into question. (Uh. I've heard.)

No. I will not be ashamed. I will confess it proudly! For I am still a rewatcher. A rereader. A redoer. If I merely like something, perhaps not so much. But if I love something? Oh, yeah. Once is never enough. I've read

Ender's Game and *On Basilisk Station* upwards of a hundred times each; I've seen *The Matrix* and *The Fifth Element* at least fifty; and I have been through all ten seasons of *Stargate SG-1* enough times that I can probably name the title of every episode in the series and tell you on which numbered disc it can be found. It doesn't matter that it was years, if not decades, ago that I first fell in love with these books, or movies, or TV shows. I revisit them now like old friends, and whenever I do, it's like coming home.

Is it quite the same when I return, as I inevitably do, to the TV shows, books and movies of my younger years? No, of course not. Returning to childhood realms in adulthood, and complete with adult sensibility, cynicism and discernment, can indeed be problematic, and I'll not deny it. Looking at a show like *Pokémon* or *Thomas the Tank Engine* with educated eyes, you can't help but come away with the impression that the moral of those series was: "Hey, kids! Slavery is cool!" French scholar Antoine Buéno's sociological treatise *Le petit livre bleu* (*Little Blue Book*) calls The Smurfs racist, misogynistic and virulently anti-Semitic, wherein he also maintains that their society was "an archetype of a totalitarian utopia"… and, yeah, okay. Read *Narnia* now and all the religion parable stuff hits you on the head in very disturbing, indoctrinating ways, and dear God, has anyone seen the original *Tron* lately? The lightcycles looked way cooler than *that*, right?

But just because we, as children, were oblivious to the sinisterly didactic themes of our entertainment, or were blinded by then-amazing technology that now looks laughably quaint, it does not necessarily follow that those shows we once loved have nothing to offer us now. Not at all.

Think of it like this. You're a child of say, five or six, and you watch an episode of *The Simpsons* with your family. You laugh at Bart's cheekiness and Barney's bodily functions and are entranced by all the pretty colors. You think *Itchy and Scratchy* is a really cool show. Then, you watch that same episode again at, say, sixteen. And now, you get the sight-gags. You understand the double entendre and the metaphor and you realize that *Itchy and Scratchy* was, in fact, a damning indictment of the mindlessly violent, allegedly kid-friendly cartoons that had come before it.

Revisiting all childhood fare is like that. There's always something new to discover. (Although, admittedly, most of it isn't quite as multi-layered as *The Simpsons* in its heyday.)

My opposition in this debate would have you fear a return to that simpler, happier time. He warns direfully of the disappointment you'll feel when you discover that — shock and horror! — your preferred Saturday morning cartoon followed a predictable formula. But of course all of those shows adhered to formulae. Guess what? So do most of the shows we watch now! *The X-Files* was basically just Scully going: "Silly Mulder, this strange tale of mutants/aliens/magic can't possibly true… wait, this autopsy makes no sense!… man, it's dark in here… okay, I admit it, you were right about the mutants/aliens/magic… am I in hospital again?" Hell, even *Firefly* — much beloved of yours truly as well as my formidable opponent — followed a very definite pattern:

MAL: Let's do crime.
ZOE: Yes, sir.
WASH: I'm a way better pilot than him.
MAL: You're a slut, Inara.
INARA: You know you want me.
KAYLEE: He does! And I want Simon. Oh, no, the engine's on fire!
SIMON: I have an awkward romantic chemistry with my sister.
JAYNE: What is the most inappropriate thing I can say right now? I am compelled to say it.
MAL: Damn, double-crossed again! Killed a man. Whatevs.
BOOK: You rascal.
RIVER: The stars sound like purple. I might kill you all tomorrow.
MAL: Isn't my ship beautiful?

Are you saying no one should ever watch *Firefly* again, dude? Never?

I will concede, here, that the antics of former idols of mine, like the Teenage Mutant Ninja Turtles, The Fraggles, and even Roger Ramjet, are not quite the thrill ride they once were (unlike the adventures of the crew of *Serenity*, which is always a good time). Going back and rewatching those Disney movies about the kids from Witch Mountain recently, I had to wonder at my hopeless devotion to them as an impassioned eight-year old. But I am not sorry that I gave them another go, and I will never stop looking backwards to where I, in my thorough-going geekhood, came from — even as I eternally look forward to the next big thing. I will continue to discover anew the wonders of Prydain and Eternia, of Care-a-Lot and Fantasia (the *NeverEnding Story* one, not the Disney one; the latter is just Fucked. Up.), and in the process I will happily take off the rose-colored glasses that my opponent fears to shed and appreciate these beloved works for what they truly are — even as I remember them fondly for what they once were to me.

© Rachel Hyland, 2017

COPYRIGHT PROTECTION
PATENTLY ABSURD
by B. C. Roberts

It is in many ways difficult to debate the merits of intellectual property. Intellectual property is a topic of some vastness incorporating copyright, patents, and trademarks, along with specific legislative schemes for things like circuit designs and common law actions like passing off. We can ignore these latter schemes as being extremely complex and not covering the sorts of creative outputs relevant to this debate. Further, there is little that is controversial about trademarks (except for trademarks on common words like Harry Potter), so we will leave it to one side as well. Patents are so irremediably broken as a way of dealing with inventions – most particularly pharmaceuticals – that it hardly seems like an argument worth making. I direct you to every human rights article written on access to medications in the developing world to deal with that topic. Only someone who supports having children die of preventable causes supports patent protection as it currently exists in the world.

Which leaves us with copyright protection. Though intellectual property commenced life in 1624 in England with the Statute of Monopolies, that statute only covered patents and not copyright. The first copyright statute was the Statute of Ann in 1709, which prohibited the unauthorized copying of books. Before this time, governments in Europe would provide monopoly rights to print a book to a particular printer, but this was part of a regime of censorship whereby individual book printers and booksellers were licensed by the city and that license would be revoked if they were found to publish work critical of the government. The Statute of Ann granted copyright privileges for 14 years for new books and 21 years for books already in print.

Which is all a nice history lesson, but let's get to the point. What are the aims of intellectual property protection and does the current regime effectively achieve those aims? The aims of copyright protection from the first legislation through to today can be summarized under two headings:

1. To compensate the creators of creative works for their investment in the creation
2. To incentivize the creation of creative works

Now, if intellectual property protection does not achieve these aims, we can safely conclude that the existing regime is a failure. I follow the critical theorist Raymond Geuss in rejecting the need to provide an alternative scheme – the claim that one cannot criticize the status quo without an alternative is how those who benefit from the status quo put off criticism.

On to the aims.

1. Does intellectual property compensate creators of creative works for their investment in the creation?

The first thing we need to consider under this heading is the way in which copyright provides financial compensation. When one creates a work one is granted a monopoly right over the reproduction of that creative work. Copyright does not protect the characters created (hence fan fiction) but only the specific expression of the work. This does extend cross-media so that a person cannot make a film which is substantially similar to someone's book, or a song from a painting and so on. This monopoly right is granted for the life of the author of the work PLUS an additional fifty years; conceivably, this can amount to well over one hundred years of protection (a good deal longer than the Statute of Ann – which, incidentally, was the law in force when writers like Wordsworth, Keats, and Jane Austen were writing).

Now, nothing in the provision of this level of protection examines the actual investment of the authors in their creation of the work. A piece of awful self-indulgent Plath-esque poetry written by a depressed teenager in English class is granted exactly the same level of protection as a multi-volume history of the Roman Empire. If the aim were really to compensate for investment and effort, we might expect any consideration at all of the actual effort expended in the awarding of protection.

2. Does the provision of intellectual property protection incentivize the creation of creative works?

The most enduring argument for intellectual property protection is that if authors/inventors are not provided with a monopoly right over their creation, then they will not create, and the world will be a worse place for the lack of arts and inventions. This argument is patently absurd (please pardon the pun).

Every single day people write amazing works of admirable sophistication and post them to the internet for people to read freely. None expect to receive financial compensation for their work; they write to express themselves, to tell stories to be involved with groups of like-minded individuals. More fan fiction is written than original fiction; clearly, there are other incentives at play here.

My favorite example of the stupidity of the incentive argument is that almost all of the people who actually create medical breakthroughs receive no money for them. Almost all medical research work is performed by researchers in universities and drug companies who do not get to own the intellectual property of their own creations (that going to their employers instead). Professors in university search for a cure for cancer not because they will be rich (because they won't) but so they can be the person who cured cancer. And, no offence, but the work to cure cancer is considerably more important than works of popular fiction. If these people will provide medical breakthroughs without intellectual property incentives, surely we can expect Joss Whedon to get over me downloading an episode or two of *Buffy*.

To go back to fan fiction: though you might concede that people write without financial incentive, you might also suggest they would be mortified if their work was copied and passed off as being someone else's. This surely is proof that people care about copyright. Maybe, but not quite. Passing somebody's work off as your own is rightly the target of moral censure and the reason we have the pejorative term "plagiarism." We don't need 100 years of copyright protection to defend against plagiarism – and anyway, what possible harm can plagiarism cause after we are dead? In a school, if a student plagiarizes they usually fail or are required to resubmit. If they were pursued for breach of copyright, the original author would be entitled to damages for lost revenue. Ummm. That seems to be kind of a problem, since in most of these cases the work being plagiarized wasn't going to make any money. Plus, who on earth would want to launch expensive legal proceedings because somebody copied their essay about the unseen vampire in "The Fall of the House of Usher"? And it holds true in fan fiction as well. When somebody copies another person's work, the original author wants "justice" in the form of an apology, a retraction, and recognition of themselves as the true author of the work – preferably as quickly as possible. The legal protection of intellectual property rights simply does not provide that.

So where are we at? The two rationales normally put forward to justify intellectual property just do not fly. It does not compensate people based on effort and people clearly do not need copyright or the promise of riches to inspire creative works.

There are a couple more arguments to deal with before we can finish, though. One is the issue of stealing from artists; the second is the problems associated with intellectual property rights. Let's look at the latter first.

Copyright is a legal right. It is not some free-standing moral principle. What that means is that if you believe your rights have been violated, get prepared to go to court. This is shit for the artist seeking to protect their work because it is a huge waste of time and money and unless you are super successful (at which point I don't properly understand why you care so much: Anne Rice, do you really need another mansion?); legal proceedings are pretty much prohibitively expensive. And it is worse for the individual who has downloaded the work who is now treated like an awful criminal. I think everyone agrees that paying $200,000 in damages for downloading a few songs off Limewire is a total overreaction and completely disproportionate to the damage suffered by the artist.

The other thing about the legality of intellectual property is that the rights granted are, by their very nature, assignable. What that means is that some bunch of douchebags running a record company make all the money while the artists receive somewhere between twenty cents and a dollar for each album sold. This is not some contingent corollary of the existing system – it is necessitated by the status of intellectual property as rights. Just look at every other type of property in the world.

Which brings us nicely to the issue of stealing from artists. The single group of people most responsible for stealing from artists are publishers, be they book publishers, record companies, or whoever. When I found out about the two zombie books written by my adversary in this debate under the pseudonym Mira Grant, the first thing I did was go to a torrent site and download them. Then, of course, our illustrious Editor-in-Chief was outraged and sent me an Amazon voucher and told me to buy them all legit-like. Which, incidentally, I did. But I would love to know how much of the twenty dollars I spent on Amazon actually went to the author. And then I would much prefer to send that money directly to the author (though I'm not sure you can Western Union amounts under a dollar) and not subsidize some fuckwit editor's coke habit.

In summary: for the first time in history, the internet is making it possible for the creators of works to connect directly with their public. And some are starting to do so. When Radiohead released their album *In Rainbows* online with a "pay what you think it's worth" price, they sold considerably fewer copies than they had of earlier albums and yet made considerably more money. Artists and writers who hang onto copyright as their way of doing business are just as anachronistic as the MPAA going after every person who downloads a song illegally. Why stay beholden to publishers who see artists as product to be sold? Especially if you are offering online versions anyway?

Intellectual property is obsolete when it comes to copyright (and patents are downright murderous).

COPYRIGHT PROTECTION
THEFT IS THEFT IS THEFT
by Seanan McGuire

Okay, wow. First off, a few statements:

1. I am pro-copyright. (There's a shocker.) I am pro-copyright both because I work VERY HARD to create the things I create, and because I enjoy having this mysterious ability I call "feeding my cats." They are all the size of small yeti. If I don't feed them, they will devour me.

2. Being pro-copyright is not the same thing as being pro-endless extensions of the initial copyright law, la la la, let's keep this bitch in a box forever. While I wouldn't necessarily be thrilled about going back to a twenty-one year copyright period for new books, I'd be perfectly happy with life of the author plus ten years for the estate to get itself in order. Saying that being pro-copyright means you're in favor of every copyright extension forced through by corporate interests is a bit of a misnomer.

3. I do not think the word "incentive" means what my adversary thinks it does.

Let's discuss.

Author Compensation, or, Feeding My Cats

According to my adversary, one of the reasons that copyright doesn't work is because it doesn't pay out in a way which is matched to the effort put forth by the creator.

So, here's the thing. If I spend five years writing a book that is like removing a bone from my living flesh, leaving gaping wounds and lots of blood behind, and you spend three weeks writing a book that flows through you like a wind from Heaven, and the books are of equal quality, we will get paid roughly the same by traditional publishing for our books. My book represented a great deal more in the way of time and effort, but publishing, like the honey badger, doesn't give a shit; publishing wants to see the pages.

In a way, writing is a lot like being on a reality show. I watch *America's Next Top Model* pretty faithfully, and every cycle, there's a girl who doesn't really have to do anything. The judges call them "natural models," and while they don't usually win (they're not dramatic enough to take home that brass ring), they almost always go on to healthy careers in the modeling industry. Other girls struggle and fight for every photo shoot. And if you don't watch the episodes—if you just look at the pictures they post at the end, showing the "best shots" of the week—you can't tell those girls apart. The amount of effort they put out is extraneous. The finished product is what matters.

My books are pretty straight-up genre fiction. I write urban fantasy and I write science fiction; they're mass-market paperbacks; you can find them on the shelf at your local S-Mart. The first volume of my October Daye series, *Rosemary and Rue*, represented ten years of work. No, you didn't read that wrong. TEN YEARS. Ten years is a very long time. And while I won't say that I would have been sad if my publisher had gone "wow, ten years, here's a million dollars," I'm not upset that they didn't do that, either. The fact that I had to learn how to write a good book does not mean they need to pay for my learning curve.

The most recent October Daye book, *One Salt Sea*, took about eight months to write; most of the reviews agree that it's the best book in the series so far, which I find reassuring, since any creator wants to improve. But eight months is a lot less than ten years! Should I have received eighty cents for every ten dollars that I was paid for the first book? Would that be what's fair here?

I write distressingly fast under any circumstances; sometimes this makes me do more work, since I overshoot my marks, but once I learn where those marks are, I get very good at hitting them every time, and I do so very, very quickly. Some of my best friends are the same way. Some of my other friends move more slowly, at everything from a stroll to a creep. They invest more time in their work. They invest more hours of their lives. Do they deserve to be better compensated, since I just "dashed it off," while they really worked?

The question of effort-for-compensation is something which arises only in the creative fields. People don't refuse to pay for their furniture because it was put together by a team of factory workers, none of whom put forth a huge amount of specific effort; they don't refuse to buy toys because they were made by machines. Higher quality things will wind up being worth more, and there is no direct correlation between "took longer to make/took more effort" and "better end result."

People Give Away Fanfic for Free, and That Means Copyright Is Useless

My path to becoming a professional author followed the path tread by so many before me: I wrote fan fiction. I wrote lots and lots and buckets and buckets of fan fiction, and I posted (or published—I overlapped the era of the paper 'zine, even if only by a few years) my work for free. I was drunk on creation, and those were wonderful days. You can probably find my fanfic if you look, and you can still read it totally for free. Just please remember that you're looking at a span of creative development that lasted about fifteen years, okay? Some of it is ass.

When I was working in other people's worlds I, like everyone else in my community, knew that I didn't own these characters. I didn't own these settings. What I owned was my own unique approach to them, and that was the "product" I had to "sell." I sold it! I had a wonderful time selling it. And never once did I think "oh, wow, the quality of this piece of Buffy the Vampire Slayer fic is so great that the original work is no longer owned by Joss Whedon."

Fanfic is successful for the same reason that works like *Shakespeare in Love* or *Pride and Prejudice and Zombies* are successful: because it gives us something familiar to hold onto the second we walk through the door. When I sit down to write a piece of fanfic, I don't have to capture or entice my audience. I already have them. I say "this is a piece of *Barry Ween* fic," and lead off with "Boy, eighteen, hair in spikes, eyes like holes," and they already know that I'm writing a story set after the original series. They know that Barry is still going crazy. They know so much, because it was handed to them by our shared cultural base in the original series.

Very few of the people I know go out and read fic based on series they don't already follow, unless they are following the author of that fic. In that way, fanfic writers become a weird sort of ad exec, selling other people's dreams by showing them through the prisms of their own.

I am not going to claim that fic requires no work: I wrote it, I know it requires work. I am not going to claim that it's the easy way out: I dare anyone to read some of the truly transformative, introspective material that's out there and say that anything about it is "easy." But I am going to say that, because we have a pre-existing relationship with the settings, we are more willing to walk through that door, and that saves the fanfic author a certain level of work in trying to lure us in.

A better example of people giving something creative away online for free, while also getting buy-in for a universe that requires that lure, would be the web comic. Web comics are very rarely derivative (anymore—many early web comics were basically fanfic with pictures), and are often based around very complicated, original worlds. While there have been, and continue to be, pay sites, web comics continue to proliferate, and even to thrive. Isn't that a ringing condemnation of copyright?

Nope. Most really successful web comics have healthy merchandise lines of T-shirts, books, mouse pads, even jewelry and plush toys. They make back their time investment on sales and in-page advertising. Even the "big kids" of the web comic world have figured out how to monetize their landscape, and have, in so doing, really recreated the TV advertising and merchandising model. They're not books. They're shows that move very, very slowly.

Thirty Minutes or It's Free

One huge freedom of fanfic that I no longer have was partial posting. When I was working on a really long story, I could put it up one chapter at a time, essentially serializing it. I was able to share my work slowly, and people were always grateful for the next piece. Try doing that with something that's been paid for. No, really. I dare you. Unless you're working in an inherently serial medium, like television or web comics (both graphic, rather than purely textual), you're going to have issues.

"Crowd-funded novels" often follow the one chapter at a time model, not releasing the next piece until it's been paid for. This is about the only way you're going to see the piecemeal approach working in original fiction. Which takes us back to the "fanfic is free, why isn't your novel?" My novel isn't free because I had to write all fifty chapters before I was allowed to publish it, and that took time and effort and editing and sleepless nights and anxiety and a lot of other things.

When I take the money, I take the deadlines. When I take the deadlines, I take the copyright protection, too. I am a protected investment, and I am okay with that.

Pathogen Party!

You may not know this, but I study infectious diseases for fun. So when I was reading my adversary's initial argument, and hit this piece, I choked on my soda. To wit:

> *"My favorite example of the stupidity of the incentive argument is that almost all of the people who actually create medical breakthroughs receive no money for them."*

I…uh…WHAT?!

Those people are being paid for their work. They are doing the scientific equivalent of "work for hire," like when a good friend of mine gets paid to write *Star Wars* novels, the copyrights on which she does not own. I want to write media tie-in novels for a show called *Haven* someday, just because I love it, and if I do that, I will not own those copyrights.

Disney animators don't own the characters they're paid to help design. Chris Saunders is one of my personal heroes, and he doesn't own Stitch, the little blue alien that he created. Why? Because they were on salary to create. If you want to pay me eighty thousand dollars a year to create something for you, I'll create it, and the fact that I won't own that copyright is not proof that the system doesn't work.

Arts and sciences are connected, but they have never been identical. Saying that someone will work toward a cure for cancer without compensation is not the same thing as saying that I should finish my series without a guarantee of compensation. As my adversary says, curing cancer is more important. If I cure cancer, I have a lifetime of paid speaking engagements and Nobel Prizes ahead of me. If I finish this book, I have the hope that I will get to write another book. That's it.

Oh, and Theft is Theft is Theft

Again to quote:

> *"To go back to fan fiction: though you might concede that people write without financial incentive you might also suggest they would be mortified if their work was copied and passed off as being someone else'."*

You want to see vicious? Watch a fanfic community where someone has just used someone else's OC (original character) without permission

Fanfic is not plagiarism. Plagiarism is not fanfic. Attempting to conflate the two at this stage just muddies the waters—and every fanfic author I've ever met who was plagiarized has brought the hammer of censure down hard. Maybe they didn't get monetary compensation the way that they would have if they'd been working for pay, but their grievances were heard.

Why the Successful Sue?

My adversary very accurately states that if you believe your rights have been violated, you'd better get prepared to go to court. He then asks why the really successful people—the ones who can win—bother, since what, do they need another mansion? The answer is simple: they bother because they can win. They bother because I, as a relatively new author, can't win. They are acting to protect the industry as a whole, and yeah, they're probably a little upset, since nobody likes to be stolen from.

(I am aware that not every illegal download is the equivalent of a sale. I am also, sadly, aware that my speaking out on the pro-copyright side means that a great many people will probably go "yay, let's torrent her work, that'll show her." To those people I say: please don't. Please stop, and consider that I have cats to feed, I have a mortgage to pay, and I don't come into your home or office and steal the value of your work. Just because I would never have let you clean my teeth, style my hair, or fix my car if I couldn't make you do it for free, that won't make it less of a theft.)

People who stand a chance in hell of winning these suits bring them because they want to make it clear that things have consequences. Maybe you violate my copyrights a thousand times and not get caught. Maybe you'll get caught the thousand and first time…and maybe that will be the time when I'm in a position to sue. Do you really want to roll those dice?

Stealing from Artists

My adversary says, again, quoting: "The single group of people most responsible for stealing from artists are publishers, be they book publishers, record companies or whoever."

He follows this up with, "When I found out about the two zombie books written by my adversary, the first thing I did was go to a torrent site and download them."

Um. Gee, thanks?

My publishers do not steal from me. My publishers pay me to do the thing I love. My publishers are also a business, and they have associated operating costs. Let's look at what it costs to make a book appear on a torrent site, shall we?

Advance to author.
Editorial review.

Copyediting.
Commission of artwork.
Cover design.
Printing.
Shipping and storage.
Advertising.

All these things make the book not suck. What other costs does my publisher have?

Rent.
Salaries.
Health insurance.
Internet and phones.
Electricity.

I am happy to have my publisher use me to make money to keep the lights on so that they can keep printing the books I love to write. It's an ecological balance, and no, I am not stolen from or screwed. And none of my editors have coke habits, despite my adversary's implication.

How much did I make when he finally bought those books of mine legitimately? About seventy-five cents a copy. Not a huge amount, I admit. But I got an advance from my publisher, and I sell a lot of books because I have a publisher. My first book—the one where I had no name recognition at all—sold more copies in its first week than my most popular fanfic ever had hits. The scale is very different.

Would Radiohead have made all that money for *In Rainbows* if they hadn't started out in traditional music publishing? No. I don't think so.

Copyright can be abused. Copyright should not be used to punish fanfic authors or to beat people like a club. But it should be used to protect creators, and it should keep my work mine until my death, if not after. The arguments used to justify violation of copyright have a lot in common with the arguments I used to get from the kids I went to school with when they wanted my lunch—"I want it, you have it, it should be mine, it's not fair." I worked for that lunch. I worked for my copyrights.

Please stop arguing that I shouldn't be allowed to feed my cats just because you've decided this is a brave new world.

© *Seanan McGuire, 2011*

THE DARK KNIGHT (AND HEATH LEDGER)
MASSIVELY OVERRATED
by Kate Nagy

The Dark Knight is an overrated movie. Oh yes, I just said that. And the late Heath Ledger's Oscar-winning portrayal of the Joker is also overrated. Yes, I totally went there, too. That's my story and I'm sticking to it.

Understand that I'm not saying *TDK* is a bad movie. It's not. It's…fine. Watching it is a perfectly adequate way to waste a lazy Sunday afternoon. But the enthusiasm – no, make that the worship the film has generated from critics and cineastes far and wide is entirely disproportionate to its merits.

Consider: although *The Dark Knight* drew eight Academy Award nominations and won two (including the aforementioned Mr. Ledger for Best Supporting Actor), in 2009 the Academy of Motion Picture Arts and Sciences announced that it would change its rules to permit the nomination of ten films in the Best Picture category, partially in response to the outcry that arose when TDK failed to bag such a nomination. Its worldwide box office has exceeded a billion dollars to date. I don't know exactly how DVD sales have looked but I can pretty well guess. People love this movie.

Except I don't.

Here's why:

It's too damn long.

The Dark Knight clocks in at a robust 152 minutes and it seems half again as long. It "ends," what, four times? Between the Joker and the Mob and poor Harvey Dent and Commissioner Gordon, there's way too much going on. Any one of those things all by itself would have been the basis for an excellent movie. But put all together, they make a film that's simply overstuffed.

It's worth noting that this is not a problem unique to this Batman movie, or even to this superhero movie. It's pretty common for filmmakers to try to cram everyone's favorite villains in. But it is a problem.

It's hard to care about any of the characters – even the good guys.

For one reason and another, it's hard to care about almost anyone in the movie. Maybe it's the fact that the preponderance of plot and whizz-bang action sequences leaves little room for character development. Maybe it's the fact that the title character sports an oddly depressed affect throughout, like he spent the entire shoot snorting barbiturates. (Christian Bale is a

65

good enough actor that despite everything, he does give an entirely serviceable performance, but we've all seen numerous times that Bale is capable of a lot more than "serviceable.") Among the other actors, Gary Oldman is adequate but largely forgettable. Maggie Gyllenhaal does what she can with a seriously underwritten role (Nolan tends not to do particularly well with female characters anyway – yes, I went there, too). Michael Caine and Morgan Freeman are never boring on screen but they're not in this one that much and Cillian Murphy and William Fichtner are criminally underused. I'll get to Ledger in a minute. The only one I cared about by the end was Harvey Dent.

As Harvey Dent, Aaron Eckhart managed to upstage at least two Oscar winners and create an interesting and even tragic figure. I was firmly in his corner for most of the movie and actually thought that his eleventh-hour conversion to the dastardly Two-Face was an entirely reasonable response to everything he had been through. I was pulling for him against Batman, in other words. I'm not sure I was meant to be.

It's even hard to care about the Joker.

Heath Ledger was a gifted young man who turned in a groundbreaking, nuanced, heartbreaking, unforgettable performance… in *Brokeback Mountain* (2005). As far as *The Dark Knight* goes, I know that it's geek heresy to even think this, but really? Ledger doesn't create a character, he gives a performance: his Joker is a mumbly, twitchy, inexplicable bundle of tics, about whom it could reasonably be observed that the apparent inability of the assorted heroes to take him out in the first five minutes of the film casts serious doubt on their competence as professional crime fighters.

I blame the writers, personally. Ledger didn't pull that particular Joker out of his back pocket, I don't think. – Oh, and maybe the director, a little bit, for not reining Ledger in just a tad. Either way, it's one of the more over-praised performances of the past decade.

It just takes itself too seriously.

"Because he's the hero Gotham deserves, but not the one it needs right now. So we'll hunt him because he can take it. Because he's not our hero. He's a silent guardian, a watchful protector. A dark knight."

These majestic words – which close the film, so they're the last thing that the viewer comes away with – are spoken in reference to… a guy dressed up like a bat who chases around a guy dressed up like a clown.* Meditate on that for a minute.

Is it possible to explore serious themes within that sort of context? Of course it is. Comics in general have often served up their action and adventure with a side dish of That's Something To Think About. But these things can be carried too far, and *The Dark Knight* is absolutely brimming with angst, and darkness, and gloom. I cracked a smile exactly once – when Wayne absconded with the ballet – and while I never expected the movie to be a comedy, I also didn't expect it to be as heavy as a Russian epic. Bruce Wayne is a man of tremendous wealth and power whose alter-ego makes good people's lives better using some of the niftiest toys ever engineered. Is it too much to ask that we get to see him, I don't know, enjoy himself just a little bit? *The Dark Knight* is relentless; evil is everywhere and good people either get mowed down in its path (Rachel Dawes), give in to the darkness (Harvey Dent), or get blamed (Batman). That's a lot to hang on… a bat and a clown.

Again, I'm not for a minute saying that *The Dark Knight* is a bad movie. It's not. It definitely has its moments – the "two ferries" sequence is nicely played, and Eckhart and to a certain extent Freeman and Caine turn in fine performances. And all those Oscar noms I mentioned above? They're mostly in the technical categories, and deservedly so – the movie is expertly crafted. It's… fine.

But that's really my point: it's fine. That so many people think it's this amazing and incredible masterpiece largely represents a triumph of marketing, or something. Is the state of genre cinema so dire these days that "competent" now passes for "brilliant" and "not terrible" is automatically considered "Oscar-worthy"? I refuse to believe it.

The Dark Knight is simply overrated, and Heath Ledger is overrated in it.

*Credit where it's due: I'm not the first person to make the observation about the bat and the clown; I think I got it from a poster on Pajiba.com. I wish I had said it, though, because it sums things up so perfectly.

© Kate Nagy, 2011

THE DARK KNIGHT (AND HEATH LEDGER)
OSCAR-WORTHY AND MORE
by Jason Murdoch

Okay, let's clarify to begin with: I'm not a raving fanboy. I enjoyed Adam West's *Batman* for the tongue-in-cheek series it was, and whilst I'm generally a fan of Tim Burton's work, I struggled with his incarnations of the Bat: they just didn't give me a reason to watch, apart from the typical hyper-realistic visuals. As for the Joel Schumacher ones.... well. They were Joel Schumacher.

Enter Christopher Nolan and Christian Bale. Finally, a storyline that provides motive and characters that you can understand. Something as dark and gritty as Gotham on the brink should be.

So, Batman Begins sets the scene.... What now?

I want more from a sequel than just the same good guy bashing a different bad guy. I want it to go further. I want it to give me some new ideas. This is why *The Dark Knight* succeeds.

True, there are a few characters to get our heads around. More than characters, though: each one of these individuals encapsulates a possible future for Gotham.

Gordon

Here's the good guy, the run of the mill cop with unquestionable morals. Gordon's the guy that will look out for the people, because he is one of the people.

The Joker

Here's our ultimate villain. The guy without rhyme or reason, the guy that just wants to watch the world burn. In the Joker's hands, Gotham goes up in flames. There's no hunger for power; he is the essence of pure anarchy. It is a simple beauty. But more of Ledger's Joker in a bit.

Harvey Dent

The glorious dictator, ruthless, charming. He wants to rule, and realistically will ensure that Gotham will prosper... but at what cost? He is almost too good to be true, a veritable white knight, at least at the outset. His is probably the most interesting storyline, probably because there's the most progression here, from the "two-headed" coin that stands for certainty to how that certainty is tested and eventually gives way to chance. Here the shining beacon of hope is tried, tested, and found wanting. "Understandably so," you may think, but if this is what the shining light ends up as, maybe Gotham doesn't need one to start with?

Then we have the namesake of the film:

Batman

Still the antihero, the hero Gotham needs, but the one it will inevitably turn against. What we are treated to is a comparison between Batman and all these characters, and we have to question which one is best for Gotham.

Each one of these is more than just a character: they are an idea, a possible future. They each challenge the viewer to take sides, some easier than others. What's amazing about each one of these characters is that they're all only human. There's no radioactive accident, no phenomenal cosmic power. Just people, and the choices they make.

Sure it's a long movie; well, maybe for Gen Y, for whom instant gratification is not quick enough. Yes, they are obviously setting the background for future movies. This takes away from the shiny things and explosions slightly, but is this such a high price to pay for a quality storyline next time? Or are we content to watch Michael Bay movies for the rest of our lives?

All this (and more) in a movie about a clown and a guy in a bat suit.

And then there's Ledger.

Let's call a spade a spade. Would as many accolades have been given to Ledger for his portrayal of the Joker if he were still making movies? Probably not. Same could be said for the *Mona Lisa*, and the question asked: is it in its rarity that lies its value, or is it inherently valuable in its own right? True, Ledger's death gave the movie a lot of hype, and probably didn't hurt his award nominations. (Or, to continue the comparison, Da Vinci's auction values.) Life lost is tragedy, but that isn't the question under debate.

Traditional villains, especially in superhero movies, have adhered to a certain formula – an over-the-top, egomaniacal, power-hungry, revenge-driven, manipulator-type character is what we have come to expect. What Ledger does so well here is break this mold. There's no power, no money to be gained from his plans. He isn't a one dimensional character out for revenge because Spider-Man killed his fathe... err... sorry, wrong movie. He is literally out to create chaos for chaos' sake. What's even scarier about this character is that he is so effective at it. He's not super-strong, he has no real powers, so how does a villain that is no more than human walk into an underworld meeting, make a pencil disappear, and stroll out again? How does he survive? It's because he's already doing what no one else is game to do. No one is game to call his bluff, because no one, not even the viewer, is quite sure if he's bluffing. Ledger manages to convince us that it's possible. This "mumbly, twitchy, inexplicable bundle of tics" (as my opponent would have it) seems like a raving idiot, but is already one step ahead. There is method to the madness, an understanding of how people will react to his plans, and a perverse pleasure in playing the puppeteer with puppets that could kick his head in if given the opportunity. Think of Hannibal Lecter: not a particularly physically inspiring individual, yet one of the scariest villains to grace the silver screen. Yeah, I just drew that comparison.

In short, is *The Dark Knight* the greatest movie ever produced, bar none? No. I don't think any of us are kidding ourselves there. But does it MORE than deserve the repeated accolades that it received?

Yes.

For a movie about a guy in a costume to take an audience on this much of a journey, for a movie about a clown to offer an audience this much, to go beyond the classic good guy-bad guy storyline and provide viewers with characters that represent more than people, and to do this convincingly with astounding visuals, and an atmospheric soundtrack rather than a theme song, *The Dark Knight* has proven to be a great movie.

On top of that, Ledger's performance was nothing short of inspirational. And neither are over-rated in the least.

DISNEY
TINKER BELL IS REALLY A SUCCUBUS
by Sara Paige

I grew up around a lot of Disney, and it played a bit of a role in my childhood. In the 80s, the Disney Channel was a pay channel, like HBO for kids, and it didn't have commercials. My mom paid extra for it so that we could have programming to keep my sister and I occupied while she did stuff. And unlike Nickelodeon, Disney didn't promote kids talking back or being rude to authority figures, so it was a bit more parent-friendly.

The bloom was off the rose for Disney and I when I was 10 and *The Little Mermaid* came out in theaters. I thought the original Hans Christian Andersen ending was full of poetry, and the happy ending for Ariel made me feel cheated of something grander, more majestic than just getting Daddy to fix it and make everything better.

And that's when I started to feel like I was living in my own version of the movie *They Live*, a science fiction movie in which the main character finds out that the ruling class is actually made up of aliens. Like the characters in that movie who get sunglasses that allow them to see the reality of ugly alien invaders, I felt like my initial disappointment with Disney movies set me on the track to seeing the tarnish Disney was selling as fairy dust.

It's not just retelling fairy tales, Greek myths, and even historical facts and so totally getting them wrong or missing the point. (I shudder to think of the amount of kids who think Pocahontas hooked up with John Smith. Gross.) For years Disney has done its best to promote itself as "family-friendly" while doing its level best to extract as much money as possible through a machine that's about as impersonal as it comes. Disney sells magic, but what it really deals in is exploitation on all levels, from its employees to its consumers.

First, let's talk racism, mostly because talking about the sexism is so easy; it's like shooting fish in a barrel. For a really long time, Disney traded in some pretty obvious white supremacist tropes. Good characters had light skin, bad ones were dark. There were no Disney films featuring protagonists of color until recently, and even then the first one, *Aladdin*, was pretty racist. There are some Arabs I've met who never saw *Aladdin* because their horrified parents wouldn't let them. I mean, check out the opening lyrics to the theme song:

> *O, I come from a land, from a faraway place*
> *Where the caravan camels roam*
> *Where they cut off your ear*

If they don't like your face
It's barbaric, but hey, it's home.

Where they cut of your ear if they don't like your face? Really, Disney? And while it's nice that they changed this on the DVD, it doesn't completely make up for the fact that the bad guys are more Arab than "Just call me Al" Aladdin, who is made out to be much more American, lighter skin, accent, and all.

And while it's nice that Disney has tried here and there to make up a little for the racist characterizations of African Americans in movies like *Song of the South* (which I first saw as a kid on the Disney Channel), *Dumbo* (those crows!) and even the hyenas in *The Lion King* (Cheech Marin and Whoopi Goldberg sounded more "ethnic" than the very white actors playing Simba and adult Nala), it took them until 2009 to have an African American heroine? And don't even get me started – again – on *Pocahontas*, which was just another fantasy about how white people were so awesome to Native Americans... until we killed them all. Except that last part is never mentioned in Disney.

As for the sexism: look, is there a single movie where a woman isn't waiting for the prince to come? Even the lionesses in *The Lion King* had to wait for Simba to rescue them from Scar, although they were hunters who outnumbered him. To make up for Disney's decades of propping up "good girls" who passively wait for a man (usually by being asleep), Disney has now overcompensated with feisty female tropes as a prop so they can continue to render female characters as two-dimensional with some sort of prop. Belle likes books! Mulan can fight! See, they're not totally sexist anymore! But they still need their prince. Not to mention that the more non-Caucasian a woman is, the higher probability that she will be sexed-up (Esmerelda, Jasmine, Megara), and interestingly enough, less likely to become a princess.

As for the princesses – it's a great way to exploit our girls and put them on the right track to always wanting to seek a prince and wear ill-fitting costumes. I'm glad they are able to make $3 billion off the backs of young girls' self-esteem.

But outside of the movies, there is real life, and what goes on behind the scenes. In the real business world, Disney pays employees in a way that I've only seen in the non-profit world, with something called psychic income. Psychic income means that they trade on their branding in order to pay less for labor. But unfortunately, no one can eat that or pay the rent with it. At MBA career fairs, Disney is one of the few companies that recruits for an unpaid internship. The theme park cast members are some of the lowest paid employees in the US.

In fact, on job boards, the pay is a universal complaint, as well as the hours required and the cronyism. My favorite statement on a job site that captures the essence at a job at Disney? "...If you don't have family or friends and don't celebrate holidays, work/life balance is perfectly fine… Career potential is good. You can definitely grow if you are close with the managers and are on their good side." Sounds like that Disney magic!

Last, let's talk about the customers, too. I've been to Disney World twice and Disneyland once, all three times as an adult. As a marketer by trade I have rarely gotten a chance to be in such a well-run, cunning machine determined to extract every last cent from a human being. From the second people enter to the time they leave, the advertising and brainwashing do not stop. It's relentless: to buy merchandise, to buy candy, to get preferential treatment on rides. There is little Disney doesn't have to sell you, and they will sell it to you at massively inflated prices. When I go there, I may not believe in magic, but by the time I leave, I believe wholeheartedly in capitalism's ability to make a buck.

I also watch people at Disney theme parks. I see hordes of people go in happy, with excited smiling kids. On the way out they, more often than not, are angry, tired, and poorer, while the kids are cranky and throwing screaming tantrums. And that's the crux of the matter, isn't it? Disney welcomes you in under the guise of believing in fairies and magic and pretty (usually white) princesses, and then it sucks the life out of you. It is the corporate equivalent of a succubus.

Look, if people want to believe in Santa, I let them. If they want to believe in the power of positive thinking, I keep my response (mostly) in my inner monologue. But Disney is a charmer; it's a conman who sucks you in with sweet promises and then spits you out again. And before we drink the fairy-laced Kool-Aid, we should know that Disney is not in the business of helping people "believe," it's very much in the business of making money for its shareholders at the expense of people on all levels, and it doesn't care who – or what – it exploits.

© Sara Paige, 2013

DISNEY

WHERE DREAMS COME TRUE

by Kellie Sheridan

For a company that has helped shape generations of childhood memories, Disney sure has to spend a lot of time defending itself against all kinds of accusations. Sure, things in the Magic Kingdom may not be perfect, but the outlook it projects to children and adults alike is invaluable. For me, being exposed to Disney's brand of magic did so much to shape the grownup I turned into. I've seen most of the animated movies multiple times, made two trips to the parks in Florida, and still own a few T-shirts with Disney characters on them. Okay, maybe I'm not what you would call one hundred percent grown up, but with Disney you don't have to be.

Watching countless Disney movies turned me into a fan of fantasy and storytelling, and showed me the place magic still has in our decidedly un-magical world. While movies like *Alice in Wonderland* and *Peter Pan* were my gateway to bigger and bolder fantasy adventures, it was never just about escaping into other worlds. It was about beating the bad guys, or thinking my toys and/or pets were having conversations I just couldn't hear. It was about endless possibilities. Although I grew up to be a creature of logic and habit, Disney taught me to imagine, and for that I will always be grateful.

So, where's the harm? In recent years there has been a growing sense of outrage at some of the messages Disney movies present to their young audiences, but like everything else in life these messages are what you make of them. It's easy to cry "sexism" when looking at the early Disney princess movies, or "racism" when watching most of the movies that feature characters with any skin color that isn't white (or beige, as rendered by animation colorists). But each of these movies is a product of the time in which they were created, and not something to be over-analyzed decades later. It's a little late to be up in arms about the way women were portrayed in the 30s, 40s, and 50s – an issue that certainly wasn't limited to these movies. That's a much bigger issue, and hardly something you can pin on Walt Disney Productions. If you're watching these movies and primarily seeing these politically incorrect *faux pas* instead of things like a story about a boy with a genie, who has to figure out that being himself will get him farther than pretending to be rich and famous, then you're probably too cynical for this particular brand of fantasy anyway.

I won't deny that there are layers of sexism buried in the Disney vault. But again, a lot of this has been a product of the times, and of debilitating social norms where a movie with a male lead can be marketed to any and all while prominent females are likely to cut that market share in half. The important thing is that as the times changed, so did the characters. And is it really such a bad thing that Disney went out of its way to create dynamic female characters like Mulan and Pocahontas in order to correct past mistakes? No, sir.

And if characters like Cinderella and *Sleeping Beauty*'s Aurora are all bad, then why do they still resonate with so many children? Little girls today are encouraged to be self-sufficient, strong and just as kick-ass as little boys, so it isn't that they're hoping to sit on their hands until their prince comes along. And really, I don't think it was ever about that. Being a Disney princess is about knowing that no matter if you're a princess, a gypsy, or a French book nerd, you're special. We've seen it throughout all generations of Disney movies, with both male and female characters. No matter who they are (male, female, adorable talking animal), or where they start out, by the end of the movie they've done something awesome! That's what kids (and adults) are taking away from all this.

You hear a lot of people complain that Disney has butchered their favorite stories, myths and fairytales. And in a lot of cases, they definitely have, but if you can look at the Disney versions as separate entities, you can begin to see their value. Disney strives to create movies that can be enjoyed by the whole family, and let's be honest... the original ending to *The Little Mermaid*, or most of the Grimm fairy tales, really don't work for all age groups. Disney is there to create a world of fantasy that helps us remember that good can trump evil, even if it doesn't always, and it has managed to do just that again and again. It's up to our parents and history teachers to tell us what really happened to Pocahontas and her people; there is no rule saying children can't be exposed to both versions of each story. So how is Disney's decision to lean towards the positive really harming anyone?

The added bonus is that Disney movies can serve to get people interested in the original stories. Disney's version of *Hercules* was one of my favorite movies growing up. I watched it again and again, becoming obsessed with the Greek gods, and going on to read the original myths in my spare time, something I may never have done if it weren't for Disney (okay... and possibly *Xena*). And personally, I'm glad that my initial initiation to the myths didn't involve Zeus' rape (essentially) of Hercules' mother. Can you really blame any company that markets products to children for excluding that and other such details?

As for the corporate side of things, once again many of the arguments that are made against Disney are things that really need to be analyzed on a much larger scale. Yes, families enter Disney theme parks happy and energetic, and leave exhausted and ready for some serious alone time. How is that any different than spending a day with children at a shopping mall or a birthday party? Kids can be exhausting, and when there's a lot going on they are liable to get over-stimulated. They're still going to come away from their Disney vacation with fantastic memories and stories for their classmates about how they met Princess Tiana, which is why their parents decided to make the Disney pilgrimage in the first place. Seeing the magic of the movies "come to life" can do wonders for any child's imagination, and that's well worth the headache.

And yes, Disney is out there to make money and sell products. Just like everybody else. I won't even argue that they're selling products in order to make money to continue their mission to spread love and magic. I'm not quite that naïve. I will argue that they've put forward a brilliant marketing campaign that has lasted generations and served to make Disney an integral part of childhood. They sell products and movies that people love, and I won't begrudge them a profit on that, especially as they aren't the only ones to benefit. Putting on a princess dress can make a little girl feel like she's capable of anything, and if Disney can give her that feeling, it's something to be proud of.

So yes, Disney is not a perfect, altruistic entity. It's a corporation. It makes money in exchange for its employees' hard work. But at the end of the day, it offers something valuable in exchange for our hard-earned cash, everything from a secret belief in magic to a great movie to a chance encounter with a princess. Disney may not be for everyone, but over seventy-five years after their first movie was released, Disney still resonates with people of all ages as it continues to spew out imagination and a positive outlook. So hand me my glass of fairy dust-laced Kool-Aid, because from toddler to crazy old cat lady, there will always be room in my life for a little Disney magic.

© *Kellie Sheridan, 2013*

DISNEY AND *STAR WARS*
THEY CAN'T DO WORSE
by Kim Sorensen and K. Burtt

KIM:

By now everyone knows that Disney has purchased Lucasfilm. Now, along with Pixar and Marvel, Disney owns *Star Wars*. The deal includes not only *Star Wars* but also other businesses operated by Lucasfilm, including LucasArts, Industrial Light & Magic and Skywalker Sound. Disney and Lucas reached an agreement, Lucasfilm was sold for $4.05 billion cash and stock. If there's one thing George Lucas's inflated ego didn't need it was more money.

This is a statement that Lucas released about Disney's purchase:

> *"For the past 35 years, one of my greatest pleasures has been to see* Star Wars *passed from one generation to the next. It's now time for me to pass* Star Wars *on to a new generation of filmmakers. I've always believed that* Star Wars *could live beyond me, and I thought it was important to set up the transition during my lifetime. I'm confident that with Lucasfilm under the leadership of Kathleen Kennedy, and having a new home within the Disney organization,* Star Wars *will certainly live on and flourish for many generations to come. Disney's reach and experience give Lucasfilm the opportunity to blaze new trails in film, television, interactive media, theme parks, live entertainment, and consumer products."*

He sounds so douchey—however, this Geek vs. Geek isn't about George, it's about Disney and how awesome it is that they now own Lucasfilm.

When you look at it financially, Disney made out like a bandit. *Star Wars* alone is worth more than $4 billion. However, most of us nerds are less interested in the financial aspect of the deal; what we care about is what it means for one of our favorite franchises. Disney has already released a statement saying that they plan to release another trilogy of films, with *Star Wars: Episode VII* being released in 2015. The Star Wars website has also confirmed that Michael Arndt will write the script for *Episode VII*. Arndt won an Oscar for his screenplay for *Little Miss Sunshine* and he was nominated for an Oscar for his screenplay for *Toy Story 3*. I loved both of these movies and I'm excited to see his take on the *Star Wars* universe. No director has been confirmed yet, but considering who else has directed a Disney film – cough *The Avengers* cough – I'm hoping/wishing/praying for Joss Whedon. Although no matter who directs the film, I don't think anyone could ruin *Star Wars* as much as George Lucas did.

There are rumors all over about Luke, Leia and Han being much older so that the original actors could reprise their roles. Harrison Ford has even stated that he would be interested in playing Han again. *Harrison Ford wants to be Han again!* Ford has been notorious about hating being called Han and questions about *Star Wars*, yet now he wants to reprise his role. I guess Disney *can* make miracles happen.

Disney also has control over LucasArts video games. So far the MMO *The Old Republic* is still going strong. Before the great purchase, LucasArts had a project in development, *Star Wars 1313*, an ambitious cinematic action game the studio premiered at this year's E3. A LucasArts spokesperson said the Disney acquisition shouldn't affect that game's development. "For the time being all projects are business as usual," he said. "We are excited about all the possibilities that Disney brings." So it seems that Disney will finish that project, though there has been a lack of conversation about other such games, like *Monkey Island*. With that said, the purchase is still new, and anything could happen.

The most significant lack of conversation concerns Disney's attitude to Indiana Jones. Disney has made no announcements about Lucas's other successful franchise, but there are some issues with Paramount Pictures over the rights. However, after *Kingdom of the Crystal Skull*, I'm okay without another Indy movie for a while.

Another thing that has not been addressed yet is what is going to happen to *The Clone Wars* television show. It's shown on Cartoon Network and there could be some difficulties there. Neither has there been mention of the live action television show that Lucas had planned to develop. Maybe in the coming months Disney will address some of these lingering questions.

I know lots of people don't like Disney owning Lucasfilm. I know that Disney is a big evil corporation and everything they do is bad. I can completely understand those points, but they gave us *The Avengers* and they're going to give us more *Star Wars*. Call me a sheep but I'll be in line for tickets as soon as possible; you know, if the world doesn't end.

I'm ecstatic that Leia is now a Disney princess. I just hope Luke, Leia, Han, Chewy, or other characters show up in the next *Kingdom Hearts* game.

© *Kim Sorensen, 2013*

K.:

So, the Disney/Lucasfilm deal is such big geek news that this argument will need more than one Geek Speaker to handle it all! It's that epic!

As my esteemed colleague on this side of the debate has said, Disney is a big, evil corporation. But in this particular case, I think this is a good thing. A big corporation such as Disney means that multiple people will always be involved in big decisions. No more will one person have complete control. That might not always be the best thing... but we all know what Lucas did with *Star Wars* when left to his own devices. One hopes that with this new arrangement, we won't have to deal with such travesties again.

Why? It is to Disney's benefit to make the best movie(s) possible. They want money. *Star Wars* can make them money. Pissing off the fans is not the way to make them money. So rather than having some harebrained idea ("Jar Jar," anyone?) and running with it because "it's my movie and by God I'll do what I want with it!", Disney execs will do their best to make a movie the fans (and everyone else) will like.

And one big part of that is the fact that someone other than Lucas will be writing and directing. My colleague has already eloquently discussed the writing aspect and touched on the director (really, how awesome would it be for Joss to do *Star Wars*?!) – but it's worth reiterating. As I discussed in my review of *Episode III*, many of the serious issues with the new trilogy were with the direction. Lucas was far more focused on cool special effects than he was about, you know, directing. Disney-backed movies shouldn't have that problem; they'll find someone who can, you know, direct. No more wooden performances. No more cheesily-given lines ("NOOOOOOO!!!"). For that alone, the Disney deal will be worth it.

But there is more to it than just the movies. And not just the video games and TV shows as well. What better company than Disney to provide real fan experiences? Think of how cool *Star Tours* was when it first opened at Disneyland; what can Disney do with the entire license and brand? They could add an entire land to Disneyland now! Tomorrowland, Frontierland, Adventureland, and now Far-Far-Away-Land! (Errr... Long-Time-Ago-Land?) You want to be a Jedi and go through an adventure of some sort? Disney can make that happen! You want to fly X-wings? Disney can make that happen! You want to hunt Ewoks to show you have better aim than the average stormtrooper? Disney can make that happen! And not only can they make all that happen, I'm betting that they will! (Even the Ewok thing, though it might have to be on the secret side...).

Two final reasons that are worth discussing. For one, despite the aforementioned doucheness of Lucas... he does recognize that he doesn't actually need the $4 billion. So, what is he doing with it? Investing most-if-not-all of it into educational initiatives. Go him! How can you complain about $4 billion to charity?!

But the biggest reason that the Disney/*Star Wars* combination is awesome? The songs! It's Disney...of course there will be songs in the new movies! Can't you just imagine "Phil Collins sings *Star Wars*"?! By golly, I'm going to pre-order that CD right now!

DISNEY AND *STAR WARS*
AN EMPTY, SUCKING FEELING OF DISQUIET

by Rachel Hyland

You know, at first I felt quite positive toward the idea of Disney's purchase of Lucasfilm, and consequent control of the *Star Wars* universe. After all, as my formidable opponents in this debate cheerfully point out, the folks at Mouse Central can clearly do no worse to the franchise than its creator. I am one of the many – many, many, many – who believe that *The Empire Strikes Back* is the best of the films in the Jedi/Sith sextuplet largely because someone other than Lucas directed it. Because, as he has proven many a time, George Lucas has become such a bad, terrible, godawful director that even Michael Bay looks down his nose at him whenever they have their weekly poker game with Brent Spiner and Will Smith, and other people associated with sentient robots. (You know this happens.)

But the more I thought about it, the more I started to get that empty, sucking feeling of disquiet in the pit of my stomach, and the grim taste of foreboding in my mouth as I reluctantly contemplated the dangers ahead. And it is not for the reasons that you think. I am certainly not one of the anti-establishment anarchists who rail against the corporate hegemony of Disney (which not only owns Pixar, US network ABC, and all things Marvel but also such stalwarts as The Muppets Studio, ESPN, and hey, even Baby Einstein) and who apparently want us all to live in a Marxist idyll in which we each contribute our best to the common well without thought for personal gain, a bunch of mindless Actives in a world-wide Dollhouse. The fact is – and this may be revealing a little too much about my personal politics here, but oh, what the hell – our established mega-capitalism, as long as it is well-regulated, is A-OK by me, and if a huge multi-national conglomerate wants to swallow up sundry smaller conglomerates in order to bring me the very best in summer blockbuster entertainment, then dude, who am I to protest?

With that in mind, then... what could possibly be my problem? I mean, I am the person that just yesterday commented to a friend that, actually, I don't think living in a dystopian, corporation-controlled society (like that of *Rollerball* or, say, *Wall-E*), would really be all that bad. So why am I suddenly so very concerned that Big Bad Disney has its money-grubbing hands all over that midi-chlorian-laden galaxy far, far away?

Well, folks, it's simple. The fact is, I love Disney. And I am scared that *Star Wars* is going to ruin it. Or at least humble it a little.

The problem is, you see, that Disney's record with science fiction has been... well... less than stellar (do, please, ignore the pun). Especially when it comes to live action. Probably the best of the bunch would have to be *Flight of the Navigator* and – this is true – *Sky High*, which are both pretty fun movies but are not exactly *Inception*, now, are they? I mean, if you go way, way back to the 70s, some claim could be made for the superior sci-fi stylings of *Escape from* and *Return to Witch Mountain*, but even then the remake does much to sully even those venerable classics. Otherwise, what else do we have? *John Carter*? (Not as bad as everyone says, but not exactly a triumph.) *TRON* and *TRON: Legacy*? The appalling L'Engle adaptation *A Ring of Endless Light* or, worse, the film version of *My Favorite Martian*? The Disney Channel Original Movie *Halloweentown II: Kalabar's Revenge*?

Now, personally, I love a Disney Channel Original Movie, the more preposterous the better. I can even find redeeming virtues in all of the above mentioned critical and/or box office failures; yes, even *TRON: Legacy*. So if Disney does what it does to *Star Wars* and turns out a terrible stinker, I will personally probably love it all the more, such is the perverseness of my tastes. But there are hardcore Warsies in the world that I fear would not be so eager as me to find the silver lining in the besmirched Cloud City.

My opponent K. says (and I'm paraphrasing) that it's a good thing Disney has wrested the *Star Wars* universe away from George Lucas because surely their many-heads approach will be better than his one. Kim brings up the tremendous success of *The Avengers*, and by extension to the general awesome of Marvel Studios' output, noting that even under Disney control fan-friendly fare has been achieved and expectations exceeded. Herein lies a conundrum. Y'see, much of what has made the movies Marvel has most recently produced so good is that they have been carefully monitored by the folks at the home office; much like Pixar has John Lasseter at its helm despite its Disney overlords, Marvel still has the dedicated likes of Stan Lee involved in the projects. But here, without George – as ultimately disappointing as he may have been – Lucasfilm is a ship without an iconic captain; it is Apple without Steve Jobs, Angel Investigations without Angel, which may give Disney all the reason they need to appoint someone of their own that they can trust. And if, as K. suggests, Disney is all about the money, then the live-action director who has without a doubt made the most of that for the company in recent times? Kenny Ortega, helmer of all three *High School Musical* films. (He made the third one for $11 million and it earned over $250 million at the world-wide box office, and that's before you factor in merchandise and DVD sales.)

Am I saying that I don't want to see *Star Wars* as envisioned by Kenny Ortega? Of course I am not saying that! I want to see that more than almost anything. But I fear I am well and truly in the minority there, and when it comes to the *Star Wars* faithful, I cannot imagine anything more likely to infuriate their stormtrooper-clad, lightsaber-wielding souls. My main worry is that my beloved Disney may be the loser in this expensive gamble, as much as may be the die-hardiest of *Star Wars* fans. If Disney fucks this up, it's hard to predict what those people might be capable of.

Sure, when it comes to their universe, *Star Wars* fans seem to be a forgiving bunch; even when the movies were a travesty, they've remained true, we've seen it happen three times already in living memory (arguably four; some have their reservations about Jedi). But until now they have had the somewhat cult-like figure of George Lucas to revere and to follow; theirs not to reason why. But when, if they don't like what ends up on the screen they can direct their hatred at a faceless corporate entity, and one many of them objected to taking over their beloved playground in the first place, I think we can safely assume that Disney could find itself the object of boycotts, picketing, who knows what all?

There is no fury like a geek scorned.

As if that weren't enough to give any dedicated Disney-ite pause at this very idea, there are two other points I would like to address. One, my opponent Kim says she is "ecstatic" that Leia is now a Disney Princess. And two, my opponent K. (an enigmatic first initial to a name long shrouded in mystery...) suggests that the Disneyfication of Star Wars is a happy day because now there will, "of course," be songs in the proposed Episodes VII, VIII and IX. To both of them I say: no, and no. I will not have it. First of all, to be a Disney Princess, one must clearly be the central figure of one's own story, and anyone who claims that the star of the earlier trilogy (and, really, the latter, as well) was not R2D2 is obviously blind to nuance. And second, the only good Star Wars-related song is a parody song, like Weird Al Yankovic's "The Saga Begins" ("My, my, this here Anakin guy, maybe Vader someday later...": Genius!), and should never be sung in earnest. Or did the *Star Wars Holiday Special* teach us nothing?

I mean, just imagine what fresh hell could be wrought by setting lyrics to the Cantina Music.

© *Rachel Hyland, 2013*

DOCTOR WHO
WHY REBOOT *WHO* RULES
by Rachel Day

You really can't be British and ignore the cultural phenomenon that is *Doctor Who*. One of my earliest memories is hiding behind our horrendous orange patterned sofa scared of the Daleks (in my parents' defense, it was the 70s). That memory is closely followed by another of the Fourth Doctor (Tom Baker) turning into the Fifth Doctor (Peter Davison), who was really my Doctor. So, Classic *Who* definitely has a place in my heart and was part of my childhood, and I wouldn't change those memories for the world.

But I also vividly remember that Classic *Who* lost the plot, jumped the space shark and became more about the Doctor's costume than a serious drama, albeit one aimed primarily at children. While I don't deny that without the great concept, many years of existence, and cultural fondness for the Classic run, Reboot *Who* wouldn't exist at all, Reboot *Who* is the reason why *Doctor Who* lives on and may yet get the chance to continue for many more years to come.

I'm not going to disparage Classic *Who* either for the dodgy effects, obvious men-in-costumes-aliens (although the Licorice Allsort monster kind of does deserve a mention), or the sometimes flaky set design. After all, Classic *Who* never had the benefit of today's technological advances that Reboot *Who* enjoys – and I'll even concede that Reboot still does have all of the same, despite the better production quality. Let's face it, there's only so far CGI can go in making a space-flying police box look realistic.

Nor am I going to argue that the Doctors are better in the Reboot, or even that the companions are better in the Reboot. All the Doctors have their followings, as do all the companions, and frankly everybody is entitled to their favorite without getting into a "yours is so much better than mine" debate.

That said, let's focus on why Reboot *Who* rules, and which reboot I mean. The TV movie of 1996 really failed at rebooting the franchise and kind of falls into the crack between Classic *Who* and Reboot *Who*; betwixt and between, as they say. Reboot *Who*, for me, is the TV series which launched in 2005 with the Ninth Doctor (Christopher Eccleston) to the present day. It could also be argued that the TV series has rebooted twice; once with its launch, and again with the advent of the Eleventh Doctor (Matt Smith)… but let's not open up that particular can of worms.

The Last of the Time Lords

From the start, Reboot *Who* took a more serious tone than its Classic forefather. The new series had a darker edge as it focused on making the Doctor the last of the Time Lords. The Ninth Doctor was recovering from the loss of Gallifrey and his part in the end of the Time War – as evidenced in the episode "Dalek" (S01E06). The Doctor went from being a renegade, very clever Time Lord who stopped by and helped out in crisis situations to being the last of his kind. It made the Doctor a more tragic and vulnerable figure. The angst of being the last of his kind has made for great drama, particularly in the Master (Derek Jacobi/John Simms) storyline that ran through Season 4 with the Tenth Doctor (David Tennant) and culminated in the great three-part "Utopia/The Sound of Drums/The Last of the Time Lords" (S03E11-13), as well as the Tenth Doctor's demise after preventing the return of the Time Lords ("The End of Time"). Even the Eleventh Doctor has had to deal with it, in "The Beast Below" (S05E02).

Reinventing the Monsters

If the Doctor was given a more serious edge, so too were the monsters that had, by the end of the Classic run, become something of a running joke. Exhibit A: "How do you outrun a Dalek?" Answer: "Go up a flight of stairs!" So, the monsters were given an overhaul. Old favorites the Daleks got hovering ability allowing them to chase people up those stairs – but importantly continued their galactic domination efforts, including stealing entire worlds. The Cybermen became all the creepier for the lobotomy of real people involved. The Master, as played by John Simms, became a truly disturbed sociopath. But there has also been the introduction of new threats such as the Weeping Angels in the award-winning episode "Blink" (S03E10), the Ood and more recently, the Silence.

Adult Notes in a Family Show

In taking the show to a more serious place, Reboot *Who* has found that very fine line that Pixar movies excel at walking: namely, keeping an adult audience interested while retaining its mandate as a family-, and importantly, children-friendly show. The storylines have become much more complex and filled with depth. A good example of that is the outstanding "Vincent and the Doctor" (S05E10) where the Eleventh Doctor meets Vincent Van Gogh (Tony Curran). Written by guest writer Richard Curtis (*Blackadder*, *Four Weddings and a Funeral*, *Love Actually*), it explored the art and work of Van Gogh and his mental illness.

Companionable Relationships

In keeping with the adult notes, the relationships between the Doctor and his companions have been explored much more intensely in Reboot *Who*, with romance more overtly on the menu: from the Ninth Doctor's infamous kiss of life with Rose (Billie Piper) in "The Parting of Ways" (S01E13) to the whole Rose-Doctor angst through Tenth's tenure which included a side-trip into Martha's (Freema Agyeman) one-sided Doctor crush and a best mate deal with Donna (Catherine Tate), to the Eleventh's Doctor's friendship with Amy (Karen Gillan) and Rory (Arthur Darvill), and his recent locking of lips with the enigmatic River Song (Alex Kingston), Reboot *Who* has discovered romance in a way the Classic series always eschewed.

Conclusion

While there can be no doubt that the new incarnation of the show will always owe much to the brilliant concept of the Doctor, the TARDIS and the love created by Classic *Who,* but the classic form ultimately failed to be something that audiences wanted to watch. Reboot *Who* regenerated the franchise into a serious sci-fi show that is more popular than ever and shows no sign of stopping.

Classic *Who* is dead. Long live the Reboot!

© *Rachel Day, 2011*

DOCTOR WHO
WHY THERE IS ONLY ONE *DOCTOR WHO*
by Seanan McGuire

My opponent in this debate makes the extremely valid point that "you really can't be British and ignore the cultural phenomenon that is *Doctor Who.*" I don't know any *Who* fan, old-school or new-school, British, American, Canadian, Australian, or hell, Martian, who wouldn't agree with this. *Doctor Who* has never been nearly as big of a deal in the United States, where it was relegated to public television stations at unusual hours of the night or morning, to be discovered by bored kids searching for treasure on one of the few channels that was almost never forbidden. For American fans growing up in the eighties and nineties, *Doctor Who* was absolutely an integral part of our childhoods.

Rachel then goes on to say that classic *Doctor Who* "lost the plot," becoming "more about the Doctor's costume than a serious drama." That is where we must, alas, part ways. Because as far as I'm concerned, not only did *Doctor Who* hold onto itself all the way through to the bitter end... which wasn't an ending after all, since it was followed by the New Adventures and the Missing Adventures and the TV movie and the Big Finish Audio Adventures. Just like the Doctor himself, *Doctor Who* never truly died.

It just regenerated.

See, I don't believe that there's such a thing as "Classic *Who*" and "Reboot *Who*," any more than I believe that the First Doctor and the Eleventh Doctor are totally different men with totally different histories and backgrounds. They are the same being, renewed and changed to suit a new time, a new set of challenges, and a new sort of storytelling model. Times change. It's unavoidable. And as with anything that gets involved in a wibbly-wobbly, timey-wimey sort of thing like television standards, *Doctor Who* had to change with them.

So this is my position: I am not going to insist that any single Doctor is better or worse than any other single Doctor (although I naturally have my preferences, and they're pretty much all prime numbers, which amuses the crap out of me). I am not going to argue that any companion is better than any other, or that any one story defines "the true spirit of *Doctor Who*." Instead, I'm going to try to explain why this is all a single line, one that loops and twirls back on itself like a ball of yarn getting all twisted and tangled in the wind.

Summer Belongs To You

So there's this show that has absolutely nothing to do with *Doctor Who*, despite having several time travel episodes and occasionally making *Doctor Who*-related jokes, because the show was created by enormous geeks and I respect that. It's called *Phineas and Ferb,* and the basic conceit is that these two boys, in an effort to have The Best Summer Ever, create amazing machines and have incredible adventures every single day for the duration of their summer vacation. The theme song flat-out says: "There's a hundred and four days of summer vacation, then school comes along just to end it / So the annual problem for our generation is finding a good way to spend it..."

Some of the adventures are pure hammered awesome, like when the boys built a roller coaster and threw a musical to go with it, or when they built a giant robotic shark, or when they staged a come-back tour for their mother, who was a 1980s pop idol (and who else feels old now?). Other adventures are sort of forgettable, which is why I can't think of any to list here. But they're all part of what makes *Phineas and Ferb* such an awesome show, and part of what makes it so much fun to keep watching. You know they've built things before, but what you're here for is the thought of what those crazy kids are going to build next.

So, *Doctor Who*. See, there's this old alien dude, right? He's lived a long time, and he's tired, and he's pretty sick of being surrounded by idiots... and he has a granddaughter whom he loves very much, and he doesn't want her growing up like this. He wants her to see the world. Hell, he wants her to see all the worlds, in all the times, forever. So he steals a time machine, and he steals his granddaughter, and they take off running like their feet are on fire. And it. Is. Awesome. Those early adventures (the ones that survive) were the sort of storytelling and narrative that was appropriate for the time. This was an era where adults didn't admit that they wanted to watch the big blue box bob through time and space, so they pitched the show at kids—an investment that would eventually lead to *Doctor Who* becoming one of the only shows to raise its own fanbase, aside from the soap operas.

Time Makes You Bolder, Children Get Older...

...and we were all getting older, too. As the core audience for *Doctor Who* grew up, they brought in new threats, new storylines, and yes, a new Doctor. The Second Doctor didn't have a granddaughter to educate. Instead, he had companions to annoy, and a whole big universe to pick apart with a grin on his face. The stories got more adult, the scripts got more complex, and everything got a lot more immediate. For all that *Doctor Who* was a black-and-white show at the time, it was going through its own version of what happened when our four-color comic book heroes discovered that sometimes, it was okay to have a shade or two of gray. It wasn't an overnight change. Neither was our way of looking at stories.

The Doctor was always, and is always, a trickster-hero of our time, rather than one for his own. When we needed him to be a teacher and a father-figure, he was. When we needed a romantic, he was that. And when we needed a hero broken enough to let us past his walls, he was that, too. He changed because we changed. We changed the way we wanted our stories to be told, we changed the things we wanted those stories to contain, and we changed our expectations.

Absence Makes the Heart Go Wander

So here's the big deal breaker for some people, at least where the classic/reboot divide is concerned: the gap between the TV movie and the 2005 series. And it's true, in the United States, there wasn't much that got you your *Who* fix during that time. But the Eighth Doctor (Paul McGann, confirmed canonical in the new series) was there the whole time, keeping the adventure alive in the Audio Dramas from Big Finish. The Time War was set up in those stories. The fanbase was kept active and engaged by those stories. And when the time was right to change again, Eight became Nine, a war became war's aftermath, and a big blue box appeared again.

Conclusion

Doctor Who changes. That's what it does. And without denigrating either classic or new *Who*, I say that the changes are what makes it all one story, and what will continue to make that story awesome.

© *Seanan McGuire, 2011*

FAMILY GUY
MAKING US DUMBER
by Amy Sharma

"The Simpsons as conceived by a singularly sophomoric mind that lacks any reference point beyond other TV shows."
— Ken Tucker, Entertainment Weekly.

I used to like *Family Guy*. I mean, the premise of Stewie and the dog has potential. The jokes at times made me laugh out loud.

But then it started to grate on me. I really didn't like Peter or Chris. Why do they exist? Why are they such large goobers? How can an unattractive nitwit like Peter land Lois? Why are they telling the same joke over and over? Why are they reminiscent of the jokes we all told in third through seventh grade? Why do I feel dumber after having watched an episode?

And then, thankfully, rather early on in the show's lifetime, Fox axed it. Yet such a cry went up from the masses that a few years later they reinstated it. Unfortunate, because Fox also axed *Futurama* and *Firefly* in their prime, but ignored that fan outcry for life after death. (Though *Futurama* would later go on to find a new home at Comedy Central.)

Which again proves that Fox prefers fart jokes to anything remotely clever. Stooping to the lowest common denominator or never underestimating the stupidity of the American people seems to be their business strategy. But it's worked for hucksters like P. T. Barnum and the Republican Party for quite some time, so I guess I can't really blame them. *Family Guy* rakes in viewers, which equates to money. Still, the fact that it is still on TV is a pox on the American people (that's right kids, who needs discussion of the wars or a balanced budget when we have bigger fish to fry: the existence of *Family Guy*!).

Why oh why is this show so bad? Let's find out...

To begin to formulate my argument, I googled "*Family Guy* Haters." And the haters had some good points. Specifically, that if the jokes make you think, the show is creative. But when was the last time a *Family Guy* joke made you think, even just a little? "Never" is the appropriate answer.

However, the haters on discussion forums aren't really the best sources for me to quote in this argument, because they can't really spell and they use "retarded" as a derogatory remark. A lot. And it's typically spelled wrong. This proves two things: 1) even some stupid people (who are its target audience) don't like *Family Guy* and 2) the People's Internet isn't always what it could be (see 99.99% of tweets).

I needed some more ammo, because calling this show "retarded" is stooping to its own level. And it's mean to actual developmentally-disabled people. After some more digging I found the gem of a quote at the beginning of this article as well as some stuff from Trey Parker and Matt Stone who, aside from being the creators of *South Park*, are notorious *Family Guy* haters. I'll let Wikipedia summarize:

> *"In a 2006 interview, Parker and Stone stated that they dislike having their show compared to* Family Guy. *After the episode "Cartoon Wars" aired, Parker states they received support and gratitude from the staffs of* The Simpsons *and* King of the Hill *for 'ripping on'* Family Guy.*" Parker and Stone clarify their opinions of* Family Guy *in the DVD commentary for the episodes. They say that, although they respect it for its fans and making people laugh, they ultimately hate the show itself and have absolutely no respect for its writing, given its overuse of gag humor that has nothing to do with the story."*

And that, dear readers, is the crux of it: *Family Guy* is like Mad Libs. Remember those? I do, because they now appear as the toy in Chick-Fil-A kid's meals. It's the perfect analogy. I imagine a majority of the writers all work at separate cubicles and come up with 10-30 second vignettes/jokes (30 seconds is pushing it) that are then put into a database tagged by their length and theme: i.e. sex joke, fart joke, swimming in raw sewage joke, *Star Wars* joke, Britney Spears joke, etc. Then, the main writers sit down and say: "This week's episode is about Brian buying a hot dog at 7-11." After that, the story line appears:

> Brian walks out the door to 7-11, along the way he pets a dog and picks his nose [flash to 30 second bald guy joke.]

> He arrives at 7-11, [flash to 10 second Britney Spears joke] and then he debates getting chili on the hot dog [flash to 20 second Star Wars joke. You thought I would say sex joke because of the hot dog? Or fart joke because of the chili? My friends, that is entirely too related to the main story line.]

> Etc., etc.

You get the point. The jokes in brackets are then filled in by a random number generator attached to a database. Not a bad idea. Saves on labor and actual thinking. Except this is a TV show with an actual budget, not an inexpensive activity book that was designed to entertain kids on car trips before the advent of portable DVD players and tablets. For goodness sake people, you are getting paid, you have university degrees! TRY!

Let's look at two example quotes from the show:

Quote 1

> **PETER:** Lois, you know my rule, you are only allowed to sleep with three people besides me: Gene Simmons, John Schneider or Boba Fett.

BOBA FETT: All right! Goodbye virginity!

Quote 2

PETER: Huh, I wonder what Scooby and the gang are up to?
[Scooby-Doo theme plays]
TV ANNOUNCER: We now return to *The Scooby-Doo Murder Files*.
FRED: Gee whiz, gang. Looks like the killer gutted the victim, strangled him with his own intestines and then dumped the body in the river.
VELMA: Jinkies! What a mystery!
SCOOBY-DOO: *[jumps into Shaggy's arms]* Arroo!
FRED: You're right, Scoob, we're dealing with one sick son of a bitch!

Two things to note: 1) these aren't really that funny and 2) they could have appeared in the same episode. One, say, about library books.

My kid watches this BBC show *In the Night Garden*, and we always joke that they only filmed about an hour of footage, and then they re-splice it, add different narration, and *voilà!* New episode. It is a show that makes me want to poke my eye out with a pen. But it's a kid's show, aimed at the two-year-old market. Two-year-olds are far more interested in bright colors, songs, and bouncing balls. They care not for jokes (let alone clever ones) or plot lines. *Family Guy* is meant for a slightly older market. Yet they don't put in any more effort or sophistication.

Now, one can make the argument that *30 Rock*, *Seinfield* and *Futurama* are quite random as well. But upon closer inspection, it is apparent that thought went into the seemingly random story lines. In the end all the random jokes and tangents are pulled together in a relatively nice bow. Or in the words of Bender at the end of "300 Big Boys": "Finally, closure."

And that is why *30 Rock* is loved by critics everywhere. It is clever. It makes you think. Now, I am not saying all sitcoms need to be completely cerebral (and yes, I've seen the *Family Guy* episode where Brian makes Peter seem smart by forcing him to watch *Frasier*). But, I am saying they should at least ask you to think, just a teensy bit. Surely all that production money is going to writers with more than two brain cells and not monkeys in a room trying to bang out Shakespeare?

Of course, this may be a losing battle. If *Family Guy* is gone, we'll still have *The Real Housewives of XYZ* and the Kardashians (can someone make them stop breeding? That isn't helping), and we will keep getting dumber. But *Family Guy* has writers; it pretends to be a real show. People compare it to *The Simpsons*, *Futurama* and *South Park* as if they are peers. They aren't. Stop pretending this is better than reality TV. It isn't. Stop telling me it is good. It's not. Let's just relegate it to where it belongs: at the bottom of the TV cesspool with all the other garbage.

FAMILY GUY
FREAKIN' BRILLIANT
by Kim Sorensen

I am a *Family Guy* fan. I have been a fan since its premiere. To be honest, I had low expectations. I had thought it was just another prime time cartoon from Fox, similar to *The Simpsons*, which I had not enjoyed nor watched in years. I was incredibly wrong in my assumptions. *Family Guy* was a blast of comic brilliance that came out of nowhere and went unheard by an audience still enraptured by the antics of *Friends*. At first it all appeared relatively routine, even – as many have accused – a rip-off of *The Simpsons*. Fat, child-like, head of household Peter Griffin (voiced by creator Seth MacFarlane) screws things up while doting wife Lois (Alex Borstein), put-upon daughter Meg (Lacey Chabert, later Mila Kunis) and genetic copy Chris (Seth Green) look on. Also in the mix is genius homicidal infant Stewie (MacFarlane) – one of the most deserving break-out characters in TV history – and Brian (also McFarlane), the family's talking dog.

Yes, the characters sound like clichés, but that's the point. MacFarlane uses them simply as archetypes as the show regurgitates every pop culture childhood memory to create a full-length parody of 70s and 80s sitcoms. Although I would say that it is not a simple parody but a satire. Just as Archie Bunker was a product of the 50s values being imposed on by a changing 70s culture, *Family Guy* is about the new millennial values juxtaposed on sitcom camp of the last century. In MacFarlane's world there are child molesters on *Lost in Space* and *Eight is Enough* actually refers to disciplinary beatings.

Yes, *The Simpsons* has covered similar ground, with a particular emphasis on random flashbacks and fantasy scenes. But with *The Simpsons* in a creative tailspin for the last decade or more, MacFarlane and crew have swooped in to fill the gaping void. To out-Simpson *The Simpsons*, if you will. What MacFarlane brings to the table is pitch-perfect comic timing, an ability to know how quick to cut or how long to drag out a particular bit to get the laugh, along with an utter fearlessness. From bits in which Jesus Christ turns water "into funk" to when daughter Meg finally makes some friends (but who are really in a suicide cult), *Family Guy* isn't just freakin' brilliant, it is one of the funniest things to ever grace TV.

At one point the show was canceled, only to be renewed at the eleventh hour. And then it was canceled again, and brought back supposedly by strong DVD sales. There are people who say that after its resurrection, *Family Guy* hasn't been the show it used to be. I would argue that the show is the same, but there *are* subtle differences. Characters have changed. Stewie is less British, less psychotic, and more of a homosexual caricature. MacFarlane never quits with the equally humorous and offensive gags.

He has given to us multiple episodes of an unhinged James Woods who is defeated by a trail of candy. Jesus has returned to Earth and Peter found him working in a record store. Robert Downey Jr. stars as Lois's long-lost brother who has been locked in an asylum because he murdered fat guys. There are amazing scenes straight from movies: Chris's first day of high school he gets paddled, a la *Dazed and Confused*; Brian and Stewie destroy Peter's record, taken frame-for-frame from *Office Space*. As a fan of those movies it is a funny reference/homage. Of course not every episode is amazing, but when a show has had eleven seasons, that's going to happen.

One of my favorite things about *Family Guy* is MacFarlane's ability to make fun of the show and of himself. At one point Peter threatens to fire Lois, and when she replies that he can't fire her he responds with two words: "Lacey Chabert." MacFarlane's bantering with Seth Green is always funny. The two argue back and forth over *Robot Chicken* and who has done better parodies of *Star Wars*. Lois sums up the main point of *Family Guy* and lots of MacFarlane's writing in general when she says: "We get it, you watched TV in the 80s."

I will acquiesce that MacFarlane is full of himself, and that the show has lately been more topical and overall is not as humorous as its earlier seasons, but I still enjoy it. I still laugh. Even though some episodes are down-right dark (like the episode "Brian and Stewie" where the two get locked in a bank vault), MacFarlane uses *Family Guy* to try out new things.

Sometimes they work and sometimes they don't.

Like it or not, *Family Guy* is a huge part of pop culture, and has made Seth MacFarlane such a major player in Hollywood that he was selected to host the 2013 Oscars. It led to two other successful shows for MacFarlane, *American Dad* and *The Cleveland Show*. It has become one of the most recognizable shows on television and one of the biggest cult shows ever, and it's still better than most "comedies" being shown on American television, whether animated or not.

© *Kim Sorensen, 2013*

FILM ADAPTATIONS
IS NOTHING SACRED?
by Kate Nagy

Generally, when a director announces that s/he is filming an adaptation one of my favorite novels, my response is cautious optimism, and sometimes even wild enthusiasm. I was all about Gary Ross' *The Hunger Games*, for example. Indeed, I've been known to joyfully fantasy-cast some of my favorites. At the same time, I firmly believe that There Are Some Things Man Was Not Meant to Know, and that one of those things is how Athansor, the flying white horse at the heart of Mark Helprin's classic *Winter's Tale*, would look soaring across the big screen in high-definition with surround sound at my local multiplex. And yet, this is exactly what we have to look forward to in 2013, when Warner Brothers' planned adaptation, written and directed by Akiva Goldsman (*Batman and Robin*, *Lost in Space*, *I Am Legend*), arrives in theaters.

Call me narrow-minded, call me unimaginative, call me small-souled, call me anything you like, but I'm begging you, producers, writers, director, actors, cinematographers, sound mixers, boom mike operators, key grips, best boys, caterers, and on-set animal monitors associated with this film: please, please, don't go through with this. *Winter's Tale* is not just any book, and trying to depict its many subtleties and complexities on film is a terrible idea, start to finish.

I'm not going to summarize the novel's plot; if you're unfamiliar with it, you really should read the book. But rest assured, this film is real and it is coming. Multiple sources report that filming will begin this fall in New York; Colin Farrell has signed on to play anti-hero protagonist Peter Lake, joined by Russell Crowe as crime lord Pearly Soames, and *Downton Abbey*'s Jessica Brown Findlay as heroine Beverly Penn. Will Smith and William Hurt are also reportedly on board.

So... big studio... experienced writer... solid cast. What could possibly go wrong with this?

First of all, while there are some gorgeous set-pieces I admit I'd enjoy seeing onscreen (Peter Lake hanging from the Zodiac above Grand Central Station comes to mind), the book as written doesn't seem to be particularly screen-friendly. For one thing, it is thematically dense, containing a lot about the true nature of justice and whatnot – maybe I'm a snobbish cynic (okay, no "maybe" about that), but I just don't see Hardesty's search for something as abstract as the Perfectly Just City resonating with a lot of moviegoers. Hell, I'm not sure I'd go see a movie about that myself if I weren't familiar with the source material.

Also, the book is stuffed with… stuff, and a lot of the best stuff would have to be dropped if there would be any hope of bringing in a film under three hours. I shudder to think what will end up cut… the Baymen? Jesse Honey and his all-purpose reepschnur? Craig Binky? How could this movie even be made without Craig Binky and his blind bodyguards? (I still giggle at "Alertu" and "Scroutu.") I suppose they could do a very bare-bones time travel adventure with Peter Lake and Beverly in the past, Hardesty and Virginia in the present, and some sci-fi trappings (the bridge of light, etc.) thrown in. It might even be a colorful and moving experience. But it wouldn't be *Winter's Tale*.

In short, this is a book with a whole that is much more than the sum of its parts. What holds those parts together? Helprin's language. How do you translate his dazzling prose onscreen? I think you can't, unless you're trying to make an art film, and Akiva Goldsman… doesn't make art films. What does Akiva Goldsman make? Well, he made the Will Smith vehicle *I Am Legend* a couple of years ago – you know, the one where he completely changed the ending of Richard Matheson's original novella, thereby obliterating, I don't know, THE ENTIRE POINT OF THE SOURCE MATERIAL.

Ah, yes… let's talk for a minute about the ending. In the book, our heroes, in a boat, are lifted high into the sky over the burned-out ruins of Manhattan and then set gently down in the middle of the Perfectly Just City. Also, and I can't stress this enough, it's left ambiguous as to whether the hero and heroine reunite. Which is part of the point! It's important that we decide for ourselves! But do you seriously think any major studio is going to greenlight a big-budget time-travel epic in which the hero and heroine DON'T reunite?

So, in sum, I'm picturing a sumptuous, pretty, well-acted movie that oversimplifies the book's sprawling plot, systematically strips the narrative of all subtext and thematic resonance, decimates the ending, and generally leaves the audience saying WTF. But, hey, there'll be a flying horse! Maybe he'll fly over the audience! In 3D! I'm betting this will be released in 3D. Oh, lord. (*buries face in hands*) I'm not sure what Helprin was thinking when he sold the rights. Maybe he's trying to buy his own island or something.

It's true that I'm not altogether comfortable publicly pooping all over a movie that doesn't even have a release date yet, and I'm well aware that I may be back here a year from now begging Akiva Goldsman's forgiveness and eating a mouthwatering meal of crow. Yet somehow I doubt it. Akiva, I'm talking to you: It's not too late. Pull back now. Adapt another one of Helprin's novels – *A Soldier of the Great War* would be a good one, everyone loves war stories, you could keep the same cast, even – make a billion dollars and buy Helprin that island. But please, I'm imploring you, do not mess with *Winter's Tale*.

FILM ADAPTATIONS
NO, NOTHING'S SACRED
by Rachel Hyland

I have to confess that I am not as enraptured by Mark Helprin's 1983 novel *Winter's Tale* as is my opponent in this debate. Kate lists it as her favorite novel of all time, rhapsodizing at length about its language, its imagery and its unforgettable characters. As one more newly come to the book – not released in a new edition since 1995 but now, of course, available for your favorite e-reader – I can say that I enjoyed it, for all its convolutions, and I am certainly in awe of Helprin's linguistic panache, but not only do I have no objections to the proposed filmic adaptation, I also actively encourage director Akiva Goldsman and co. to go forth and bring on the flying horse in what Kate believes is inevitable 3D.

But the essence of the question here is not specifically whether *Winter's Tale* would make a good movie (though I think it's certainly very possible, and most particularly that signing Russell Crowe as the charismatic and utterly mad crime kingpin Pearly Soames is a triumph of the casting director's art), but more generally whether the attempt should even be made. Kate claims that the book, as written, is "unfilmable," and she is terrified to even contemplate which parts of the narrative will be, of necessity, lost to accommodate a reasonable running time.

Now, look, I am as much of a pedant as anyone when it comes to seeing my favorite books translated onto the screen. I sat through *The Golden Compass* and was furious that Phillip Pullman's celebrated ambiguity and allegory became a hodgepodge of ill-conceived action sequences, and I was just as downcast as anyone by the gouge-your-eyes-out awfulness that resulted when director Chris Columbus was let loose on Asimov's short story "The Bicentennial Man." But by no means do I feel that the limitations of screen time, budget, studio interference and, it must be said, imagination, all of which often lead to the excision and alteration of some treasured moments of literature – really, Peter Jackson? You couldn't fit Tom Bombadil into your sixteen hour movie? – incontrovertibly mean that we should never allow these hallowed tomes to be adapted, and thereby capture a broader audience.

Take, for example, comic book movies. Some years back, I went head to head with our Will Cashin over the respective merits – or lack thereof – of the movies made from properties in both the Marvel and DC universes.

Will put forth the argument that the quality of DC's output (*Superman*, Burton's *Batman*, *The Dark Knight* trilogy) trumped the quantity of Marvel's, especially given the many failures on the latter's resume: *Howard the Duck*, *Daredevil*, et al. Even stipulating to that – which I don't: *Swamp Thing*, *Steel* and *Catwoman*, anyone? – I still maintain that it is far, far better for the attempts to be made than for the stories to lay fallow, inviolable, accessible only to we few comic book nerds.

My argument ran thusly:

> *"Now, this may merely be because I happen to be a chick who likes comic books, but I applaud this general broadening of comic familiarity... [because] anything that engenders an awareness of any comic book among the general populace is a Very Good Thing. As comic fans, I think we're all better off the more widely known the objects of our affection become...*
>
> *"My learned colleague has leveled many charges at Marvel's head in his diatribe on this issue, his main one being that Marvel irresponsibly offers up its characters willy-nilly for adaptation and that DC is to be commended for keeping it's sacred. I disagree. Sure, the efforts to film our heroes may occasionally bring the various comic houses and/or titles into disrepute, but I'd rather they at least try to deliver their stories unto the populace than hoard them away all safe and sound to be enjoyed only by those already in the know."*

I feel the same way about books. Sure, there are risks inherent in the adaptation of any written work, and certainly we have seen our share of disasters (repeat offender Chris Columbus and his Percy Jackson travesty comes immediately to mind), but isn't it better that word of these works be disseminated throughout the world via the medium of movie studio advertising budgets than for them to languish, often uncelebrated, on the shelf?

There are many, many movie and TV adaptations that I, personally, wish had never been made. *True Blood*, for example, where Charlaine Harris's Southern Vampire Mysteries series has been turned into a Blood! Sex! Death!-fest I cannot abide. (True, the last few books have lost their way, but the show never, for me, found it.) I hated the movie version of *Eragon*, thought the lame attempt at conveying the wonder of Neil Gaiman's *Stardust* on screen was a joke, and if I may be permitted to journey a little outside of our purview for a minute, felt that Karen Joy Fowler's lyrical novel *The Jane Austen Book Club* was robbed of all its depth and portent when thrown up on the screen, regardless of how much one might like Hugh Dancy and Maria Bello. (And one does.)

But as exercises in broadening the reach of the works on which they are based, the movies made of them – be they ever so unsuccessful – can only be a Very Good Thing. A studio has only to announce that they are going into production on a movie for film buffs' ears to prick up; add that it is a movie based on a novel, and suddenly there is a resurgence in book sales, especially when that "Now a Major Motion Picture" sticker is affixed, or the novel is released with a film tie-in cover.

I mean, I had never read, nor even heard of, Mark Helprin's *Winter's Tale* until Kate's enthusiastic exhortations made me take a look… and I am the Editor-in-Chief of a magazine dedicated to all things in its fantastical genre. Just think of all of the potential readers out there who are similarly unaware of this novel's existence, and in whom will be aroused curiosity whenever the movie trailer first makes an appearance, and the book is made newly prominent on shelves everywhere.

Often, of course, the property under adaptation will already by immensely popular: your *Harry Potter*s, your *Twilight Saga*s, your *Hunger Games*. But how many people do you know who read the latter trilogy simply due to the imminent movie, or even subsequent to having loved it? The movie – which, itself, was considered somewhat problematic in early discussions, due to all the kid-on-kid violence – led the trilogy back onto the best-seller lists, and while I think we can all agree that it wasn't kind of *The Hunger Games* to cause people to then read the idiocy that is *Mockingjay*, the fact that dystopian fiction, and YA dystopian fiction at that, was brought into the forefront of the popular consciousness through the success of this film can only be applauded.

I don't like *True Blood*, but I like that it has, in some measure, legitimized Urban Fantasy. And for all my issues with *Game of Thrones*, the fact that it has brought Epic Fantasy to the masses in a way not seen since *Lord of the Rings* makes me happy. So maybe I'm not so much the *Winter's Tale* fan, maybe I am not as protective of its integrity as is my counterpart in this discussion, but nevertheless, I want to see this movie made as much for the medium's power to promote works of our beloved, often ignored, genre as for any inherent value to be anticipated in the film itself.

My favorite book of all time is Orson Scott Card's *Ender's Game*, and when the long-awaited movie adaptation of that, currently in post-production and with a 2013 release date, makes it to the cineplex (oh, frabjous day!), I will be first in line. Forget that it has Gavin Hood, of *X-Men Origins: Wolverine* infamy at the helm. Forget that much of it feels unfilmable. (The Battle Room? Doing that justice will take technical wizardry I don't think yet exists.) Forget that casting it as written is well-nigh impossible. (Lucas searched the world for a mini-Anakin and ended up with the wooden witlessness of Jake Lloyd. A juvenile military genius like Ender was doubtless far out of reach, let alone Bean; which is probably one reason they made the children of the novel into teenagers.) And talk about kid-on-kid violence! Nevertheless, I still want to see what can be done with it onscreen, for good or for ill, and I want to see that movie tie-in novel released with a new cover and the words "Now a Major Motion Picture" enticing in new readers, and I want *Ender's Game* to be as ubiquitous on bookshelves as are the collected adventures of the kids at Hogwarts.

Though if they'd let Chris Columbus direct it – remember, the guy also managed to make *The Philosopher's Stone* boring – then I'm not sure I could've been held responsible for my actions.

© Rachel Hyland, 2012

FILM CRITICS
WAY TOO SERIOUS
by Jason Murdoch

Movie reviewers take themselves too seriously.

Okay, so I'm aware of the hypocrisy of this piece. I'm also perfectly aware that I've almost "turned on my own kind," since reviewing movies is a lot of what we do here at *Geek Speak*. But frankly, it's a fact. My esteemed colleague and distinguished movie reviewing machine, David Baldwin, will argue that their/our role lies in informing audiences, holding the industry accountable, deconstruction and discussion, and yes, a little entertainment. It all sounds sooo noble and insightful and academic.

But this is rarely the case.

Okay — so "entertaining" sometimes happens, I'll give you that one. But back to the point.

Think back to the last few film reviews you read (even, I'm afraid, including the ones in this very magazine), by which I mean reviews of regular Hollywood studio pictures and not, say, some new, much-hyped indie on its way to Sundance. Now, how many of these reviews of Hollywood's output were actually positive, without even a hint of malice or contempt? Maybe, a couple… if you're lucky. (And one of those is definitely *Wonder Woman*.)

Now, how many of the following terms ring bells?

Disappointing
Plot-holes
Unfortunate
Incomplete
Poor character development
Underwhelming
Half-baked
Second-rate
Unfocused
Rehashed
Unoriginal
Uninspired
Bloody fucking awful

The list goes on… but you get what I'm saying.

The issue here is that people go to the movies to be ENTERTAINED. Not to pick apart the cohesiveness of the narrative, or every line of dialogue, or every improbable action sequence. But reviewers? It seems to me that's exactly why they go.

So let's say I'm planning to see a movie. I get online and check what's showing at my local cinema. I YouTube the trailers, then Google a couple of reviews.

This is the beginning of the end.

Say I really liked *Deadpool*, so I check out the Rotten Tomatoes score for another Ryan Reynolds comic book movie, *Green Lantern*. Maybe I even skim over some of the more prominent review abstracts: "Misfire," "Overstuffed," "Clumsy," "Conceited."

Hmm. Pass.

If this was a one-off occurrence, reviewers could be forgiven. But it is more often than not. So much more.

Now, imagine if you will, a different place. A magical world full of open-mindedness, and people who took things as they were intended. Tricky, I know, but you can do it! Go on, close your eyes… oh wait, you're reading this… um.. open them… OPEN YOUR EYES!! You can't hear me, can you? *Le sigh*.

Okay — I'm going to assume you have enough nous to have ignored the eye-closing bit. So back to the topic at hand. Let's say the reviewer(s) who had previously shot down my *Green Lantern* enthusiasm had realized that it was a movie based on a comic book! And not just any comic book, mind you, but one with a fairly "out there" background story — aliens, magical rings, all sorts of craziness. I mean, this is a complex mythology that's not just asking you to accept the idea of a single "superman", but shows you different worlds, a variety of alien lifeforms, a ring that turns into a light gun, and all sorts of other completely out there and unbelievable shit!

Unless I'm a complete and utter moron, I should already have a fairly good idea what to expect from a movie like this. Why, then, do I need someone to tell me how the movie doesn't have the plot, character development or emotional involvement of something like *The Shawshank Redemption*, and is therefore undeserving of my time?

Of *course* it's hard to swallow, it stretches the concept of "suspension of disbelief" to the edges of its definition. That's kind of its purpose; and in this scenario, my imaginary reviewer, the one that DOESN'T take him- or herself too seriously, knows this, and takes it into account. So instead of drowning me in their negativity, the reviews I read let me know that it's a fun movie, that it explores the idea of overcoming fear, that it gives you the full backstory of the Green Lantern world, that you'll see an epic amount of (not entirely terrible) CGI, and that you'll get to see Ryan Reynolds in another role that lets him deliver the fast-paced, witty dialogue we've come to expect.

Suddenly, I may be inclined to see the movie, since ALL THESE ARE THINGS THAT I AM INTERESTED IN!

I already knew it was most probably never going to be an Oscar-winning classic — it never set out to be. A movie like Green Lantern is SUPPOSED to be light-hearted and imaginative, featuring all manner of explosions, aliens, and shit that is completely un-fucking-believable, in the both the literal and figurative senses.

For too long have reviewers placed unrealistic, unattainable, and plainly ridiculous expectations on movies, especially the popcorn blockbuster movies without which no holiday season is ever complete. And for some reason, they attack sci-fi, fantasy and horror films with even more righteous film school fury than any other genre.

In Australia, we call it Tall Poppy Syndrome. "Michael Bay earns more than me so I'm going to cut down his movie — even if it is one that is clearly intended to be taken with a light-hearted barrelful of salt — with as much scathing sarcasm and wicked, learned wit as I can muster. Yeah, that'll fix him."

To sum up: Too serious. Too long. To busy thinking to just watch.

Enjoy a fucking movie already.

© *Jason Murdoch, 2017*

FILM CRITICS
USUALLY RIGHT
by David Baldwin

I cannot stop reading my opponent's musings on why film critics take themselves too seriously. It caught me off guard, and I have been reading it over and over again at length trying to comprehend his disdain for this breed of writer. While I will not disagree with the idea that some do take themselves way too seriously (especially that clever punster and thesaurus enthusiast Armond White), there are quite a few that do not.

The film critic is a necessary — "evil" if you will — to the film-going enterprise. They help us make conscious decisions in the films we watch (at least, most of the time), and wade through the crap and typical Hollywood filth so that we do not have to. While some people may not need to be told that a movie like *Zookeeper* is not on par with *Schindler's List*, there are others who really do need to hear that *Rise of the Planet of the Apes* is just as great you might have heard (I saw it specifically because the critics and audience had nothing but amazing things to say about it). And it's not just big budget films — critics also help shed light on must-see indies and those random obscure films that go on to become some of the most beloved films of all time. Would anyone have given

Smith, Wright, Nolan, or Tarantino a chance if they had not heard the buzz coming from film critics? Would the general public know who Leone, Truffaut, or Kurosawa were, without the mentions from critics?

And the beautiful thing about film criticism is that it is two-fold. If your friend asks you about a steaming pile of putrid junk you absolutely loathed, are you really going to hold back on ripping it apart, or are you going to encourage them to see it anyway, form their own opinion, and waste their hard-earned cash in the process? If you are talking about films, and engaging in a discussion on reasons why you love or hate movies, then you are essentially acting the same way as a critic does. Now, you may not be paid for it, but you are doing the exact same job telling the audience what you thought worked and did not. And as I have never met someone who has watched a movie and then was physically unable to tell me their opinion on it afterwards, I would register a guess that everyone who has ever watched a film has acted like a critic at some point in their lives.

I remember when I started writing film reviews. I wanted to meld my love for creative writing with my enthusiasm for film. I was an authority in my circle of friends, and God knows I watched enough of them — so why not? I never really put a thought to what people would think of my reviews, or if they would disagree horribly with them. I just saw them as a fun exercise to get my feelings and opinions out there. I not-so-secretly hoped people would read them and actually take my opinion into account before they went to the multiplex, but it was never a crucial thing to me. And I am pretty certain there are a lot of critics who feel the same way — they just want to gush about their favorite topic, and hope it helps influence someone to watch or not watch based on what they say. We need to remember that despite their hate and disdain for certain films over others, film critics are fans of film above anything else. Otherwise, what right do they have to be writing about it?

But I could go around and around in circles talking about why you should listen to film critics, and why they are crucial to the film-going process. What it comes down to is this: it is the job of the reviewer to be able to decipher plots, spot great acting, and know what is entertaining and what is not. I know I have made special concessions in the past, knowing full well a movie is not for me, but knowing it will specifically appeal to others (most of the *Fast and the Furious* films come to mind). It really is not fair to discount their opinions just because they may not know a lot about the source material for a film, or be a fan of the genre. A great film, one that is truly entertaining, should be able to take its viewer on a journey that explains everything they need to know to understand the film, and to make them not care about the genre, but instead care about what is happening and why. The best films I have seen in the past few years have been examples of genres I used to hate and still do.

This may turn some people off, and make them immediately agree that critics are elitists, and that it really should not matter what they think of a movie. And to that, I say kudos, but wade with caution. I am all for ignoring critical opinion and going into films willing to give them a chance to prove themselves. It happens from time to time, but more often than not, the critics are usually right. They see countless more films than you do on a weekly, monthly and yearly basis. They will always have a good idea of what works and what does not. And while their opinions may not necessarily reflect those of the public, it is still really unfair to discount what they have to say. It is just as important as what we think of a movie.

In the age of the internet, everyone is a critic. We now have the ability to easily get our thoughts published in some manner, whether it is by blogging, writing on message boards, writing for awesome online magazines founded in countries that are half a world away from us — the possibilities are endless. The question at the heart of this debate should not be whether film critics are too serious, but if they are slowly becoming obsolete in favor of user-generated content that is saying the exact same thing, minus some of the eloquence. I go to Rotten Tomatoes on a weekly basis to check out what the critics are saying about new films, but just as frequently, if not more so, I go to IMDb to check out what the users are saying. Because if someone there is telling me that a goofy movie the critics are panning is actually enjoyable, I may just decide to take the plunge and watch it. That does not, however, negate the opinion of the venerable writers whose *job* it is to tell me what they think of a film's merits, outside of what its intended audience may be.

Oh, and for the record: fuck *Green Lantern*.

© *David Baldwin, 2017*

GAME OF THRONES
A PAINFUL EXERCISE IN DREAD
by Rachel Hyland

I was inveigled into reading *A Game of Thrones*, the first in George R. R. Martin's phenomenally successful *A Song of Ice and Fire* series, by *Geek Speak*'s own K. Burtt. An ardent Martin fan, if not necessarily a bona fide member of über-fan club Brotherhood without Banners, he had mentioned the series so glowingly so often that I finally couldn't take it anymore; I hated being so out of this geek-*zeitgeist*-y loop. So I read the first book. And cried almost the whole way through. Threw it across the room a couple of times when it got particularly misogynist/rapey/child molest-y. (Plus, butcher's boy/direwolf kill-y.) Then I read the second book, and the third, crying all the while, throwing across the room all the while, and when I eventually got to the then-most recent fourth, I felt like Martin and I were engaged in a sado-masochistic relationship from which there didn't seem to be any escape. And by the time the (very long-awaited) latest tome in the series, *A Dance with Dragons*, was released last year, I was looking forward to it with perhaps the same enthusiasm I do a trip to the dentist or cleaning out my fridge: as a necessary evil, but one that I knew would ultimately give me a feeling of virtuous satisfaction.

Well, except for all the misogyny/rape/child molestation.

Before *A Dance with Dragons*, though, came the much-celebrated television adaptation of the first book, airing on premium cable channel HBO, starring big name actors and going all out to turn this elaborate Epic Fantasy extravaganza into their latest crossover hit. Their earlier success adapting Charlaine Harris's popular Sookie Stackhouse series into the even more popular *True Blood* doubtless paved the way here, demonstrating to network suits that cult-like works from somewhat marginalized subgenres could be turned into programs with a much wider appeal, especially if they should just happen to involve bunches of attractive people getting all kinds of naked at the drop of a... well, anything. Throw in as much taboo sexual activity as one could possibly muster – in *True Blood*, blood-drinking, multiple partners and, let's be honest, necrophilia; in *Game of Thrones*, incest, gang rape, voyeurism and a whole bunch of sex workers – and hey, you have a ratings winner.

Is *Game of Thrones* a quality show? Sure. Does it have excellent production values, a talented cast and some clever effects wizardry? Absolutely. And is it faithful to the books, in the most fundamental of ways? Definitely, although I do think they have gone overboard with the sex stuff, and quite why practically every incidental female character we get to see lounges about doubtless freezing cold castles and the like –

remember: winter is coming – without a stitch of clothing on I can only ascribe to an HBO-mandated ratio of breasts per minute.

And yet.

I cannot bear to watch *True Blood* because of the myriad changes made between the page and the screen. I love the original series of books dealing with Sookie, Eric and the gang – although, like many of us, I am finding the latter ones to be something of a chore – and so the manner in which her often simply-told tales, in which the prosaic and the extraordinary are juxtaposed in fascinating and hilarious ways, has been transmuted into a Sex! Blood! Death!-fest with little more to recommend it than the finely-honed abs of the admittedly-beauteous Alexander Skarsgård, has left me less than impressed. But with *Game of Thrones* I find that the opposite is true; I stopped watching it entirely, only two episodes into its recently-completed second season, because it is, quite simply, *too* faithful to its source material.

I know, this sounds like an outright impossibility. How can a filmic adaptation of a much loved/admired/respected work be *too faithful?* Well, that's the thing. *A Song of Ice and Fire* is not that much of a loved/admired/respected work... by me. Oh, the first one, sure. I'd never read anything quite like *A Game of Thrones* – still haven't, really – and I would still consider myself an adherent, if only for its courageous and utterly what-the-fuck? beheading of lead (if dimwitted) protagonist Ned Stark. But as the series goes on, with yet more adolescent girls fiddled with and rapes attempted/pondered/described and the only woman with any power in the Seven Kingdoms made crazed and drunk – because, it seems, a mere female could never bear the weight of such an important duty as the one she's been scheming to acquire for decades, even though her insane thirteen-year-old son somehow managed it – it all becomes, quite frankly, icky. With way too much pedophilia. And don't even get me started on Chosen One Daenerys and her "saving" of the "savages." A cringier apologia for missionary, conquistador zeal, both personal and at the government level, I have hardly ever read. If this weren't a totally feudal society, and she the alleged heir to its highest office, I would expect to see her soon start spouting an earnest desire to bring democracy and the free market to the middle of this "East" in which Her Blondness spends so much of her so-valuable book time, all the better to win the war over there so that she doesn't have to win it at home. (USA! USA! White people! USA!)

I stopped watching *Game of Thrones* Season 2 because, assuming it to be as faithful to its source material – 1999's *A Clash of Kings*, AKA Medieval Stratego, and Arya Running Away From Stuff! – as was Season 1 to its (and it was cool that they kept in the beheading of Ned Stark, I must concede), I just knew I was going to get very, very mad—and you really can't throw your more modern television across the room without technical mishap, as perhaps one might have done with an old cathode tube*.

(And heaven save me from Season 3 and zombie fricking Catelyn. Just when you thought she couldn't get any more frustrating and shrill…)

Breaking my objections to the TV series down to their most fundamental level, I find that while I was compelled to read the subsequent books in the series, having embarked upon this dark and depressing fantasy adventure in the strangely addictive first, to now relive their harrowing events in all their gut-wrenching, bile-inducing, infuriatingly horrible glory, whether on the page or on the screen (and this last despite how hot the guys who play Jon Snow and Robb Stark are) is just not something I can bring myself to endure. Why, then, subject myself to such a painful exercise in dread?

Will I read the sixth and seventh, and supposedly last, books in the series, whenever they should deign to grace our shelves? (Titles we have, *The Winds of Winter* and *A Dream of Spring*, although no projected release dates as yet, of course, because jeez, it's barely been a whole year since the last book was released, what more do you people want?) Oh, probably. If for no other reason than to find out if, as I have long suspected, Jon Snow – really the only character at this point worth caring about, since Tyrion married Sansa (ugh! Sansa!), Bran turned cannibal, Arya turned assassin, and Brienne (ugly, ugly Brienne; because a woman can't be hot *and* good with a sword) fell for Jaime – is the son of deposed, mad-'cause-of-incest-we-assume king, Aerys Targaryen, and Ned Stark's sainted dead sister, Lyanna.

Probably through rape, of course. Sigh.

On the other hand, maybe I just… won't. And one day, if they ever make *Game of Thrones*, Seasons 6 and 7 – presumably entirely recast, since even the kid who plays Tommen will probably be nearing retirement age by then – perhaps I'll then see the value in watching them.

(That said: Peter Dinklage as Tyrion? AWESOME.)

© *Rachel Hyland, 2012*

GAME OF THRONES
A STORY THAT BEARS REPEATING
by Regina Thorne

For my ninth birthday, my father bought me a one-volume edition of *The Lord of the Rings*; I lugged that thing around with me for two weeks, locking myself in the bathroom and taking a flashlight to bed so I could read uninterrupted by such trivial concerns as meals and getting enough sleep. My fortnight's journey with Frodo to Mount Doom gave me a temporary crush on Legolas and a life-long love of fantasy fiction. But it wasn't until I was in my early thirties that another work of fantasy fiction, the first three novels of George R. R. Martin's series *A Song of Ice and Fire*, induced the same urge to read until dawn to find out what would happen next, and the same sense that this world really existed, somewhere beyond my reach, and that it would endure in my mind and imagination long after I turned the last page.

What made *A Song of Ice and Fire* so special to me? The best fantasy fiction, including Martin's work, asks Really Big Questions or focuses on Big Themes (the kinds of questions and themes that a lot of the "literary" fiction I also read often avoids) in a high-stakes world. As Cersei Lannister says "In the game of thrones, there is no middle ground. You win, or you die." (Sometimes you win or your entire family, civilization, race or species dies.)

Martin's Big Questions and Big Themes happen to include two that I find particularly resonant: the first is the conflict between societally acceptable codes of "honor" in a feudal society and what we, the readers, perceive as morality (even if that morality is distant or foreign to many of the actors within his story.) Again and again, the characters of *A Song of Ice and Fire* are forced to choose between obeying the dictates of honor and obeying the dictates of morality, beginning with the "original sin" of the series: long before the series begins, Jaime Lannister kills the King to whom he had sworn absolute loyalty. (Only much later do we learn that the king intended to destroy an entire city and all of its inhabitants.) During the first book, Ned Stark is faced with the same dilemma: while his refusal to countenance the assassination of Daenerys is both honorable and moral, his silence to King Robert on the subject of Cersei's treasonous, incestuous adultery is moral – he doesn't want the blood of her innocent children shed – but not in accordance with what Westeros at large would perceive as honorable. In the second and third books of the series, we watch Jon Snow forced to break his oaths in order to safeguard the kingdom he has sworn to protect. And on the opposite side, the knights of Joffrey's guard who beat the helpless Sansa Stark are honorably fulfilling their vows to obey their King's command when everything we know and see argues that they are a pack of morally bankrupt weasels. "Whatever you do," Jaime Lannister says, "you're forsaking one vow or another." I find the ways in which Martin's characters try to resolve this dilemma – or are broken by their inability to resolve it – extraordinarily compelling.

The second overarching theme of Martin's series is best summed up in a quote from one of the most sympathetic secondary characters in the series: "We are only human, and the gods have fashioned us for love. That is our great glory, and our great tragedy." Nearly every character in the novels is motivated in one way or another by love, be it romantic or familial, eros or agape, and its lack. Love motivates acts of selfless courage and horrifying violence; the lack of love blinds even astute judges of human nature to the motivations of those around them.

Of course, neither of these themes would mean anything if I didn't almost uniformly love the characters Martin has created (in some cases I love to hate them, but I still find them fascinating to read about, even if it's only because I keep hoping that they will finally, finally get their comeuppance). Even secondary or tertiary characters like Maester Luwin or Mirri Maaz Duur or the Queen of Thorns have such distinct personalities on the page that I find myself wanting to know more about them beyond it. Lastly, unlike many male authors of fantasy, Martin excels at creating believable and differentiated female characters, ranging from the politically astute great lady Catelyn Stark to the naïve yet honorable warrior Brienne of Tarth to the teenaged Sansa Stark and her sister, everyone's favorite tomboy, Arya. Love or hate them, they are each fiercely individual, as unique as the male characters in the story.

Are the books perfect? Of course not. Although I sympathized with Daenerys in the first book, I think the sections told from her point of view are the weakest in the series. This may be partly a result of the limited third person point of view structure of the novels; unlike the other locations in the story, until Book 5 (which I'm just getting around to reading) there are no other points of view for the events that occur in Dany's milieu. There are fewer correctives to what she gets wrong (unlike the overlapping POVs for events set in Westeros or even at and beyond the Wall, where we have Jon and Sam.)

I also think the world-building is weaker on the other side of the Narrow Sea. Although I can see how the Dothraki are modeled on the Mongols (down to "Khal" for "Khan"), the other civilizations of Essos are a bit of a hodge-podge, with things that look like Italian city states on one side (if Braavos isn't based on Venice, I have a bridge over the Grand Canal I'd like to sell you) and on the other side Assyria/Babylon.

In addition, a frequent criticism of Martin is the amount of violence (particularly the threat of sexual violence against women) and more generally the sense that the books are incredibly depressing, with the "bad" guys getting away (often literally) with murder and the "good" guys made to suffer over and over again.

On the first point, I agree that there are many instances of either the threat or actual sexual violence against women (though mercifully, these are not carried out against characters like Arya or Sansa, or point of view characters in general, although there's a whole nasty sub-area of marital sexual violence in the relationships between Khal Drogo and Daenerys and Cersei and Robert Baratheon). Although I certainly understand why other people don't see this in the same way that I do, I appreciate the verisimilitude – for lack of a better word – of this fantasy world, which was something entirely new and different for me when I first read these novels. In other words, I liked that Martin chose to remain true to the zeitgeist of the medieval Europe in which he set his fantasy. Too many fantasy writers want to use this kind of faux-medieval setting so they can have knights and swords and courtly love and end with the rightful King (or much more rarely Queen) attaining his/her throne, without considering the plagues, starvation, religious fanaticism, and general cruelty and carelessness of these systems of governance in our own world.

Regarding the second criticism of the general sense that these books are depressing and so dark as to be almost nihilistic: well, yes, they are really dark and depressing and I live in dread that my favorite characters are not going to make it to the next book. Yet somehow, for me, the underlying theme of the story is not so much "horrible things happen to everyone, especially those who don't deserve them at all," and more something that Martin himself once said: "All of us have the capacity for good and all of us have the capacity for evil ... the battle between good and evil is waged every day within the individual human heart." To me, that message, that we are all capable of choice (at least until we're brutally murdered in the game of thrones, or by supernatural beings who are really, really cold), is strangely hopeful and not depressing at all.

When it comes to HBO's *Game of Thrones*, I owe my enjoyment of the series (and my occasional disappointment with it) to my love of the books on which it's based. On the one hand, it's amazing to see this brilliant cast in roles they seem born to play, the incredible production values, the stunning locations and cinematography of the series and the evident care with which even the smallest prop has been conceived and constructed. On the other hand, sometimes I find that the version of the characters and their motivations I carry in my head and heart is hugely divergent from that of the showrunners and although in some instances I like their versions better (e.g. Theon, Stannis, Cersei) in others, I vastly prefer the characters as I interpreted them from the books (such as Catelyn and Robb Stark.)

Nonetheless, I eagerly await Season 3 (and hopefully far beyond) to see some of the most memorable moments from these books brought to life for me. And if the show messes things up, well, I always have thousands of pages of the text to read and read again.

© *Regina Thorne, 2012*

HARRY POTTER
OVER-RATED AND JUST NOT VERY GOOD
by K. Burtt

There hasn't been a book series in recent memory that has made as profound an impact on the world as J. K. Rowling's *Harry Potter*.

This depresses me.

There are a great many books and book series which are better-written and more enjoyable for both kids and adults that now seem to be shuffled to the side, discounted, and/or otherwise had their significance reduced or ignored due to the sheer amount of press that *Harry Potter* has received.

Now, I will say upfront that I don't completely hate the *Harry Potter* series. The first few books were decent for what they were, and it's not like I would rather have my armpits infested with the fleas of a thousand camels than even think about reading a *Harry Potter* book again, but the series overall is so fraught with issues and problems (and I say that not just because it is fun to use the word "fraught") that I find it quite undeserving of the praise and hype that still gets heaped upon it.

So here, presented to you in some kind of particular order (though what kind of order is up to you to determine), are all the various reasons why I find the *Harry Potter* book series to be completely overrated and just not very good.

The Main Character

Yes, Harry himself — he who managed to get his name at the beginning of the title of every single adventure (not even Indiana Jones managed that feat!). I don't think he makes a good main character, for a few different reasons. For one, he's not really that good at anything. Okay, yes, he is good at flying, I grant you that, and one could claim that he is also good at the Patronus charm, though I could counter that by saying that was just a function of him being taught it earlier than the rest of his class and having the chance to practice. Other than that, what was he good at? Magic? Schoolwork? Mischief? It always seemed that all other characters just assume that he's good at any/all of the above, so there never is any reason for him to actually *be* good at any/all of the above. I'm not saying that he necessarily should be, or that the main character in general needs to be "The Best" or anything, but throughout the series, Harry is touted by others as being a wonderful and excellent wizard for no discernible reason.

What also bugs me is how it seems most everything that occurs for Harry is directly due to others. Hermione is the power behind most magic and essentially all schoolwork; Harry's skill at sneaking around is solely due to his invisibility cloak (with help from the Marauder's Map – now that's a nifty piece of work; why couldn't Harry and his friends try to create something like that?!); and even his defeats of Voldemort are due to outside circumstances.

But all this, annoying as it is, wouldn't necessarily be a huge problem if it weren't for Harry's attitude.

His attitude, particularly in the middle books, removed any sense of connection I felt with the character. For a series to work, one needs to like the protagonist, and starting in the fourth book, there is little to like. I found his apathy in *Goblet of Fire* to be rather grating — here he is in what is supposed to be this grand spectacle and trial of wizarding (more on that later. Oooh… foreshadowing), and he does… nothing. He has to be hand-held and guided through the entire thing. Granted, he is participating in the Tri-Wizard Tournament (Quad-Wizard Tournament?) against his will, but couldn't he at least try to put in a little more effort himself to be prepared for the various tasks considering how "dangerous" they were?

But apathetic Book 4 Harry doesn't hold a candle to angry, arrogant, bratty Book 5 Harry. If apathetic Harry made me similarly apathetic toward him, angry Harry made me actively dislike him. After all he has gone through in the previous books to that point, don't you think that he would take a second to attempt to look at the bigger picture and not be so completely selfish? Perhaps try trusting Dumbledore? Stop lashing out at his friends?

"But wait!" you say, "He's just acting out like a normal teenager would!"

Ah, I'm glad that you brought that up, as that brings me to my next problem with the series.

The Transition from Children's to Young Adult to Adult

Since when is Harry a normal teenager? Considering the circumstances, his sullen, bitter, sulking self just seems out of character. But it's just a symptom of a bigger issue. As the series progresses, J.K. Rowling tries to transition from a Children's series to a Young Adult series to a more Adult series, and she isn't particularly successful at doing so. Children's literature is full of black and white situations. The good guys are obviously good, the bad guys are evil caricatures, and the situations are regularly completely and unreasonably over-the-top (well, "unreasonable" from the standpoint of more adult fiction – perfectly reasonable for children's). Look at the first book in the series: how Harry has been living in a tiny cupboard under the stairs when we first meet him, the lengths to which his uncle goes to keep Harry from receiving his invitation to Hogwarts, or how the best traps that the top professors could come up with to protect the Sorcerer's (or Philosopher's, if you prefer — not that I, as an American, have any idea what that is, apparently) Stone are ones that could conveniently be bypassed by 11-year olds. That's not a slam against the first book by any means – children's fiction can (and possibly should) be over-the-top. The problem comes in when grey areas are added. If you are not going to be as over-the-top, then you need to be not over-the-top. Mixing some grey areas with the black/white caricatures just results in the mess known as Book 5.

Look at the character of Umbridge, as an example. She is ridiculously exaggerated as a villain, getting away with much more than she should be able to (how does she cancel the entire Quidditch season? As big as Quidditch apparently is, wouldn't the entirety of the alumni of Hogwarts object?), which — had she been introduced in the first or second books — would have fit. By Book 5, however, when the series has supposedly turned more adult with more grey areas, this caricature of evilness just seems quite out of place. Obviously (and disturbingly) so, in my opinion.

But it is not just the over-the-top-ness portion of this mix that doesn't quite work. Take Harry's father. As the series progresses, Harry continually learns the ways that his father wasn't perfect. Okay, fine, learning one's parents aren't perfect is part of growing up. The problem is how it is handled. I never felt like there was a good reason for this. Is it just to help Harry grow up? Possibly, but why not then give some good along with the bad – as the series progresses, Harry doesn't really gain any new insights or stories about good things his Dad did, just how he mistreated Snape in school. So, was the reason to give backstory and motivation for Snape? Possibly, but as we learn, his motivation was more about Harry's mom than his dad. It really just boiled down to "Dude, your Dad was a jerk!" and that was it. An attempt to add some grey that didn't really have any purpose.

And not having a purpose leads me into my next point:

Plots that Don't Make Sense

Some of the plot points of the books make so little sense that it took me out of the story — I was too busy saying "Now wait a minute..." One example would be the Tri (Quad) Wizard tournament from Book 4 (you knew I was getting back to this). So students from two other schools are forced to come to take classes (are they even taking classes?) at Hogwarts just so that one student from each school can participate in this grand challenge that only entails three tasks over the course of the entire school year? And all other students aren't allowed to take part in their normal activities – such as Quidditch – because of this? Really?

Well, that doesn't make much sense, but once again, Book 4 fails to hold a candle to Book 5 in that department (I didn't like Book 5 at all. Could you tell?). In particular, the infamous Prophecy at the center of the entire book (and in some ways, the center of the entire series). The problem is that this prophecy doesn't really mean anything. It essentially says that Voldemort and Harry will fight to the death. Deep, that. So why exactly do Dumbledore and everyone keep that from Harry? Why does it matter so much to make sure Voldemort doesn't hear the end of it? If it's really that big of a deal, why couldn't the good guys destroy the recording held at the Ministry of Magic? The big fight at the end shows that those globes were easily destroyed, and they already had a copy themselves in the form of Dumbledore's memory. The entire conflict of the book could easily have been avoided by one 30-second conversation. The phrase "Gah!" was heard loudly and quite possibly repeatedly upon finishing Book 5.

Another question: At the end of Book 5, doesn't Dumbledore promise not to keep things from Harry anymore? So why does he *immediately* start keeping things from Harry in Book 6 about the Horcruxes? Why drag out that whole plot/discussion throughout the course of the book when he could sit Harry down and explain things in one go?

There are lots o' questions that can be asked such as these. What they all have in common is:

The Writing

I just don't think J.K. Rowling is a good writer. She has a great imagination and sense of whimsy (usually), but being whimsical can't make up for weak writing. Besides the aforementioned plot issues, questionable character decisions, and attempts to transition from children to young adult to adult, other examples of her writing style that just don't work would be the way she handles character deaths. An example: Sirius' death at the end of Book 5. He is stunned and falls through the curtain between life and death? That's it? What could/should have been a dramatic and poignant death (ignoring how ludicrous the plot was that lead to it to begin with – see above) is just plain stupid. I honestly expected Sirius to come back in some form or another by the end of the series, which would have somewhat justified how he "died," but nope, 'twas not to be, and that "death" really was final.

And the dichotomy in how the various deaths in the final book are handled is rather strange. Some have the proper weight (such as Snape's), but others are mentioned almost in passing, enough so that whilst reading it, I didn't even realize the characters were, in fact, killed – Tonks and Lupin, for instance.

One of the overall issues with the writing is Rowling's penchant for going for convenience rather than consistency. She invents new uses for magic to be used in specific instances seemingly without thinking of how that would affect or change the world she's created. An example: how wizards travel. In Book 2, the floo network is introduced. Book 3 has the Knight Bus. Book 4 has portkeys. And Book 5 and beyond focus on apparating. Why do these earlier options exist considering these later

113

options (and why, with all these travel possibilities, do students at Hogwarts still travel by train)? I suppose you could try to come up with reasoning behind each, but it just seems like Rowling needed other ideas in later books to fit the plot points she wanted to make — it was purely a matter of convenience.

Another example: the time-travel device that Hermione uses in Book 3. That's some pretty freakin' powerful magic there, and yet it never shows up again in the series despite many instances where the ability to go back in time even an hour would have helped considerably. Why didn't it? Because it was needed for the Book 3 plot but would have interfered with the later plots! Same with the truth serum (veritaserum, I believe it was called) introduced in Book 4. It appears in Book 5, true, but the sheer existence of such a potion seems like it would have made a lot of things in the wizarding world much easier (couldn't it have proven that Sirius was innocent, for instance?) and yet was only used for certain plot points only.

It reminds me of the episode of *The Simpsons* with Lucy Lawless at a Q&A at the comic book store. She is asked all sorts of nitpicky questions from *Xena* fans, and her response is along the lines of "whenever you notice an inconsistency – a wizard did it" which lucky for J.K. Rowling is an eminently usable excuse for lazy writing.

But it's not just the writing, but also:

The Editing

You may have noticed how many of my issues stem from Books 4 and 5 (and past). This, along with the fact that as of Book 4, all the books are significantly longer than the first three, is not coincidental. I first became aware of the *Harry Potter* books after Book 3 came out, which seems to be about the same time as the massive hype machine started running. As such, it seems as if the editors didn't want to tempt driving their new star writer away by daring to actually edit her work. Books 4 and 5 are way too bloated, Book 6 is just all setup for Book 7, and as for the final book itself – well, when you have entire sections about characters aimlessly wandering around wondering what is going on and what they should be doing, well, that's a sign that perhaps the book could use some trimming down.

Bottom line: the *Harry Potter* series is not bad (my esteemed colleague makes some excellent points, particularly about Hermione). It's just not that good, and in no way deserving of the hype and praise it receives. The first three books? Pretty decent. After that? Not so much. But at least the series got kids to read. Yay, reading!

Now they can go and read something worthy.

HARRY POTTER
OVER-RATED BUT STILL VERY, VERY GOOD
by B. C. Roberts

Writing about *Harry Potter* is a daunting task. So much has been written already both in support and against. For every person who loved the novels and the world they created, there are just as many (just like my colleague who opposes me in this argument) who find the series over-rated. But despite all this, let's wade once again into the mire that is writing about *Harry Potter*.

First things first. *Of course Harry Potter* is over-rated. This has nothing at all to do with the series itself and everything to do with the hype surrounding it. It is a publishing house's job to create publicity around a product, and just like everything else in the history of marketing, there was some exaggeration (no, Coca Cola will not make you cooler). So claiming that *Harry Potter* doesn't live up to the hype is a non-argument – it can't, the second coming of Christ couldn't.

So the question is really whether or not *Harry Potter* the series is any good at all – or more specifically, does the good outweigh the bad. And I think the answer to this is very strongly in the affirmative.

Let's start with Harry Potter as a character. Harry is not the most gifted wizard, but he is the guy who comes through in a pinch. When it's balls to the wall, Harry time and time again finds a way to survive. He's often lucky — and he always has excellent support — but at the end of the day Harry has that unshakeable self-belief and determination which is common to all great heroes. He isn't the Spider-Man "sit around and feel sorry for myself" type; he's the Batman "use any trick that works" type. And with that comes a fair amount of hubris. When Harry gets thrown into the Tri-Wizard Tournament and doesn't try very hard, it's because he's Harry Fucking Potter, doesn't everyone remember that he killed a basilisk with a sword? And this is one response I find entirely credible. At the age of ten Harry is thrown into a world where he's Jesus Christ, where he is, really, more important than those around him. Now, when sportspeople are put in that position they become self-centered arrogant twits (hello, Tiger), and across the fourth and fifth books Harry does the same. It's hard not to be a narcissist when everyone tells you every single day that you're better than everyone else. But it never gets out of control. His crush on Cho and his awkwardness with her is the perfect example of this.

Then there are the support characters. There are so many amazing characters in this series that it's near impossible to select just a few for special mention. The standout, though, is Hermione Granger. More than anyone else in the entire series, Hermione really demonstrates the possibilities of magic and how incongruous that is with the Muggle world. Hermione begins the series with large buck teeth despite her parents being Muggle dentists, but after Draco Malfoy curses her and makes the teeth grow longer and longer, Hermione has Madame Pomfrey shrink the teeth down to a normal size. Her parents would be horrified. Hermione's shining moment for me, though, comes in the final book. Everyone important is at the Weasley's house for Bill and Fleur's wedding when Death Eaters attack and everyone scatters. Hermione disapparates with Ron and Harry, the two boys have nothing with them but the clothes on their backs, and they wonder how they will get back to the Burrow to collect everything they need for the quest ahead:

> *"Undetectable Extension Charm," said Hermione. "Tricky but I think I've done it OK; anyway, I managed to fit everything we need in here." She gave the fragile-looking bag a little shake and it echoed like a cargo hold as a number of heavy objects rolled around inside it. "Oh damn, that'll be the books," she said, peering into it, "and I had them all stacked by subject…"*

It's brilliant and so is Hermione. Sure, Harry's name is the one of the front of the book, but Hermione's awesomeness is hardly an argument against the greatness of the series. The same goes for all the other marvelous support characters. From Hagrid to Professor Trelawney, Grawp to (my personal favorite) Gilderoy Lockhart. They are all masterful creations, each believable within the logic of the series, always hitting just the right level of strange and extraordinary, but also with real world counterparts.

But far and away the shining achievement of the *Harry Potter* series is the creation of the perfect fantasy world. For every child who reads that first book, when Hagrid breaks into a far-flung shack on a rocky island and tells Harry that he's a wizard, there's the same excitement that magic could one day appear in their world and spirit them off to the most wondrous of schools. Harry's world is so close to ours that the possibility of the one spilling into the other is always tantalizing.

The most impressive thing about Hogwarts and the entire magical world in *Harry Potter* is the way that it blends the real world into the imaginary. It isn't just that Hogwarts is the most exciting place to go to school on the planet or that flying on a broom and repeatedly saving the wizarding world (sometime around the end of each school year) is fantastic, but rather that it all seems so possible and well, so British. It seems, in the context of the novels, perfectly obvious that British wizards would drink cups of tea and eat bread-and-butter pudding. They could have the house elves prepare anything in the world, real or imaginary, but they stick to what is widely recognized as one of the worst cuisines in the world. God love 'em.

Sure, the novels go from being simple children's fiction to more dramatic young teen fare and along the way things get longer and darker, but the consistency throughout the series is not lost. The blend of crazy and mundane stays well balanced and I particularly love the wizarding version of a police state that we get towards the end of the series. Umbridge, for example, is at once surprising in her cruel punishments and penchant for pink and at the same time entirely predictable as the archetype of the government agent who takes her job too far and too seriously. At every stage she is an imaginative creation and a carbon copy of South American fascists.

No writer in any genre has managed to create such a complete, coherent and compelling world. The rules of magic are set out very early on and consistently applied (unlike the disaster that is the His Dark Materials series) and we are never provided with random new rules that we are just expected to accept (à la Artemis Fowl). The wizarding world is at all times simultaneously fantastic and completely believable, and that is a feat not to be sneezed at.

© *B. C. Roberts, 2010*

THE INHERITANCE CYCLE
ACCOMPLISHES NOTHING
by Gabrielle Lissauer

The Inheritance Cycle, by Christopher Paolini – *Eragon*, *Eldest* and *Brisingr*, so far – is a series riddled with plot holes, triteness, purple prose and flat characters. The storyline itself is stolen from *Star Wars* and the world is a patchwork quilt of almost every fantasy story you can think of.

Eragon is, to hear the author tell it: "… an archetypal hero story, filled with exciting action, dangerous villains, and fantastic locations. There are dragons and elves, sword fights and unexpected revelations, and of course, a beautiful maiden who's more than capable of taking care of herself."

What he describes as the archetypal hero story is not the archetypal hero story, but instead a list of clichés that are often found in archetypal hero stories. The hero's story does not need dragons, elves, sword fights, dangerous action, and exciting villains. The hero's story only needs the hero character going on a journey or quest to discover something and then return triumphant changed by his new knowledge. As Joseph Campbell wrote in his 1972 essay collection *Myths to Live By*: "A hero ventures forth from the world of common day into a region of supernatural wonder: Fabulous forces are encountered there and a decisive victory is won: the hero comes back from this mysterious adventure with the power to bestow boons on his fellow men." There's nothing in there about villains, getting the girl, or anything like that. What Paolini has done is taken the skin of the hero's journey and called it the entire animal.

From its outset, *Eragon* is rife with problems. From poor use of imagery ("The Shade hissed in anger, and the Urgals shrank back, motionless." – how do you shrink back and remain motionless at the same time?), to the language spoken by said Shade looking like a cat walked across the keyboard, to a bizarre ignorance of just how riding a horse works (how exactly can one have a "lap" when astride?), it's just really, really bad. And the series only gets worse from there.

One of my favorite examples of just how bad it gets is the series' ineffective archvillain, Galbatorix. There have been three books out of a planned four, and he has yet to make an appearance. No one even really talks about him. In the first book the one thing we learn about him that makes him currently evil is that he makes people pay taxes. The land has been at peace for a hundred years. He has absolutely no real impact on titular alleged hero Eragon's life when the book starts.

Instead of feeling like Eragon has to defeat this Evil Emperor from taking over the world, instead we have Eragon trying to over-throw a man who has successfully ruled his kingdom peacefully for one hundred years. Sure, it might be said that he gained his kingdom through violence, but then, look at the United States of America. How was it created? Why, the colonists rose up, killed a bunch of people, and created a new country. Galbatorix may not have gone about his gaining of the kingdom in the best of ways but we know little about how the world was beforehand. What we do know is from people who are biased and lost the war. We also know that the so-called greedy emperor has left the elves alone, left the dwarves alone and left the human country of Sudra alone even though it would be easy to crush. He doesn't seem to have any interest in moving beyond his boundaries.

This is the lay of the land when the book starts. You would think, then, once Eragon becomes rider of the dragon Saphira, Galbatorix would rush to gain the Dragon Rider's trust before others did. Instead, he sends minions after Eragon who don't engender much in the way of trust, and they insist on Eragon joining the king without giving him much incentive to do so. Killing Eragon's uncle also wasn't the smartest thing to do.

The one time we "see" Galbatorix is in *Brisingr* when he fights against Oromis – the last elf dragon rider – using the body of Eragon's half-brother Murtagh as a mouthpiece. He expounds on things that he should have said to Eragon two books earlier:

> *"There is no need to continue fighting me. I freely admit that I committed terrible crimes in my youth, but those days are long past, and when I reflect upon the blood I have shed, it torments my conscience. Still, what would you have of me? I cannot undo my deeds. Now, my greater concern is ensuring the peace and prosperity of the empire over which I find myself lord and master. Cannot you see that I have lost my thirst for vengeance? The rage that drove me for so many years has burned itself to ashes. Ask yourself this, Oromis: who is responsible for the war that has swept across Alagaësia? Not I. The Vaden were the ones who provoked this conflict. I would have been content to rule my people and leave the elves and the dwarves and the Surdans to their own devices. But the Varden could not leave well enough alone. It was they who chose to steal Saphira's egg, and they who covered the earth with mountains of corpses. Not I. You were wise once before, Oromis, and you can become wise again. Give up your hatred and join me in Ilirea. With you by my side, we can bring an end to this conflict and usher in an era of peace that will endure for a thousand years or more."*

What good is it for him to say this to Oromis, when Oromis is already arrayed against him and has been for years? The likelihood of trying to change his mind is slim to none. But if Galbatorix were to say this to Eragon, there might actually be a chance that this could sway Eragon's mind. This is highly unlikely, of course, as Eragon isn't allowed to stray from the Hero's path and have doubts about what he's doing for long; and as a result, he is, in many ways, a more visible and effective villain than Galbatorix ever was.

We see his actions constantly. We hear him say similar things that Galbatorix does, that he wants to bring peace to the land and free it from the grip of war. But whereas we never see Galbatorix do anything evil, we see Eragon snapping the necks of soldiers he could have avoided meeting in the first place, and invading a man's mind and taking fierce joy out of it before casting a spell on him that forces him to walk – blind – hundreds of miles to the land of the elves. Gleefully, almost, he kills the last two members of a species, ignoring their last request to be remembered, something that would be so easy for him to do.

And he just doesn't care. Never once do we see him regret his actions. He cries more over killing birds than he does over killing a man.

In the meantime we do not see Galbatorix do anything. Paolini says that he wants to save him for the big reveal at the end, but there has been no build up to him. No wondering what will happen when we see him. No rumors that he's trying to do something to stop Eragon. Or of any big plans. His reactions are even reasonable to what is being forced upon his kingdom. He's putting down a rebellion, a threat to his rule; a peaceful rule at that. And yet Eragon is the "Hero."

To paraphrase Mark Twain: A tale shall accomplish something and arrive somewhere. But *The Inheritance Cycle* accomplishes nothing and arrives in air.

Which is the best way to sum up this series.

THE INHERITANCE CYCLE
IS REALLY SOMETHING
by Rachel Hyland

I know I'm probably reading too much into it, but I quite love Christopher Paolini's runaway hit YA series, *The Inheritance Cycle*, for the very reason that my learned opponent in this debate most hates it. She takes issue with the fact that the so-called hero of the piece, Eragon, seems to be equally – if not more so – villainous than our supposed villain, the dastardly Galbatorix.

That's exactly what I like about it. I like that Paolini has taken a whole lot of very familiar Fantasy tropes, along with more than a dash of *Star Wars* (which itself borrowed liberally from assorted mythologies, along with *Flash Gordon*) and then has presented us with something we've not often seen: a Bad Guy who thinks he's a Good Guy, who is being treated as a Hero but could also be considered a Villain.

I liken it in my head to Greek Heroes of old, your Achilles and Hercules and such. According to history, those guys sucked. They murdered indiscriminately, raped, pillaged, what have you. But according to popular culture – indeed, even according to the culture of their time – they were true Heroes, because they kicked major ass. History, as we are so often told, is written by the victors, and Eragon is clearly bound for Varden glory; from their perspective, he is a liberator, a warrior, their version of the King Under the Mountain, their Knight on a White Horse (or in this case, blue dragon).

Galbatorix has all the trappings of an archvillain; most of his minions are hideous and they all speak ugly languages, and he's shut himself away in a fortress. Eragon's allies would seem to be of the Light, all elves and dwarves and noble savages and such. And yet they're the ones making war; one man's terrorist is another's freedom fighter. The road to Hell is paved with good intentions. You can't make an omelet without breaking some eggs. All of these proverbs and more apply to the Varden's actions in this ongoing struggle for control of Alagaësia.

Taking out the in-depth analysis of perspective and motivation from these books, The Cycle breaks down like this: *Eragon* is your pretty standard Coming of Age Hero tale, and hey, that orphan kid is special!; *Eldest* starts off slow and yet somehow frantic and confusing but comes about with a rousing battle and a whole "Eragon, I am your brother" thing by the end; and *Brisingr*... well, hey, flaming sword!

I'll not deny there are definite signs of immaturity in Paolini's writing style, and much of his plot elements are glaringly familiar. His prose is simple and his word choices even more so, and it certainly isn't an uncommon occurrence to encounter an ill-used word or misplaced punctuation mark. Despite these flaws, these books have proven to be tremendously popular amongst the young people, and have spawned their own cottage industry. There's even a book called *What Will Happen in Eragon IV: Who Lives, Who Dies, Who Becomes the Third Dragon Rider and How Will the Inheritance Cycle Finally End?*, by Richard Marcus, released in 2009 and purporting to discuss such burning questions as "Are Eragon and Arya destined to be together?" and "Who are the Grey Folk, and what role will they play in the battle between good and evil?" And speaking of evil: "Will Eragon and Saphira triumph over evil to free all of Alagaësia?"

(Um... yeah. I would hope so. Otherwise, I will totally be on the other side of this debate. I mean, I'm all for subverting convention, but come on!)

What Harry Potter did for modern wizardry and *Twilight* did for vampires, *Eragon* and its successors have done for dragons. For any kid who missed out on Lloyd Alexander's *Chronicles of Prydain* series, or Robert Asprin's *Myth Adventures of Skeeve and Aahz*, these Inheritance books – for good or ill – are many a neophyte's entrée into the magical realm. Elves, mythical creatures, dark sorcery, royalty, Rightful Heir – these may all be very familiar elements to those of us steeped in this tradition, who have lived and died at the hands of such masters as Tolkien, McCaffrey, Feist, Jordan and Eddings, but to these new readers, Paolini's world works as a kind of My First High Fantasy.

Wherein lies much of its appeal – for me, at least. Paolini, whether he knows it or not, is working on several levels here. On one, he's created an imitative, but exciting withal, adventure that is accessible to even the most mundane-minded youngster, and on another, he's subverted an entire genre and created a so-called hero who is almost the epitome of an anti-hero.

I keep coming back to the brilliant (and sadly out of print) novel *Villains by Necessity*, by Eve Forward. In this clever twist on Fantasy convention, a troupe of out and out Bad Guys – a thief, an assassin, a sorceress, a centaur, a pagan worshiper, etc. – must save the world; good has triumphed, and all of existence is about to disappear unless balance is restored.

In the minds of those agents of Good out to defeat them, our little cadre of scoundrels must be stopped at all costs because they are the black hats, inherently evil, and so any purpose for which they unite must be dread and deplored. But unless they perform a small act of evil, a greater evil – the end of the world – will come to pass.

What we have in *The Inheritance Cycle* is just such another flash of inspiration; and for all that I concede the series labors under many, many weaknesses, I also claim that its biggest strength comes out of them, if only you can squint your eyes a little in order to see it.

© *Rachel Hyland, 2010*

LOVE IN SFF
AWESOME WOMEN FALLING FOR LOSERS
by B. C. Roberts

Love stories are a staple of any genre and have been a mainstay of literature for as long as people have been writing, or even when they were still reciting the latest in epic poetry in classical Greece. But it seems that today in Science Fiction and Fantasy (SFF) there is a real surplus of what I am going to call "touching love stories." These are the ones where the two lovers must conquer some great obstacle in order to be together and that having conquered that obstacle things turn out perfectly romantically (which either means everyone dies, a la *Romeo and Juliet*, or they live happily ever after, a la *Much Ado About Nothing*).

There are no two stories in SFF bigger right now than Harry Potter and *Twilight*. But I'm going to ignore them both. It's just too easy to complain about the monstrous stupidity and offensive sexism (not to mention ludicrous celibacy) of the relationships in *Twilight*. Similarly, complaining that Hermione falling for Ron is like *Nikita*'s eponymous heroine falling in love with Nameless Henchman Number 4, or *Chuck*'s Sarah going for Morgan, is just too obvious. So instead I want to talk about *Avatar*, *Underworld*, *The Fifth Element* and, pushing the boundaries of what counts as genre, *Salt*.

The theme in all these movies is that a strong, fabulous, independent woman falls in love with some type of loser, and this incredibly unlikely love interest is either used to drive the action or resolve the major conflict. But it's not just that I object to awesome women falling for losers. We've all seen it and at some point you either get really bitter or you learn to live with it (or you use it to your advantage... but I wouldn't know anything that). It's that basing a movie on an unrealistic love story does more to make a movie feel unrealistic than Ben-Hur wearing a wristwatch. As much as we all love to see humans flying through space or weaving magic in castles, there is a base expectation that humans continue to act relatively consistently with how they act now. This is the complex counter-factual at the heart of all genre: "If I was a starship commander would I have sex with every hot alien I met?" The answer is "Hell yes!," and therein lies the inherent believability of the greatest space sleaze of them all, James T. Kirk. But consider the opposite side of the equation: '"Would I, as a woman/hot female alien, who is otherwise strong, independent and has the respect of my people, fall for an outsider who can bring me only trouble and a strange-looking human/alien hybrid baby thing?" I don't think the answer to that is so unequivocal. Hence, if you expect the audience to buy the fact that someone with everything to lose from a relationship is nevertheless going to throw herself, blue booty and all, right into it, you really have to convince us.

So let's look at the motivation for Neytiri (Zoe Saldana), the main blue character in 2009's *Avatar*, falling in love with Jake Sully (Sam Worthington), poster boy for advocacy group "The disabled can land hot chicks too, but only if they're another species" (look them up). Neytiri knows that Jake is an outsider and allied with the people who are destroying the rest of her planet. But, through the magic of the montage, the two spend enough time together to fall madly in love, mainly because Jake is basically proficient at being a Na'vi. What about all the Na'vi who are awesome at being Na'vi? Surely that's hotter than an outsider just being OK at it? Of course she falls in love before Jake tames that really big flying thing and proves to be a great Na'vi. Are we supposed to assume that she could see within him all along and knew that he would be great? Is that something we really believe? Every woman I have ever met who has been convinced that she sees within her loser boyfriend the prospect of greatness ends up being sorely disappointed. So does Neytiri forget he's one of the humans? Or that the other humans have been largely banned from the tribe?

Maybe I'm just failing to appreciate the awesome power of the montage.

The other major problem is SFF is that with all the effort being put into the creation of an interesting alternative world, the love of the central characters is simply taken for granted without any real explanation. In 2003's *Underworld*, for example, Selene (Kate Beckinsale), who has spurned the advances of every other vampire for centuries, falls for a human who has been bitten by a werewolf. Being bitten means that the human, Michael (Scott Speedman), will inevitably turn into a werewolf—the very creatures that Selene has devoted her life to wiping out. More than any other vampire, Selene hates the werewolves, but is willing to risk it all for this human. Sure, he turns out to have the potential to turn into some super-cool vampire/werewolf hybrid, but Selene's in love before she knows any of that. So what are we meant to believe, that deep within a hundreds-year-old vampyre there lurks a winsome girl just longing for the right man to come along? The love story here is jarring, not because *Underworld* is a bad movie (as my opponent hurtfully claims) but rather because it is otherwise a very good SFF movie. The motivation of every other character is clear, the motivations of Selene in every other respect are clear. But what we get at the centre of the movie is a love story that is there just because love stories are supposed to be there.

Which brings us to *The Fifth Element* (1997), a truly classic SFF movie in which Bruce Willis again proves that among all the 80s action heroes, he's the only one who can step outside his core genre and pull it off. Again, the central love story is one of opposites attracting. Korben Dallas (Willis) is ex-Special Ops, now driving/flying a taxi. One day, through the sort of luck one would only find on the screen, damsel in distress Leeloo falls through the roof of his cab. It's kind of an "of all the taxicabs, in all the cities in all the world…" moment. From then on Dallas goes to great lengths to help Leeloo save the world, his prime motivation being that she's hot. And let's be honest. It's Milla Jovovich at her best; who wouldn't fight a few aliens to tap that? Where it all gets a bit unbelievable is when Leeloo, having experienced the worst that the universe has to offer in terms of evil people trying to kill her, and having learnt all about the atrocities of the 20th century (in the future, computers only show history up until the turn of the millennium) Leeloo has to make the choice between letting humanity rot and saving every rotten one of them. And what is the defining moment in her choice? It's that the love of Bruce Willis is more profound than World Wars and a variety of genocides. Really? Won't somebody please make a movie where humanity is damned, love isn't enough to overcome evil, and everyone dies?

And finally, just a quick word about *Salt*, a 2010 movie I've only just seen. Angelina Jolie plays Evelyn Salt, a Russian sleeper agent who is activated and told to kill the Russian President. Evelyn is married to a German arachnologist, Krause (August Diehl), who was an asset she seduced in order to get access to North Korea. She falls for him and agrees to marry him when he campaigns for her release from North Korean prison (where she was being horribly tortured), after both the CIA and KGB leave her for dead. So, just for a change, here is a pretty believable reason to fall in love with someone. For some reason I haven't been able to fathom, though, marrying Krause makes her side with America rather than Russia. Long before the Russians kill Krause (at which point her loyalty to America is assured), Evelyn decides to disobey her Russian handlers and not to kill the Russian President. The audience is expected to accept that love explains all decisions, even when it explains none, or at least not why one choice would be made over another equal one. If anyone has a good answer for this, please e-mail me.

I have now had the opportunity to read the hugely entertaining opposing piece for this month, and I agree completely with our Rachel Day that a good love story can make an average movie into a great one. I have my doubts about whether *The Mummy* falls into that category, but nonetheless I take her point. For her few examples, though, the weight of unbelievable, poorly-conceived, poorly-detailed love stories in SFF clearly falls to my side. Sure, love stories can be moving but, as my counterpart points out, love stories get put into every genre as a matter of course. And oftentimes, rather than driving the action or drawing the audience in, they're just stupid.

LOVE IN SFF
LOVE IS A VITAL ELEMENT
by Rachel Day

Needless to say, I'm going to have to respectfully disagree with my colleague's erstwhile argument that there are too many "touching love stories" in the SFF genre. Love is a vital element within genre because well-drawn believable characters have relationships with others that resonate with and draw an audience into the story, and that's not going to change any time soon. Where would the world of sci-fi and fantasy be without Han and Leia, Bella and Edward, or Kirk and Spock? (OK, so maybe I made the last one up, but that relationship is a serious bromance by anyone's standard).

The problem, B. C. argues, is too many "touching love stories" which focus on soul-mates overcoming epic obstacles on a journey of destiny to be together; to which I reply: well, it never harmed the popularity of Shakespeare's *Romeo and Juliet* any – or to make this genre, the popularity of Mercedes Lackey's Valdemar series. Indeed, a good love story can make even the crappiest film, TV show or book of any genre better, and a great love story can make it popular beyond the wildest dreams of its creators. There's a reason why romance is the best-selling genre of published fiction; why shipping (the active fan support for a particular relationship) is such a widespread fandom activity; why film producers insist on including a romance sub-plot into all genres that aren't romance itself. Love equals money in the business of books, film and television.

But let's talk some specifics: my colleague isn't going to tackle Harry Potter and *Twilight*, and neither will I. Primarily because I would argue that Hermione ending up with Ron is nothing but a contrivance to ensure Harry ended up with someone else and its only obstacle being Ron acting like a prat. And as much as I enjoyed the *Twilight* series, I still deplore Bella changing herself to be with Edward (possibly I'm wearing my Team Jacob t-shirt right now).

However, neither am I going to talk about the films that my colleague covers because; firstly, what's the fun in that?; and secondly, with the exception of *The Fifth Element* I haven't actually seen them. Yes, yes, I will get around to watching *Avatar* one day, but why anyone would willingly watch *Underworld* or *Salt* is something of a mystery to me. *[You*

MUST watch Underworld *immediately! – Ed.]* Except to say that while I do have my own issues with *The Fifth Element* – Korben Dallas (Bruce Willis) being revealed as ex-Special Ops being one of them, (like the leading man having a crack military background isn't an over-used trope in the genre at all) – I have no issues with the improbable love story in what is ultimately a camp not-to-be-taken-seriously movie. Boy meets girl. Boy falls in love with girl. Boy finds out girl is an artificially created life form meant to save the world. Girl saves the day with the Power of Their Love. What's the problem?

Since my opponent chose four films to illustrate his point, then so too will I: the *Star Wars* saga, *WALL-E*, *Batman Returns*, and *The Mummy*. All four are wildly different, hugely successful and yet have at their heart a "touching love story."

The Mummy actually has two "touching love stories" at its heart: one in the shape of the relationship between American hero Rick (Brendan Fraser) and ditzy but incredibly smart Evelyn (Rachel Weisz), and one in the history of Imhotep (Arnold Vosloo) and Anck-Su-Namun (Patricia Velásquez). Both face epic obstacles and have a destined love. The latter is a tragedy with two corrupt lovers; the former, a happy-ending fairy tale for opposites who attract. Both are integral to the plot, to the characters' motivations, to providing angst and tension in amongst the action sequences. Both give the movie some depth beyond an enjoyable romp. *The Mummy* would be nothing without its touching love stories.

The same goes for *WALL-E*. Yes, it is an animated film but it's robots in space with an apocalyptic Earth. Regardless of the environmental and dieting messages embedded in the movie, the heart of it is the "touching love story" between WALL-E and EVE. They meet and face epic obstacles, but eventually get their happy ever after. I cried. I'm not ashamed to admit it. OK, maybe a little ashamed, because they are at the end of the day animated robots, but seriously, the scene where EVE fixes WALL-E and he doesn't remember her? I'm welling up just thinking about it. Their love gives the movie emotion and drama; it elevates the fairly twee plot and makes me want to hug an automaton of some kind.

Obviously, I'd much prefer to be hugging Han Solo. Ah, the epic love of Han and Leia, which survived getting captured by the Empire, Han being frozen in carbonite and Leia almost falling out of her gold bikini. Where would the original *Star Wars* trilogy be without the sub-plot of Han and Leia's "touching love story" — and the admittedly slightly icky triangle when Luke turns out to be Leia's brother?

The best of the shaky prequels (and what saved them from being complete tripe in my opinion) is the romantic tragedy of Anakin and Padme. Their forbidden love and the desperation of Anakin (Hayden Christensen) in wanting to save Padme (Natalie Portman) enabling his fall to the Dark Side, only for his fall to be the catalyst for her death, is actually heart-tugging. It makes the eventual redemption of Darth Vader/Anakin in the saga even more poignant.

Poignant and tragic are also words to describe the "touching love story" between Catwoman (Michelle Pfeiffer) and Batman (Michael Keaton) in the fabulous *Batman Returns*. It is often heralded as the best of the Batman movies, and I would argue the reason for that is the incredible relationship that evolves between these characters. I love that final scene in the Penguin's lair when she kills Shreck (Christopher Walken); the desperation of Batman in revealing his own identity in trying to reach out to her, her wanting to give into him but ultimately refusing to trust him and deny her nature. TRAGIC!! (Yes, the caps lock is necessary.)

The common element in all these films is that the "touching love story" is believable on some level. And while I admit some of the genre romances out there leave a lot to be desired in terms of believability and are just badly drawn, badly written and badly executed, the SFF genre as a whole would be a much poorer place without the touching love stories that are great; that pull at the audience's emotions and make us cry; that provide a window into humanity that we can relate to in stories that otherwise present us with strange new worlds. If for every *Underworld*, I get a *Batman Returns* – well, I can live with that.

© *Rachel Day, 2010*

MARTIAL ARTS MOVIES
WHATEVER
by Kate Nagy

Many times – in fact, I would go so far as to say most times – our "Geek vs. Geek" feature has been privileged to offer you, the reader, some of the most passionate and thoughtful arguments to be found for or against a book series, a movie, a trend, a legal issue, or even a specific season of a cult television show. These remarkable documents often represent the culmination of years of feverish devotion to the cause and hours of deep meditation on the subject, as well as the distillation of fierce debate with the writer's family, friends, and on-line communities. The writers, in other words, are Experts, and they would like you to know that they have something important to say.

This time out... not so much.

Well, I take that back. I don't doubt my opponent's commitment and expertise for one hot minute (and neither should you). But unlike his, my attitude toward this month's topic – martial arts films – can be summed up in a single word: "Whatever."

I'm not sure how to justify my complete and utter indifference toward this entire, wildly popular genre. I mean, I don't hate these movies. I admire Ang Lee's masterpiece *Crouching Tiger, Hidden Dragon* as much as the next person. I consider Jean-Claude Van Damme's magnum opus *The Quest* one of the best Bad Movies ever produced. Music from *Dragon: The Bruce Lee Story* holds pride of place on my iPod, and the sight of Christian Bale clad in a pristine white afternoon suit and swinging his arms with dogged determination as he shoots out all the monitors in the Tetragrammaton building at the end of *Equilibrium* never fails to lighten my heart. I don't necessarily take these films (*Crouching Tiger* excepted) particularly seriously, but I don't loathe them.

But I don't love them, either. In fact, I usually don't think about them. Why? Maybe it's because, as a general rule:

Martial arts movies tend to privilege fighting over plot

And dialogue. And realistic characterization. And – sorry, Jean-Claude – acting. And after a while, all that fighting, no matter how amazing and balletic, becomes kind of a snooze. (At least in *The Quest*, Van Damme changes it up by fighting a series of opponents utilizing completely different styles.) Now, admittedly, this is an issue in all action movies. Even in *The Avengers*, which I otherwise loved, there came a point near the end where I was like "Can we stop blowing shit up now and force Loki

129

to the negotiating table? Maybe bring Odin in as facilitator?" But it is definitely an issue in martial arts films.

It's a man's world

Women are under-represented in these movies and that's a plain fact. I know, I know: Here's the part where my opponent invokes the sacred names of Michelle Yeoh, Ziyi Zhang, Lucy Liu, and Uma Thurman. And points out that I just said I liked *The Avengers*, which only had one female character of real note. And reminds the readership that I've never expressed an objection to an overabundance of hard-living male characters in a fictional context before. All true. And yet, your typical martial arts movie consists of a sketchy and frequently preposterous plot moved forward via sequential scenes of dudes beating the shit out of one another in increasingly lurid and inventive ways.

Which reminds me:

Violence is boring

This sort of goes back to my first point, but I think it's really at the root of my *ennui*. Aside from the rather questionable message that these films put forth – Want to win the heart of the haughty princess? Better go kick some ass! A drug dealer has set up shop on your street corner? Call in the ninjas! – it's just tedious to watch all these fights, unless they're really unusually beautifully choreographed (*Crouching Tiger*), audaciously over-the-top (*Equilibrium*'s Gun Kata, which never get old), or move the plot forward in a material way, as opposed to, you know, *being* the plot.

So at the end of the day, it comes down to a question of taste: While on an intellectual level I can appreciate Jet Li's intensity and Jackie Chan's work ethic, I usually find these movies repetitive, silly, and dull. And with all the other movies out there – genre and non- – that I want to see, these rarely if ever burble up even to the middle of my "to-see" list, let alone the top.

Unless Gun Katas are involved. Then – I have to confess – I'll be first in line.

© Kate Nagy, 2012

MARTIAL ARTS MOVIES
WHAT'S NOT TO LOVE?
by Jason Murdoch

Let it go on the record that I have a deep-seated passion for movies from this particular genre. From early Shaw Brothers films, through to modern day blockbusters, nothing quite tickles my pickle like a good (or really bad) martial arts action film. Now, I understand that this particular style of cinema isn't for everyone, that's fine. But let's not let an ignorance of the brilliance behind the scenes shape our distaste.

The thing is, if you look hard enough, there's something here for everyone. Whether it's the cinematic wonders of the likes of *Hero* or *The House of Flying Daggers*, whether it's the story of someone overcoming odds (*The Karate Kid* anyone?), or the hilarity of sooo many Jackie Chan films, what's not to love?

Okay, I'm not completely brainwashed. I'm not suggesting that there aren't a significant amount of martial arts movies with the primary goal of showcasing amazing fights and generally providing eye candy. But they're not kidding themselves. They're not hoping for an Oscar. Is this so bad? But let's be real here, there is also some amazing cinema that includes martial arts sequences. Let's not get caught up in the worst of the best.

Here's the thing. I have little interest in chess, so I put no effort into understanding it, I don't try and appreciate the subtleties, the discipline required to play at a top level. I don't care if some Spanish priest had an opening move named after him, and that's still used to this day. So, when someone makes a movie about chess and I happen to watch it, I make no effort to grasp the concepts, to appreciate the years of practice it takes to play a game of chess with such skill. All I see is guys moving pieces around a board, I yawn, dig into my bucket of popcorn and think about the scathing review I'm going to write. But this isn't the fault of the movie.

The writers, directors, producers etc. all know they're releasing a piece of cinema that will have a specific and somewhat limited target audience. They're okay with that. They don't expect everyone to want to see it, or to understand what they're trying to achieve. Enough of chess though, there's not nearly enough physical violence for my tastes (unless we're talking Wizard Chess, but I digress).

Martial arts movies are as amazing as they are because they allow us to believe one thing. That a person, one tiny person can stand up to anyone. That they can make a difference. That they can overcome what seem to be insurmountable odds. And they can do it whilst kicking some serious portions of ass! What martial arts movie have we seen that isn't about one character pushing themselves beyond the limits of normal humans, to stand up to something? I'm struggling to think of one.

Here's what I love about the martial arts genre:

The moral of the story is always about believing in yourself, choosing the honorable path, or something similar. That's not a bad thing

Let's go back to one of the classics: *Bloodsport* (1988). Sure, Van Damme's acting is aneurysm-inducing, but the basic premise is that a child was given a chance to learn an ancient art. He showed the discipline and strength of character to earn the respect of his teacher. He then fights adversaries that he shouldn't be able to defeat (especially after the whole being blinded thing in the final fight scene) and overcomes them because his motives are pure.

We all wish that we had that kind of discipline, the physical and mental fortitude to pick ourselves back up and beat the odds. We want to believe that we could save our loved ones, stand up for the little guy, maybe even exact vengeance. It's all rather disgustingly noble and idealistic, but really as people, don't you want that? Wouldn't that be all sorts of cool?

Visually, martial arts are stunning

That's all well and good, but this is a movie; do we really just want to see some guy getting the snot kicked out of him by another guy? The thing with audiences is that they easily become complacent. When was the last visual effect that actually wowed you? Been a while, hasn't it? (The giant sentient robot changed from a truck too quickly – come on, who has said it? Admit it.) It takes a lot to impress us nowadays. Martial arts movies have been having the same trouble for quite some time, but this is one area of cinema in which they are always trying to up the ante. From Kung Fu to Wing Chun to Karate to Ninjitsu to Krav Maga, the varieties of martial art are as varied as their movie plots are not; the stars of most martial arts movies are incredible specimens, with astounding speed and accuracy and flexibility and strength in real life as well as on film. Watch *Police Story* (1985), and have a look at exactly what Jackie Chan puts his body through, look at the body control, the skill, think of the hours of practice it would have taken to master those moves. Then think of how long it would have taken to translate those moves into a fight sequence with a chair, and a step ladder, and the comedic timing. The time taken to choreograph, rehearse, refine, and perform in front of a camera with everything that could go wrong. HOW is that boring? How is that anything but absolutely freaking amazeballs?!

Culturally, martial arts in film let different regions show the world something they have to offer

Let's take an Asian import, *Ong-Bak* (2003). This movie was a cultural phenomenon. It brought the art of Muay Thai to the western world in a digestible form, so that people would stand up and take an interest, and maybe even look at visiting Thailand. It was more of a tourism venture than a blockbuster. As an aside, Tony Jaa blows my mind. Forget the fight sequences (as if you could), look at the chases, watch the superhuman skills, the timing, the acrobatics employed. We're amused for a minute whilst watching people get chased through the streets. These people train for years to get to a position where they would even think to attempt performing these stunts. Surely anyone can appreciate that?

"Martial Arts" isn't necessarily a genre, but it does make other genres better

The big thing is, "martial arts" isn't really a genre, per se. Sure, there are a significant number of movies centered around martial arts (or martial arts tournaments), but realistically we can't call something like *Rush Hour*, with Jackie Chan and Chris Tucker, a "martial arts movie;" it's a comedy that features martial arts. We can't call *The Bourne Identity* or *Taken* "martial arts movies"; they're action movies with some pretty amazing Krav Maga sequences. So where do we draw the line? Where do we stop and say this movie is only about martial arts, and therefore not of interest to someone of my opponent's tastes? Surely we can't say that about *Kill Bill*; yes, it features quite a significant number of fight sequences, but it also has a plot, it has characters, it is more than martial arts. Same goes for Jet Li's breakout hit, *Once Upon a Time in China*. Is my esteemed colleague saying she wouldn't want to watch this acclaimed, objectively awesome experience because it features a large helping of martial arts? (After all, she seems to LOVE *Equilibrium*.)

So really, let's look at what the inclusion of martial arts has done for modern action films. I'll return your attention to the *Bourne* series, to the *Taken* movies, and then also to the *Dark Knight* films, and a rather overlooked one, the comic book adaptation *A History of Violence*. There are no wire stunts here, no unbelievable cinematics of people fighting over rivers, or treetops, a la *Crouching Tiger, Hidden Dragon*. There *are* some intense martial arts though. I would even go as far as to say that the use of the styles of martial arts included in these movies are somewhat character building. You can see to what extent these characters are willing to go to achieve their goals, whether that be survive, save their family, generally protect Gotham, whatever. The styles are fast, they're brutal, they aren't flashy – just like the characters utilizing them.

I could go on, but the long and the short of it is we watch movies to escape reality, to be entertained, to be challenged. What's more entertaining than someone who can knock you out in the first two seconds of a fight after doing a backflip double kick to the underside of your chin?! (*Bloodsport II*, if memory serves me correctly.) Sure, action movies might not be your cup of tea. "Asian cinema" might not be your cup of tea. I don't understand how anyone can look at amazing feats of human ability, dedication and discipline, and then suggest that they are anything less than admirable and fascinating. But if you're not prepared to make the effort, then guess what? You probably won't see why these movies are worth it.

© *Jason Murdoch, 2012*

MARVEL MOVIES VS DC MOVIES
DC: QUALITY OVER QUANTITY
by William Cashin

Before we get down to the nitty-gritty of this Geek vs. Geek battle, let's take a moment to acknowledge how far comic book movies have come. Only a few decades ago we were looking at the sad demise of the *Superman* movies. *Batman* (1989) saved the "industry" for a while and made what was to come possible. But why was and is there an "industry" at all? Making movies from source material known only to those on the fringe of society (there you go, Will, offend your audience in the first paragraph…) doesn't seem like much of a business model. And whilst you could at least rely on the fact that most people had at least heard of Superman and Batman, what would attract the general public to anyone else?

A Marvel supporter, like my formidable opponent, would argue that this question has been answered. And to a small extent I agree. Certainly *X-Men*, *Spider-Man* and *Iron Man* amply demonstrate that you can make successful blockbuster movies from comic books that had been around for at least fifty years but still hadn't managed to work their way into the mainstream (perhaps this is a bit harsh on Spider-Man, but come on, how many would have heard of Tony Stark before the last few years?). So, it is possible that good comic book movies are possible despite a lack of interest, or knowledge about the source material.

A DC movies supporter, like, well… me, would argue that for every success there have been at least ten failures. And it's only going to get worse. The comic book movie industry is ramping up like never seen before, and Comic-Con is now a required stop for A-listers on the movie publicity tour (even if your movie has dubious connections to comic books), but still there are few signs that we have actually learnt anything. Most comic book movies are still god-damn awful.

And why do I think they are awful? Because it seems like people think they can just convert any old comic book into a movie. Some comics, no matter how good they are, simply don't translate to film, no matter how much money or how many scriptwriters you throw at it. I believe DC knows this, and so is hesitant to rush its material onto the silver screen. Marvel, however, is either ignoring this wisdom or simply doesn't care, and is planning to flood the market with what will mostly be terrible, but sadly profitable, blockbuster fare.

In summary, DC has decided for a quality over quantity motto, and Marvel has gone for your wallet, not showing a care in the world for how bad its movies are.

In truth, Marvel isn't entirely to blame for this development. Certainly my opponent will bring up *Superman IV*, *Return of the Swamp Thing*, *Catwoman*, and (shudder) *Batman and Robin* as examples that DC can also make movies for profit with little regard for the necessity of a coherent storyline. But DC has moved on from this terrible phase (we all did crazy things in the 80s and 90s we are not proud of), and has shown much more patience since then. Marvel has therefore had the benefit of hindsight and yet has made, and is in the process of making, the same mistakes.

Alright, that's enough serious talk. Let's get to the whole point of writing this article; making fun of some truly horrible Marvel movies.

That Marvel has built their "movie empire" on the back of the "success" of the "movie" *Blade* truly does warrant a re-questioning of the laws of physics (vampirism itself doesn't seem to follow the second law of thermodynamics). How the hell did that happen? And with Wesley Snipes of all people, who would later go on to make memorable direct-to-DVD classics such as *The Marksman*, *The Detonator*, and *The Contractor* (am I alone in believing that these three had the same script?), *Blade: Trinity* and the not-at-all-timely comedy classic, *Honey, I Forgot to Pay the Taxes Again So I'm Going to Jail!*

And yet it did. *Blade* finally got Marvel off the ground following the false starts of *The Punisher* (1989), the unbelievably racist *Captain America* (1990) – of which the less said the better – and *Fantastic Four* (1994). No, not the one in which Jessica Alba gets her kit off, but the unreleased low-budget movie where a bunch of D-grade actors were tricked by the producers into making what they were told was going to be a blockbuster release, but was really just a piece of junk that served only to keep the rights to the Fantastic Four franchise with the studio.

Blade was followed by *X-Men*, which I have to say, I do like. It didn't try to do too much, unlike its sequels, the promising but largely unsatisfying *X2* and the woeful, self-destructive *X-Men: The Last Stand*. *X-Men* had a story, and didn't compromise it with having to go into the back-story of every single character (a tough task in what was essentially an ensemble movie). That said, I would have liked to see in Magneto's Brotherhood of Mutants line-up both Quicksilver (a core BOM character) and Scarlet Witch (because she is hot). But if they had appeared, it wouldn't have been as good of a movie.

Spider-Man, too, is actually a good movie. There, I said it. That's the most you're going to get from a pro-DC fan. It does what Marvel does best: have a superhero who is fallible because of his humanity. But I'd also argue that *Spider-Man*, like *Batman* and *Superman* before it, was a massive hit because he is the closest Marvel has to a household name, which is what is needed to really rake in the big bucks. *Spider-Man* is still the highest-grossing Marvel film at the US box office, and the second most successful comic book movie, behind, of course, the king of comic book movies, *The Dark Knight*.

And this is the point where things start to go pear shaped for Marvel. With *Spider-Man* being such a huge financial success, clearly there was pressure to get as many of Peter Parker's stablemates out there as possible. And this was somewhat understandable; comic book movies were finally "in" again, after being nearly killed off by *Batman and Robin*. But rather than wait until they had some decent scripts to use, I suspect a lot of these movies went into production on little more than a whim. How else could you explain what was soon to follow?

Since *Spider-Man*, there have been nineteen films in eight years from Marvel, including a staggering ten sequels and three reboots, with *The Punisher* getting rebooted TWICE. And how many did DC put out over the same time? Only seven. Five, really, if you don't count *Watchmen* and *V for Vendetta* as DC movies (*V for Vendetta* was published under its Vertigo imprint, and *Watchmen* was published before the Vertigo imprint was even around), which I believe most people wouldn't, given their content. (Likewise, I haven't counted *Kick-Ass* as a Marvel movie, which was published under its Icon imprint). There is also no apparent easing off from Marvel, with five more films slated for release in the next two years, and several more in development.

And in those nineteen films there are some truly shocking ones. It would take far too long to detail as to how near universally all of these films manage to both suck and blow at the same time. But the worst of the worst would have to be:

Hulk

Being Marvel comics' second biggest name, you'd think they'd make sure this worked. Going with Ang Lee was a bold step, but clearly there were way too many spoons stirring the broth on this one. A truly woeful film, made more woeful by trying to make a movie principally about a large, green monster who acts with uncontrollable rage and is capable of unbelievable death and destruction....into a PG-13 film. The scene that best sums up my uncontrollable rage against this movie? When the Hulk throws a tank about a mile into the side of a mountain, the producers, with their minds obviously transfixed on the movie ratings, felt the need to include a bit with the people inside the tank saying over the radio that they are all okay. Ah… no, you're not okay. You've just been turned into Hulk Play-Doh.

Daredevil and *Elektra*

Uggh. I don't even want to remind myself of how bad these were. I remember watching Daredevil with a fellow *Geek Speak* contributor, looking at each other, constantly asking ourselves "They didn't just do that, did they?" CGI that was truly laughable, and pathetic storylines that made no use of the darkness of the *Daredevil* and *Elektra* comics. I didn't even get to the end of *Elektra*, so if it got better I apologize (I severely doubt it). I did, however, last long enough to see Ben Affleck's cameo, which must rate highly on a 'least effort put in for a cameo' scale. As of 2005, my worst three movies of all time were *Hulk*, *Daredevil,* and *Elektra* (soon to be joined by *Transformers*).

Ghost Rider

No, just…no. Move on, there is literally nothing to see here.

The Punisher: War Zone

I haven't seen this film, but I think it still deserves a mention, because it again highlights how simply inept the Marvel business model is. There was no one, bar a very small minority of hardcore Punisher fans, that actually wanted this movie. Hell, I'd argue even they didn't want it, after seeing Punisher ruined twice before with their 1989 and 2004 efforts. The only thing I'd credit Marvel for with this film is letting it have an R rating. But that is where the kudos ends. The movie's director was essentially cut out of editing by Marvel execs, and its writer Kurt Sutter chose to remove his name from the writing credits, believing he didn't deserve credit for the film as the shooting script was nothing like the screenplay he had turned in to Marvel. So, with all this, it should come as no surprise that it made less money at the box office than any other wide-release Marvel film.

And of course, there are the many soul-crushing sequels. It would be easy to ridicule *Blade: Trinity* as the most obvious example of Marvel spewing out drivel with no script only for the purpose of taking more money from our wallets (I'd like to point out I haven't paid to see a Marvel film in a long while), but that would let movies such as *Fantastic Four: Rise of the Silver Surfer*, *Spider-Man 3*, and *X-Men: The Last Stand* off the hook from being seen as the drivel they truly are.

So how is this any different to the DC meltdowns of the *Superman* and *Batman* franchises of the 80's and 90's? Consider that in both cases, despite the phenomenal successes of the first films, DC did not rush many of their other characters onto the silver screen. Between *Superman* (1978) and *Superman IV: The Quest for Peace* (1987) only *The Swamp Thing* (1982) and *Supergirl* (1984) were made (I'm going to make no attempt to explain or defend *Supergirl*; yes, it is terrible). And no other DC movies were made between *Batman* (1989) and *Batman and Robin* (1997), apart from the low-budget *Steel*, also released in 1997. (I'm not going to get caught up defending this one either. Shaq? Really?) Remember that Marvel would later make EIGHTEEN films over the similar period of time. So, both of *Superman IV* and *Batman and Robin* films really just failed under the weight of being sequels, which happens to the best of movie genres (I still stand behind *Godfather III*, though I know there aren't many who support me).

So why are DC movies any better? or "I still remember Richard Pryor"

In contrast to Marvel, DC treated the success of *Batman Begins* (2005) very differently. The financial success of *Spider-Man* made DC reconsider the Batman and Superman franchises, thankfully so, because it would have been a shame to leave Batman how it had ended. Of the two resultant reboots, *Batman Begins* and *Superman Returns*, arguably only *Batman Begins* succeeded (*Superman Returns* isn't a bad film, just not a good one; it tried to do something different not seen in other comic book movies, which perhaps the audience wasn't up or ready for yet).

Just on *Batman Begins* for a moment: some might say that it took a leaf out of the *Spider-Man* movies and endeavored to make the very human Bruce Wayne more the main character instead of the "Caped Crusader." I think this goes some way to discredit some of the excellent storylines going on in the *Batman* comics during the late 90s and 2000s, which no doubt were aimed at reminding readers that Batman was never meant to be the pitiful Batman seen in *Batman and Robin*. The *Hush, No-Man's Land* and *Jason Todd* story arcs are all fantastic, and along with the brilliant miniseries *The Long Halloween*, these brought the mafia and hoods back to the streets of Gotham, who would be used so superbly as core elements of the *Batman Begins* and *The Dark Knight* storylines.

For me, what separates DC from Marvel is what it did next, following the success of *Batman Begins*. Or more importantly what they didn't do. They didn't make any films.

Hang on? Whoa?

Think about it. Remember how many times you heard a *Wonder Woman* movie was about to be started? It never happened. Reasons differ depending on whom you listen to, but most revolve around DC execs not being happy with the scripts. If this is even 10% true, it's 110% more restraint than Marvel execs ever showed. Joss Whedon was for a long while tied to a potential Wonder Woman movie, but never managed to convince DC to move forward with his ideas. Marvel instead signed him in a heartbeat and had him paraded along with the actors also signed up for an Avengers movie that has no script. Hmm.

Other DC movies importantly not made before their time: a Flash movie (there are so many Flash characters nowadays, where would you begin?), both a Shazam movie and then a Black Adam movie (the Rock as Black Adam...brother, please!!!); and then there was that woeful Justice League idea with D-grade actors that almost, almost was made. Boy, oh boy, did we dodge a bullet there.

And why weren't these made? DC figured out that these movies either weren't up to scratch, or the general public wasn't ready for them. I'm not saying I don't want to see a Flash, Wonder Woman, or Justice League movie, I really do, but I want DC to make sure everything, absolutely everything is in place before standing up on stage at Comic-Con, and that includes having the best script ever written.

Remember that almost all of the DC comic movies in the last forty years have been Batman and Superman titles, despite the depth and breadth of the DC lineup, now nearly eighty years old. *Swamp Thing*, *Steel* and *Jonah Hex* are the only other non-Batman/Superman derived movies, and it comes as no surprise that none of these are particularly good.

The only other would be *Watchmen*, which was a noble attempt to bring an impossibly complex multiple plot storyline to the screen. It would have been easy to criticize it for what was not in the film (about 80% of the graphic novel), but for the sake of the movie storyline it was far better that only a few plots were used in the film. No doubt the near-twenty years it was in development led to the success of making sure the plot could at least be followed in one sitting. Besides, like James Joyce's *Ulysses*, how many people have actually read quite possibly the best comic of all time? And did it really matter that the giant squid wasn't in the movie?

Consider the other DC title that more than a few fan boys would kill to see. Ever since it was published, many have wished to see Frank Miller's *The Dark Knight Returns* up on the big screen. An old, angry Bruce Wayne returning to the cape to reclaim Gotham, taking on a corrupt US government and Superman. Yes, Superman. Rightly recognized as one of the best graphic novels of all time, so why no film yet? Apart from the fact it would be difficult to explain to (most) audiences why a Batman, completely non-canon to the Batman in *Batman Begins* and *The Dark Knight*, was beating the crap out of Superman, the reasons why the story worked so well as a comic book would be the same reasons, much like *Watchmen*, why a movie adaptation couldn't ever get the whole story across.

Conclusion

In summary, I believe DC makes better movies, not just evidenced from the ones it has made, but the ones it hasn't. This ensures that, for the most part (there will always be movies like DC's *Jonah Hex* and Marvel's *Punisher: War Zone*), DC will continue to produce quality movies at the expense of quantity. *The Dark Knight* is a perfect example of this.

In contrast, Marvel will continue to flood the market with more generic, mind-sapping yawnfests. And even if the occasional one is okay (*Spider-Man*, *Iron Man*), there will be plenty that aren't. If any of the next ten movies Marvel makes over the next three years are decent, I'll be surprised. *The Avengers* movie is doomed to fail, not at the box office, but almost certainly critically. And from what we've seen of the *Thor* footage so far, that doesn't look promising either (anyone else think Anthony Hopkins is channeling Prince Vultan from *Flash Gordon*?).

DC, meanwhile, are working away on what they hope will (finally) be their third film franchise after *Batman* and *Superman*, that being *Green Lantern*. And good luck to them. They've waited until filmmaking technology would be good enough to bring Oa and alien green lanterns like Kilowog, Tomar Re and Boodikka to the screen properly, and they've stuck to just one Lantern, Hal Jordan.

All we can do now is hope it doesn't suck… like almost all Marvel films do.

© *William Cashin, 2010*

MARVEL MOVIES VS DC MOVIES
MARVEL: PERSISTENCE OF VISION
by Rachel Hyland

Look, I really dislike the *Daredevil* movie. I'm no fan of *Elektra*, or *Hulk*, and I'm not too hot on the first *Fantastic Four* or the third *Spider-Man*. *Ghost Rider* was just plain wrong, and *X-Men: The Last Stand* literally had me in tears. Honestly, I was so disappointed by the idiocy being enacted on the screen that I cried, right there in the theater. (*The Matrix Revolutions* had the same devastatingly embarrassing effect. You know you're pitiful when the ten-year-old kid in the next seat hands you a tissue.)

So, I am not about to take up the cudgels of defense against the many slings and arrows rightfully flung at the collective awfulness of more than one Marvel-based film. They don't deserve it. I will even go further and suggest that *X-Men Origins: Wolverine* is among the worst offenders; it was bad enough when they foisted Ben Affleck onto us as my beloved DD, but presenting us with boy band reject Taylor Kitsch as my equally-beloved Gambit was simply unpardonable. (Though, admittedly, Ryan Reynolds as my also beloved Deadpool couldn't have been more perfect. And yes, that is almost the extent of my comic crushes: Hawkeye, John Constantine and Raphael the Teenage Mutant Ninja Turtle round out the set.)

But, y'know what? It's all too easy to bring down the hammer on Marvel movies. Fish, barrel; ducks, line. I mean, *Blade: Trinity*? *Punisher: War Zone*? Are they trying to punish *us* in some way? Have we done them some massive wrong? Is this retribution for illegal downloads?

140

It's equally easy to take aim at some of DC's more ill-advised endeavors: *Swamp Thing* (and the *Return* thereof), *Supergirl, Steel, Catwoman*, the Joel Schumacher *Batman*s (*Batmen*?), *Jonah Hex*. It could be argued, and successfully I think, that per capita, Marvel and DC movies are equally as guilty of poor judgment – and the cynical exploitation of their characters' fans – as each other.

So let's contrast, instead, Marvel and DC's respective successes, and see what we have then, shall we?

Let us first take a quick look at the history of comic book cinema. The early years amounted to film serials like 1941's *Captain America* and the 1951 theatrically-released TV pilot *Superman and the Mole Men*, which led to the iconic series starring George Reeves. (Can you imagine a time when you had to go to the movie theater to watch a TV show?) 1966, of course, saw the release of the Adam West- and "Bat-Shark Repellent"-starring *Batman* film, and the late 70s brought several edited versions of the *Spider-Man* TV series to theaters.

But the modern comic book movie era really began in 1978, with Richard Donner's *Superman*. It was an auspicious beginning for DC aficionados, with the film racking up fourteen weeks at the top of the US box office and even being awarded a special statue at the Academy Awards. There followed, in 1981, *Superman II*, and there can be no doubt that Terrence Stamp's General Zod is still one of the great movie bad guys of all time. Things didn't really go too well for DC movies after that until 1989's Tim Burton-blessed *Batman*, in which Michael Keaton gives a thoroughly engaging interpretation of poor little rich boy Bruce Wayne, and Jack Nicholson's version of The Joker (I'm sorry, spirit of Heath Ledger, but it's true) proves to be the definitive comic movie supervillain.

In the meantime, we Marvel-types were treated, in 1986, to the celebrated box office catastrophe that was *Howard the Duck*.

Personally, I happen to love the story of that little alien ducky tangling with Dark Overlords of the Universe and 80s soft-rock girl bands. (Shut up!) But it must be conceded that *Howard* has become a by-word for filmic failure, and the sword-and-sorcery Schwarzenegger vehicle *Red Sonja*, which preceded it by a year and is based on the Marvel character of the same name, is likewise reviled and disdained (when it is remembered at all). And 1989, which brought such renown to DC and all its works with its Prince-soundtracked, Caped Crusader-y blockbuster, gave unto the dedicated Marvel fan... Dolph Lundgren in *The Punisher*.

Had this debate taken place in, say, 1990 (which it could well have; do you remember any such conversation, Will?), then I would clearly have been forced to retire from the lists with nary a shot fired in the struggle. My deep and abiding love of *Howard the Duck* notwithstanding, there is no way whatsoever I could have sustained an argument for its superiority over the *Superman* and burgeoning *Batman* franchises. But since this debate is taking place two full decades later, I can most assuredly make a very strong stand in this epic battle. Because things have improved a lot for us friends of Marvel, cinematically, and yet for the DC-inclined amongst you... not so much.

I have spent the better part of this past month or so in watching, mostly re-watching, every comic book movie based on either a Marvel or DC comic ever made. (It's a hard-knock life, folks.) That's twenty DC-based movies – counting *Watchmen* and *V for Vendetta* – and twenty-six for Marvel. Taking a "best for last" approach, I started with DC, and at the logical place: *Superman*. I watched all four Christopher Reeve installments (*Superman III* might be my new favorite: Pamela Stephenson is a laugh riot, which I don't think I've ever fully appreciated before), and 1984's *Supergirl* for the first time since I was about 12 – wow, Helen Slater is pretty! And even though I haven't included it (nor the film serials, nor the 60s Batman movie) in DC's total, I came upon the George Reeves-starring *Stamp Day for Superman*, a 17-minute 1954 short film that is part propaganda, part infomercial ("The United States Treasury Department presents: *The Adventures of Superman!*"), and you simply must check it out on YouTube this instant.

In this bizarre outing, Superman foils a robbery in which a guilt-ridden first-time hoodlum laments: "I should have learned to save and handle money a long time ago, then this wouldn't have happened!" Back at the *Planet*, Jimmy Olsen shows off his new typewriter (it's the size of a first generation DVD player, but he gushes wonderingly: "I can almost carry it in my pocket!"), which it turns out he was able to afford because he bought Treasury Savings Stamps each week when at school. "That's very interesting, Jimmy," says Clark (is it?), and is inspired to write a feature article on "... how kids help themselves and Uncle Sam by buying bonds and stamps." Lois, of course, soon gets kidnapped – and remember, this thing is only 17 minutes long; Jeepers, Miss Lane! – which leads to my favorite Lois line ever: "I obviously don't have any brains, or I wouldn't be here." Yeah, no kidding. But Superman saves her and then flies to a local school and exhorts the kids to save themselves. "So, boys and girls, be super citizens and have a super future by saving regularly with United States Savings stamps at school." It's absolutely shameless... and yet still better than *Superman Returns*. (I'm sorry, Bryan Singer, but it's true. George Reeves is no Christopher Reeve, Dean Cain or even Tom Welling, but he beats Brendan Routh by a Kryptonian mile. Hell, even Jimmy's typewriter has more screen presence than that inscrutable automaton, and I was never so glad to have wrapped up a franchise marathon as when the final credits rolled on that 2005 nightmare. Also, Kate Bosworth? Really?)

And then I moved on to the Bat. From Keaton to Kilmer to Clooney to Christian Bale, I immersed myself in Gothic Gothamness, following up those six flicks (*Batman Returns* is definitely my favorite) with Halle Berry rocking the leather in 2004's much-maligned *Catwoman*. (Bad, yes, but not nearly as bad as everyone says.) Wes Craven's 1982 *Swamp Thing*, and its even more lackluster 1987 sequel, *Return of the Swamp Thing*, I had never seen, so they came next and I begrudge every second I spent in sourcing them and then sitting through their never-to-be-sufficiently-accursed unpleasantness. I watched *Watchmen* again, and was equally apathetic about it as the first time; I saw *V for Vendetta* again, and liked it better the second time around. (Natalie Portman is still woeful, though. And I had thought she couldn't get any worse than as tragic, woebegone Padme.) Then I checked out Shaquille O'Neal in 1997's *Steel* for the first time (was he cast in it 'cause of the rhyme?), and laughed so much at the campy nonsense that I feared I'd end up committed: "I never could make free throws." Ha! Happily, I saw *Jonah Hex* when it was out in theaters a few months back (happily, for the purposes of this endeavor, not happily as in, "Yay, I spent money to watch *Jonah Hex*!"), and so was able to complete the DC cycle in its entirety – it's not out on DVD yet, and piracy is wrong, kids.

Want to know which DC movie I enjoyed watching the least? Well, stipulating to the *Swamp Thing* debacles, I'd have to say that honor belongs to the "biggest comic book movie of all time," *The Dark Knight*.

Now, I will confess that part of this is that, much as I admire Maggie Gyllenhaal in all her indie-darling glory, I missed Katie Holmes's presence as crusading attorney Rachel. Still another part is a lingering sadness over the untimely demise of Heath Ledger (which made Terry Gilliam's brilliant *Imaginarium of Dr. Parnassus* likewise something of a trauma). But most of it, I think, is that *The Dark Knight* just isn't all that enjoyable of a movie. Go ahead, watch it again. I dare you. Once you get past the hype and the unexpected humor and the wonder of the performances – from Bale and Ledger to Aaron Eckhart and Cillian Murphy, they are universally great – what you basically have is *One Flew Over the Cuckoo's Nest* meets *Escape From New York*, with lashings of *A Tale of Two Cities* thrown in. ("'Tis a far better thing I do than I have ever done...") Sure, the first time through, *The Dark Knight* was a blast, a thought-provoking exercise and a rumination on the nature of good and evil, but once you've been blasted, had your thoughts provoked and are done ruminating, there's not much left to really, well, like. Watching *Batman Begins* again was unrewarding but not irksome; watching *The Dark Knight* again physically hurt, because I remembered worshiping at its altar just as most everyone else was doing back in aught nine, and I now had to confront the possibility that I had been so very mistaken in my sentiments. Seriously, I had more fun watching *Catwoman*; was more enchanted by *Steel*. And *The Dark Knight* is the best, most acclaimed and highest-grossing of all DC's output.

Let's cross over, now, to the Marvel side of the DVD shelf. (What, you don't keep yours separated?) Leaving aside the aforementioned 1980s flicks, and also forgetting about the 1990 direct-to-video *Captain America* – a feel-good if culturally insensitive World War II action romp; "Gee whiz, we gotta get going, Mr. President!" – and the unreleased 1994 *Fantastic Four* movie (in which Victor von Doom and Reed Richards are a slashfic waiting to happen), things really kicked of theatrically for Marvel with 1998's *Blade*. Pitting Wesley Snipes, at the height of his ass-kicking appeal, as vampire hunter Blade against then-hottest of the hot Stephen Dorff as arch-nemesis Deacon Frost was a master-stroke, and despite not staying true to the character at all (what the hell's a *half-vampire?*), it racked up an impressive showing at the box office and ushered in a new age of Marvel cinematic supremacy. At a time when the DC side of the fence had just gifted us with the turgid excrescence that was (and remains – trust me) *Batman and Robin*, Marvel Studios, in their first co-production, proffered a bona fide action-fest that drew a wide audience among both comic fans and non.

After all, prior to his movie, Blade was hardly well-known outside Comicville. In fact, he wasn't that well known in it, either, being one of the more obscure heroes to come out of Marvel's 1970s monster books, and having spent pretty much a decade in exile after Dr. Strange killed off all the world's vampires in 1983. So DC's biggest successes had come from Batman and Superman, their two leading lights (Wonder Woman is probably the comic house's other big name, thanks mainly to the Lynda Carter series of the 70s), whereas Marvel was able to field such a depth of talent that it was able to bring a second – or even tenth – stringer off the bench and make him a star. A star so popular that his follow-up adventure, 2000's *Blade II*, was the #1 movie at the US box office on its release, and made even more money than its progenitor. (Yes, I know, *Blade: Trinity*. Horrible. Let's move on.)

2000 also saw the release of Bryan Singer's glorious *X-Men*, and that, my friends, is where our tale really puts our good guys (Marvel) in an unassailable position as the leaders in this particular field. Again, inspired casting helped make *X-Men* a success – the person who tapped Hugh Jackman for the role of Wolverine, after Dougray Scott dropped out, deserves some kind of statue erected to them somewhere – but it also served to introduce the general movie-going public to the "team" concept in comics, helped establish a universal knowledge of things like mutant powers and adamantium and the hotness of cartoon characters, and generally made comic book lore accessible and even interesting to those who would have considered themselves above such things before *X-Men*'s premiere.

Now, this may merely be because I happen to be a female who likes comic books, but I applaud this general broadening of comic familiarity.

While I realized in the late 90s that I am by no means alone – thank you, internet! – being a girl and proudly owning a mint copy of *Vampirella #1* was something that I spent my adolescence aware was Just Plain Weird. So perhaps I am speaking as the closeted teenager I once was (funny how I was unashamed to own a Mariah Carey album, but hid my *Dark Horse Presents* collection away in embarrassment) when I say anything that engenders an awareness of any comic book among the general populace is a Very Good Thing. As comic fans, I think we're all better off the more widely known the objects of our affection become; even the fact that there is much distinction between the Marvel Universe and the DC Universe is slowly being recognized by those who have yet to claim allegiance to either nation. With the advent of star-vehicle blockbuster comic book movies from both sides of this debate, the comically uninitiated are slowly cottoning on to our little slice of illustrated life, and I think that is only to be encouraged. Comics are the new vampires; there's a type for every taste in literature, and therefore a type for every taste in film. Non-Marvel/DC (proposed mashup name: DCarvel) gems like the *Hellboy* movies, *Sin City*, *Mystery Men*, *Kick-Ass* and *Scott Pilgrim* illustrate that comic books provide ample fodder for any number of movie-going demographics; and even the problematic non-DCarvel (wow, it's catching on already!) adaptation attempts like *Judge Dredd*, *Constantine* and *From Hell* have at least, like their DCarvel counterparts, raised the profiles of graphic novels (and by extension, their fans) throughout the mundane world.

My learned colleague has leveled many charges at Marvel's head in his diatribe on this issue, his main one being that Marvel irresponsibly offers up its characters willy-nilly for adaptation and that DC is to be commended for keeping it's sacred. I disagree. Sure, the efforts to film our heroes may occasionally bring the various comic houses and/or titles into disrepute, but I'd rather they at least *try* to deliver their stories unto the populace than hoard them away all safe and sound to be enjoyed only by those already aware.

Where some might see judicious restraint in the actions of DC – and its parent company, Warner Bros – in refusing to bring out a JLA, Wonder Woman or Black Adam movie, I see only cowardice. I see a lack of faith in its product, and in its fans. When the Golden Age of Marvel movies began in the late 90s, the Big 2 the comic house could claim were – I would contend – Spider-Man and The Hulk, if only due to the Saturday morning cartoon (and theme song) of the one and the Lou Ferrigno TV series of the other. Iron Man was pretty damned obscure indeed before Robert Downey Jr. signed on to play him, and as far as anyone outside of the four color brigade was aware, Daredevil could just as easily have been a movie about Evel Knievel as my Man Without Fear. (And, oh, don't I wish it was!) Man-Thing, who got himself his very own – deliciously dire – Sci-Fi original in 2005, is so esoteric a character as to basically be an extra. But Marvel, and sundry other producers, saw potential in these relative unknowns and others like them. They then sought to bring these heroes to the public's notice, and it seems they'll keep on bringing them to the public's notice till the public takes proper... er... note.

It's called persistence of vision, and I consider it a very worthy trait.

The 2003 *Hulk* didn't succeed, despite having Ang Lee at the helm and starring Eric Bana and Jennifer Connelly? Let's do it again, with Edward Fricken Norton in the role – he is beyond compelling in 2008's *The Incredible Hulk*, and his absence from the 2012 Avengers line-up is a tragedy. The Dolph Lundgren 1989 version of *The Punisher* didn't appeal? Let's do it again in 2004, with the beauteous Thomas Jane donning the signature skull-decorated T-shirt that Lundgren unaccountably spurned. And when that didn't work? (Though, I have to tell you, it continues to work for me.) Let's try it again again, in 2008, this time throwing in a whole lot of cursing and a far burlier leading man. I look forward to the inevitable Punisher reboot a few years hence, with, oh, I dunno, Zac Efron to star. If at first you don't succeed...

In the meantime, bring on both an *Iron Man* and *Fantastic Four 3*, Marvel! (I fell in love with *The Rise of the Silver Surfer* anew on re-watch, and not only because Norrin Radd is yet another of my comic book crushes; yeah, I lied before.) Bring on *Thor* and *Captain America* and *X-Men: First Class* and – my God! – a Joss-directed *Avengers*, and that long-proposed *Red Sonja* reboot (with or without Rose McGowan). Give us an Ant-Man movie and a Scarlet Witch movie and a Black Widow movie and *X-Men Origins: Gambit* (re-cast, hopefully), and keep 'em coming.

And, DC? Don't be such pansy asses. Ryan Reynolds as Green Lantern's a start, but come on! Don't be afraid to let your lovelight shine. Get yourselves a Teen Titans movie and a Flash movie and an Aquaman movie (if you get Vincent Chase to star, it'll be killer) and, oh, I don't know, a Vulcan movie or something, and don't be so terrified that they'll fail.

As they say, any publicity is good publicity. And on that count alone, Marvel wins this one hands down.

© *Rachel Hyland, 2010*

MEDIA TIE-IN NOVELS
WHEN THEY'RE GOOD, THEY CAN BE AMAZING
by Geonn Cannon

When I was a kid, *Quantum Leap* was appointment television. I would get comfortable in my chair, set up the VCR, and I would record every single episode. I even cut out the commercials and, in a sign of just how obsessed I was, I would edit the tape so that the leaps came together flawlessly. I would pause on the leap out, and then I would start recording in the middle of the leap in on the next episode. It wasn't always perfect, but the few times it was, I was very proud.

So naturally, my love couldn't be contained by just watching the show. This was before I started writing, but fortunately the producers of the show had okayed a publishing company to put out tie-in novels. I had already read a few *Star Trek* tie-ins (my other big sci-fi love in my formative years... *TNG*, not *Original Series*, please), so I jumped at the chance to read Sam Beckett's further adventures in paperback form.

To this day, the *Quantum Leap* novels are still a perfect example of tie-ins done right. There's very little continuity to worry about and any issues can be explained by Sam's Swiss-cheese memory. The very basis of the show sets itself up for original novels very well: every new life Sam leaps into is basically an original story idea. You just have to add in the leaping facet and everything else will fall into place.

But the novels did more than that. They did what the show couldn't by taking us into the future (1999... cough) with Al Calavicci, Verbeena Beeks, the sentient computer Ziggy, and all the other characters who were mentioned but all-too-rarely seen. The novels gave us a peek at a broader world by showing us the people Sam had left behind. His friends, his wife, his coworkers who were desperately trying to get him back while helping him with his unofficial mission through time. The books were extremely well done, and even gave us a satisfactory end to the series, with *Mirror's Edge*.

Quantum Leap was a great series, and the books carried on that tradition by adding to it with a broader vision of what was really happening with the characters. It didn't ignore Sam's leaps; some of the novels could easily have been turned into episodes. But it was that added insight to what happened after Al stepped through the glowing door that really made them special.

These days, it's not rare to find books for a wide range of series on the shelves at your local bookstore. USA is a very prolific producer of novels based on their shows – *Psych, Monk, Burn Notice* – as is Syfy: there are even *Eureka* books! Of course, the former WB was an industry leader with their books based on *Buffy, Angel, Charmed* and the like, a tradition continued by the CW with *Smallville, Supernatural* and *The Vampire Diaries*. And *Doctor Who* novels? There are hundreds of those things. *Star Trek*? Thousands.

Plus, the *Stargate* universe joined the mix not once, or twice, but thrice.

The first tie-in novels for *Stargate* were a continuation of the movie. Their worthiness is dependent on whether or not you prefer the movie to the TV show. The books have their problems (language being a big part of it, given what the humans call the feline-type aliens they encounter), but it's drastically different from what Brad Wright and Jonathan Glassner created on Showtime.

The second attempt was a categorical disaster. An author who shall not be named (Smashley McConnellsky – also responsible for five of the lesser Quantum Leap outings) was hired by a company to produce the novels without ever having seen a single episode. Rather than rectify this by actually watching the series, she ventured forth into the mix and produced four laughably godawful parody novels that include the same characters as the show. I call them a parody because that's the only way I can justify their existence. One novel refers to Amanda Carter, while another mentions Daniel's blond hair. Yeah. Those didn't last very long, and now they are treasured, if just for the humor aspect of it all.

Fortunately, a company called Fandemonium figured out the correct formula: hire fans, and then edit your freaking books. That would have solved a lot of the first company's problems. The readers might not always be happy, but at least – for the most part – the books get the important things right. But when they don't, oh... oh, we will not let it go because they should know better this time.

That's the fine line that tie-in novels have to walk. With shows becoming increasingly serial in nature, with ongoing plots and story arcs, these novels have to slip in undetected. They have to include a book-length story with at least a drop of character growth, and then they have to leave everything the way they found it when they're done. That's a lot to keep balanced. Adrian Monk can't discover a vital clue to his wife's murder in a novel, and Michael Westen can't ferret out an explanation of his burn notice.

The reset button is where a lot of tie-in novels fail. There's no drama or suspense, no real worry that they might not get out of this one because... well, if Carlton Lassiter got shot, that would probably have been shown during an episode of *Psych*. So the reader goes into the novel knowing that everything will be fine at the end, which might make you wonder why to even bother with the book at all.

The answer is perspective. Like with the *Quantum Leap* books where we followed Al to the future, the tie-in novels bring new points-of-view to the table. Every *Monk* book is narrated by his nurse, Natalie. We get to see her as a struggling single mom with a singularly frustrating boss. We have an outsider's perspective of Monk's antics that we don't get from the show. In the show, the camera focused on Monk so that even when he was standing alone, we were with him. The books make it easier to take that step back and become a witness to it from the outside.

A tie-in novel also lets you get into your favorite character's head. You can hear their doubts and fears, the things they might not necessarily let show. A look of concern on Amanda Tapping's face as we cut to commercial might turn into a page and a half about why Samantha Carter has doubts about a current mission and why she's willing to go along with it anyway. It tells a story rather than showing it, allowing you to become a bigger part of it than you would have been otherwise.

Tie-in novels aren't always good. Sometimes they're appalling. (I'm looking at you, *SG-1*'s *Power Behind the Throne*) But when they're good, they can be amazing. The best thing a tie-in novel can offer is a reunion. When a show goes off the air, that's it. The stories are done. But with tie-ins, *SG-1* and *Atlantis* live on. The teams are still going through the gate, *Atlantis* has been continued with the amazing Legacy Series that shows us what happened after the series finale. And there are so many other shows – and indeed movies – that get further escapades in print form, besides.

Tie-in novels are usually produced quick and cheap. They'll most likely never win any awards, and there's always just a little bit of a guilty pleasure when you're caught reading one of them. But that's a small price to pay to spend a few hundred pages with some old friends having new and exciting adventures together.

And yes, I still have the complete collection of *Quantum Leap* books on my shelf.

© *Geonn Cannon, 2011*

MEDIA TIE-IN NOVELS
NOT WORTH THE PAPER THEY'RE PRINTED ON
by K. Burtt

Despite seeming to concede victory to my opponent right off the top, I must say that I am not wholly against the idea of media tie-in novels. The concept behind them doesn't scare me to the point that I am considering dressing as a tie-in novel for the next Halloween to frighten the neighborhood kids. I don't have such fear and loathing when I contemplate the existence of tie-in novels that I have to check my surroundings to make sure I'm not in Vegas (though, if I were? Sweet! Vegas, baby!). Nor do I even find myself filled with so much abhorrence and revulsion that the only thing left to do is to create a brand new online magazine to vent about it, pulling in an international writing staff to help out (hey, it happens more often than you'd think!). But though my hostility has yet to reach those levels, I just don't think tie-in novels are worth it.

My opponent has generously pointed out several of the issues that occur with most tie-In novels already: they're quick and cheap, they either have to push a big reset button at the end of the book or really screw with canon, and many aren't worth the paper they're printed on. Let's look at some of these issues a little more closely.

For one, the original creators of the TV show or movie(s) are rarely involved in tie-in novels. The creators don't pay much attention, if any, to the specifics that go into them (perhaps giving an okay to the general plot ideas at most.). Think of the fan uproar that occurred when news broke that the original producers of *Buffy* wanted to make a new movie – one that did not include Joss Whedon. The fans knew that any *Buffy* without Joss isn't really *Buffy* at all. So why accept *Buffy* books without Joss? I mean, a book could be good and have the right tone, style, feel, even dialogue of the TV show or movie, but without the original creator involved, or at least a member of the writing staff, any such attempt will feel false to begin with. Heck, look at the *Buffy, Season 8* comics (no, really, go look at them)! Joss was involved for most of it, even writing many of the issues. And it worked – it was Buffy. But some issues were written by others, with no *Buffy* connection…and it didn't always work. Or look at the *Aftermath* comics of *Angel*. Joss isn't involved in those. And…they're kind of odd. They just don't have the right feel to them.

And without the creator involved, the likelihood exists that a tie-in novel can really screw with canon. You can have things happen to characters that never would have occurred on the show; characters will make decisions or act in ways that don't ring true. It's annoying when an episode of a TV series has characters act, well, out of character. It's noticeable and frustrating. So when such a book is written, there are two options: It's not part of canon at all, which means the book is effectively professional fanfic and should be ignored from here on out (and if so, why does it exist at all, other than to make money?) Or, it *is* part of canon, and just like that you not only irritate the fan base but potentially color their views of the original TV show/movie.

That latter aspect is a danger area inherent in one of the "pros" of tie-in novels, as discussed by my opponent: that we can get insight and perspective into favorite characters through a novel, perspectives that you don't get from watching on screen. This is true... but what if that insight *doesn't* ring true? What if you have in mind a certain motivation for a character, and then some author comes along and assigns some completely different motivation? It's going to color your view of that character from then on out, even if you do your best to tell yourself "oh, well, that didn't really happen. That's not what they really think." So yes, it can be quite interesting to get insight you didn't have before, but the risk exists that it would be insight that messes with your entire view of the character and/or show (which might sound a little extreme, but you just know it's happened).

Now, I realize that everything I was just saying relies on a lot of "what ifs". Kind of a worst-case-scenario for the media tie-in novel. I am aware of that. And I will even now admit that of the tie-ins I have read, some weren't terrible, and I even thought that a few were particularly excellent. Peter David did quite a good job with some of his *Star Trek: The Next Generation* novels (*Imzadi*, for instance, deserves all the accolades it has received), and the *Heir to the Empire* trilogy (i.e. the *Thrawn Trilogy*) of *Star Wars* books by Timothy Zahn set a high bar that few (if any) have been able to reach – perhaps that's only because those particular books, which kicked off the entire "expanded universe" of *Star Wars*, were written with the explicit and direct consent and blessing of George Lucas, however. But tie-ins of that caliber are few and far between. As my opponent said, "Tie-in novels are usually produced quick and cheap" and "They'll most likely never win any awards." And this is really my biggest problem with them. They exist only to make a buck, without regard to quality.

In the world of video games, it is a known fact that games based upon movies (or TV shows, but mostly movies) will suck. It's a fact of life. (And the reverse is usually true, as well.) Any gamer who knows anything about video games knows this. There are exceptions, sure, but I doubt any gamer will ever buy a tie-in game, even if he/she is a huge fan of whatever movie/show the game is based on... unless they are convinced by respected reviewers that "actually, this particular game is pretty good! How weird is that?"

I think it's the same for tie-in books. They are only written because the studio/publishing house thought that they could make an easy buck off fans. Its telling that these books are mostly written about genre or otherwise cultish shows; a fanbase that will fork out hundreds for a three-dimensional chess set or a replica of Fray's scythe will buy anything, seems to be the thinking. Most books are written by relatively unknown authors, they're often quite short, and there usually doesn't seem to be much thought put into them: often, they are full of glaring errors that would horrify even the most casual fan of the show. There really is a lot of junk out there. For every *Imzadi* there are a depressing number of *TNG* books where Data uses contractions; or *Stargate* books where the author thinks two-way travel through a wormhole is possible; or *Buffy* books where soulless Angel's name is spelled "Angeles". (From what I've been told... I don't read these. Obviously.).

And even when decent books of this type are written, they could well then refer to events of past books (the aforementioned expanded universe *Star Wars* novels are quite guilty of this), meaning that to fully understand what is going on, you would need to wade through all the junk anyway.

Back to the video game comparison: a bad tie-in game shouldn't really have an effect on the opinion of the original subject, but tie-in books can. Add that to the fact that many if not most are just not all that good to begin with – why bother at all? For me, I have better things to do with my time than go through a sea of media tie-ins in the hopes that I'll come across one that even approaches the standards of the TV show or movie on which it is based. Thus, I have stopped reading them completely. They're just not worth it.

Having said all that, if only there was some kind of place one could go, perhaps some sort of online magazine on the world wide web... a "webzine" if you will... where books can be read and reviewed by others, people who are both fans and incredibly articulate and insightful, thus allowing one to find out ahead of time if a tie-in novel is actually one of the worthwhile ones. Man, that'd be pretty sweet.

© *K. Burtt, 2010*

THE MID-SEASON HIATUS
A NECESSARY EVIL
by Kate Nagy

Recently, *Geek Speak*'s estimable Editor-in-Chief, Rachel Hyland, wrote a passionate diatribe against the increasingly common practice on network television of airing a certain number of episodes of our favorite shows and then abruptly taking a lengthy break: the dreaded "mid-season hiatus." She variously referred to the hiatus as "torture," "a travesty," "annoying at the best of times," "just plain stupid," and a practice that "sucks ass." One might reasonably infer that she doesn't care for it all that much.

You know what? I don't like it either.

A mid-season break is a complete pain in the ass. Everyone knows that. Nobody likes a hiatus, least of all a show's devoted fans.

Nevertheless, a hiatus is not the end of the world. In some cases, it may even be... not such a bad thing. Herewith, my reasons why a mid-season hiatus, while painful, sometimes has its place in the grand scheme of things.

First, just to put things into context, a few words about why we have hiatuses (as Rachel asked: hiati?) to begin with. At the risk of stating the glaringly obvious: It would be really nice if a network's principal objective were to create Art or tell a cracking good story or even entertain the fans. But we all know that this is not the case. Don't get me wrong: if those things happen nobody objects, and in fact everybody's life becomes a whole lot easier. However, everything the network does, they do with the goal of making money. In a very real sense, their bottom line is their bottom line.

Of course, the best way to pull in large sums of money is to post excellent ratings and thereby drive up ad revenue. Now, I'll be the first to admit that this is an imperfect paradigm: ratings are basically a 20th century tool in a 21st century world. The Nielsens have become a little more sophisticated in recent years (they can track DVR usage, for example), but not much. In any case, fewer people are watching their favorite shows as they air; we're catching them on DVD, or on hulu.com, or in bits and pieces on YouTube, or even – well certainly not any of *us*, but maybe some of those other people – through various extralegal means. In most of these cases, the viewers are skipping the commercials altogether. (Oh noez!)

In fact, so many people are turning to these new technologies to meet their viewing needs that I'm pretty sure that the networks (no matter what they say) have no idea how many people actually watch their shows each week. I'm also pretty sure that at the end of the day they don't especially care, since they still have a fairly good read on how many people are watching each show as it airs, when those all-important ads are broadcast.

From an artistic standpoint, then, the system is seriously flawed. Unfortunately, it's what we have to work with. So with that in mind:

A hiatus can give a sinking ship the opportunity to right itself

There are several people near and dear to my heart (don't worry, I'm not naming names) whose initial forays into higher education were spectacularly unsuccessful. These individuals arrived on campus anticipating four years of academic glory, but quickly found that tedious activities like going to class and studying for exams cut into their chillaxing, partying, and general hanging-out time to an unacceptable degree. Eventually, their respective Administrations invited them to take a semester or two off to reevaluate their priorities. In short, their academic careers were placed on hiatus.

Was this annoying? Disruptive? A little embarrassing, even? Sure. But look what happened next: most of these people returned to college and suddenly became academic superstars. Dean's list; advanced degrees; interesting and fulfilling careers. Getting bounced from school was no fun for anyone, but the time off allowed them to retool, to think about what was going wrong, and to strategize about how to make it better.

So it is with some television shows. For example, after four episodes, *V*'s ratings were dropping like a stone and its quality could have been charitably described as uneven. When it came back, some months later, it was with the fast-paced, exciting "Welcome to the War." Ratings for that ep were decent, although not spectacular; still, if (as early indications would suggest) the showrunners used the hiatus profitably, word of mouth will almost certainly give *V* a boost.

Do the networks always take advantage of a hiatus to make improvements to the shows? Shyeah, right. But the hiatus at least gives the illusion of a fighting chance for improvement.

A hiatus, properly used, can build buzz

How do you make something really desirable? Take it away and make it really hard to get. And then put your PR team to work. Look at *Lost* – they're not doing a hiatus in this, their final season, but they did make their faithful wait eight long months between seasons. Eight months! And how many magazine covers did the show have? How breathlessly did *TV Guide* and (in particular) *Entertainment Weekly* cover the lead-in to the beginning of the new season? By the time "LA X" rolled around back in February, *Lost* fans had been worked into a fever pitch of anticipation, a level of energy that has sustained us through the season's ponderous middle stretch.

A hiatus creates a vacuum in which new interests can flourish

A hiatus represents the perfect opportunity for the frustrated geek to branch out. Rachel's article is full of useful ideas – graphic novels! Compilations! YouTube! Fanfic! Or even…dare I suggest it…discover a whole new show. When your show falls off the radar, it makes space for something new… and occasionally, something good. It's worth noting here that *Buffy the Vampire Slayer*, *Dollhouse*, *Numb3rs*, *Quantum Leap*, and *Terminator: The Sarah Connor Chronicles* all originally debuted at midseason.

A hiatus can create marketing opportunities that bring needed revenue to the networks

Remember, fewer people are viewing the commercials, so bushels of ad money are less certain… and somebody has to pay Joseph Fiennes' salary. That's why, for example, *FlashForward* has famously released a DVD of the first half of Season 1. Artistically this is a boneheaded decision, particularly given the fact that the first half of Season 1 of *FlashForward* could and should be marketed as a surefire cure for insomnia. (Strategy, people!) But newcomers to the show who pick up the DVD in the bargain bin at Target may actually enjoy it – you never know – and might be inspired to watch the second half of the show live. And if enough people do that, *FlashForward* could hang on for a second season.

Yay?

A hiatus is better than the alternative

Close your eyes and just imagine. *Firefly* isn't gone forever. It's just on hiatus!

There. Aren't you happy now?

THE MID-SEASON HIATUS
JUST PLAIN EVIL
by Rachel Hyland

Consider, if you will, that a trusted confidante of wants to introduce you to someone new. At first, you may be reluctant: perhaps you have enough friends; perhaps, even, this new person sounds a lot like someone you already know. But you keep hearing how great they are, how much you'll love them, how completely blown away you'll be. Others weigh in on the subject, seemingly disinterested yet knowledgeable souls who tell you that this new person is your kind of person, that you'd really be missing out if you didn't at least meet them for coffee. So, finally, after everyone has been going on about it for weeks, you finally succumb to the many blandishments and meet this much-heralded stranger for the first time.

And after a bit, you really start to like this new acquaintance of yours. It isn't too long before you call them friend. You become interested in their life and their loves, you get invested in their happiness, you really care about their trials and their triumphs. And then, just as you feel you're starting to get really close, just as a bond is formed and a trust circle is enclosed, your new best friend just up and disappears from your life for weeks, months, at a time.

Are you still their friend?

Or, to continue the analogy, consider someone you've known for a while —years even. They've been good to you, and you like them ever so. You've stuck with them through the good times and the bad (sometimes very bad), you've given them your time and your devotion and even your forgiveness, and you have expected nothing but a little courtesy in return. Then they suddenly go off the deep end, make promises on which they don't deliver, make you crazy and frustrated, hurt you with their selfish disregard for your feelings, until you finally just get tired of all their bullshit and take the ultimate step in severing all ties: delete them from your Facebook.

Right?

That's just how it is with TV shows that go on hiatus. (Yes, we finally got there, people!)

TV shows lose viewers for three main reasons: poor quality, timeslot changes, and mid-season hiatuses (I'll ask again: hiati?). Occasionally, all three of those circumstances will apply (hello, *Heroes*), but often all it takes is the dratted last item on that saddening, infuriating list.

I've said it before and I'll say it again: the mid-season hiatus sucks. It sucks in every conceivable way, from sucking the intensity out of a thrilling narrative to sucking the interest out of the casual viewer. (Well... okay, it sucks in every conceivable way but the literal one.) And it's all very well to act as a network apologist, to give reasons like revenue and retooling and revitalizing the fanbase, but no matter what the justification, there can be no justification. Because...

A hiatus can give a sinking ship the opportunity to, well, sink

FlashForward came back last month from its much-touted stint in rehab with an awesome double episode that almost nobody watched. Why would they? ABC certainly hasn't made it Must See TV. Taking it off the air for four months did nothing to make anyone want to watch it more. It's going to take a miracle to save *FlashForward*, and considering the excellent caliber of the episodes since its return, this is clearly a case of the mid-season hiatus sinking, not saving, this metaphor.

V, meanwhile, may have taken a lengthy time off for its own bout of detox, but why did go to air in the first place? ABC declared, in

156

September, that the show would only be offering up four episodes before heading off to Promises (for, what, Scott Wolf-addiction?), and *V* didn't even premiere till November. So ABC already knew there was trouble in Visitor City (they were the ones who fired half the production staff and demanded the rewrites), and yet they still showed us the fruits of what they considered dubious labors anyway. They could hardly be surprised by the low ratings. Seriously, if the network that airs it can't commit to even a half-season of a show, then why should we?

A hiatus can make one forget when the damn thing is on

DVRs are a miracle invention. They, along with iPods and the Wii Fit balance board, convince me beyond all doubt that our society is enjoying the fruits of recovered alien technology. But DVRs are a double-edged sword when it comes to TV viewership. On the one hand, yes, they will happily tape those things that you ask of them, with nary a word of complaint (unlike your much put-upon parents or roommate). On the other hand, those things that they tape will often be watched with a thumb on the remote's Fast Forward button, to skip past all those pesky advertisements. Advertisements for, say, the mid-season return of some show you once watched so faithfully. Some show that has subsequently changed timeslot, or that your DVR has completely forgotten about during its long absence. And so when days or even weeks later someone asks you what you think of the latest *Fringe* episode and you had no idea it was even back on, how likely is this hypothetical you going to be to tune in now? I'll tell you: not very.

A hiatus creates a vacuum in which new interests can flourish

Absence, despite the cliché, rarely makes the heart grow fonder. Out of sight, out of mind is far more apropos of, well, people, and in the case of television shows (especially troubled, uneven, depressing little shows – yes, I'm talking to you, *Stargate Universe*), a mid-season hiatus can lead its viewership to realize, hey, I don't need this frustrating nonsense! I've got important laundry I could be doing, taxes I could be filing, MTV reality shows I could be watching! The fact is, we television viewers are creatures of habit. We watch *The Simpsons* because that's what we do on a Sunday night, not necessarily because it's essential to our being (anymore). And when our habit is broken, when the show we were expecting is no longer so there, we will often move on to something else and never look back. Hey, we're fickle.

A hiatus can kill momentum

The networks know not what they do. They have these tremendous talents at their disposal, these creators and writers and producers who build up elaborate storylines with killer intricacies that they weave into the fabric of their universes, and which we then weave into our lives. The excitement is palpable, breath-taking and immediate, as they amp us up to a heightened state of interest and awareness that has us craving the next episode... and then, BAM! Hiatus, leaving that craving unsatisfied for weeks, even months at a time. Is it any wonder that the mid-season return of every show ever has lower ratings than before it took a break? One can only sustain a feverish state of suspense for so long before one is forced to quit, cold turkey. The networks are like drug dealers, getting us hooked on the high and then withholding the good stuff to drive up demand.

Should it surprise them that we get over our dependence with the help of a 12 Step Program... or, at least, a rival television program?

A hiatus is better than cancelation, but can easily lead to it

The parable of *Firefly* is an argument against the mid-season hiatus if ever there was one. It barely made it to mid-season itself, but has sold so well on DVD that it illustrates the point very effectively: it takes time for any show to build an audience. And when that audience is built, it likes things to unfold in a consistent, timely and efficient manner.

Why watch a show on TV if you know that all it's going to do is vex you with its programming vagaries? Since you know that it's likely to be released in a box set in a few months anyway – and if not, there's always the download alternative (whether legal or otherwise) – you'll be able to watch every episode at your leisure. Why, therefore, put yourself at the mercy of revenue-hungry network execs, constantly being tormented with reruns and pre-emptings and at least one hiatus, when you can simply wait and see it all at once? Or perhaps come to the conclusion that it's not worth seeing at all?

In conclusion, the mid-season hiatus is just one more nail in the coffin of broadcast TV. It is one more reason people have not to watch these shows as they air, instead of waiting till they're available in a more-preferred, less-interrupted format.

And that is so, so sad. It is a vicious cycle. People don't watch good TV shows because the breaks are so annoying. Then people get annoyed because there are no good TV shows. This is not the fault of these anonymous people. It is the fault of the networks. It is the fault of the bean counters and the ratings calculators who are, as a whole, thoroughly misguided as to what the people actually want. It's the fault (at least, in part) of the damned mid-season hiatus.

I've said it before and I'll say it again: the mid-season hiatus sucks.

© *Rachel Hyland, 2010*

MOVIE TRAILERS
ARE THE WORST
by Rachel Hyland

"So, what time does it *actually* start?" Thus I have asked pretty much every person who has ever sold me a movie ticket. Because sure, the advertised kick-off might be 7:50 PM or some such, but rare is the cinema at which the show you paid for actually begins at the appointed hour. Like buying a glossy magazine and having to leaf past seventeen pages of hair product before you even reach the masthead, a typical trip to the movies comes along with up to thirty minutes of commercials — the worst of which, in my opinion, being the ones for other movies.

Trailers. My *word* do I hate them.

I don't think it's always been this way. As a kid, every moment at the movie theater was a joy, a rare treat of which I wouldn't want to miss a single moment, and often the trailers were the closest I would come to watching these forthcoming films for several years. And the trailers – or previews, as we call them in my homeland – that presaged each video rental, back when that was a thing, were not only thrilling enticements to the next one, but also very often an indicator of your current choice's quality, or lack thereof.

But as time went on, I grew increasingly disenchanted with the trailer in all its forms, to the point where I now refuse to even enter the movie theater before I am sure they are over. (And yes, I have missed the beginning of more than one as a result; what DID happen with Peter Parker's parents in *The Amazing Spider-Man*? I've been meaning to check...) Many is the friend I have sent in ahead of me while I wait anxiously outside, trying – and usually succeeding, though I don't mean to brag – to time my entrance perfectly, sitting on the aisle so as to disrupt as few people as possible with my tardy (on time) arrival.

Going to the cinema with me is far more problematic than it probably should be.

The thing is, I just don't understand why anyone would want to watch the trailers. Oh, I get why the film companies make them – they need to advertise their goods, after all. But WHY do people seek them out, and obsess over them, and create elaborate fan theories from them long before the film they are pimping is even available for pre-booking?

Why open yourself up to such disappointment? Why engender a fever pitch of anticipation that is sometimes YEARS away from being sated? And, most significantly, why invite anyone to spoil plot points, dialogue and sometimes entire scenes from a movie you're probably going to see, regardless?

In our recent Geek vs. Geek on *Suicide Squad*, our Mark Ritchie lamented the finished product's lack of resemblance to the series of kick-ass trailers released in the months leading up to the film's premiere. He (rightly) suggests that the footage used in the trailers should have been present in the film; essentially, that the filmmakers pulled a bait-and-switch, false advertising at its worst. I entirely concur: a trailer should at least resemble the film its promoting, and having now seen some of the judiciously edited works of trailer art to which Mark was referring, I can see where his disappointment lies. But here's the thing. Almost all the footage in the trailers is in the film, it's just cut so evocatively, and set to such incongruous yet perfect music, that these scenes sing with a life and frenetic vigor the movie could not hope to match without inducing seizures. I'll admit, I didn't love *Suicide Squad*, even going into it blind, but I still had a pretty good time with it, most probably because everything in it was new to me; Harley's crazy-eyed quips, Diablo's pyrokinetic flamboyance and Deadshot's astounding feats of marksmanship undulled by repetition.

This is a common problem with viewing trailers, I think. You take away that joy of discovery in seeing something for the very first time, projected on a big screen with surround sound as was intended, rather than, say, on your phone.

Take, for example, three of the biggest film releases of the past year, *The Force Awakens*, *Captain America: Civil War* and *X-Men: Apocalypse*. I went into all three having avoided the myriad of pre-release marketing – which, especially in the case of *Star Wars*, was surely some kind of midi-chlorian-infused miracle – and so stared at the screen in wonder as Han Solo boarded the *Millennium Falcon*, as Spider-Man swung into action, as Wolverine escaped from Weapon X's compound. Coming at all three completely cold, I was able to judge them solely on their merits, their surprise reveals coming as actual surprises and their shortcomings evaluated by what was on the screen, and not in comparison to the highlight-reel version seen on some other screen beforehand. Sure, I still had baggage with *Civil War* – the comic book kind, to which the movie was spectacularly unfaithful – but at no point was I cross with the movie because it didn't live up to its hype. Because I had managed to avoid the hype entirely.

But I'll be honest. None of this is why I really hate trailers.

I just don't like spoilers. AT ALL. I would rather be unpleasantly surprised than have a single moment's amazement taken away from me, and since I have a solid plan, somewhere in the back of my head, to someday watch ALL the movies, I don't want to have a single one of them ruined by – and you know this happens – seeing a preview so thorough you feel like you don't even need to see the movie anymore.

Am I suggesting film companies shouldn't make trailers for their forthcoming releases? Of course not. For a start, I actually don't know anyone else who shares my intense hatred of them, and I would hesitate to deprive others of their weird need to pre-watch all the good bits. I am also aware that some people prefer to choose from among the various cinematic offerings rather than just assay it all, and so for them a good, bad or even indifferent trailer can help narrow down the field.

What I would like is for the advertised movie time to actually BE the movie time, but with the theater opening, say, half an hour earlier for anyone who wants to be inundated with scenes from the next big blockbuster and reminders to switch off their cell phones. (We know, okay?)

Then I never need miss a pre-credits sequence again. But until then: totally worth it.

© Rachel Hyland, 2017

MOVIE TRAILERS
ARE ESSENTIAL
by Mark Ritchie

In a world… where trailers can be filled with all kinds of spoilers and false promises, one man sets out on a journey to discover why he feels the still have an important place in the cinema-going experience. Brace yourself as he goes head to head with *Geek Speak*'s dark overlord herself – a wordsmith who openly admits to missing portions of the film she's gone to see to prevent seeing scenes from other films (!) – in one of this year's most anticipated Geek vs. Geek titles.

Okay, full disclosure: when I was initially asked where I stand on the topic of movie trailers, I quickly realized that, actually, I hadn't paid much attention to them in the past either way. Not really. Some were great and some were bad, but whatever the outcome, trailers were simply part and parcel of the movie-going experience for me – snippets of future releases, which served to complement the film I intended to see – and made me all the giddier for it.

Having lent it a bit more thought, I've come to realize that there's a process involved here, a certain kind of anticipation that builds up that serves only to add to my excitement of the feature I'm about to watch. Take horror films, for example; watching a slew of scary trailers right before your intended fright fest sets the dreaded tone immediately, putting you in the perfect mood to be scared out of your wits. When it comes to superhero flicks, however; well, that's an entire spectacle in and of itself! This year alone I have died, been resurrected, and died then again over the fact we have finally gotten to the stage in film where a *Batman v Superman* preview can play back to back with an *Avengers* film that teases the appearance of Spider-Man, as well as an *X-Men* story that finally tackles ~~Ivan Ooze~~ Apocalypse. How could anybody not want to see that unfold before their very eyes?

It could be argued that I'm diluting my cinema experience as a result of watching these trailers, but I just don't see it that way. It's exciting being teased about certain films that have only just finished post-production, it serves to energize my interest in the project, and I would much prefer to experience the trailer for myself rather than having the information slowly trickle down to me as the months push forward – from social media posts and various movie sites covering on-set visits, to casual conversation between like-minded friends – it would be too tall of an order to avoid any and all spoilers.

Er, as a quick aside, I would be remiss if I didn't mention that I have been burned quite recently by the flames of spoilers, however, particularly for *Batman v Superman* ('cause they went ahead and showed absolutely every bloody surprise the film had going for it!) and *Suicide Squad* (which I touched upon elsewhere – a case of the trailer outshining the film), so I am willing to advise caution when it comes to trailers, especially for blockbusters. (And most definitely if it's for a franchise that you adore.) I usually bank on the fact that, typically, I will have forgotten almost everything about the trailer by the time the film hits the cinema, but with these two DC titles, I just couldn't resist temptation, the hype was just too real, and so I lapped up any and all media relating to them: teasers for teasers, teasers for trailers, actual trailers, TV spots, TV spot compilations, people reacting to teasers for trailers – I was a fiend! I definitely have learned a lesson that less is more, and that I shouldn't watch trailers over and over (and over!) so close to a film's release date. My bad.

But trailers do have purpose beyond the obvious marketing opportunities. They are there to keep you informed, to keep you in the loop. I most definitely always know what's going on down the pipeline when it comes to my mainstay genres (thanks, in part, to Marvel's pissing contest with DC as to who has the longer release schedule), but when I venture outside of my comfort zone, outside of the realm of sci-fi and fantasy, that's where trailers for me become an essential part of my itinerary. I don't think I ever would have even known about *Rust & Bone*, now one of my favorite films, had it not been for a trailer I caught when I went to see *The Hunt*. More recently, though, I hadn't heard a lick about *Eye in the Sky*, a film with an intriguing premise but one I would have happily passed on had it not been for such a compelling trailer. And I'm totally glad I went to see it because it is one of the stronger thrillers released this year. So there's definite advantages to checking out movie previews—they can provide a great opportunity to expand your horizons when it comes to cinema.

As well as giving me goose bumps and chills and squee-inducing moments, I think that, practically speaking, there are many uses for them, too. Because in an idyllic world, more people would utilize the time allowed by trailers to tear open ALL of their paper wrappings for their sweets and crisps and various other loud confectionery that they managed to sneak into the screening. They would cherish this time and use it to nip to the loo, or check a last-minute text, or settle down overly curious kids, or chat softly with friends, or get all of that pesky sneezing and coughing out of the way. I don't ask for much, I just politely ask that people get their shit together before the film starts. Trailers allow people to breathe and get settled in for main event.

Spoilers are just the worst, and I think that we can safely agree that trailers that detail more than they should need to be stopped. But I find that the majority of trailers made nowadays to be extremely polished, with most of them capably balancing the fine act of enticing an audience yet remaining mysterious. With blockbusters, it's easier to expect a higher risk of being spoiled, 'cause execs want to lure audiences by revealing some of the biggest treats within the film, but overall, I find that the execution behind most other trailers keeps me engaged, and excited for the movie's release, and will keep getting me into the cinema on time, because I don't want to miss a thing.

MIYAZAKI
WHENCE ALL THE LOVE?
by Rachel Hyland

It always comes as a surprise to me when I actively detest something beloved of my friends. Hell, it comes as a surprise to me when I actively detest something beloved of the random guy next to me. I think I tend to be pretty easy-going, able to find at least some measure of entertainment in even the most ludicrous of fictional endeavors – and sometimes to find even a good deal of entertainment there, depending on just how ludicrous we're talking. Oh, I've hated stuff. Violently, vehemently hated stuff, and have then sprayed forth my vitriol on the subject for all to see. But even when trapped in the accursed depths of saccharine angel-filled YA nonsense I can usually find shades of meaning, a clever one-liner, or at the very least a well-placed apostrophe on which to hang some semblance of enjoyment, and to engender in myself the merest whit of tolerance for whatever torture is then unfolding before my reluctant eyes. I mean, even when savagely critiquing *Thor*, as is often still my wont – that is a pain that lingers – I am prepared to concede that Chris Hemsworth possesses a mighty impressive set of arms.

Which is why I find it very surprising indeed that I must tell you, vehemently and violently and having thought about it a very great deal, that I just do not like a single thing about a single one of those pesky Hayao Miyazaki films everyone has long been raving about – like, at all – and I have no idea whatsoever why they are all so popular and acclaimed. None.

It's mortifying.

Now, look, in most everything in life, I am happy to stand as an individual, that guy in the crowd in *Life of Brian* objecting "I'm not." There are many examples I could cite here that would handily illustrate my contrariness to the dictates of what is considered capital-G Good in our genre (Love: *Howard the Duck*; Hate: *2001*; Love: *Roswell*; Hate: *Game of Thrones*; Love: *Gen13*; Hate: *Watchmen*), and about none of these am I ashamed. My tastes are vast and eclectic, and hey, I do read, and watch, and listen to, quality, high-brow-approved fare from time to time. It's not all spaceships and vampires, you know. (Occasionally, there's also magic.) But in no particular do I feel so at odds with the geektelligentsia as I do regarding my perplexity at the general and abiding respect and love widely held for the output of Studio Ghibli, and of Hayao Miyazaki in particular.

Lord knows, I have tried. I have watched every one of the things, determined each time that this time, finally, I will relate to the characters or grasp the subtext or find glory in the choppy, haphazard animation and be able to, at last, declare myself a convert. It's like how I've spent years sporadically trying to train myself to like coffee, a thoroughly disgusting beverage that I feel certain is just a massive practical joke being played on me by the population at large. "Oh, sure, we love coffee," most everyone in the world pretends, while in reality they're all sipping on Chai Latte and laughing behind their hands when I am served battery acid, each ensuing grimace only contributing to their amusement. Similarly, I am almost convinced that everyone who claims to be so enchanted with the works of Miyazaki – the disturbing *Ponyo*, the nauseating *Nausicaä*, the god-awful *Princess Mononoke* – are secretly running some kind of *Truman Show*-esque scam, where I am being observed for my reaction to peer pressure, and the day I am unable to take the constant assault on my nerves and finally break down, saying: "Wow, now I get it, that fighter pilot guy being a pig is brilliant!", the man behind the curtain will shut the experiment down and it will be revealed that these so-called works of genius were actually intended as the worst animated movies ever, like in *The Producers* with that musical about Hitler.

(I promise, I am not nearly as paranoid as the above makes me sound.)

But I quite honestly just don't get it. At first, when I watched *Spirited Away* and thought: "wait, this crap won an Oscar?!", I figured I was perhaps just suffering from a distaste for badly-dubbed foreign film and so watched it again in its original Japanese, with subtitles. It didn't help. Also, damn it, I cut my eye teeth on badly-dubbed foreign film, most especially a whole bunch of "you killed my father!"-style kung-fu (plus, hey, *Monkey Magic*!), and the disconnect between the characters' mouths and their words never bothered me overmuch there. So, no, that wasn't it. I mean, the voice of James Van Der Beek starred in a recent English dub of *Castle in the Sky*, and I love The Beek, yet even that wasn't enough to make me not regret the two hours I spent slogging through it, every minute longing for the end to come.

Nor was it any problem I had, or have, with anime. I have long loved *Sailor Moon* and *Astro Boy* and *Neon Genesis Evangelion* and a plethora of others; add into the mix more recent outings like the late Satoshi Kon's 2006 masterwork *Paprika*, which I utterly adore, and I hope it becomes clear that this isn't some kind of bias of mine at work. It's not the medium, it is the message: I. Just. Do. Not. Like. These. Movies.

Not a one of them. From *Mononoke* (boring) to *My Neighbor Totoro* (creepy) to *Howl's Moving Castle* (stultifying) to *Porco Rosso* (annoying) to *Ponyo* (creepy again), their long expanses of silence peppered by nonsensical dialogue, their constant discordant notes struck by everyone yelling at everyone else for no apparent reason, their frankly eye-searing color palate (or washed out, eye-watering color palate: cf. *Ponyo*), and their parade of outrageous caricatures masquerading as characters all combine to make each Miyazaki/Studio Ghibli film with which I subject myself an utter displeasure from beginning to (merciful) end. The only Ghibli offering I haven't quite minded was the latest one, *The Secret World of Arrietty*, which I didn't actually abhor. But it's based on the children's novel *The Borrowers*, and really, I'd rather just read *The Borrowers*, or even watch the not entirely successful 1997 John Goodman attempt at a live-action adaptation. And *Arrietty* wasn't directed by Miyazaki, anyway.

Does this place me in a very profound minority? Probably. Will I continue to try and change my own mind, to at last see what everyone else (allegedly) sees? Sure. But for now, and in every way, I am most strenuously anti-Miyazaki – well, his works, anyway; I'm sure he's a very nice man – and I am tired of apologizing for it.

© *Rachel Hyland, 2012*

MIYAZAKI
IS AWESOME!
by K. Burtt

I must admit that I am a little confused by the very existence of this Geek vs. Geek. We're arguing about Hayao Miyazaki? This to me is like taking sides on whether or not people should spend their free time punching puppies. Aren't we all on the same side on this? So I guess there are two categories of people in the world: either you are a fan of Miyazaki… or you're Rachel.

But since she is the one who controls the button that opens up the large vat of irate alligators above which we, the staff, sit, I should thus attempt to argue my side anyway (even though we all know the truth here: Miyazaki is awesome!).

So what is it about his movies that make them so effective? There are quite a few reasons, but probably the first is the sense of wonder that his movies evoke. If you think about the imagination and the whimsy that the Harry Potter series is credited with – Miyazaki's movies are like that. (Only, you know, better… but then my issues with HP are well-documented.) From the grand – such as the Toxic Jungle from one of his first movies, *Nausicaä of the Valley of the Wind,* or the first time we see the titular castle from *Castle in the Sky* – to the whimsical and cute, with the little bobble-head forest spirits in *Princess Mononoke* or the coal puff-balls in *Spirited Away* – Miyazaki takes full advantage of the blank slate that animation allows for to highlight his imagination.

And the universes he creates are quite fantastical, and yet they just *fit*. Having a man turned into a pig during an alternate-1920's post World War I world (in 1992's *Porco Rosso*) might seem like a strange, and possibly off-putting setting, but it works. Same as the Steampunk world from *Castle in the Sky*, considered an early example of the genre in movies. All of the strange creatures found in the monster-filled bathhouse in *Spirited Away* all feel like they belong; the setting just feels natural to the viewer. (Of course there should be giant walking heads! Why wouldn't there be?!) The fact that viewers are drawn into his world(s) to that extent is a testament to Miyazaki's skill.

And it is his skill that we are talking about. Another thing I quite appreciate about his movies is the direct role that he takes. Most of his movies are ones that he both wrote and directed, thus giving him near full control over making sure his vision made it to the screen. And it isn't just writing and directing – he is known for reviewing and (sometimes even) re-drawing every single animation cel used. He is quite hands-on. (And it doesn't hurt that his movies predominately still use hand-drawn cels with only some CGI used in certain instances). As a comparison: in general, which episodes of *Buffy* were the best? The ones written and directed by Joss Whedon, of course! Same effect with Miyazaki – the movies are better, tighter, and just more fun because of his direct and complete involvement.

The characters Miyazaki creates are all quite relatable in a variety of ways, which make his movies that much more effective. I mean, who hasn't been a young witch trying to make her way in the world just like Kiki? Or been exiled from their village and sent on a quest (but having demon-enhanced vorpal arrows!) like Prince Ashitaka? Or a mercenary fighter pilot who was turned into a pig? Er... um... okay, bad examples. Don't look at the specifics, but delve a tad deeper. The young witch Kiki is a teenager just reaching that point in life where she is trying to find herself – where do her talents really lie, and how can she fit into the world? *Princess Mononoke*'s Ashitaka finds himself trying to explain an outside view to people dead set in their ways. Chihiro, the protagonist in *Spirited Away*, starts out as rather an annoying child, but starts to learn what it means to grow up. Written down like this, the characters sound like they could be rather cliché and/or yet more examples of coming-of-age stories, but they are (almost) all handled in a way that fit quite well in their respective worlds and still draw the viewer in.

All of the above is just fine and dandy, all good reasons to enjoy Miyazaki's movies, but none of those are the biggest reason I am a fan. That reason is the ambiguity inherent in his movies. Things are not always black and white. In fact, in many instances, there aren't even obvious antagonists, no one like a Snidely Whiplash or a Dirk Dastardly to sit there and say "Curses! Foiled Again!". The characters that fill the antagonist role in his movies usually have good qualities as well.

This is best seen in *Princess Mononoke* (my personal favorite of his movies), where Ashitaka finds himself trying to stop the war between the Forest Gods and Lady Eboshi, the leader of an iron works. The seemingly obvious "bad guy" is Lady Eboshi – particularly when one thinks about the environmentalism themes that run strongly through Miyazaki's movies. Eboshi leads teams to clear away the forest to allow for more iron mining, thus upsetting the forest gods and, well, anyone who likes trees. But the reasons that Eboshi does this is to make a living for the people under her protection: former prostitutes, lepers, and other assorted people otherwise ostracized from society. Eboshi has good intentions in what she does – if she doesn't help them fend for themselves in whatever way they can, then what hope is there for these outcasts? At the same time, the forest gods (in particular the wolf goddess Moro) have decided that all humans are evil and deserve to be killed. There is good and bad in almost every character. It adds a level of complexity that many other animated movies geared toward kids lack.

What that leads to is that adults can enjoy his movies just as much as kids do. Most Disney-esque animated features can be enjoyed by adults, certainly, and will throw in a lot of humor to aid in that effect, but Miyazaki movies have that extra layer of meaning. His movies aren't just for entertainment, though they certainly are entertaining. And for that reason, I am a fan. As should you be. (And c'mon: demon-enhanced vorpal arrows! How can you not?!)

REWATCHING TV
A WASTE OF PRECIOUS TIME
by B. C. Roberts

Once upon a time there was a TV show called *Buffy the Vampire Slayer*. You might have heard of it. For seven seasons it consumed the *otaku* of the western world with its edgy take on adolescence and its super-hot titular character. Well, actually, it consumed us for three seasons and then it got a bit disappointing but we all kept watching thinking it would get better until finally we couldn't explain why we kept watching since it clearly wasn't.

Now, I particularly really liked the third season of *Buffy,* and recently a friend gave me a copy of it. Not on DVD of course, because I am morally opposed to purchasing something when it can be obtained for free. Anyway, I dutifully copied this season onto my hard drive and looked at it briefly before... I went off to watch something I hadn't seen before.

Without being too philosophical, our time on this earth is relatively brief. We only get eighty or so years to experience everything that art and literature have managed to produce in the last twenty-three centuries. The odds are stacked against anyone getting even close to just keeping up with all the new shows that go to air every week, let alone going back to the classics. Do we really have time to re-watch Buffy angst over Angel after he comes back from Hell? Or Xander and Cordelia to-ing and fro-ing about getting together and then Xander getting busted making out with Willow and so on and so forth? When I haven't even finished reading *War and Peace* yet? Or, to be less pretentious, when I have never even watched *Alias*? There is always something new to experience, something that has the potential to add to me as a human being. Watching something I have already seen can never achieve that – I have already seen it, I already know what's going to happen.

That being said, I also oppose going back to watch a show that I missed when it aired that is anything less than an absolute classic. What would I gain from going back to watch triple (or was it quintuple?) agent Sydney Bristow and the various stuff she did which was no doubt a bit sexy (though less sexy than just watching porn) and full of action (though less action than watching an early Jackie Chan movie)? The answer, I am afraid, is absolutely nothing. Whatever would be the point? There are hundreds of shows soon to air as the ratings season starts back in the US and I have no chance of keeping up with them. I will struggle to fit more than a few into my life as it is, why would I go back and watch something (and watch out for the key word here) OLD?

Because ultimately, I think this is the problem. Stuff that is old is automatically less interesting than stuff that is new. Why is this? Because watching something old is, always in some respect, an act of nostalgia. And nostalgia is the single most pointless of human self-indulgences. I could be watching Season 3 of *Buffy* right now thinking about who I was then and how I have changed in the intervening decade and you know what? I would gain absolutely nothing from the process. For two main reasons. First is that nothing about re-watching a show can change how I was then and reflection on who I am now is mostly aided by my reaction to the new. Second is that Joss Whedon is not Aristotle or JamesJoyce. Close re-reading of his texts do not reveal a nuanced and insightful commentary on human nature—his work is not the study of fields like philosophy or social theory. Study of Whedon is relegated to the "mongrel domain" of cultural studies (to quote Pierre Bourdieu), which has made an academic discipline of everything. Thus studies of *Buffy* detailing "depictions of teenagers in 90s pop culture" are a far cry from studies of social justice or philosophical meaning.

This is not to say that one should prohibited from engaging with popular culture. There are even some movies I like enough that I have seen them three or four times. But if a person chooses to re-watch a television season of somewhere between 12 and 24 episodes, they cannot pretend that doing so is akin to re-reading the *Nicomachean Ethics*. And if it is not a study, then what does re-watching amount to? In short, a waste of precious time. Time which could be spent learning or watching something new. Being human is a restless search for the novel, the undiscovered. Re-watching TV is its antithesis. Re-watching a TV show treats life like an endless expanse of time to kill; as if there is nothing better to do than wait for your life to slowly end.

Soon enough we will all be dust and our beloved, oft-watched boxed set of *Firefly* is going to be sitting forlorn in the $3 bin of a second-hand shop. And every hour we wasted re-watching that episode where we almost thought that Mal and Inara were going to kiss is an hour less we were doing anything even remotely worthwhile, useful or... gasp!... entertaining.

© *B. C. Roberts, 2011*

REWATCHING TV
FINDING YOUR HAPPY PLACE
by Geonn Cannon

Nostalgia is dumb. Why bother looking back when there are new and exciting experiences happening right in front of you? So don't buy TV shows on DVD. Also, throw out your wedding album, trash that high school yearbook, and tape over those old home movies (but not with TV shows). My esteemed colleague believes there are far too few minutes on this Earth to "waste" it re-watching a TV show. I respectfully disagree. Yes, every fall I have a minor panic attack when I think about all the new shows coming on and the precious amount of time I have to watch all that I want. But just because there's a new crop of shows doesn't mean you have to turn your back on the favorites of yesteryear.

The first show I actively collected on DVD was *Stargate SG-1*, because it was not only my favorite show, but I honestly believe it changed my life. At the beginning of their eighth season, I embarked on a trip to a convention. My first convention, my first trip out of state (and out of the country). It was really my first time away from home in a new environment where I wasn't my parents' kid or my brother's brother. I was just me, with nothing but myself to rely on, and it was immensely freeing. What going to college must have felt like to smart people. While there, I took a brief side-trip to a small island that sparked an idea, which grew into a story, which became my first published novel.

Stargate SG-1 REALLY meant something to me. The characters and the stories were like old friends, and some days I just long to revisit them. It doesn't matter that I can quote lines, it doesn't matter that I know exactly how Sam Carter is going to save the day or that I know Daniel Jackson really is going to die this time (no matter how briefly). What matters is revisiting that world and seeing the characters you fell in love with. Watching one episode can remind you of the years you spent carving out an hour of your Friday night to take another trip through the Stargate.

We don't have perfect recall. Like my colleague says, there are so many new shows coming out that eventually even my quotable knowledge of *Stargate* begins to fade. I'll forget a favorite joke. I'll be fuzzy on the details. So maybe I'll go back and find an episode that isn't quite so clear in my mind and I'll take a refresher course, and it's almost like watching it again for the first time. An episode that I wasn't completely in love with the first time takes on a whole new life on DVD.

When you're watching a show you love week-to-week, you're a slave to the schedule. If a bad episode comes along, or if it just focuses on a character that's not your favorite, then that's your fix for the week, like it or lump it. But on DVD, that episode is just one of twenty or so. You give it a bit more leeway. And maybe, just maybe, you'll realize that you didn't give it a real chance.

The main argument against rewatching TV shows seems to be "You've already seen this, what's the point?" But it's not rational, it's love. It's comfort food. Sure, the upcoming show *Person of Interest* looks exciting, but so did *Undercovers*. Sometimes you want to watch a show where you know the good guys win and have fantastic snark while doing it. Favorite TV shows are like a comfy sweatshirt. It just makes you feel good to have it back. You know how the *Leverage* team will pull off their con, but that doesn't make it any less exciting to watch them put it together. In some ways, it's even better because you are actually in on the con this time around. You can see all the little traps and pitfalls that you (and the bad guy) overlooked the first time.

Which brings me to my next point: spoilers don't spoil. There was recently a new study that revealed people enjoy a story more when they know how it will end. When you're watching something for the first time, you're anxious. Knowing how it will all turn out relaxes you and allows you to fully enjoy the ride. I may not fully support that theory for first-time viewings, (spoil me for *Sanctuary* and you die, simple as that) but it definitely holds up for repeat viewings. You can relax and get into the story, and that's why people buy TV shows on DVD. It's why people buy books, for the inevitable re-read where they can focus on the story a bit more. The first time through, you're building the house. The second time through, you get to appreciate all the small touches and accents. And these days, with shows becoming more friendly to season-long arcs, you can watch it all from the beginning and pick up the clues you missed the first time around. Shows like *Lost* almost demand rewatching the entire series every now and again.

And the best thing about not only watching but owning your favorite TV shows is converting friends. Maybe one of my friends never saw *Better Off Ted* just because of crappy scheduling or bad advertising (I watched the darn show, and even I'm not sure what day it aired). But I saw it, and I loved it, and I bought the DVD set as soon as I could. And maybe one of your friends sees the set on your shelf, or maybe they realize you're watching a show that barely limped through two seasons before getting axed, and they decide to give it a shot. And now it's shiny and new to them.

I'm not saying run out and buy every season of every show you like. I love *The Office,* but it's on cable way more than enough for you to get your fix. But what about shows that aren't being repeated? I used to love *The Invisible Man* on Sci-Fi, but it's never shown. I recently got the DVDs and I'm falling in love with it all over again. Ten years on, I've forgotten a good chunk of what happened on that show. That's why I'm so eager for a

Terriers release. That show will never be reaired in syndication, and I'm worried one day it won't even be found on the interwebs. Sometimes shows just disappear, and DVDs are a safeguard, promising you'll always be able to find that one episode of that one show you truly loved even if no one else even remembers it.

Sometimes when you buy a TV show on DVD, the episodes are almost like a bonus feature. Maybe you're really buying the commentary, or the behind-the-scenes footage. Maybe the actors and writers went to the trouble of making original webisodes that you can see for the first time in all their glory.

And leaving one of the most important points for last... making a TV show is expensive. Watching on the interwebs for free is fine, but it does nothing for the cast and crew, and it gives the studio very little incentive to keep the show around. When I really love a show, I have no problem shelling out forty or fifty dollars so I can have the show I love while at the same time giving them a little money to keep the show on the air. If you think DVD sales don't matter, watch the latest new episode of *Family Guy* or *Futurama* and get back to me.

I'm not including the benefits of watching on DVD versus watching live – no insanely irritating bugs in the corner (I don't WANT to watch *Ghost Hunters International*, so stop covering up a quarter of the show I DO want to see with those pop-ups), no commercials – because that's not the issue. The issue is shelling out your hard-earned money for a show you've already watched.

I take pride in the fact that I've seen every episode of *Stargate SG-1* at least five times. I can quote Aldo Raine's full speech from his first scene of *Inglourious Basterds* ("My name is Lieutenant Aldo Raine, and I'm putting together a special team and I need me eight soldiers. Eight. Jewish. Am'rican soldiers.").

New is great. New is exciting. What's old to one person may be new to someone else. I'm just getting into the original UK version of *Life on Mars*, and I'm doing it on DVD. But just because something is new doesn't make it inherently better than something you've already seen. I'll take the pilot of *Lost* over any single episode of *Undercovers*. We revisit the things we love. We refresh our memories of characters, stories, quotes because sometimes life is long. Life is busy. And we need to turn the page back and think, "Oh, yeah, *that's* why I love Sam Carter."

No one can buy every single show they like on DVD, it's just not feasible. But the shows you love, the shows that in five years you may have an itch to see one more time... those are the shows that are worth paying a little money for, just so you'll always have it.

Shh, shh, hold on... this is my favorite part.

SLASHER FILMS
TERRIBLY ADDICTIVE
by David Baldwin

How does one write something positive about a subgenre of horror filmmaking the premise of which can basically be reduced down to one deranged individual systematically murdering a group of rather clueless others? Sure, the slasher film genre is one that likely will never disappear, but how does one really explain their enjoyment of the genre? Is it even possible?

Intellectually, I hate slasher films. Like, really hate them – but to the point that I love to hate them. No matter how bad each may be, I keep going back again and again, thinking the next one will provide me with the worthwhile experience the last one did not. I continue to be disappointed, but despite this, there is just something about the genre, something I cannot put my finger on, that draws me irresistibly back to the theater for the next attempt. I do not tend to revisit the same movie twice, but I will always watch new films that come out in this particular field. In fact, I doubt I have watched nearly as many films from any single other genre than I have with slasher films. They are always in abundance, and every year brings a new supply fresh for the taking.

One of the more obvious reasons for this, I think, is the sheer creativity. In any half-decent slasher film, the killer has to take out his/her victim in some form of visually exciting display every single time. There is no room for a lousy or half-assed kill. Even the most gruesome of death scenes in these films has some element of theatricality. And for the most part, filmmakers will spend almost the entirety of their efforts in making sure these scenes, above any others, look the best. Forget the plots, forget the character developments – the kills are what make these films fall in line with their brethren, and are at the heart of what makes the genre tick. And much like myself, audiences eat them up. What's not to love, when a movie starts off with an innocent scene of one or two people just hanging out, only to soon find themselves sliced and diced into tiny pieces in the most ridiculous fashion ever?

Another reason I enjoy these movies is just how captivating I find some of these killers. Freddy Krueger is one of the most interesting film characters ever created, and seeing Robert Englund take on the character in six sequels and one spin-off will always be a much more worthwhile experience than the latest cookie-cutter comedy or huge miss Oscar-baiting drama. The plots may get sillier, the characters may even barely fit into the grand scheme of things, but seeing Freddy at his consistent best will always be a treat you just cannot replicate in any other genre of film.

174

And the list goes on: Jason Voorhees, Michael Myers, Leatherface, Pinhead, Jigsaw, Chucky (who still terrifies me to this day) – the possible additions are just endless. These are just the killer characters I picked off the top of my head in ten seconds.

But I think this is also where the disconnect comes in for me. As much as I enjoy watching films starring these wacky characters, none of the movies in which they star are particularly very good. They are good for what they are, perhaps, but it is always puzzling that they were ever deemed good enough to inspire endless amounts of sequels, or even warrant the endless number of remakes (I can already sense a *Saw* remake waiting in the wings). Sure, they are fun to watch with a group, or sometimes on your own for a light chuckle or two, but nothing more. It truly is a genre whose enjoyment comes squarely out of how you feel towards what these films are selling. You need to be able to cheer for the villain. You need to be able to withstand horribly concocted drivel masquerading as the stuff of nightmares.

The exception to all of this can be found in the original slasher horror film, which is nothing short of a masterpiece. No, I am not talking about John Carpenter's *Halloween*, and I am not even going to touch Tobe Hooper's *The Texas Chain Saw Massacre* (but will point out that both are better than their modern remakes). No, I am talking about Alfred Hitchcock's *Psycho* – widely regarded as the first movie to kickstart this killer craze.

But while *Psycho* may be responsible for much of what has come after it, it also acts as a bit of an anomaly when discussing the phenomenon as a whole. It follows the conventions of slasher film in that it has a mysterious killer taking out unwitting individuals in various gory ways, but that is where the comparisons between it and its later facsimiles start to dissolve. For one thing, it is not okay to hate this film. For another, every single element, every frame, has become legend. Norman Bates. The Bates Motel. The shower. Janet Leigh. A boy who loves his mother. This is truly ground zero for slashers, and is the one movie every new effort sets out to (or should set out to) top. They all fail miserably. Even Gus Van Sant's 1998 shot-for-shot remake, featuring a rare freaky dramatic performance from Vince Vaughn, did not even come close to comparing to Hitchcock's original. Hell, even *Psycho* has a handful of crappy sequels made specifically to cash in on the original's wild popularity. It is doubtful any slasher film will ever come close to topping its greatness.

The in-thing among slasher filmmakers since the mid-1990s has been the use of self-parody, and the deliberate camping up of everything. It works out for some movies (I will always hold a special place in my heart for *Jason X*, where Jason Voorhees gives up his time in Camp Crystal Lake to go kill teenagers on a futuristic space station), and not so much for others (the less said about *Seed of Chucky* the better). It makes for an interesting experience each time, because this is one genre that is always reinventing itself in order to stay current, to stay in touch with the audiences. It also leads to experiments like *Wes Craven's New Nightmare* and *Behind the Mask: The Rise of Leslie Vernon*, and right away, you can hark back to how creative and theatrical these horror film tend to be.

Yes, I find it fun to hate on these films, but there really is something inherently intriguing about the genre as a whole, in its innovativeness and its ability to shock, and in how enjoyable it is to watch these films. I am currently in the middle of watching all of the *Halloween* films. And while none of them are all that great, I still find something endearing about Michael Myers' need to kill.

And, hey, if you can find the comic genius in watching a hulking monster in a hockey mask murder a young woman by beating her against a tree while wrapped up in her sleeping bag, then clearly you can appreciate the genre for what it is and sets out to do every time.

SLASHER FILMS
JUST TERRIBLE
by Rachel Hyland

I still remember the first slasher horror movie I ever saw. I was twelve years old, and it was at a sleepover for my friend Belinda's birthday party. The movie chosen for this occasion was *Friday the 13th Part II* – I can only suppose because Belinda's mother hated mine, and wanted to bury her under a mountain of therapy bills – and as we all sat there watching this heretofore forbidden fruit, dosed up on sugar and adrenaline and the grown-upness of it all, I had never been more terrified of anything in my life.

As the foreboding music eeked its way towards each gruesome kill, I covered my face with my hands so repeatedly that my cowardice drew the notice of the assembled pajama-clad girls. Much teasing ensued, but despite it revealing me as a Grade A chicken, I simply could not watch. Eventually, I couldn't even stand to listen. I excused myself to go to the bathroom and just stayed there until another friend came to check up on me half an hour later, presumably to make sure I hadn't been waylaid by a hockey mask-wearing lunatic on my way back (and if they're reading this: hi Bea and Sam!). I could not be coaxed out of the bathroom until I was at last assured the movie was over and that those big-haired teens at Camp Crystal Lake had squealed their last.

Needless to say, slasher horror and I have not been on good terms ever since.

Now, admittedly, I had always been one of those scaredy-kids who'd hide behind the couch during *Doctor Who* (for me, it was always the fearsome Cybermen who sent me diving for cover). And my parents, while very liberal and careless with my viewing habits by today's standards – I knew all the words to the raunchy *Grease* soundtrack by the time I'd turned 6, and by 8 I knew about exciting career opportunities in exotic dance and prostitution from watching *Flashdance* and *Risky Business* – were not themselves fans of the horror genre, and so I had not really been exposed to it. But my reaction to this movie, far different from that of the other girls watching it with me – and who were equally inexperienced of such things – cannot be so simply explained.

It was not the blood and guts that disturbed me, though to be sure, I liked it not. It wasn't even that damned effective score, which definitely accomplished its dread purpose in raising my pulse rate dramatically. No, I hated this first taste of the slasher movie genre because everything that was happening in it was just so *wrong*. There was this guy gleefully slicing up innocent youth and it seemed we were supposed to be happy about this – even supposed to be cheering him on. I wasn't happy. I wasn't cheering. I was aghast. Just why, I wondered, was the senseless slaughter of these unfortunate teenagers being so... celebrated? Why was this bloodthirsty villain being made out to be a hero? Did no one else consider the inevitable sadness of these kids' parents? Did no one else wonder how many lives would be destroyed, due to this one criminal's insane acts of random violence?

Okay, yes, even then I had too many thoughts.

Since this unsuccessful first attempt, there has, of course, been more than one chance for the genre to redeem itself in my eyes. As I grew older, it became a social necessity to watch horror movies – that was far from the first sleepover at which such a trauma had to be endured – and I had to find mechanisms I could use to cope with them rather than hiding in the bathroom for hours at a time (though *Halloween* left me with no alternative. It was either that or poke out my own eyes with a nail file.) The only way I managed to get through these movies was to de-humanize the people in them. I would make of the killer some kind of monster hunter and of his seemingly blameless prey merciless demons in disguise; in that way, I could cheer for Michael Myers or Alex Hammond or Leatherface and somehow make it through the awfulness, if not happily, at least without complaint. (I must admit, this mind trick never worked with Freddy – but then, Freddy was somewhat supernatural himself, and also enjoyed the benefit of the occasional pithy quip; of all these movies, I found the *Nightmare on Elm Street*s the least arduous.) Since I reached adulthood, I can count on one hand the amount of slasher horror movies I have seen, and not a single one has changed my mind on this topic... which is not to say that I don't often enjoy movies from the horror genre.

I love the *Evil Dead* flicks and most anything featuring vampires, and I don't mind a good ghost story (though one particularly foolish solo viewing of *The Ring* led to a week's worth of nightmares). I love, love, love the creepy subtlety of (most of) M. Night Shyamalan's work; and then, of course, there's all things Hitchcock, who was a genius and a wonder and is the person I always choose in one of those hypothetical "Who would you most like to have dinner with, dead or alive?" scenarios. On TV, *Buffy* and *Supernatural* have been known to scare the bejeezus out of me and yet I adore them both with an almost unnatural passion, and I am even a huge fan of *Dexter*… which is odd, because it is the very human nature of their anti-heroes that is what so disturbs me about the slasher horror genre as a whole.

Now, I don't want to go all televangelist fake-moralizing here, 'cause those people are just tiresome. To be clear, I don't think that slasher movies are any more to blame for the evils that men do than I believe *Grand Theft Auto* will make kids grow up to be amoral, drug-dealing carjackers. Humanity dealt with crazed killers long before Hollywood made them cool, and the fact that there are more serial killers nowadays (with a goodly percentage coming out of America) can be more reasonably attributed to a massive rise in worldwide population and standards of living than it can to, say, Wes Craven's body of work. But I do think that slasher horror movies, with their gratuitous bloodshed and focus on the cult of the killer – and innate sexism, though that is somewhat beside the current point – cannot help but desensitize us to the suffering of others, and perhaps even suggest a viable career option to anyone already that way inclined. Craven's *Scream* is a terrific movie and I love it a lot, not only for its amusing self-referentiality and its clever, clever twists, but because it also highlights the genre's biggest danger: not everyone has it in them to be a conscienceless killer, but for those few that do, a steady diet of scary movies would probably act as a pretty decent guidebook of how to best go about it.

I concede without argument that horror, as a whole, plays an essential role in narrative fiction, especially in the way that its monsters often act as compelling metaphors for our manifold human frailty and vice. But the subgenre of slasher horror does nothing but provide us with detailed and almost loving depictions of senseless, needless human evil – and I think there is enough of that in real life.

© *Rachel Hyland, 2012*

STAR TREK VS. STAR WARS TREK!

by Rachel Hyland

First, let me make something perfectly clear. I don't hate *Star Wars*. The original trilogy is a pleasant enough way to while away some geekly time — Han Solo is the BEST; the prequel trilogy is good for a laugh if nothing else — and Ewan McGregor rocks the hessian with Mustafarian lava flow-level hotness; *The Force Awakens* is amazing; I am very fond of R2-D2; and I don't even mind a little time spent in the company of animated Ani in *The Clone Wars*. (If only Hayden Christensen had been that animated!)

With all of that stipulated, however, let me tell you why *Star Trek* is so very much better than *Star Wars* that even a malfunctioning emotion chipped-Data wouldn't find it funny.

Now, I could go on here about Jar Jar Binks and shameless videogame-selling pod race wankery and racial stereotyping and wooden performances and the like, and all you Warsies out there know that all of it would be very well-deserved. But harping on about the disasters that were the prequel movies feels a lot like shooting Mon Calamari in a barrel; few of you are fans, and even despite the dizzyingly bad plotting and searingly awful dialogue — by turns tedious, overly-technical and melodramatic — at least those movies have the virtue of kickass special effects and unintentional comedy value. So I will, instead, focus on the original trilogy. The Holy Trinity. The one that has spawned countless pilgrimages and Stormtrooper costume purchases and trading card collections and comic book titles and tie-in novels and theme weddings and conventions and action figures and more than is perhaps necessary episodes of *Family Guy* and *Robot Chicken*.

I guess that's what I don't really understand. Whence the obsession? Especially when it comes to my biggest issue of the whole Warsian ideal:

The Force.

When the dismissive Han said, in the original movie, to a Luke all hopped up on Jedi-envy: "Hokey religions are no match for a blaster at your side, kid," I couldn't agree more. The whole Force rigmarole is hokey, and simplistic besides. *I was born with a gift... I can use this ephemeral power ... I am therefore worthy to defend the galaxy!* Think about it: how do you get to be a Jedi? An innate talent is trained and exploited. (Or used with no training at all, if you're Rey.) And how do you get into Starfleet? You study hard. *Star Wars* champions an elitist aristocracy; there are princesses and lords and inherited prestige. *Star Trek* is all about the meritocracy; even an illiterate Ferengi* can aspire to a place in Starfleet, if he applies himself.

And, you know, if you're gonna have power-though-magic (and that's essentially what The Force is; magic in space) you shouldn't then disenchant it with a whole sciencey explanation. Midi-chlorians! How terribly, depressingly dull. Oh, wait, I was gonna give *Wars* fans a pass on *The Phantom Menace*, et al, wasn't I? Oh, well. I won't bring it up again.

I mean, it's not like the many incarnations of *Star Trek* haven't had more than their share of woes, and ones that I have always struggled to justify. Inconsistent characterization, blatant plot holes and continuity errors, abhorrent objectification of women, and often pitiful attempts at comedy are only some of the crosses Trekkies have had to bear over the years. The original *Star Trek* was hampered by its labored format; *Star Trek: The Next Generation*, by its aggressive political correctness; *Star Trek: Deep Space Nine*, by its unsubtle religious allegory; and yes, by the end of the frustrating *Star Trek: Voyager*, I'll admit I was mostly still watching just to see seven-year veteran Ensign Harry Kim (Garrett Wang) get a damn promotion. (I'm not going to dignify *Enterprise* and its insane captain with even more than another passing mention; if *Star Wars* fans can ignore their prequel nonsense, then we Trekkies can ignore ours.)

But at the same time, *Star Trek*, in all its incarnations, set the benchmark for intellectual and provocative drama. These are shows that deal in elegant metaphor with some of the biggest issues of our time. Inequality, racism, terrorism, tyranny.

Star Trek — even bad *Star Trek* — gives us people we care about as they pursue humanity's quest to explore the unknown. It gives us fallible yet honorable heroes and visionaries, out there in the wide dark seeking only to learn about our universe, looking for the now famous "new life and new civilizations." And, yes, much of that new life is remarkably like the old life, just with funny hair; but some of it is emphatically not. The Horta are rocks. The Q are beings of pure energy who exist on a higher plane. The Changelings are essentially one big pool of sentient goo. *Star Trek* led us not only to ponder the big questions like what it means to be human, but also had us wondering exactly what constituted life itself.

It was, it is, a show of big themes. Themes of unanimity, freedom, equality and friendship. They are enduring ones — ideas that lift the spirit, and ignite the soul.

What are the themes of *Star Wars*? That even whiny kids can grow up to be heroes if they have the right genes? That your sister is totally doable? That if some dude you don't even like falls out a window you should go off and start slaughtering children? (Sorry, I know I said I wouldn't bring up the prequels again, but come on! Poor little padawans.)

Also, *Trek*'s ultimate villains? Just way, way creepier.

Take Vader. Quite frankly, I just don't get what all the fuss is about. What's the big deal? Sure, he's a bad guy, sure he has a shadowy past, sure he's deadly and ultimately conflicted and the end result of fear leading to anger and anger leading to the Dark Side. But you know what? I'll see your Vader and raise you the Borg.

The ultimate in "This Could Happen to You" parables, these cyborgs are on a quest for "perfection," which they believe will be gained by forcibly assimilating others into their Collective. They are emotionless, senseless drones, working as one to achieve the impossible. They come not to convert but to conquer, and though Voyager managed to demystify them to the point of dullness, they still remain the most chilling of all possibly futures sci-fi has shown us. (And if you think it unfair that I offer up an entire race in rebuttal to one man, then I give you one word: Khan. No, wait, sorry: Khaaaaaaaan!)

I could go on, but I will instead merely ask you to consider this: *Star Trek* is such a glorious playground that J. J. Abrams and his minions were able to produce their magnificently rebooted 2009 alternate universe version of past events in which everything old is new again. But what happened when George Lucas attempted to go back and alter the past of his universe?

He made Greedo shoot first.

By virtue of that fact alone, *Trek* wins.

© Rachel Hyland, 2017

STAR TREK VS. *STAR WARS* *WARS*!
by Sara Paige

The truth is, I was a Trekkie long before I ever liked *Star Wars*, and really only fell through the black hole of *Star Wars* fandom in the past year. I have about 50 times the amount of nostalgia for *The Next Generation* and *Deep Space Nine* than I do for any other piece of science fiction television.

For me, the problem with these comparisons is that they are kind of apples to oranges, or rather, science fiction to fantasy. Because that's the debate, right? *Star Wars* is not science fiction, it's fantasy in space, and *Star Trek* is just fiction in space. And the problem with science fiction is that when we argue about what's better, it always comes down to well, it's not fantasy. I mean, it has rules, after all. Of course, those rules oftentimes violate all actual rules of physics, but at least it's not that flighty fantasy crap. And people who care about that sort of thing can justifiably go clutch their pearls in the corner and have the vapors about mystical force energy.

Except here's the thing: fantasy is actually more fun. You can make things up, create entire rules with their own physics and then mess around with those rules sometimes. And you can see it in the first argument in this debate. The discussion of how great *Star Trek* is takes up about 5% of the piece. And you want to know why? Because *Star Wars* is simply more fun. I grew up on *Trek*, but you know what? When I fell for *Star Wars*, I fell way harder than I ever fell for Captains Kirk, Picard and their ilk. *Trek* is like the dependable, sleepy partner who wakes up at 6:00 sharp, makes coffee and goes to work in data entry and comes home at 5:30 every day. If you've seen *The Original Series* and *The Next Generation*, then *Deep Space Nine* and *Voyager* are not a shock, you know what is most likely to happen: interesting moral tales using alien diversity. The costumes are the same, the characters resemble each other after a while, and it's a really safe place to come back to.

Star Wars is not dependable: it is completely bonkers. *Star Wars* has fourteen-year-old Queens of planets who are elected and have term limits. *Star Wars* has evil politicians plotting for decades for total Galactic control. *Star Wars* has Space Monks with laser swords upholding peace and justice who rest their entire future with a whiny farmer kid and a princess. You never know who is going to get a limb chopped off, who will go bad (or come back from being bad), or what new familial tie will spring up. I feel like I'm on a roller coaster and I don't know if there's a loop or a dip coming because who really knows with this saga? Of course the movies are polarizing, but that's part of it. Who is really talking about Captain Janeway fifteen years later? Now how about Darth Vader? Greedo Shot First (or at least at the same time) has been A Thing for nearly twenty years and there are clearly people still not over these five seconds of film. Has there ever been anything in *Trek* that's stirred up that much emotion about anything?

The thing is, in *Star Wars*, there's so much there. Every single movie feels like at least three movies in one; they are just that dense. I can come back every time and see something I missed the other ten times I saw it. I can see them in three different viewing orders and get something new from the experience. Don't even ask yourself if *Star Trek* can do that — can any piece of media other than *Star Wars* really do that? And this is why fantasy always wins. Fantasy is just more interesting than science fiction. That doesn't mean sci-fi is bad by any stretch of the imagination, but it's why J. J. Abrams's *Star Trek* did okay, and his *Star Wars* busted every movie record out there. There's not even a comparison, and it hurts my younger Trekkie self to even compare the two, but there you have it. Sorry, *Trek*.

© *Sara Paige, 2017*

STARGATE UNIVERSE
WHY I HATE *STARGATE UNIVERSE*
by Rachel Hyland

It is not in my nature to leave a story incomplete. I never walk out of movies (even when that movie is *Aeon Flux*), or stop buying comic books (even when that comic book is *Spider-Man Loves Mary Jane*). I watched *Star Trek: Voyager* to the very end, and even managed to somehow stomach *Enterprise*. Hell, I'm still reading *Anita Blake, Vampire Hunter* novels, and those things are basically just porn, now.

But I'm afraid I just cannot stick it out, this time. This time, one particularly beloved franchise has gone too darned far. Oh, I'll still buy its tie-in novels, and listen to its audio dramas, and re-watch the adored original series over and over (and over and over), and its first spin-off series... well, at least over once. But I will not – will not! – subject myself to another episode of the thrice-damned, ill-conceived lunacy that is *Stargate Universe*.

I just can't do it. I am ashamed of myself, but there it is. I just... hate it.

Even *Stargate Infinity* was better.

Stargate SG-1 is one of the finest science fiction series of all time. It is complex, thought-provoking, humorous, and innovative. It is big on the whole "humans are awesome" motif that is prevalent in a lot of sci-fi — which I shouldn't like so much, but I can't help the way it sings to my soul — yet it also asks the big questions, and insists that you care about the answers; makes you laugh and think and feel, and fall completely in love with its main characters. Plus, that Michael Shanks (Dr. Daniel Jackson) is adorable.

Stargate Atlantis, meanwhile... well, it's a lot like *SG-1*, except set in a different galaxy, and spends less time on tree-and-rock-filled alien worlds. While definitely second in my estimation to the original, it still has a core of genius to it that makes it compelling viewing. There are bad guys to overcome, relationships to fret about, matters of morality, expediency, politics, and self-sacrifice to ponder. Plus, that Joe Flanigan (Col. John Sheppard) is adorable.

And at first, I have to say, I kind of loved *Stargate Universe*, too. How different it was! It was complex and dark, disconcerting yet entertaining, with strong performances and unconventional story-telling. It was a new twist to the Stargate mythology, all these people stuck on the Ancient ship *Destiny*, out on their own, not knowing whither they were going or how they were going to get home. Yes, it was vaguely reminiscent of some other popular sci-fi shows (*Voyager, Battlestar*

Galactica, and *Farscape*, to name a few), but if it owed a debt to any of them, it paid it by astoundingly owing no debt to its direct progenitor. Plus, that Brian J. Smith (Lt. Scott) is adorable.

For the first four episodes, I actually kind of loved it. For the next couple, I... didn't mind it. After that, I remained, at least, willing to give it a chance. And now... well, now, I'm afraid I really do hate *Stargate Universe.*

Here's why:

The Affair of a Commanding Officer with a Subordinate

I will not deny that I am among the legion of viewers who have always wished that SG-1's Jack O'Neill (Richard Dean Anderson) and Samantha Carter (Amanda Tapping) would someday get together. Of course, I know it's against the Air Force regulations to which they are subject, and I know the creators of the show have said they'll never let us see it happen (which is why the gods invented fan fiction, I suppose), but hope does indeed spring eternal. I just really, really want those two to get their happily ever after. (When you've saved the world a dozen times, surely you deserve it?)

However, when watching *Stargate Universe*, it feels like... well, it feels like I am being chastised for ever wanting that at all. See, in this new *Stargate world*, the very married Colonel Everett Young (Louis Ferreira) has clearly had some illicit... er... debriefings with the lovely young Lieutenant Tamara Johansen (Alaina Huffman) in the past. She had even resigned from her position under his command in order to escape the sleaziness of it all, before being forced to accompany her erstwhile paramour into inadvertent exile aboard the *Destiny*.

I want to be clear that I have no objection to their rule-breaking affair itself. What I object to is the fact that, by making it all so tawdry and cheap – not to mention debilitating for the both of them – the creators seem to be implying that such a relationship between O'Neill and Carter (he, an older Colonel, she a young, blonde officer under his command) would have been so, as well.

Watching Young and TJ in post-post-coital action, full of regret and remorse and ridiculousness, I feel like I'm being admonished for the wishful shippy thinking that was a big draw card for me throughout the ten years of *SG-1*. And this from the people who gave *Atlantis'* Dr. Rodney McKay (David Hewlett) a gorgeous girlfriend in the person of Dr. Jennifer Keller (Jewel Staite), who actually chose him over the manly form of Ronon (Jason Momoa). Talk about your wish-fulfillment fantasies! What's that? A room full of science fiction writers makes the girl choose the science nerd with the personality disorder and citrus allergy over the tall, muscled jock with the kung fu moves and the really big... weapon? Astounding!

But, hey, speaking of Jack and Sam...

Wasted Cameo Appearances

While the Daniel Jackson *Introduction to the Stargate* collection was a pretty nifty touch, cameo-wise, in the *SGU* series premiere, the misuse of Samantha Carter and Jack O'Neill in that same premiere was nothing short of criminal.

Leaving aside the asinine dialogue of the previously sharp-as-a-tack O'Neill (of which, more anon), let's focus on the fact that they were both in the same scene, and yet there was not even an inkling that their relationship might finally be something more than professional. At least in Season 4 of *Stargate Atlantis*, when Carter took over the base as commander, they threw the shippy viewer a bone with the presence of a framed picture of SG-1-era Jack O'Neill among her possessions. In *SGU*, nothing.

But, hey, speaking of Jack...

What in the Hell has Happened to Jack O'Neill?

Now, I'm not talking, here, about the pasty skin and doughy form of Richard Dean Anderson. The man's in his sixties, and the late-middle-age spread and pallor in his cheeks are perfectly consistent with a desk-bound Air Force General who has always had a particular fondness for pie, cake and Froot Loops. (And who has, no doubt, been "eating his feelings," pining away for his beloved — and apparently unattainable — Carter.) Sure, his cracked voice has him sounding more like he should be shooing kids off his lawn than commanding Earth's first line of defense, but that's okay, too. Richard Dean Anderson, well-matured or not, is ever a joy to behold, and certainly isn't the problem I now have with General Jack O'Neill.

It is the quality of the lines he was given. Or, more particularly, the lack thereof.

When, in the first episode, "Air, Part 1," Colonel Young shows a modicum of humility and questions his own ability to lead such a disparate team of castaways out in the wide black somewhere, Jack objects that he, too, was ill-equipped for his first mission through the Stargate. "I think the bottom line is, none of us are qualified," he croaks. What?

When, in the episode "Earth," Young objects to a risky, baby boffin-sponsored plan to get his crew home, and wants to discuss it first with said crew, Jack tells him – despite his years of managing SG-1 and the SGC as a kind of collaborative effort: "You're in command of that ship. It's not a democracy." Huh?

And then Jack goes and replaces Young as commander of the *Destiny*, via remote-controlled avatar, despite its inevitable effect on morale, and is later somehow astounded when the young scientists' plan to get everyone home doesn't work. (Did he even discuss its viability with Carter?)

I have never been so mad at Jack O'Neill. Not even when he made it with that Laira woman on Edora.

Okay, sure, maybe it wasn't all his decision to completely override the operational authority of the man in the field. But the Jack O'Neill we used to know would have made it his decision. And when later in that same episode, Young (in his meat suit), stands in front of a room full of Air Force-types and basically tells O'Neill to shove it in the snippiest fashion, and O'Neill merely grimaces as the recalcitrant *Destiny* commander stalks away, all I could think was: "No way would Jack take that! But he totally deserves it!" It's like they want us to despise O'Neill now, to like Young more than we like him, to move on from the old Colonel we loved so much, and suddenly take up with the new. (Perhaps that's why they called him "Young"? To emphasize that O'Neill is kinda "old"?) It really is the lamest attempt ever at passing the torch.

Plus, look at who it's being passed to! I mean, really, who are these people Jack has working for him, nowadays? As head of Homeworld Security, he has jurisdiction over all SGC-related personnel. Sure, the pesky International Oversight Advisory probably weighs in more often than not, but it's gotta be pretty much Jack's show. And, for some completely incomprehensible reason, he has elected to put his trust in some really unworthy candidates. Young was even, by his own admission, Jack's first choice to lead the expedition that eventually led to *Destiny*! (Wow. Good call, there, General. Really.)

But, hey, speaking of those unworthy candidates...

Anti-heroes (who are More Anti than Hero)

Are they kidding us with these guys? Is this some kind of stylized, space-set homage to Quentin Tarantino? It's a prank! A lark! Or possibly just a self-assigned challenge, to see if these characters can be set up to be such unmitigated bastards that they are hated the world over, and then later redeemed through the clever use of sympathy-arousing backstories.

Maybe the *Stargate* brain trust didn't want to rest on their laurels. Having previously been successful in making Rodney McKay into a worthwhile human being – and even making the supercilious IOA tool Richard Woolsey (Robert Picardo) marginally likeable in Season 5 of *Atlantis* – perhaps they wanted more of a challenge.

Forget McKay or Woolsey... it will take a redemption on the level of *Buffy* and *Angel*'s Wesley Wyndham-Price to make most of the *SGU* characters even passably, remotely, imaginably appealing.

To begin with, there are your Lesser Evils: your Sergeant Greer (Jamil Walker Smith), your Lt. Scott, your Drs. Volker (Patrick Gilmour) and Brody (Peter Kelamis). They're all just garden variety annoyances: Greer with his barely-leashed homicidal rage; Scott with his pretty, but vacant, eyes and Barney Stinson ways; the Drs. with their intellectual self-righteousness and put-upon martyrdom. Annoying, all, but not the worst of it.

That falls to the Unholy Trinity.

First, Dr. Nicholas Rush (Robert Carlyle) is Rodney McKay without the wit, charm, and basic human decency. (There was a time I would have said that Rodney McKay was Rodney McKay without the wit, charm, etc.) Rush is a spineless, heartless, worthless individual, whose scientific curiosity and furtherance of his own agenda takes precedence over the lives of anyone on the ship. Even a Cylon would find this guy calculating and detached. As a kid, he probably pulled the wings off butterflies.

Next, the libidinous Colonel Young is a weak and uninspiring commander, with a chip on his shoulder and a barely repressed megalomania, who, in the midseason cliff-hanger, left one of his crew – a troublesome one, admittedly, but still a human being – stranded on an alien world with little or no supplies. (Of course, we all know Rush will get that old beater of an alien ship to fly and go find *Destiny* in it, but that's hardly the point, is it?)

And finally, back on Earth – most of the time – is Colonel Telford (Lou Diamond Phillips), a brown-nosing, vindictive and moribund specimen who appears to have a crush on Young's wife, along with a vendetta against anyone who has ever thwarted his august authority.

Wow. Of such outstanding quality is the US military made. Apparently.

But, hey, speaking of Rush, Young and Telford...

Big Name Stars

Could this be the reason that these three major characters are such jerks? 'Cause they're portrayed by proper, recognizable Hollywood-types, who perhaps demanded complex and interesting roles if they were to deign to appear in a Syfy original? One of the great things about the other *Stargate* series is that you might have recognized a few stars (Richard Dean Anderson was MacGyver, of course; Don S. Davis [General Hammond] was Scully's dad in *The X-Files*; and Joe Flanigan played Jen's love interest in *Dawson's Creek* one time), but by and large it was a feast of new talent. Sure, there'd be the odd guest star you'd know from other Canada-shot shows (More *X-Files* alums, people from *Andromeda* or *Due South* or *Viper*), and sometimes the new-blood approach backfired (as in the case of the first season *Atlantis* failure, Rainbow Sun Franks as Lt. Ford). However, I'd rather the occasional mistaken casting than to have had more well-known names take the roles of Vala Mal Doran and Cameron Mitchell away from cult-favorite *Farscape* refugees Claudia Black and Ben Browder.

But these three stars of *Stargate Universe*... they're just not quite so cult-y.

Robert Carlyle, of course, played the eponymous character of Hamish Macbeth in the popular British series, as well as appearing in bona fide hits like *Trainspotting* and *The Full Monty*. He was in *The Beach* with Leonardo di Caprio, *The 51st State* with Samuel L. Jackson, and he even played a Bond villain! (Admittedly, it was in that one with Denise Richards as a nuclear physicist, but still.)

Lou Diamond Phillips first got his break in the late 80s, playing tragic Latin popster Ritchie Valens in *La Bamba*, which he followed up with *Young Guns* (and its sequel), as well as a legion of bad, bad movies, including my personal favorite item on the Diamond Phillips resume, *Bats*. (Giant mutated bats and *Starship Troopers'* Dina Meyer: what's not to like?) More recently, he was seen in an episode of *Psych*, which I consider pretty much the pinnacle of success.

Ferreira's probably the least known of the trio (possibly because of his uncertainty as to his name: dude, is it Louis Ferreira or Justin Louis? Pick one!). He's one of those Hey, I Know That Guy! guys, whom you see in something and can't quite place, but you refuse to cheat and use the IMDb, and so you lie awake until it finally comes to you in the middle of the night that he was in an episode of *The Pretender*, or *The Sentinel*, or *Two Guys, a Girl and a Pizza Place*.

But, hey, speaking of the middle of the night...

Darkness

Okay, we get it. You're on a largely empty, millennia-old ship in the void of space, with little power and no control over your destination. Rations are scarce, tempers are on edge, and all is very possibly lost. You're light years (light decades?) away from home and hearth, friends and family, Taco Bell and TV. Existence is futile.

But does that mean everything has to be so darned drab? So very mind-numbingly dreary? Couldn't we see a little color here and there? Color that does not come from Eli's omnipresent red "You Are Here" T-shirt, or Chloe's equally ubiquitous (except when she gets naked, as frequently happens) pink top?

All that grayness is just so depressing.

But, hey, speaking of Chloe's pink top...

Chloe (Elyse Levesque)

I guess I don't actually hate her, per se. It's more that I just don't get the point of her. Is she the every-girl thrust into the extraordinary situation, kind of the focus for the audience's own desire to be a part of such an intergalactic adventure? Is she the side-kick? The mascot? The *SGU* equivalent of a *Doctor Who* companion? Or is she just some random hot chick who does yoga and gets it on with the first available cute guy in uniform (Lt. Scott – have I mentioned that he's cute?), not seeing the worth of the adorable Eli Wallace (David Blue), and thus setting up a very tedious love triangle?

I think the actress who plays her does a fine job, all things considered (and she is, as already mentioned, really hot, and good at yoga – plus, how cool a name is Elyse Levesque?), but within the scope of the ship, Chloe is a nonentity. The most recent episode, "Justice" (01.10), wherein Colonel Young is accused of the murder of one of his own crew (yes, murder! And only half a season in!) and she is asked to defend him, reeked of what they used to call in *Star Trek* fandom BIMOL. (But, it's my only line!)

Chloe is, I feel, not only unnecessary, but also kind of pathetic. Yes, there were many non-warrior-y civilians involved in *SG-1* and *Atlantis* – Daniel Jackson, Jonas Quinn (Corin Nemec) and Elizabeth Weir (Torri Higginson) come to mind – but they were absolutely essential personnel, all bringing their specialized skills and formidable intelligences to contribute to their respective adventures. It seems like Chloe's just around to look pretty and cry a lot. And is it just me, or has she gotten to "go home" unreasonably more than anyone else?

But, hey, speaking of "going home"…

The Communication Stones

In *SG-1*, the Ancient Communication Stones caused nothing but trouble. These devices, resembling nothing more than shiny over-sized pet rocks, are the things that allowed civilian barber Joe Spencer (Dan Castellaneta) a peek inside the Top Secret workings of the Stargate Program when he was mentally linked with Jack O'Neill, and they also effectively started the war with the extra-galactic, religious-crusading Ori and their followers in Season 9. The Stones were also up to no good on *Atlantis*, where they allowed a sociopathic thief to take control of Dr. Keller and almost get her executed.

In *SGU*, they aren't outright malicious or war-starting (yet), but they do allow our merry band of castaways the opportunity to phone home. Which they do. A lot. And while this may seem perfectly innocuous, may even seem like a Good Thing, it really kind of isn't. You know what it is? It makes the start of this series feel a little like the end of *Star Trek: Voyager*, when suddenly everyone on the ship could start sending and receiving letters from the Alpha Quadrant (and poor Janeway could get dumped). It feels like… like things aren't really all that bad. They're not all alone. They're not cut off from their superiors, forced to band together to fight as one without having recourse to the rules and the regulations and the ephemeral notions of How Things Are Done. They merely check in with Earth for orders. It's just so… pedestrian.

Plus, how creepy is it that the crew members of the *Destiny* get to hang out inside other peoples' bodies? They're getting drunk in these bodies! Eating who knows what, doing who knows what… having sex

189

with people in these bodies! And what happens to the Earth-bound personnel who find themselves inhabiting someone aboard *Destiny*? Do they get to have sex? No! They just get to try and fix the damn ship, while Young and Camille Wray (Ming-Na) and their ilk get to play around with someone else's equipment.

Creepy, creepy, creepy.

But, hey, speaking of trying to fix the damn ship...

Oh, No! The Ship is Broken! Oh, Wait. Nevermind.

Millennia-old. Okay. That is old. And, obviously, it's difficult to estimate how much repair and overhaul a millennia-old ship would require, since we don't really have any technology that has lasted that long. But if there's anything we've learned about the Ancients, it's that they knew how to build stuff that would stand the test of time. Stargates. Cities. Repositories of Knowledge. Although, to be fair, Atlantis was in need of some major DIY-ing when the original Expedition first arrived there.

But it does seem as if *Destiny* is in really bad shape. Really bad. Which would be fine, if it hadn't become increasingly obvious that whatever the bother *du jour* may be, it'll be fixed with mere moments to spare. That someone will find the right component and get it back through the onboard Stargate, or the ship will solve the problem herself, or some other such improbable *deus ex machina* will occur. And we always know something of the sort is going to happen, of course, since the show could clearly not continue without its main – and most likeable – character.

It's kind of insulting, really. I mean, were we supposed to be surprised when the ship managed to recharge its batteries in the corona of a sun? When Scott found the so-needed lime in the desert? When Young and Scott found a water supply on that ice world? I hope not! But I fear so. However, we can't be, because there is no real tension, and there is no real tension because there is no chance of failure. And that's fine for incidental side-plots of an episode – like we never thought Daniel was actually dead, or that Sheppard was actually prematurely-aged by the Wraith – but not when that very uncertainty is apparently the only point of the story.

But, hey, speaking of insulting...

People

The *Stargate Universe* creators appear to have missed the memo: humans are awesome. Or, at least, we are in science fiction. That's why so much sci-fi resonates so strongly, keeps us reading and watching and buying and obsessing. But it's not merely that humans are awesome; after all, there are humans all over several galaxies, according to the *Stargate* canon. It is that the humans from *Earth* are awesome, able to come in and kick serious alien bad guy butt, despite technological disadvantages and political machinations, and seeming to have no idea what we're doing. We manage to lead a Federation of Planets, or build an interspecies collaborative space station, or bring the feared legions of the hated alien foe to their knees, all after leaving our own planet eons after the other participants in the Galactic Village. We go out into the universe, and we make it our own.

You know why? 'Cause we're awesome.

In *SGU,* however, the humans from Earth are not quite so awesome. (Not even the ones we had previously considered awesome; damn it, Jack!) And maybe it is, in fact, a true reflection of how people would act in this kind of circumstance. Maybe, when finding ourselves cut off from every avenue home, when every day is a battle for survival, when in an environment where no one can be sure of anything, we would all behave as selfishly, and as childishly, as the denizens of the good ship *Destiny*. It actually rings quite true. Which is just so disheartening. Dismaying. Distressing. Disturbing.

And if I wanted my television to be those things, I would watch *The Hills*.

Stargate Universe shows us mankind at its worst, at its most contemptible, its least flattering. Not in that comfortable *Star Trek* way, where the Klingons are the violent part of our nature and the Ferengi represent greed; not even in that less comfortable – kinda racist – *Star Wars* way, where the evil Trade Federation employees evoke Japanese businessmen. Instead, *SGU* gives us a *Moment of Truth*-worthy tour through the ugliness that exists inside us all. And I just do not like the view.

To be honest, this last is what I hate most about *Stargate Universe*. I hate that, in watching it, I find myself kind of hating humanity. We suck. We are not awesome. Or... wait. Maybe we are, and it's just *Stargate Universe* that's not? Yes. I like that idea much better.

So, when *SGU* comes back from its mid-season hiatus on April 2, it can do so without me. I'll probably be watching Season 4 of *Stargate SG-1* for the twenty-eighth time.

Hell, I may even be watching *The Hills*. After ten episodes of *Stargate Universe*, I think maybe I'm ready.

In Fairness...

I guess *SGU* isn't all bad. Here's what I actually like about it:
1. The title.
2. IOA hard-ass Camile Wray (Ming-na) has a girlfriend.
3. Eli (David Blue).
That is all.

STARGATE UNIVERSE
WHY I LOVE *STARGATE UNIVERSE*
by Rachel Day

It is not in my nature to stick with something once I've decided it sucks. I admit to watching only three episodes of *Enterprise*, despite the allure of Scott Bakula. I lost interest in *Lost* somewhere around Season 2, and I barely managed one whole episode of the revamped *Battlestar Galactica* (and yes, I know it was slick, clever and well-produced; that still didn't make me like it.)

I am, however, still very much enjoying the *Stargate* franchise's new offering, *Stargate Universe*. It, too, is slick, clever and well-produced... and I love it.

My first *Stargate* romance was with the original movie. The mix of mythology, action/adventure and science fiction pushed all my happy buttons. Not to mention the friendship, romance and redemption. (And Kurt Russell looking very fit.)

The series *Stargate SG-1* therefore had a lot to live up to, but the casting of *MacGyver*'s Richard Dean Anderson as Col. Jack O'Neill was a good start. By the third episode I was thoroughly infatuated, primarily due to the chemistry between the show's four main actors (Anderson, Amanda Tapping, Michael Shanks, and Christopher Judge). For the next eight years, *SG-1* told imaginative stories with a deft mix of humor and pathos as our intrepid team explored the extraordinary. It was much cleverer than it was ever given credit for and I forgave it for sometimes ignoring characterization for plot because, even when it embraced story arcs, it was essentially an adventure-of-the-week format, and SG-1 did adventure of the week very, very well.

I will say, though, that I came close to falling out of love with the show during its Season 9 revamp. It wasn't the absence of Richard Dean Anderson – because I thought Ben Browder was a fantastic replacement – but there were too many changes, and not always for the good. Quite a few episodes stretched believability to its very limit and beyond, but I slowly found myself falling in love again – albeit in a quieter, more understated way. I was genuinely disappointed when *SG-1* was finally cancelled after its tenth season.

Stargate Atlantis and I had more of an on-again/off-again love affair. I liked the pilot episode, "Rising," but I stopped watching just before the mid-season two-parter as I was just plain bored. "But you stopped watching just when it got very good!" wailed my best friend. So I caught up, conceded that yes, "The Storm" (S01E10) and "The Eye" (S01E11) were fantastic, and carried on watching until Season 2. I hated Season 2 and its idiotic biogenic-warfare storyline. I only tuned in to Season 3 because of a lack of other things to watch, and found myself slowly falling in love again (despite the revolving door on the office of the expedition leader); I remained fondly hooked until *Atlantis* was cancelled after its fifth season.

So I was thrilled – *thrilled* – with the news that another incarnation of Stargate was on the cards. And yet... I also wasn't.

The early signs were ominous. Casting calls indicated a much younger cast than the two previous shows, and had online forums screaming that it was going to be *Stargate 90210*. Then there was the premise that the show was set on a spaceship, which seemed to disregard the major complaints about the last few seasons of *SG-1* and *Atlantis*: not enough of the Stargate, too many of the space battles. Finally, there was the *Voyager*-esque plot, which prompted the question: is there a TV rule that the third spin-off of any successful sci-fi franchise must be about a group of people stranded in another galaxy trying to get home? The only things I was really looking forward to were the announced "increased focus on character development" and the heralded return of Richard Dean Anderson as Lt. Gen. Jack O'Neill, so it was actually with some trepidation that I sat down to view the first episode of *Stargate Universe*.

I was in love after the first hour, and now (admittedly only ten episodes later), I still love it – flaws and all.

Here's why:

The Characters Have Relationships!

For years, one of the criticisms leveled at the franchise has been that there weren't enough moments between the characters; that the friendships and romantic relationships which the fans adored would end up on the cutting room floor all too often in order to make way for scenes that moved the plot forward.

Atlantis's "The Shrine" (S05E06) was applauded for the sweet moment when Sheppard (Joe Flanigan) and McKay (David Hewlett) were simply sitting on the pier drinking beer. "Why can't we have more moments like this?" was the cry. And let's not even mention the lack of one canon kiss between our universe, timeline, non-robot, non-clone, non-influenced-by-alien-virus, non-dream/hallucination Sam and Jack, which would confirm that "going fishing" together actually did mean that the couple got their happily ever after.

That's not the case on *SGU*. And it's not all about ship as in romance and sex (although there's plenty of both if that is your thing). This new show is focused on all the different relationship dynamics between the characters – everything from friendship to professional rivalry to the parent/child bond.

True, some of the relationship dynamics shown are the opposite of friendly. The rivalries between Telford (Lou Diamond Philips), Young (Louis Ferriera), and Rush (Robert Carlyle) are colored by the more negative emotions of jealousy, anger, and bitterness. And one of the most intense dynamics is between Sergeant Greer (Jamil Walker Smith) and International Oversight Advisory bureaucrat Camile Wray (Ming-Na), who clearly can't stand each other. But this is great. People don't always get along like the Brady Bunch, especially people who wouldn't normally choose to be together. My main criticism of *Voyager* was how quickly the conflict between Starfleet and the Maquis was set aside; there seems little danger of that in *SGU*.

There are also some wonderfully positive dynamics highlighted in *SGU*, too. One of my favorite scenes to date is the sacrifice of Senator Armstrong (Christopher MacDonald) to give his daughter one more day of life. It's powerful, moving, and at the same time incredibly uplifting because this is something with which many parents (and children) can identify.

After only ten episodes, there is a veritable smorgasbord of such moments to choose from: Eli (David Blue) meeting Chloe (Elyse Levesque); Greer fighting with Rush; Scott (Brian J. Smith) confiding his own losses to Chloe; Eli making cookies with his mother; Chloe confiding her fears of uselessness to Eli; Camile cooking with her partner Sharon (Reiko Aylesworth); Sharon breaking down after Camile leaves; Young giving Greer a pep talk when he's disturbed by failing to protect the others in an alternate timeline, and more…

Personally, I love the hinted-at-but-not-yet-completely-confirmed relationship between TJ (Alaina Huffman) and ship's commander, Colonel Young. There's a real friendship and caring between the two – a sense that it wasn't simply the tawdriness of a broom closet quickie that led them to stray from the Regulated path. It's the subordinate-and-CO affair that was denied to Sam and Jack, and that's actually why I love it. Partly, because it elevates Sam and Jack by comparison: not only because they held to their honor and duty (unlike some), but also because it illustrates the messy consequences that may have unfolded if the two of them had ever just screwed… er… the Regs.

And, speaking of Jack and Sam...

Cute Cameo Appearances

The benefit of seeing the *Stargate* franchise continue is that there's always the possibility of seeing more of my favorite and much-loved characters from the previous shows. I've loved the cameo appearances made in *SGU* to date.

Daniel Jackson's "Stargate 101" was just *genius* (and MGM released videos of his lessons on their official *Stargate* site as a bonus), but I also liked seeing Sam taking on the Lucien Alliance in the *General Hammond*, ordering Telford and Young with real authority, and her reporting back to Homeworld Security at the end of "Air, Part 1" (S01E01). Frankly, I was just delighted to see Sam and Jack in a scene together again.

As a shipper, I admit it would be nice to have seen some sign that they are together romantically, but the scene is one in which they are on duty and being professional, not to mention separated by a vast expanse of space, so…I'll take what I can get. As a bonus, Sam doesn't finish every sentence with the word "sir" and the vibe was one of surprising equality given the difference in their ranks. It's certainly ambiguous enough that I can continue to imagine them as a couple off-duty (although I wouldn't mind if the producers found some way of slipping a Sam and Jack kiss into *SGU* in the future).

And speaking of Jack…

The Return of a Serious Jack O'Neill

Personally, you could just have Richard Dean Anderson turn up, say nothing and I would still be one contented bunny. The man still has the most gorgeous pair of… brown eyes. And having met him briefly at Avalon a couple of years back, I have to say in the flesh he's got stacks of sex appeal that literally turned women – including myself – into gibbering idiots (and I don't turn into a gibbering idiot easily). Even at sixty, the man can melt chocolate because he just has that indefinable something.

Lt. Gen Jack O'Neill isn't Col. Jack O'Neill. The character has evolved and is now the Man. He's beset by the IOA and the President, politics and practicalities, rather than having the freedom out in the field to do his own thing. And yet, the core of Jack remains the same. He always was a serious military-minded man with a scathing sense of humor for anyone he didn't immediately like or respect. One of the best moments in the pilot for me was hearing Jack's retort to Eli when he says he needs to check out the document with his lawyer: "And by lawyer, I assume you mean mother," Jack drawls caustically.

I'll concede that the other episode to really showcase Jack, "Earth" (S01E07), has issues in terms of plotting (too much Earth and not enough *Destiny*), but I liked Jack giving Young a much needed kick up the butt about his command authority on the ship. There's no doubt in my mind that had Jack ended up on the *Destiny*, it would have been under military command and there would have been no question about it. SG-1 always had a military commander and, despite occasionally listening to Daniel's civilian objections, it certainly wasn't a democracy under Jack's command even if it evolved that way under Carter – and, later, Mitchell.

There's also no doubt in my mind that Jack meant the reassurance he gave Young that (to paraphrase) Colonel Carter had saved his ass dozens of times with wacky science (and, yay for Jack even mentioning Sam). Even if the scientists' idea was out there, it was worth at least trying it.

And when Young finally steps up at the end of the episode and effectively sticks it to the briefing room and its occupants, you can't tell me there's not a hint of pride in Jack's eyes; he's certainly quick to back-up Young against the IOA guy. Also, I can't see Jack tolerating Rush's behavior on the ship any more than Young does. Maybe Jack wouldn't have left him behind on a planet to rot as Young seems driven to do at the end of "Justice" (S01E10), but Jack could be just as ruthless when he needed to be: he closed the iris and knowingly killed a man (OK, so Alar was the equivalent of that world's Hitler, but still); has shot most of his team when they've been infected by alien entities; and was prepared to blow up a ship with Daniel on it to save people. And let's not forget that Jack himself once conceded that he'd done some damn distasteful things in the service of his country. He's not a Boy Scout.

My main complaint of the Jack in *SGU* so far is that I want more of him. I love his scenes with Young but I'd like to see him doing more with the other characters too.

And speaking of characters…

Characters First, Heroes Second

SGU has a completely different approach to characters than its predecessors and this is a very good thing. One of the most irritating things about *Stargate Atlantis* for me was the cookie cutter approach taken with the main characters: One snarky male commander – check! One alien warrior – check! One genius scientist – check! One civilian with diplomacy skills – check! One fiercely dedicated Chief Medical Officer – check! Yes, they did mix it up some but overall, Team Atlantis looked very similar to SG-1, and the new characters they tried (like young and enthusiastic Lt. Ford) seemed lost in the mix.

All the main characters in both *SG-1* and *Atlantis* were painted in broad brush strokes as "heroes" with attention only paid to back-story or motivation when it was required for the plot. Now, don't get me wrong, that worked for both shows – even if fans complained vociferously at times – but this time out, the *Stargate* creators have really focused on developing characters first and heroes second (or third, even). The characters are being portrayed with flaws and strengths. All have had their weaknesses, but all have also had their moments of glory, of true heroism.

Young may cross the line in leaving Rush behind, but on a separate occasion he risks his own life to rescue Lt. Scott and get them both back to the ship. He's consistently shown as having the loyalty of his officers and command; of trying to be fair in his approach to life on the *Destiny*.

Scott might have given in to a quickie in the broom closet and have issues with contraception, but he steps up to take control in the first few hours on the *Destiny*, risks his own life to get lime and water for the ship, and tries to do the right thing when he finds out he has a son.

Chloe may lack a purpose on the *Destiny* but she's aware of that and is trying to find one, whether that's helping TJ, volunteering to gather food, and even defending Young at his trial in "Justice." Let's not forget she also gets to wallop Rush and generally call him on his logical if emotionally-cold decision making.

Greer may have a temper that lands him in the brig but he's fiercely determined to protect others, can invent a really cool flame-thrower, and has a hidden spiritual side that sees him get naked to face his death (note to producers: this should definitely happen more often).

And speaking of Greer…

Relatively Unknown Actors Stealing the Show

Yes, yes, yes – we all know Robert Carlyle can act and he rightly deserved to pick up his Best Actor Scottish BAFTA for *The Unloved* last year. His incredibly deft performance of Rush is no surprise, and we would expect decent performances from the likes of Lou Diamond Philips, Louis Ferreira and Ming-Na. But it's a joy for me that it's the lesser known (if at all) actors who are quietly stealing the show

Jamil Walker Smith has to be the best find ever. His portrayal of Greer is one of the things I love most about *SGU*. I believe he is Greer head to toe. But it's not just him. While I could also talk at length about Brian J. Smith, Elyse Levesque and Alaina Huffman, I'll just focus on one other: David Blue's Eli.

The actor has had to anchor much of the first season so far, given that his character provides the everyman point of view essential to describing the Stargate universe to the audience. Eli also provides the comic relief, the pop culture references, and a nifty red t-shirt with the ironic strap-line "You Are Here." Two performances of Blue's stand out for me: in "Light" (S01E05), where he manages to convey Eli's disappointment at Chloe choosing Scott and being relegated to "best friend" position without saying a word; and in "Time" (S01E08) where Eli opens up to TJ and reveals the truth behind his mother's illness…

And speaking of "Time"…

"Time"

Personally, I think the eighth episode in *SGU*'s first season is one of the best the franchise has produced. Everything about the episode is quality.

The story is clever, makes full use of the Stargate and its lore, and is packed full of character moments as the crew of *Destiny* face death at the hands of creepy alien monsters in one timeline, and a deadly alien virus in another. Common enough sci-fi settings and situations, yes, but the focus is on how people reacted. And not only that, but it treats the audience as intelligent. The time travel element throws up all kinds of questions and the ending is a huge shock! It's up to the viewer to work out for themselves that the crew would receive the message they needed in order to survive for the following episode.

I love being treated as intelligent. I love that answers are not spoon-fed to me. No, it's not always a comfortable transition from the old *Stargate* format, but "Time" truly showcases how brilliant *SGU* can be

And speaking of brilliance…

TJ

TJ rocks.

The character has had some of the best moments in the show so far: knocking out Telford with a sedative when he misuses Young's body (a move of which I think Janet Fraiser would have been proud); standing face to face with an alien life-form with a sense of wonder; bluntly telling Greer she doesn't trust him (and Greer accepting that); saving the *Destiny* by getting the little sand aliens into a container and off the ship; fake smiling at Chloe's gushing about the love-fest with Scott; and breaking down in a corridor after being unable to save her patients… She's one of the most likeable characters on board and it's no surprise that when producer Joseph Mallozzi recently asked on his blog which character people would like to see more of, TJ led the pack by a long way.

Much of the credit for that is down to Alaina Huffman's performance. She has managed to convey TJ's military side and competence yet also her vulnerability and uncertainty. There's a humanity, compassion and caring about TJ that sets her apart from the others. She also has an appealing ordinariness when she talks of how her father, a tailor, taught her how to stitch. She's a fantastic character.

Then there's the whole Young thing and the mystery of actually what went on between the two of them… did they, indeed, screw… (wait for it)… the Regs?

And speaking of screwing the Regs…

Controversial Topics

I love how *SGU* isn't afraid to raise the controversial topics.

The suggestion of an affair between Young and TJ is one of those questions. *SG-1* shied away from showing Jack and Sam together partly because of concern over the reaction the real Air Force might have had to the storyline of two officers engaging in fraternization. *SGU* doesn't concern itself with that; it seems to be tackling the storyline anyway. And there are other controversial questions being posed: "Air, Part 2" (S01E02) asks that perennial question: if you had to sacrifice one person so everyone could live, who would you sacrifice? In "Light" (S01E05) the question is flipped on its head: if you had to choose which few would be saved and make it to a lifeboat, how would you make the decision?

But the use of the Communication Stones is probably the most controversial of all: if your consciousness switches bodies with someone else, what rights do you have in your new body? Do you have the right to get drunk? Do you have the right to cuddle up and exchange kisses with your other half? Do you have the right to have sex? (As amusing as it was, I could have done without seeing Telford and Young swap back and forth during the make-up horizontal tango Young engaged in with his wife.) The idea is icky – really, really icky – but it's meant to be. It's meant to throw up the question of what is acceptable and what isn't. It's meant to challenge us. Would you want to swap bodies with someone if it was your only way home? Would you volunteer to swap bodies with someone if it was their only way to visit home? How far would you let someone else go in your body? How far would you go in someone else's body?

Maybe we don't agree with the answers that *SGU* is suggesting the characters have made but just because we don't agree with them doesn't necessarily make those answers wrong. After all, if we were stuck on a ship thousands of light years from home, maybe our thinking wouldn't be so different.

But, hey, speaking of the ship…

The Nature of *Destiny*

Just how cool is *Destiny*?

The last time I fell in love this way it was with *Airwolf* (the very cool futuristic helicopter that was central to the TV show; plus the show itself, obviously).

Destiny is old. Falling-apart old. She's grimy, dirty and a bit battered. But she's one of the first ships built by the Ancients and she's definitely a mystery waiting to be unraveled. Then there's the total ambiguity over whether she's aware. Is she just going about her pre-programmed business heedless and unconcerned about the human inhabitants crawling through her corridors? Or is she actively trying to ensure their survival?

She stops at one planet because they need lime but she sets them a time limit so they almost fail to make it back to the ship before it zips back into FTL. Did she do it because Rush told the ship it needed lime? Or because she was just going to stop there anyway? Did she know the planet with the alien monsters held the antidote to the virus they acquired from the water planet? Or did she stop there by chance?

And not only that, but she refuels by flying into a sun! A very awesome concept that has been explored before in science fiction lore, and here SGU shows us just how awesome it is because we see it. The special effects when the Destiny zips around a gas giant and stops by a sun are astounding; the beauty and magic of space realized on screen, and we get to experience that, as do the stranded humans on board...

And speaking of humans...

Humanity

Stargate Universe has taken the franchise back to its roots and put the regular humanity of today at the front and centre of its storytelling. After years of our heroes becoming blasé about being out in the galaxy, kicking alien butt and mastering alien technology with ease, *SGU* takes us back to the early days when SG-1 went blundering around the galaxy with no idea what they were doing and what was really out there.

We're only ten episodes in but we've already had some incredible human acts: Senator Armstrong sacrificing himself for others; Greer determined not to leave Scott behind; Rush eschewing a place in the survival lottery; Young determined not to leave Scott behind; Sharon being strong for Camile; and Lisa Park comforting a crying TJ, to name only some. The best of humanity is on show, and, okay, I admit, so is the worst of humanity, but am I the only one who loves that? *Stargate* was never meant to show us the utopian image of Earth humans so embodied by the *Star Trek* franchise. This is us now.

I'm fairly certain life aboard *Destiny* is a pretty accurate representation of what would happen if a bunch of us did get stuck out in space on an Ancient ship. We can be selfish and petty; some of us wouldn't be able to take the pressure. Admittedly, *SG-1* and *Atlantis* primarily showcased this side of humanity in the past through pseudo-villains such as Kinsey, Maybourne, Woolsey and Kavanaugh (and even McKay when he first appeared), but they are among the most love-to-hate recurring characters the franchise has produced.

And I have no doubt that ultimately what we'll see in *Stargate Universe* will be humans rising to the challenge, overcoming their flaws and being totally awesome. Because we are. And *SGU* gets that. It's just showing us the journey, the whys and hows of getting there, how we overcome our baser instincts to become awesome, and that's what I love most about it.

That isn't to say I don't think *SGU* doesn't have room for improvement. It could:

1. Lighten up! Both literally (that is one dark, dark ship) and in terms of turning the humor dial up a notch or two.

2. Get a better balance between the episode plots and the character moments. If *SG-1* and *Atlantis* sacrificed character for plot, they seem to making the opposite mistake here.

3. Showcase its female characters more.

That is all.

© *Rachel Day, 2010*

SUICIDE SQUAD
A CRUSHING DISAPPOINTMENT
by Mark Ritchie

Leading up to the release of *Suicide Squad*, it was difficult to trudge through the smoke and debris left from the scathing reviews garnered by *Batman v Superman: Dawn of Justice*. I didn't hate that film – far from it. I felt it managed some truly iconic moments, and it made way for Wonder Woman's long overdue cinematic debut. Yes, it suffered from being over-stuffed, yet still too simplistic in its execution of highly regarded arcs from the comics; like a game of Jenga, you could feel DC wanting to build and build upon its own universe with Flash-like haste and, as with Jenga, without careful consideration and planning, it can all crumble before your very eyes. While certainly watchable – and I think we can all safely agree that Batman was awesome! – *Batman v Superman* was an expensive misstep in trying to play catch up to Marvel's firmly established film universe.

But there was a beacon of neon-light at the end of DCs bleak tunnel: David Ayer's *Suicide Squad*! It was exactly the kind of rebellious jolt DC needed to land on its feet after a dodgy dismount earlier on in the year. Trailer after trailer, *Suicide Squad* had fans foaming at the mouth. The tone of each subsequent trailer captured the essence of the comics perfectly, with some fantastic use of pop music and the kind of brilliant editing that took many clips out of context (so as to not spoil anything) but still compelled you to throw money at the screen. They were vibrant, energetic and totally badass; the tidbits of character interaction felt completely in character for each of the cast.

So why did absolutely NONE of that make it into the final film?

I can honestly say that I walked into the cinema with an open and optimistic mindset; the pre-release reviews were not going to deter me from enjoying this film. It looked fun and had a strong cast with a dependable director, so as long as I enjoyed myself, that's all that mattered. Maybe they just didn't get it. Maybe the film just wasn't for the casual crowd...or maybe, it was just a really uninspired movie. One simply destined to exist in the pantheon of comic book films (alongside *Thor 2* and *Iron Man 2*), like some forgotten piece of furniture left to gather dust in the attic.

And that's probably the movie's worst offense of all (and there are many); *Suicide Squad* may briefly flirt with the idea of being fun and edgy, but it very quickly becomes an entirely different movie altogether, one strapped for time to develop its large cast, and one that all too easily settles into mediocrity. There are many boring scenes in film. Boring! In a movie that contains a crocodile man, the Joker, and a ninja assassin, how is that even possible? Allowing twenty minutes for introductions, through mostly ineffective flashbacks, simply isn't enough to fuel the rest of the film. The entire running-time should have been an introduction to this world, into the dynamics of the group; to build this world of crooks into something multi-faceted and lived-in, but why even bother with anything like character development when you can have an electrical ring of death in the sky and Cara Delevigne dancing in a bikini?

With talks of multiple re-shoots and a tonal overhaul by studio big-wigs, naturally one might assume that the majority of *Suicide Squad*'s shortcomings stem from the fact that David Ayer's version of the film was chopped into tiny pieces. While Ayer has gone on record saying this is his cut, scenes are noticeably absent and/or short-changed. Flag's relationship with Enchantress, for example, is relegated to a pithy one-liner from Amanda Waller that's meant to qualify as character development; it's interesting to note that some of the promotional trailers showed scenes of them together romantically, and considering Enchantress is such a big element of the film, it would seem only appropriate that we get to see the woman behind the witch before things get a little too CG-heavy. I am not asking for Flag to show up with a boombox outside of Enchantress' portal and declare his love for her, I just want a reason to care. About any of them. The mission is what matters in this script; it's just a shame said mission is really, really dull.

The thing is, whether or not the film was thrown into a blender, and the final product is a diluted concoction of edits, it still doesn't take away from the fact that the script is dastardly, with dialogue that never feels believable and very rarely rings true to the characters. There's no time for witty banter because most the dialogue is made up of each character reminding the audience why we should consider so-and-so a villain in the first place. We are constantly reminded just how crazy Harley is but she barely even crosses the line into kookiness, and time and time again the audience is told that Deadshot is a murderer for hire (I felt particularly battered from this reminder). It's a perfect case of tell and not show, which is the exact opposite of what you want when you're being introduced to this seedier side of DC for the first time. Joker's relationship with Harley is addressed but never explored; we are allowed few scenes of Dr. Quinzel before her transition, and we are just supposed to accept that she fell in love with the Joker because reasons. It's a show-reel that keeps reiterating their relationship without adding anything new or of relevance. Considering just how complex their relationship is often represented, it's truly disappointing to see such a basic primer on such a lurid, twisted romance.

Considering the majority of the wafer-thin character work on display here (the merc-with-the-heart-of-gold, Harley and Joker's relationship,

Enchantress, the macguffin mission), you would think that, as compensation, we would be treated to some interesting and action-packed set-pieces. Think again! Not one character has a shining, defining moment. The action scenes are claustrophobic and poorly framed; the henchman are especially forgettable with absolutely no personality, and not one poses any kind of threat to the team. The fun in having a bunch of misfits band together against their own will is to witness the dysfunction, distrust and chaos of the initial set-up and watch as that dynamic gradually shifts into something resembling a fully-functioning anti-Justice League. But *Suicide Squad* has no time for anything of substance, not really. All of the team have one-liners and silly replies, but there's none of that juicy, seething tension, the kind you get when your significant other watches an episode of *Game of Thrones* without you. There's no concept of how bad they are or once were; they're just empty puppets, who walk from point A to point B, to advance to the next level. Rinse and repeat.

The hype was oh-so real for this movie. *Suicide Squad* opened with so much promise, so much potential. I genuinely loved the start: Harley's scenes in captivity are loads of fun, and Enchantress' introduction (specifically how – with her black hand clasping her human host's) is one of the most interesting visuals the film has going for it. Will Smith, initially, is absolutely electric as Deadshot; Jai Courtney garners some laughs as Captain Boomerang, and Viola Davis is perfect for the role of Amanda Waller. But all of these elements are quickly taken for granted: the fun fizzles, Deadshot becomes too melodramatic, and the ruthless Amanda Waller comes off as slightly ridiculous when things take a turn for the murder-y.

It is so disheartening to be writing this about some of my favorite anti-heroes and villains. When you look back at *Deadpool*, and just how crazy fucking awesome that film was and what it managed to accomplish (in terms of style, script, and box-office takings), you realize what a colossal swing and a miss it was not to treat *Suicide Squad* with the same kind of unhinged tenacity.

This is such an average film. Not bad, not good, not so-bad-it's-good, just resoundingly average. And that's probably the worst possible outcome for a fan of the original comics, or any DC fan at all.

All eyes are now on *Wonder Woman*. The pressure is on. Can the Amazon Princess bring DC to the forefront enough to be considered an actual threat to Marvel's triumphant Cinematic Universe? I hope so! The Comic-Con trailer gave me goose bumps the first time around – and still does every time I watch it. But if I've learned anything from *Suicide Squad*, it's that trailers can be very, very misleading.

© *Mark Ritchie, 2016*

SUICIDE SQUAD
WHY ALL THE HATE?
by Jason Murdoch

Okay, let's just get this out of the way: I am in no way saying that *Suicide Squad* is a Good Movie. It's not going to go down in history as one of the great examples of cinema by any stretch of the imagination. That's not what I'm saying at all. All I'm saying is, it isn't a BAD movie.

26% on Rotten Tomatoes, 2 out of 5 from *The Guardian*, and a quick hunt around the interwebs provides quotes like "a cold cup of coffee," "professional negligence" and, perhaps the most scathing, "worse than *Green Lantern*."

Harsh, people. Harsh.

I don't for a second think that *Suicide Squad* is anywhere near as bad as most people insisted. Maybe that's because by the time I'd had a chance to see it (I know, call myself a fan, then not even line up for the midnight screening... what is this?) the reviews were out, the critics had had their field day and my expectations were thoroughly lowered.

Maybe it's because I'm perfectly fine with a movie that lets you just turn your brain off and be dazzled by cyborg pirate ninja zombie wizards or implausible sentient robots, when I know that's what I'm signing up for.

But maybe, just MAYBE everyone jumped the gun a touch. Flew off the handle a wee bit.

But why? Why did everyone rage soooo vehemently about this, of all movies? That is not the fault of the movie, but the hype train.

When you are promised the world. When you are FINALLY promised a decent DC movie (*Dark Knight* franchise aside). When you see how a group of misfit little-known characters can make for an unexpected hit *cough guardiansofthegalaxy cough* and you have the right actors, the potential promised by the comics, characters that can carry a movie... AND ALL THAT ADVERTISING!!!

No wonder we expected the world.

Let's start calling a spade a spade.

Spade #1: It isn't *Suicide Squad*. It's the Harley and Deadshot show. This is fine, great even, when you know that's what you're getting. Frankly, every other actor stands firmly in the shadows of Margot Robbie and Will Smith. But those two shine.

Robbie's Harley Quinn does exactly what she should do: references enough of the core material to be true to the character's origin, whilst staying accessible enough to audiences. (Can you really imagine what the *Batman: The Animated Series* Harley voice would have been like to listen to for a whole movie?? Just take a power drill to my eardrums now.) And likewise, Will Smith does exactly what he should do: play the same character Will Smith plays in every movie he has ever been in. He's the wise-cracking, charismatic smartass he was hired to be.

Spade #2: It's not a Joker movie. He's a bit part. We forget everything we have heard about the Joker or Jared Leto's dickheaddery and all of a sudden his bit part in a movie that isn't about him doesn't make a lick of difference. Zero disappointment.

Spade #3: It's only a couple of hours. You cannot give every character the full backstory that they all need. Some get relegated. No one actually wants to sit through something that would take longer than the full Extended Edition, Director's Cut of the *Lord of the Rings* trilogy. They want to go in, get enough, and leave in time for dinner, or whatever it is that people do these days after movies. This means in the "group of heroes banding together" standard plot you HAVE to focus on a couple of key characters. Do we REALLY think that Killer Croc's backstory would actually progress the plot at all? There is a metric ton of stuff that needs squeezing in. It's a no win... put everything in and people complain. Leave stuff out and people complain.

It's very easy to sit here and carp about how the plot feels rushed, or the generic henchmen are generic. But really, let's look at what we actually receive, leaving all pre-set expectations at the door.

Delightful, shining performances by Robbie and Smith. Witty banter and one liners between the main characters. Action scenes that have explosions and gunshots and stuff being chopped up with a samurai sword. A sweet, sweet soundtrack. Special effects. A hateable baddie. All stuff a good comic book movie needs. All perfectly enjoyable.

But when what you expect is the saviour of the entire DC cinematic universe, something for the rest of the DC films to live vicariously through, drive to soccer games and scream at the ref over, push into a university degree that it doesn't actually want, because its father is an alumnus and his father before him... No wonder it acted out.

So, let's not hold our collective breaths for *Wonder Woman*. Or *Justice League*. They'll be fun. Not amazing. Maybe Momoa's *Aquaman* will be quality. Maybe they'll do a Teen Titans movie that will outshine the rest (PLEASE!!!). But if we keep forcing our own agendas, and expecting the next DC movie to make up for the back catalog, we will continue to be disappointed. Some stuff can't be atoned for.

Let them be their own movies and suddenly it's all okay.

© *Jason Murdoch, 2016*

SUPERMAN
I DON'T GET IT
by Rachel Hyland

Look, I don't hate Superman. He's okay, I guess. I mean, I liked the Christopher Reeve/Margot Kidder movies as a kid, I loved *Lois and Clark* as a teenager, and I have even been known to enjoy the odd episode of *Smallville*, 'cause boy those people sure are pretty. But I don't get what it is about this alien refugee that has made him the most recognizable, admired, and iconic superhero of our age. I don't understand why people get his symbol as a tattoo, or name their kids Kal-El (seriously, Nic Cage?), or spend thousands building their own Fortress of Solitude, all to honor him. Spider-Man, Iron Man, Hawkman, Aquaman, Ant Man, Plastic Man, Bananaman; I could more easily understand any one of those valiant costumed "men" being considered the epitome of everything that is awesome rather than Clark Fricking Kent and his cheesy all-American wholesomeness.

Now, a big part of this may just be that I am a devoted Marvel adherent, and Superman is so very DC that he might as well have those letters sewn onto his costume instead of his signature stylized S. But I like Batman a lot, and he is DC. I adore the Teen Titans, and so are they. I have recently fallen in hopeless love with Martian Manhunter, and he couldn't be more DC if he were the Capitol Building. So I don't think this is a Sharks vs. Jets kind of blind loyalty thing. I just think Superman's kind of a soulless do-gooder who is way less interesting than, say, Lex Luthor. Hell, I'd rather read of the adventures of Jimmy Olsen, boy reporter, than of his mentor and hero. (Especially as played by first season *Lois and Clark* Jimmy, Michael Landes, who is tremendous and should be in more stuff.)

Maybe it's because Superman is so very... super. Perfect. And he is therefore utterly insipid, and unforgivably predictable.

When Superman gets into a tussle with anyone not in possession of a very rare piece of intergalactic space debris, the result is a foregone conclusion: he's gonna win. When Superman gets into a tussle with someone in possession of a very rare piece of intergalactic space debris, the result is a foregone conclusion: he's still gonna win... it just takes longer. When Superman comes up against a moral dilemma, the result is a foregone conclusion: he's gonna do the right thing. (Which, more often than not, means the "right wing" thing.) When Superman – or his mild mannered alter-ego Clark Kent – gets embroiled in any kind of romantic situation with someone other than Lois Lane, the result is a foregone conclusion: they're gonna break up. (Alternate Universes or the far future

The Kingdom [1999] not included… the various times he and Wonder Woman have hooked up and had kids, that's pretty sweet.)

What else do I not find appealing about Superman? Well, there's his hokey home life with the kindly and hardworking Kents. His use of spectacles as an apparently infallible disguise. His seemingly impenetrable haze of self-righteousness. And while TV Clark Kents have been known to offer up more than the occasional quip (*Smallville*'s writers have certainly given Tom Welling more grist than his deadpan mill is perhaps equipped to handle), the Man of Steel is, in the main, so very earnest that it appears neither the concept of sarcasm nor self-deprecation has ever been introduced to him. And while comic book Clark may occasionally crack wise, Superman never does. He doesn't even speak; he declaims.

But y'know my biggest gripe about Superman? He's just so damn Messianic.

In *The Matrix Reloaded* (I know, not the most popular of movies to reference, but I really liked this part of it, so bear with me), we learn from that white clad, double-talking Architect dude at the end that the idea of "The One," that prophesied savior of mankind against the machines – whom Keanu Reeves' Neo is believed to be – is in fact a construct of the machines themselves; if humanity, so their quite admirable logic goes, believes that there is destined to come some great and powerful being who can save them from their enslavement and drudgery, then they'll be less inclined to go about saving themselves.

That's what Superman is. He's "The One." He's Krypton *ex machina*. He's the civilized and mighty and better-than-us White Knight who solves all our problems with his wondrous Other-ness so that we don't have to. He patronizes us and gives us benediction and blessing and his very presence is supposed to fill us with comfort and joy. And that kind of thing just makes me cross – and makes me like Superman not one whit.

When I mentioned this debate to new Geek Speaker and comic fan Jason Murdoch, he said dismissively: "The only time I've had any interest in Superman was during that speech at the end of *Kill Bill*."

"Yes!" I replied immediately. "Exactly!" The monologue, delivered flawlessly by David Carradine, really sums up a lot of my issues with the Man of Steel:

> **BILL:** Superman stands alone. Superman did not become Superman, Superman was born Superman. When Superman wakes up in the morning, he is Superman. His alter ego is Clark Kent. His outfit with the big red S is the blanket he was wrapped in as a baby when the Kents found him. Those are his clothes. What Kent wears, the glasses the business suit, that's the costume. That's the costume Superman wears to blend in with us. Clark Kent is how Superman views us. And what are the characteristics of Clark Kent? He's weak, unsure of himself… he's a coward. Clark Kent is Superman's

critique on the whole human race, sort of like Beatrix Kiddo and Mrs. Tommy Plumpton.

In *Superman Returns* (again, not the most popular of movies to reference... but I kind of liked this part, so bear with me) the Kate Bosworth version of Lois immediately endeared herself to me with the authorship of a piece entitled "Why the World Doesn't Need Superman," penned after the Man of Steel left us high and dry for... I dunno, some reason, I forget. Something about *Superman II*. Of course, by the end of the movie she's all in love with him again and so recants – one hopes the Pulitzer committee withdraws their kudos – and offers up "Why the World Needs Superman," essentially Geek vs. Geeking with herself, and as a result I end up hating her and the whole damn mess of a movie. I don't do well with authority and moral absolutism and totalitarian regimes. And Superman, for all that he is a benevolent dictator, is one nonetheless.

Because he's wicked strong.

Our K. Burtt, in his review of the animated *Justice League* series, pointed out how Superman's essential all-powerful, invincible.... him-ness led to more than one problem with that otherwise pretty flawless show. "One issue," said he, "is that with seven main cast members, some episodes feature only three of four of them. It's fine from a character-growth standpoint, but causes problems from a logic standpoint... kind of the 'um... if Superman were around, this would have been taken care of in 30 seconds' type of thing." Also: "... as per usual with anything dealing with Superman... he's rarely if ever allowed to unload to the full extent that he is capable of. His powers seem to be somewhat limited to just-enough-to-move-the-plot-forward, which is always kind of annoying."

It is more than kind of annoying. It's insanely so. The fact is, with Superman at full throttle, is there really any need for the Justice League at all? For any of the rest of the DC universe? Let's face it, he and his extra-terrestrially-blessed, yellow-sun-bestowed powers put pretty much every other superhero in the shade, even in his weakened post-Crisis state. My learned adversary would have it that Marvel, too, has their pinnacle of strength and superpower, The Hulk, but I would contend that his kind of indomitability is far more complex, and therefore made far more interesting, than that of his DC counterpart. (Although, to be honest, The Hulk is far from my favorite superhero, either.) Hulk may be largely undefeated, but he spends much of his time facing off against other Marvel superheroes! He, like Frank Castle, is an anti-hero, fighting his inner demons just as much as he fights with his stablemates, and that makes him compelling, even in his own imperviousness. With Superman, who is a hero on our world due to nothing more than cosmic happenstance *and* who has had most of his life to deal with this fact (and not have to deal with any guilt or self-loathing as a result of it), his complete superiority over all others isn't a cause for admiration. And, in fact, according to the kinda-sorta definitive *Marvel vs. DC* limited-series comic released jointly by both houses in 1996, Superman beat The Hulk very handily in their little encounter. "Hulk smash" is no match for laser eyebeams, super strength and flying, now is it? (Unsurprisingly, the comic fans of both houses agreed.)

So, the "hero," the "unstoppable brute" that my opponent erroneously claims to be Marvel's finest, cannot, in the final analysis, hold a candle to Superman, technically speaking – at least, not when his powers are applied with any kind of regard for continuity. Does this not rather illustrate my point? True, Superman's had his hiccups and brushes with defeat in his various incarnations, and when DC's two most revered men faced off in Frank Miller's brilliantly dystopian *The Dark Knight Returns* limited issue, the Bat- did beat out the Super-, but that was more sneaky wishful thinking than anything else, really. And true, his epic battle with Doomsday killed him in that unwontedly teasing *The Death of Superman* arc, but he got resurrected! ('Cause Kryptonians can do that, dontcha know.) Superman's such a paragon that his very existence, when applied consistently, makes pretty much everyone else obsolete... even Martian Manhunter! And maybe that's what I like least about him.

No, wait, also? X-ray vision just creeps me out.

© *Rachel Hyland, 2011*

SUPERMAN
HE'S SUPER, MAN!
by Mark Ritchie

One might think I'm at a slight disadvantage with this one at the offset: I have to defend a hero who sports flashy red go-go boots and wears his undies on the outside of his leg-wear. The cards are already stacked against me. But not to fret, for I have plenty of reasons as to why Superman – questionable attire aside – is the quintessential modern-day hero in my arsenal and, while my opposite number makes a compelling argument to the contrary, Superman is without a doubt an icon for the ages.

I should preface that I am by no means a hardcore comic-book fan. I also happen to enjoy and appreciate Marvel and DC in equal measure. (Well, almost... DC wins only by a hair.)

But I do love Superman. He may not be my favorite DC hero (that would be Batman, just so you know), but Superman represents hope, he upholds a strong moral code that's difficult not to admire, and leaving his array of impressive – who am I kidding? downright awesome powers aside – his most remarkable feature would have to be his solid set of ideals, which make him the perfect idol to aspire to. Of course, we live in a world where corruption runs rampant and the stressful situations we encounter on a day-to-day basis may not always see us at our finest, and while Superman's ideology (he is tolerant, just, incorruptible, and merciful, strives to help others, and always takes responsibility for his actions) may not always be achievable, it's a solid foundation to keep you on the right track, making him a truly inspirational figure and ensuring he's a beloved household name.

Before I continue on any further, I'd just like to tackle one point my opponent makes in her argument, before I dig into the meat and potatoes of my side of the debate. She argues, through use of various snippets of our friend K. Burtt's spot-on review of *Justice League Unlimited*, that the very presence of Superman renders the Justice League, and practically every DC character imaginable, useless, because, well, The Man of Steel has no equal – he's the strongest of the lot. And that frustrates her.

Hmm.

Let's pop on over to the Marvel side of things for a wee moment. That franchise has a pesky, indestructible brute, with limitless strength, and serious anger issues: The Hulk. He cannot be stopped. No matter what he faces, no matter how strong his opponent, it doesn't matter what is thrown at him, he can never be beaten. He becomes angrier and angrier and therefore stronger and stronger! Why even entertain the notion of The Avengers? They spend half of their time trying (and failing) to apprehend this out of control character with very little in way of a moral compass. Thor, maybe, can last a few rounds with him, but it always leads to the inevitable conclusion: Hulk smash. And smash he does. Bruce Banner is the Hulk's Achilles heel, but even so, there have been various iterations of the Hulk where the beast has managed to override Bruce indefinitely. Why even entertain any other Marvel hero, for that matter (the Hulk has taken on the lot: X-men, Fantastic Four, The Avengers, just to name a few)?

Because there are stories to be told. And there have been some fantastic Superman tales in the past. Superman is not infallible, he's not tiresomely predictable, and he has plenty of weaknesses, too (and I'm not just referring to various shades of kryptonite): magic, of course, is another main physical weakness – throw the likes of Captain Marvel at him (who has defeated the Man of Steel in the past... though it's not considered canon), and Superman is in for a bout of pain and misfortune. But on a more personal level, it's Superman's hubris that has landed him in more trouble than he probably bargained for (with Lex Luthor usually the culprit responsible for clouding Superman's judgment). He doesn't always make the right calls, and it's that very same righteousness that irks my colleague, that I find fascinating about him. As I mentioned, he upholds a commendable set of ideals, but his complex can sometimes backfire (as it during the *Justice League Unlimited* episode "Clash," in which Superman takes down half the city facing Captain Marvel, under the sure assumption that Lex Luthor had planted a bomb underneath his new settlement that he built for low-income Americans). It's also Superman's duality, and his personal affections to those close to him, thanks to his alter ego, Clark Kent, that make him such a compelling hero and his role as a superhero all the more difficult to uphold. There are many facets to Superman, and many, many threats he must face, and he constantly has the weight of the world on his shoulders, because he's the only one of his kind who can defend it. (At least on the DC side of things; there are so many overpowered Marvel Supes at this stage, I wouldn't even know where to begin.)

There is, of course, that faint echo in the back of my mind asking the obvious question: "why choose the likes of Superman, when you can have the likes of Batman?" And while I may favor the Dark Crusader over the Last Son of Krypton, there is an undeniable predictability to Bats, too. When he's not brooding on rooftops, he's masquerading as Bruce Wayne, playboy billionaire, but still very much with the furrowed brow. This is what makes Superman so awesome. Yes, he's righteous and powerful and just and that be all you can be Boy Scout, but what if he suddenly turned on the world he was sent to protect? Throughout Superman's history, there's always been some instance of him succumbing to some sort of evil, and it's in these moments we catch a glimpse of his true capabilities, and it can be frightening. It can also prove to be damn entertaining.

Take *Smallville*, for example; the best episodes from that series can be attributed to Clark's red kryptonite-induced haze, and the havoc that follows in its wake. There's plenty of other incarnations of Clark going rogue (Darkseid managed to take control of him and turn him on Earth in *Superman: The Animated Series*), but he'll always manage to overcome his oppressor and triumph over evil, and I wouldn't have it any other way.

He *is* Superman, after all. The first true comic-book savior upon which many other well-known heroes are based upon. He ignited the comic-book genre and spawned a new generation of storytelling and has provided countless stories of courage, honor and all kinds of kickassery. He is the ultimate superhero.

... Now, if only they'd do something about those blasted go-go boots.

SUPERPOWERS

WHY I'D BE A SUPERHERO, OR HOW COULD ANYONE EVEN CONTEMPLATE BEING ANYTHING ELSE?

by Rachel Hyland

Did you know that there are people who, if gifted with superpowers in some way or another (radioactive spider bite, doused with radioactive chemicals, exposed to radioactive isotopes... really, comic land would be nothing without nuclear physics), would choose to use those powers not for good but for evil? That there are those who, when immersed in a hypothetical discussion regarding said powers, deny any wish to don a mask and/or a cape to save their fellow man from miscreants and ne'er do wells, but instead would use those powers to rob banks and create havoc and generally be the dark nemeses against which all our favorite secret-identitied, selfless vigilantes so valiantly campaign?

I suppose I always knew this intellectually, on some level. The sad fact is that there are people of questionable moral fiber in the world, a reality we are confronted with every night on the news: thieves and murderers, warlords and dictators, everywhere lawbreakers just as merciless and as egocentric as even the most maniacal of fictional criminal masterminds. It stands to reason, then, that those kinds of people would be quite taken with the notion of possessing superpowers, if only to enhance their own prestige and make the subjugation of others less bothersome. But that someone I know should hold this opinion; and someone, moreover, that I would have no hesitation in characterizing as one of my very best friends... Well, let's just say, that came as something of a shock.

Do otherwise good, decent, thoughtful people *really* want to be the bad guy?

Oh, it's not that I don't understand the allure of the dark side. Ruthless Darth Vader is cooler than the whiny, sappy Anakin; unrepentant Angelus is funnier than the tortured, brooding Angel; mischievous Catwoman is sexier than the terribly earnest Batgirl. But it is one thing to find assorted villains captivating and quite another to want to *be* one of them; it's the difference between playing *Grand Theft Auto* and running down sex workers and assorted pedestrians in stolen cars and actually running down sex workers and assorted pedestrians in stolen cars. The former might be an enjoyable way to kill time living faux dangerously (or so I hear), but the latter is an anti-social lifestyle choice that can only reveal one as a homicidal psychopath unsuited to polite society.

So the fact that any fine, upstanding citizen would proclaim their desire to become a supervillain instead of a superhero, should the occasion ever arise, just doesn't make sense to me — especially a fine, upstanding citizen who, I break no confidences in revealing, has a tattoo of Spider-Man secreted somewhere about his person. If supervillains are so utterly superior, why didn't my colleague's reckless younger self have the Green Goblin indelibly marked on his body? Or Doctor Octopus? Or Kangaroo? (Okay, I get why not Kangaroo... a dude who can just jump kind of high against a guy who can swing through the city and crawl up buildings? Worst Spidey villain ever.)

Now, further discussion of the issue revealed that when he said supervillain, what my formidable opponent actually thought he meant was super-anti-hero; he wanted to use his newfound theoretical strength to cripple irresponsible energy companies and the avaricious financial sector and rid us all of the menace of international copyright law. But the difference between an anti-hero and a villain – and especially a supervillain – lies not in their intent but in their utter lack of conscience, and given that the collateral damage such a campaign of anti-trust terror must necessarily engender bothered my adversary not at all, I would suggest that "supervillain" was indeed the correct nomenclature.

It could be said (and was said, also by my opponent in this debate) that superheroes operate outside the law as much as do villains, and as such it is difficult to differentiate between them in mere words; we simply know them when we see them. I disagree—I think the main distinction lies in one word: sacrifice. A superhero will sacrifice himself for any random other with barely a moment's thought, but it is the rare supervillain who will endanger his own life/liberty/pursuit of happiness in favor of even a loved one, let alone a stranger dangling precariously from a collapsed bridge. (Which he probably collapsed in the first place.)

Sure, superheroes may, like their villainous counterparts, often do the wrong thing for what they perceive to be the right reasons, and they are just as often hunted by assorted law enforcement agencies as are their own dangerous prey – from Batman to The Punisher to Deadpool (only one of whom is usually depicted with actual superpowers, by the by), these heroes can be, and are, just as easily painted as villains. But despite their often dubious methods, each would without hesitation lay down their lives to Do the Right Thing; it's doubtful the same could be said of any incarnation of The Joker, or Jigsaw, or... who the hell is Deadpool's archenemy, anyway? T-Ray? He has so many.

The simple fact is, a superhero – however reluctantly – feels he or she must save the world, while a supervillain merely wants to take it over, and then make it over in his or her own image. As Dr. Horrible put it so concisely: "The world is a mess, and I just need to... rule it." That is very much at the core of the supervillain credo. The difference between

213

Professor X and Magneto is not in their ideas – they both want mutants to be safe and accepted by the population at large – but in how they choose to achieve their ends. The one campaigns for slow, steady change, ultimately bringing mutant and human together as one, with the strong protecting the weak for the good of all; the other wants to assert his own dominion, sure that mutants are a superior species and should therefore take their rightful place as humanity's lords and masters.

When Superman collected up all the planet's nuclear weapons and sent them into the sun in *Superman IV: The Quest for Peace*, it was an act of villainy, because not only did it give Lex Luthor the opportunity to – somewhat farfetchedly – make his own super being to do battle with poor Supes, but it took away humanity's right to make our own mistakes, imposing his Kryptonian will on ours just because he could. When, at the end of the movie, he realized that universal nuclear disarmament was a matter to be decided by nations and not by one man, he was returned to his superhero status. A superhero can make mistakes, but he acknowledges them, learns from them, is humbled by them—and often dwells on them ad infinitum until we're all ready to scream at them: "Dude, okay, you got your uncle killed, like fifty years ago, get over it." A superhero will blame himself; a supervillain will blame everyone else. Another key difference.

But to return to Superman's usurpation of the UN and his grand larceny of WMDs: when my opponent says he would use his theoretical superpowers to destabilize our banking systems and rid the world of fossil fuels and who knows what anarchistic else, what he's really saying is he believes it is one man's prerogative to determine the course of all human history based solely on his own beliefs and doctrines, and he would impose his will on us all at the point of a laser eyebeam; might equals right. He doesn't seek to save or protect on the micro level, as might, say, Daredevil stop a mugging or Wonder Woman thwart a kidnapping or The Authority prevent a planetary invasion by, uh, God. Instead, he seeks to compel obedience to his whims on a worldwide scale; the very hallmark of a supervillain.

Also, from a purely practical standpoint, deciding to be a supervillain is just pretty foolish, because eventually you will be brought to justice, though it may take decades worth of comics – or an entire movie – to do it, and even then you'll probably escape from jail or be brought back from the dead because, hey, every hero needs his nemesis. And admittedly, a superhero's lot is not always a happy one, always hiding your good deeds and staying one step ahead of the conventional law and not really getting to have henchmen. Henchmen would be fun.

Perhaps when it comes right down to it, being a superhero is less appealing than being the opposite, and I admit here and now, I would probably suck at it. Forget joining The Avengers or any of the X teams, I don't think I'd even make the grade as one of the Mystery Men, and one of

214

their members' only power is being invisible when no one is looking at him. But the alternative just doesn't bear thinking about. To quote Churchill: "No one pretends that democracy is perfect or all-wise. Indeed, it has been said that democracy is the worst form of government except all those other forms that have been tried from time to time." No one pretends a superhero is perfect or all-wise, and certainly being a superhero would have its challenges, and more than its share of frustrations. But to do anything else? To ignore your great responsibility when great power is thrust upon you, and instead become an egomaniacal, megalomaniacal madman letting power corrupt absolutely and intent on world domination, no matter how ostensibly noble the goals?

No. Hell, no. If for no other reason than the seemingly mandatory evil laughs have become just so passé.

© Rachel Hyland, 2017

SUPERPOWERS

WHY I'D BE A SUPERVILLAIN, OR THERE ARE ONLY SUPERHEROES BECAUSE THEY DON'T THINK BIG ENOUGH

by B. C. Roberts

Right now there are over a billion people in the world living on less than US$2 a day. Starvation kills hundreds of people every day. Lack of clean drinking water is responsible for at least 30,000 deaths every day. At the same time there are more people in the world who are overweight than there are people who are starving. And the fortunes of the world's richest one hundred people could lift every single person on the planet out of poverty.

Our illustrious (and virtuous) editor has laid down quite the challenge, arguing forcefully that we should choose heroism over villainy because being a super villain is just so… well… wrong. And she's right.

That's the point.

To start with the persistent argument across all of genre that humanity must be left to make its own mistakes, that every super-powered person who attempts to relieve humanity of this apparently basic human right (though needless to say it doesn't appear in the Universal Declaration of Human Rights or any other such document) is a villain.

In 2012, when Israel and Palestine were blowing each other up and posturing that considerably greater violence was to come, Hilary Clinton and Mohammed Morsi brokered a peace that neither side sought. Israel seemed hell bent on "making its own mistakes" by eradicating Palestine and Hamas was equally committed to "making its own mistakes" by bombing whatever bit of Israel it could direct rockets at. Now, nobody would suggest that Clinton and Morsi's role was anything other than coercive – without the backing of the US and Egypt, Israel and Palestine respectively could not expect to continue existing. And nobody in their right mind would say that this peace deal removed anyone's fundamental rights to anything. The entire international legal machinery is designed to prevent humanity making its worst mistakes.

When Superman destroyed all the nuclear weapons in *Superman IV* (see the opposite argument), he wasn't removing humanity's dubious right to make its own mistakes. He was helping us be the best we can be, rather than defending our worst. The Nuclear Disarmament treaties are the best of humans, but which our corrupt politics is too broken to implement. That is, the international community had already decided nukes should go, they just couldn't make it happen. When Superman decided he was in error he became less than a hero; he became a colluder with all the powerful regimes who use their position to tyrannize the weak.

Was Iron Man being a villain in his first movie outing when he intervened in an international conflict to save the inhabitants of a village? Of course not. We expect superheroes to intervene. And so, if I woke up with superpowers, I'd really really REALLY intervene. And I think it would make me a supervillain in the end.

So if the question is whether I would use super powers to intervene on a global scale and remake the world into something better rather than nab bag snatchers there can only be one answer: get the fuck out of my way.

...

OK. So hopefully you're still reading.

Let's consider how this might work. One day you wake up with the powers of Superman. We'll use Superman because when people talk superheroes he is clearly the paradigm. If you wake up with the powers of Aquaman, fine, be a minor superhero, what are you going to do really?

But you wake up with near absolute invulnerability, super-strength, super-speed, the ability to fly, laser beam eyes, x-ray vision, super strong breath and the ability to effectively disguise yourself by putting on a pair of eyeglasses. You are, in almost every way, superior in abilities to everyone else on the planet.

At first you think that you would like to help some people out. You go to school and save a few kids from being bullied. You cruise around town and stop a few car thieves and muggers. You notice that a lot of your family's friends are having their houses foreclosed upon. Your particular part of small town America has been hard hit by the local auto factory closing down and now everyone is out of work and the banks are moving in. You think, surely, with this near limitless power, I can help out the people in my town.

A few ideas occur to you. You could become a successful MMA fighter though with your strength it would hardly be fair (and potentially lethal) for your opponents. You could hold a benefit, announce your powers to the world, and ask for donations. I guess it could work, but there are a lot of houses to save. You could strong-arm the bank manager and make him back off on the foreclosures. That might work for a little while, but how long could it last?

Or you can steal some money—no, steal a SHITLOAD of money, and make everyone's problems disappear. You could distribute it in small amounts, enough to cover each repayment so that nobody need ever suspect that the lost money from that Argentinian bank heist ended up in Smallville. The criminal option is tantalizing and no matter how hard you try to think about other options you become fixated on how many awful corporations there are making so much money off small-scale tragedies like the one in your town. So you steal the money, everyone is saved, and you go back to local patrol duty, hoping that you haven't permanently tarnished your character.

You finish school and end up in the big city. Every night (apparently never needing to sleep is another of your super powers) you protect the city, but crime seems never ending and the poor just keep getting poorer. One day your best friend comes to you and tells you he has been busted for possessing a small amount of marijuana. Now, you have always supported decriminalization of marijuana and you're pretty angry that poor Jimmy Olsen is facing a stint in prison for smoking weed. You do some research online and discover that America incarcerates a greater proportion of its population than any other country and that the great majority of these are for petty drug offences.

You can see where this is going.

A tangle of corrupt officials, stupidly strict penal provisions and indifferent judges makes law reform near impossible (though you are heartened by the few states who have managed to legalize medical marijuana). One day you wonder if drugs should be legal; maybe you could even help make them legal. You are sick of hiding your powers, pretending to be mild-mannered when you could be awesome. Maybe a little bit of fear wouldn't be such a bad thing. Some of those powerful people should learn to fear something.

It's time to take the big step. It's time to be awesome. You come out openly, deciding that being a hero should be your full-time job. It turns out that crime doesn't only happen at night or on slow news days. Working a human job is just pointless, there's too much to get done. So now Superman protects the city—protects it from everyone. You set up a refuge for everyone who fears someone powerful. You tell the police that your friend will not be facing charges, they can't take him, they can't charge him, they can't incarcerate him. But that seems unfair, there are so many people unjustly imprisoned. So you bust out everyone on petty drug charges and give them a place in your refuge.

Next to go are the pimps. Sex work should be legal everywhere and men shouldn't be able to exploit women who would like to work safely, or force women into it who aren't willing. So, you take in all the sex workers and make clear that no pimps are welcome. If any pimps complain, you decide not to repeat the mistakes of so many superheroes, who are forever letting their nemeses get away and cause havoc another day. (Seriously, how many deaths are on Superman's head for letting Lex Luthor come back again and again?) So, some pimps get made an example of. If any complain, your combination of super hearing and laser eyesight make short work of them.

And so it goes on. You build a bigger and bigger city. There is no homelessness, no street violence, no domestic violence (abusive husbands fare quite badly under your reign). Drug use is legal and protected, as is sex work. Your city is starting to look more and more like a well-run Scandinavian country. As officials attempt to oppose you they are dealt with summarily. Of what importance is a mayor beholden to corporate interests? You appoint yourself mayor of the city, then president of the country. There can be no war, you can defeat any national army from the upper atmosphere with those awesome and too-often-forgotten laser eyes.

Are you a villain? In a sense, unquestionably. You violate every rule of official superherodom. You kill people. Relatively often. You have fun; not having to pretend you're a boring human, you get heaps of girls. You avoid that awkward bit where the girl you like is partly in love with both you and your alter-ego. She's just totally into all of you. Sure, you're a villain, but you're better than every superhero who never had the courage to do what you do: To genuinely use their powers to remake the world into the better place that humans wish they could but always fall short because they rely on consensus to do it.

And that's ultimately what it comes down to. There are lots of people who want the world to be a better place and a few who are powerful enough to make sure that never happens. You don't represent those in power, but you do represent a lot of others. And if that makes you a villain, well, the millions of dollars, beautiful women, and sense of accomplishment make it all worthwhile.

© B. C. Roberts, 2017

TIME TRAVEL AND FICTION
THE PERFECT COMBINATION
by William Cashin

I love time travel. Not just because we all have that secret desire in us to become masters of time, but also because it is a great topic for scientific and philosophical debate. Will time travel ever be possible? If so, how will we get around the many temporal paradoxes that seem to say it can't happen? But this Geek vs. Geek is not about that. It's about time travel in fiction. So, if you want to have a debate about the science of time travel, join me at www.iamsmarterthanyou.org/noreally/iam/.

Instead I will discuss how time travel and fiction are the perfect combination. Let's face it, everything you have probably heard about time travel came from a film or a book (unless you've read my article on Born's theory of multiple universes, on the website above). And no, the "that's just Hollywood" argument doesn't hold true. I hate to say it, but more often than not, they do put up a good argument, and expose you to some of the fantastic complexities of what time travel would be and could be, and consider time travel's many ramifications.

I'll also discuss one of the main charges laid against using time travel in fiction, namely that it is mostly used as a *deus ex machina*, and is another example of writers being lazy. Okay, this happens occasionally, but I'll try to show you that occurrences of this are few and far between, and these movies are largely seen as bad movies anyway.

But more than anything, I want to discuss some clear rules that I think you need to follow to make a great time travel film. If only everyone followed these rules, this Geek vs. Geek wouldn't be needed, because everyone would be pro-time travel in fiction.

Oh, and a MASSIVE spoiler alert for the films discussed in this article! But if you haven't seen *12 Monkeys* by now, that's your fault, not mine.

But first... lighten up

Fiction is fiction. *Of course* time travel is bollocks (or do I *want* you to believe this? Muhahahaha...), so the first thing you need to do when you see time travel in a movie is say to yourself: "Okay, let's see where this goes". Did you walk out of *Déjà Vu* when Denzel Washington was told about Snow White? No, you went along with it. Did you walk out of *Click* when Adam Sandler was handed the remote? Okay, it this case you probably should have. Even I wish I had.

By hanging around, more often than not in time travel films you get those magnificent pay offs. Such as learning that James was seeing himself in that haunting childhood memory in *12 Monkeys*, and the brain bruise you got when you consider that it was John Conner that sent Kyle Reese back into the past for him to become his dad in *Terminator*. These are the movies that make you think long and hard about them for days and weeks afterwards.

These movies work because they convince you to willingly suspend your disbelief in time travel, by specifically setting out an internal logic to their usage of the medium. And even in movies where they are deliberately having fun with what are seen as the normal "rules" of time travel (more later), they still get you to sign up into believing where they are taking you, no matter how silly things are about to get.

Think of Basil in *Austin Powers 2: The Spy Who Shagged Me*, assuring Austin about time travel by saying "I suggest you don't worry about those things and just enjoy yourself", then turns to you, the audience, and says "That goes for you all too!". Think of Rufus at the start of *Bill and Ted's Excellent Adventure*, assuring us "Don't worry, it'll all make sense. I'm a professional". That he was.

So, what exactly *is* a time travel film?

This is perhaps not a question asked enough. A lot of movies that have time travel in them, in my opinion, aren't really time travel movies. Stories that involve a character being "transported" far into the past (*A Connecticut Yankee in King Arthur's Court, Black Knight*) or into the future (*Planet of the Apes, Les Visiteurs*) are what we should actually call "alternative history" stories. In these stories, time travel has merely been a plot device to get a character from A to B, similar to a tornado in *The Wizard of Oz*, or a red pill in *The Matrix*. How exactly they got to the past or future is not important. In fact, according to these stories, it seems being knocked unconscious by a blow to the back of the head is the most common route of time travel. In this case, the *deus ex machina* criticism is probably valid.

To me, you only have a time travel story when the EFFECTS of time travel are considered. In other words, the possibilities and ramifications of time travel must be openly discussed by the characters, either in a comedic manner (*Hot Tub Time Machine, Frequently Asked Questions About Time Travel, Back to the Future*) or in a serious, earnest manner (*Donnie Darko, Primer*). And whilst you most likely won't hear the characters call them by what they are, by doing so the storyteller is getting you to consider the most fundamental concept of all time travel films: temporal paradoxes.

Put simply, temporal paradoxes are events that would seem to suggest that time travel can't possibly happen. And yet, we just can't get enough of them in our stories. There are many types of temporal paradoxes, such as:

The predestination paradox, or "whatever is meant to happen, happens"

Easily the gloomiest of the paradoxes, because it basically implies there is no free will. James in *12 Monkeys*, living in a post-apocalyptic future and haunted by a recurring dream of a man dying, agrees to go back in time to stop this future world ever happening. But all he manages to do is inadvertently create the Army of the Twelve Monkeys, and then dies in vain, as a twelve-year old James watches on. *The Butterfly Effect* is also riddled with predestination paradoxes. It's a sad paradox because despite knowing what is to happen in the future, no matter what you do it must happen that way. No matter what you try to do to change it, you were always going to do that, and your actions were always going to have no effect, or even worse, cause the future you are trying to avoid. Ouch.

Ontological paradox, or "where exactly did you come from?"

Again, there are many examples of these, but my favorite would be the "Johnny B. Goode" song paradox. Marty McFly, from 1985, plays Chuck Berry's "Johnny B. Goode" at a 1955 school dance. Chuck Berry's cousin is there, and liking what he is hearing, he gets Chuck Berry on the phone to hear "the new sound he's been looking for". So who wrote the song? Or was it ever created? The whole *Terminator* series is also built on many ontological complexes. Other than John Connor sending his soon-to-be father back in time to knock up his mum, there are also the events of *Terminator 2: Judgement Day* where scientists create what will become Skynet from the wreckage of the Terminator sent back previously. So apparently the knowledge of how to create the machines has no origin.

And of course, my nemesis, the grandfather paradox

Surely, the killer for most time-travel hopefuls. Being able to go back and undertake autoinfanticide, thereby stopping you being born and ever stepping in the time machine seems to be an open and shut case against time travel. So how do they get around this in stories? You miss, the gun locks, your granddad gets away, it wasn't actually your granddad, and so on. This solution to the grandfather paradox is known as restriction action resolution, but let's stick to time travel movies for now. Marty literally fading away in *Back to the Future* is another example, though why he faded away slowly is also interesting…

These themes are what make a film about time travel. It's not when an astronaut finds the remains of the Statue of Liberty on a beach. It's certainly not Superman circling around the Earth to turn back time. This is perhaps one of the greatest *deus ex machina* moments of all time, so much so that Superman himself is nowadays referred to as a "*deus ex*". It's an average plot device, and not even a decent "got ya" moment. It is NOTHING to do with what makes a time travel film.

First rule of time travel club. DO talk about time travel club

As I said at the start, I believe there are certain "rules" that you should follow to make a decent time travel film. Follow them well and you end up with a great time travel film. And the first rule is to make sure your audience knows that the movie is *about* time travel. Sometimes even stating the bleeding obvious is needed. You need to get across to the audience the internal logic of the movie as soon as possible. There are so many interpretations of time travel nowadays, you have to make sure your audience knows which one you are following, or how your new one will work.

For example, *Back to the Future*. It meets the rule IN THE TITLE. No one missed that one. But very quickly Doc is explaining time travel to Marty (leading to the first of many "That's heavy, Doc!" cries), and he even gives us the amount of energy needed, 1.21 jiggawatts (or is that gigawatts?). Doc serves throughout the trilogy as a guide to Marty, and to the audience, on how time travel works (what you can do, can't do, and absolutely should not do, but do anyway) in the *Back to the Future* world. He explains what would happen if you were to come into contact with yourself from the future, and explains the different alternative realities that have formed in the sequel.

In *12 Monkeys* we get the creepy scientists explaining how time travel works, by how they tell James what he needs to do (they of course do a poor effort with this, which is part of the movie's intrigue). In *Bill and Ted*, Rufus sternly tells the two that the time in San Dimas is still passing no matter where and when they are, so they need to make sure they are not late to their history presentation. Whoa? They are in a time machine, how can they be late? But in the *Bill and Ted* world, that's the rule, and it must be obeyed.

Second rule of time travel. Don't expect to succeed

Another reason I love the concept of time travel is the whole mad scientist angle. Not necessarily the kooky, loveable mad scientist that Doc Brown did so well, but a man dabbling with things well beyond his realm. Think of Victor Frankenstein creating life from nothing; a gift thought to bring great promise, but then brings unknown horrors, as seen in his monster. Time travel has been this monster for many a protagonist in time travel stories.

Often time travel is created or undertaken to try to change or stop a horrible event in the past ever occurring. But by the end we learn that all they did was at best delay the event (*Terminator, The Butterfly Effect*, the latest *Time Machine* version – terrible by the way), or at worst contribute to the event happening in the first place (*12 Monkeys, Terminator 2*), hence the pre-destination paradox. These types of stories can tell trace their heritage back to the original self-fulfilling prophecy stories, *Oedipus* and *Macbeth*.

For me, these time travel movies serve as a cautionary tale on the consequences of taking our desires too far, such as dabbling with time travel. Victor Frankenstein thought he was creating life, but by playing god he created a monster. In time travel stories, man's desire to avoid an event in the future or in the past by becoming a "master of time" only seems to ensure that the event happens. In this case it is man's desire to time travel, to control his own destiny, that is the "monster." Thus, man's most horrible creation is its unrelenting drive to seek what it most desires to the bitter end.

As Bill would say... Whoa

Third rule. Don't you dare cop out and go for the 'Hollywood ending'.

This is an important one for me, and of all the rules the one that separates a decent time travel film from a good one, or even a great one. Films that don't follow this rule are undoubtedly those that my formidable opponent has used to show how annoying time travel films can sometimes be. And for these ones I would agree. There are few things more annoying than when you willingly suspend your disbelief, thereby going along with a film's internal logic, only for the film to smash their own logic to pieces just to score a happy ending.

Most commonly this is done when a character from the future/past returns to the past/future, having left behind the new love that he/she has found, knowing that now they will be forever separated by time. And then what happens? They meet someone that looks EXACTLY like the love they've just lost. Ugh. *Les Visiteurs* is a good example of this (though, remember, this as an alternative history film so I won't defend it here).

Another film somewhat guilty of this is Back to the *Future III*. Deservedly, this series has given us some of the best time travel movies ever made, but the last scene of the last film still irritates me. Did Doc Brown really have to come back? After nearly two films of chastising Marty for wanting to use the time machine, and how he never should have created the time machine in the first place, he makes another one right at the end. Sigh. In the film's defense, I'm guessing they did this because they wanted one more scene with Doc acting as Marty's "guide," as he had done throughout the series, to tell him that his future is now his alone to write. Hmm, perhaps not worth the breaking of internal logic, but I may be in the minority there.

Time travel is by no means the only genre known to break their internal logic towards the end of the film, but perhaps this annoys me more in time travel films because you really have to invest a lot more in a time travel movie. It irritates me when you're told all along that something can't happen, and then it does. *The Lake House*: Why, oh why? If he could have just turned up like that, why didn't he just do this earlier? *Frequency*: So what, now he suddenly hasn't died from cancer and so is still alive to save the day? But then why didn't his son already "know" that? Err... internal logic failing... belief in humanity dwindling... eject... eject...

So... time travel movies are good right?

Absolutely. Look, any genre has those truly horrible films in its family, doing their best to give the rest a bad name. But I would say there are far more great time travel movies than there are bad ones. And because you have to invest more in a time travel film, when it is a good one the payoff is much greater and far more rewarding than for other genres.

And as for those movies that just use time travel as a plot device, it can be done successfully, but only with care. It is a bit of risk, but storytellers use it because they know that if it works, it really does pay off. A habitual user of this plot device is undoubtedly *Star Trek*. Consider *Star Trek Generations*. Was time travel used just to get William Shatner into the film? Perhaps. Did this lead to a crass movie? No. And *Star Trek IV: The Voyage Home*; was the need to travel back to the 20th century a bit of gimmick? Yes. Was the movie still great? Absolutely.

For me, as long as you follow the rules above, and stick to your film's internal logic, you can't go wrong. The rest is fair game. Have fun with it (*Back to the Future, Bill and Ted, Austin Powers*), make it creepy (*12 Monkeys, The Jacket*), or make your audience think *(Donnie Darko... still scratching my head over that one). Or even make a new form of time travel; there is no reason why you have to follow the logic of other films. Trust me, there are numerous volumes of scientific journals out there devoted to the theory of time travel, so you can argue almost anything.

Go ahead, give it a go.

© *William Cashin, 2010*

TIME TRAVEL AND FICTION
CAUSES NOTHING BUT TROUBLE
by Rachel Hyland

Nothing has caused more trouble in the world of speculative fiction than time travel. Well, prophecy is also a pretty big culprit, but in many ways the one is merely a subset of the other, so I'll let my original pronouncement stand.

Now, time travel as depicted on, say, *Futurama*, in which Fry is cryogenically frozen for a thousand years, or in *Demolition Man*, when

John Spartan and Murder Death Killer Simon Phoenix awake from cryoprison in a future with no crime, cause me no grief. I am likewise untroubled by the concept as used in *Flight of the Navigator* or Orson Scott Card's Ender series, where the vagaries of Einsteinian physics mean that anyone travelling faster than the speed of light ages but little while the universe around them marches on apace. Hell, all of those are basically just reboots of Rip Van Winkle, and I always loved that particular folk tale. I also don't really mind those wrong-righting *Groundhog Day*-style reliving of vital incidents stories – your *Early Edition*s, *Tru Calling*s, and *Day Break*s, etc. I mean, they don't really make sense, but neither do they offend my sensibilities.

But actual time travel? Of the kind in *The Time Machine* or *Back to the Future*, where someone builds a contraption that somehow, through the most blatant of technobabbling, manages to overcome the laws of the universe in order to physically transport a person – or ephemerally transport a person's consciousness, as seen in *Quantum Leap* and the like – to another point along the linear spectrum? No. At the risk of being like one of those naysayers who said we'd have no use for telephones, or that no one in their right mind would ever need more than 640k of RAM... absurd!

As a kid, the concept of time travel did not bother me as profoundly as it does today. I loved *Doctor Who* and the Australian TV series *The Girl from Tomorrow*; one of the favorite movies of my youth was – and remains – *The Philadelphia Experiment*, along with *My Science Project* and *Time Bandits*; I devoured such novels as Madeleine L'Engle's *A Wrinkle in Time* and the little-remembered *Kapatoo* by Ben Steed. (If you've never read it, find it on eBay now!)

But you know the single piece of genre storytelling that ruined it all for me?

The Terminator

Yes. The Terminator.

I mean, what the fuck is going on in that chronology?

Nothing that happens in those movies is even remotely possible. I don't mean they're scientifically impossible, in the way that we don't have the technology to send hot naked people through space and time just yet. What I mean is, each of those movies (and the subsequent TV show) present their own unique quandaries when it comes to the application of a little thing I like to call (because I learned it in Grade 3 Science), Cause and Effect. To wit: if the cause of the future Apocalypse is the invention of Skynet, then we must ensure Skynet is not invented in the present. But if we ensure Skynet is never invented, then how can anyone come back in time from the future to tell us to stop Skynet from being invented, since it's the invention of Skynet that leads to the ability to travel in time? And that is only the very tip of the neural net where *Terminator* tomfoolery is concerned. I mean, if sending the Terminator back in time led to the development of the technology on which Skynet was based, and then Skynet then went ahead and made the Terminator on which it was based... who the hell created the Skynet technology to begin with? Pixies?

And how was John Connor conceived? *How?*

You know what? I'm not even going to go into *Terminator 3: Rise of the Machines, Terminator: Salvation* or *Terminator: The Sarah Connor Chronicles*. 'Cause frankly I'm cross enough about this damned convoluted set of circumstances already.

Although I will quote Sheldon, from *The Big Bang Theory*: "Assuming all the good Terminators were originally evil Terminators created by Skynet but then reprogrammed by John Connor, why would Skynet, an artificial computer intelligence, bother to create a petite, hot, 17-year old killer robot?" ("The Loobenfield Decay," S01E10)

But... The *Terminator* universe is cool!

Oh, I'm not saying that I don't love all the *Terminator* stuff. Of course I do! The original is a poignant and delectable love story, *T2* is pure rollicking action fun, and while *Rise of the Machines* isn't exactly a series highlight, I think *Salvation* has been grossly maligned by the viewing public. *The Sarah Connor Chronicles*, meanwhile, was an awesome show, and I miss it still.

But in order for me to appreciate the *Terminator* universe, I have to ignore a lot. It's not just suspension of disbelief, as my opponent suggests – and which I, as a lifelong genre fan, have made into an art form; it is an almost ruthless suppression of all that I know to be remotely rational. In order to enjoy *The Terminator*, and dozens of movies and TV series and books like it, I have to disregard, or at times even celebrate, the fact that it is thoroughly nonsensical. I have to smother my intellect to the point of ruthless, tin-pot-African-dictator-silencing-opposition-style annihilation, or the mother of all migraines will stop me dead in my tracks.

I'm not sure that I should have to work so hard at not thinking about stuff in order to enjoy what is ostensibly entertainment.

Another problem I have with the whole notion of time travel is that, while it may occasionally make for great amusement and diversion, not only does it rarely make any sense whatsoever, but it even more rarely leads to anything good for its victims, or for us. Other science fiction tropes, like Alien Invasion or Evil Empire or even Humans Are Awesome, bring with them many different metaphorical and allegorical spins; they can be used to highlight the human condition, our failings and our virtues, for our long-term betterment as a whole. What's the best that time travel, as a concept, has given us? That if you don't study for your History final, you'll become a rock star?

It's a jungle out there

My learned colleague would have it that, as long as time travel movies – and by extension, we must infer, time travel TV shows and novels – manage to avoid pretty much all of the plot-devicing that makes a time travel movie what it is, then they'll all be awesome. He claims that if there is *no deus ex machina* allowed, no complete erasure of everyone's memories permitted, and absolutely no paradoxes (ontological, grandfather, causality loops, what have you) even contemplated, then, hooray, he's fixed a whole subgenre of Science Fiction and Fantasy!

The thing is... that is never going to happen. We are not dealing, here, with some utopian vision of the future in which every filmmaker and TV showrunner and author and comic editor will somehow get together and pledge allegiance to Will Cashin's Rules of Fictional Time Travel. There is no glorious, halcyon *Bill and Ted*-esque era of enlightenment coming in which we'll all be excellent to each other, party on dudes, and avoid discommoding our fellow geeks with convoluted and disingenuous time travel-related posturing. I'm not saying it wouldn't be nice. I'm just saying it is so unlikely as to be almost as improbable as actual time travel itself.

Meanwhile, this limited view he takes of the trope kind of wins my argument for me: if one needs to rigidly police this conceit's application throughout the multiplicity of creative endeavor before one can be properly content with its function, then clearly the time travel principle isn't quite as "perfect" a match for fiction as some claim.

Essentially we're being told by my opposite number that the whole idea of Time Travel in fiction is kind of a fixer-upper. *I'm* saying it's a fixer-upper! Indeed, that's pretty much the whole point of my being on this side of this debate.

Ergo, I win.

And yet, we all still lose, because until we find a way to establish those time travel rules as inviolable, we'll still have to put up with yet more profoundly headache-inducing, gut-twisting, fist-shakingly irksome and inconsistent head-scratchers.

I mean, *The Lake House* has a time-traveling mailbox in it! There is just no excuse for that.

© *Rachel Hyland, 2010*

THE *TWILIGHT SAGA* MOVIES
TEAM AWFUL
by David Baldwin

For my own sake, in case I need to defend myself against any readers who violently disagree with me, I will tell you from the outset that I have never read any book from the *Twilight* series beginning to end. I read a few pages of *Breaking Dawn* while killing time in a bookstore, but I have never, and doubt I will ever, read any of the books in Stephenie Meyer's insanely popular series. But the films are a much different story.

As an entertainment journalist, film critic, and someone who takes pride in how many films I have seen in my lifetime (the number of votes I've registered on my IMDB account suggests I am nearing 2000), I found it impossible to resist the temptation to watch *Twilight* and *New Moon* (more later on the stupidity of the "*Twilight Saga*" moniker). The publicity and hype surrounding both films was incredible, and the reactions to the trailers in packed theatres were near unbearable. While I have yet to decipher just what it is about this series that has set the world on fire (it is not like the idea of a vampire or a werewolf is new to anyone), I can say they have made for two of the worst and most disappointing films in recent memory.

So where do I start? Well, the special effects are atrocious beyond telling—some of the worst put to celluloid in the past ten years. But that is far too easy an area to pick on, especially in the wake of *Avatar*. So, thanks for spoiling us on that front James Cameron (not that there is anything wrong with that...)

The logical first thing to attack is the writing. It sucks, plain and simple. I have heard that the dialog is fairly close, if not identical, to that in Meyer's novels, but that is no excuse for how awful they sound. A trademark of the series is how deadpan and serious everyone comes off. Practically no one cracks a joke, or yet a smile; even when some of the dialogue and situations become downright ridiculous, everyone stays straight faced. Never mind the fact that I almost ruptured something from laughing so hard when Bella tells Edward that he's "beautiful" when he first shows off his glittering chest. I get the idea that it is supposed to be simple; that it is meant to be a romantic melodrama for impressionable teenage girls. As a book, this may have worked. But as a movie, a cutesy line like "Hold on tight, spider monkey!" just does not cut it. Just trying to remember some of these lines is sure to give me nightmares for weeks.

I'm already starting to cringe, and here I was just getting over Jake telling Ennis that "I just don't know how to quit you!"

Both films also suffer from being derivative, and frankly, rather boring. *Twilight* managed to keep me vaguely entertained despite this, but *New Moon* almost sent me into a coma. Some would blame that fault squarely on the films being part of a longer series, and neither being a truly complete story. But is that an excuse for either movie to just go through the motions and merely act as a set-up for the next film in the series? Should they not be able to stand on their own, and not feel as if they need to be watched in succession? This is not unique to *Twilight*, a lot of films act as filler (see *Iron Man 2, Pirates of the Caribbean: Dead Man's Chest, The Matrix Reloaded* for examples of what I mean). It just pains me to know the films need to act in this manner. That neither filmmaker – *Twilight*'s Catherine Hardwicke nor *New Moon*'s Chris Weitz – could even attempt to make the movie able to stand on its own is yet another element of disappointment for this series (but I will note that *New Moon* suffers from this syndrome a lot more than *Twilight* does).

But the writing can only be blamed for so much. The acting is truly pitiful. Let's leave out how insanely gorgeous Taylor Lautner is now that he had to push himself to ridiculous lengths to keep from being recast, and let's look away from Robert Pattinson and his finely coiffed mane. Can we actually say either of them can act? Sure, Lautner is the best and most interesting thing to come out of *New Moon*, but I would hardly call that emoting (unless taking off your shirt and putting it back on multiple times now qualifies for being the next Marlon Brando). In the original film, he had a few lines and was an otherwise throwaway character, if not for the fact that we all knew he had a bigger role in the series as it went on. In the sequel, he had significantly more dialogue, got a chance to truly brood and pine over Bella, and then sulk like a whiny child before being unceremoniously cut out of the majority of the final act. Yeah, I'm certain that is what everyone has in mind when they discuss an actor's "range."

Pattinson, on the other hand, just seems to get away with having dreamy eyes and no sense of talent whatsoever. He has no charisma or charm. He is lifeless in his role here, and never once does he make Edward's "love" or attraction to Bella not seem forced by the confines of the storyline. I am certain that if the producers replaced him with a cardboard cutout for one scene no one would even know the difference. He is just so wooden – so plain. There is no justice in a world where he can get away without the painful rejection and easy parody fodder that Hayden Christensen continues to deal with in the wake of the *Star Wars* prequels. And he actually tried! (I can only hope the new Jason Friedberg/Aaron Seltzer abomination *Vampires Suck* gives Pattinson his overdue comedic whiplash. But God help me if this is not the last movie Fox greenlights from these two plagiarists.) It is almost like Pattinson knows he is some otherworldly heartthrob to a plethora of females around the world, and knows he does not have to do anything to maintain their attention. I can only think of one scene in the two films where he shows some form of acting, even for a remote period of time.

Let me set the scene up for you.

Bella walks into the classroom for the first time, science class, I believe. He sees her and catches her scent. He goes crazy with what I can only imagine is hormonal rage, which appears to have still gone unchecked despite his having lived for over 100 years.

And then he starts humping and caressing the desk.

Now, this appears to be okay for Edward Cullen to do in the not so magical land of Forks. In real life, this guy would have been arrested, suspended from the school, expelled, or sent for a psychiatric evaluation whether this was his way of showing he was repulsed by her or not. That behavior just is not right from someone who is supposed to be 17. But somehow, this attracts Bella, and she eventually falls in love with him so hard that she cannot bear to even think about being with anyone else. She gets to the point in *New Moon* where she isolates herself from the world because she is so depressed about his leaving her, and then starts doing things that may end up killing her, just so she can live life on the edge with the minute possibility that he will come back for her (and let's not forget the horrendously acted screaming nightmare fits on the part of Kristen Stewart). What does Meyer think she is teaching all of these young, impressionable girls who fawn over the series so much? Sure, the chaste element to the story is great and all, but telling them to fall for one guy so hard that it is quits if you cannot have him? We really want to encourage that mentality?

I actually kind of dig Stewart in other films. She is great in the criminally underrated *Adventureland*, I really liked her in *Into the Wild*, and despite not being a fan of *Panic Room*, she was quite good in that too. So how can she have talent in all of those films, and just seem to be playing Bella without a shred of motivation outside of a paycheck? I blamed Pattinson's wooden delivery and zero chemistry earlier, but Stewart is just as much to blame. She brings more intensity to the role, I will give her that. But that is about all she does for it. Oh, and she plays with her hair! Yes, we cannot leave that trivial detail out of a description of her mesmerizing acting abilities in these films. Every girl wants to be in her position, but her one-dimensionality is so emotionally disturbing that it borders on actionable.

Unfortunately, no one else up to this point in the films has gotten a chance to really make something of their supporting character in the series: Billy Burke is great in his small doses as Bella's father Charlie; despite receiving an Oscar nomination and some form of credibility as an actor, Anna Kendrick (Jessica) continues to be underwritten and underplayed; Peter Facinelli (Carlisle), Elizabeth Reaser (Esme) and Ashley Greene (Alice) get some things to do, but are used more to move the plot along than anything else. I keep forgetting the enormously talented Nikki Reed (Rosalie) is in these films – more on her in a moment – but then, she could pass for furniture with how much she gets to do at any given time. I was genuinely excited for Michael Sheen (Aro) to join the cast and moderately excited for Dakota Fanning (Jane). But outside of what you see in the trailer for *New Moon*, neither of them really gets to do anything. I hope in the future films they get some sort of arc they can use to make something of their roles; otherwise, they too will be added to the list of talented, underused supporting stars.

Now the only reason I mentioned Reed in the same breath as the more recognizable names above is because of *Thirteen*. While it may have suffered slightly from being a tad exaggerated, the film was a wild, realistic, and moving portrait of what it is like to be a teenager (and it was even semi-autobiographical, giving it that much more authenticity). She worked on the script with director Catherine Hardwicke, who ended up directing *Twilight*, but was later shoved off in favour of Chris Weitz, best known for helping give us *American Pie* and the rather underwhelming adaptation of Phillip Pullman's *The Golden Compass*. I can only ask, what was the difference in making *Thirteen* in 2003 and making *Twilight* in 2008? Both are about the lives of teenage girls, the trouble they have growing up and the realization of becoming the person they want to be (which for Bella is apparently becoming an unemployed woman exercising her feminist rights to exist as the muse of a vampire and the unattainable crush of a werewolf). Yet one movie is so much better written, acted, directed and filmed than the other (I will give you a moment, but only a moment, to guess which one I am referring to). It is baffling, and makes for yet another shred of disappointment to add to the pile. (I do find it amusing and ironic to note that Reed's co-star in *Thirteen*, Evan Rachel Wood, is now a vampire on the seriously addictive *True Blood*. Now, for all its faults, at least that show knows what it is and can adjust its tone quite easily.)

As I was writing this, the official announcement came in that *Breaking Dawn* would be split into two films, much like *Harry Potter and the Deathly Hallows*. While it is obvious that Summit is merely copying Warner's marketing strategy (I am curious already if the DVD/Blu-ray releases for either series will be separate, or added together to form one movie), it just illustrates the reason why the quality of filmmaking in *New Moon* or *Twilight* did not really matter in the end. The company knows they have a cash cow, and they want to milk it for every last ounce of it's worth, and they want to do it as quick as physically possible. Why else are these films being rushed into production and released so quickly?

But I do digress. Despite the awfulness of the first two, I will watch the next three films (on DVD or Blu-ray, never theatrically) to see how David Slate and Bill Condon handle the reins of this unruly franchise. I already know that Condon will not do the reportedly horrific and gory elements of *Breaking Dawn* the way a professional like David Cronenberg, David Lynch or even Vincenzo Natali would. But then, I am already going into these films disappointed anyway, so I won't be holding my breath hoping for miracles.

Finally, what's with the *Twilight Saga* qualifier? Even though I never read the books, I knew what each entry was named, and would likely have no problem knowing which film is the next one. So why add the goofy subtitle? Does Summit really think anyone is going to mistake the next *Twilight* movie for something else? Do they really think they are going to lose out on any money by not instinctively referring to the next entry as part of the so-called *Twilight Saga*? Have you ever met anyone who had trouble remembering what the next preposterous film title was in the James Bond series? I have not, and I doubt anyone would do the same for *Twilight*.

If even I know the titles in this series then so too do the hordes of teenage girls who are its baffling target audience.

© *David Baldwin, 2010*

THE *TWILIGHT SAGA* MOVIES
TEAM AWESOME
by Rachel Hyland

Okay, I am getting sick and tired of having to defend my love of all things *Twilight*y around these parts. Especially to the males of our crack *Geek Speak* staff. It's like they are all suffering from a tragic and incurable disorder, something that requires a telethon and possibly a ribbon of some kind. Acute Edward Cullen Aversion Syndrome. They are all missing a gene, or a base-pair chromosome or something. They just Do Not Get It. That Stephenie Meyer's *Twilight* series, for all its flaws (and, oh yes, I'm aware it has many), can still be entertaining and engaging and utterly enchanting is somehow beyond their collective ken, and my love for it has therefore become a source of ridicule and disdain.

Well, listen up, boys (and, actually, yes, quite a few girls as well), 'cause I am only gonna say this... well, as many times as I need to. But listen up, anyway. 'Cause I *will* be heard.

The *Twilight* world is, in a word, fun. It is – in many more words – melodramatic and ridiculous and romantic and nonsensical and hilarious and addictive and breathtaking and unreal. It is one of those rare phenomena that deserves all the hype, because it awakens such profound reactions. Not that it is in any way high art or thought-provoking allegory, but who says something has to be either of those things to be great?

I started reading *Twilight* about a year after its release. It was really just on a whim that I picked it up in Borders, intending to just check out a page or two, see what all the (then-lesser) fuss was about. To all the people who claim that Meyer is a poor writer, I counter with the fact that I was still standing there an hour later! That is not the hallmark of a poor writer. A poor writer would not make you want to keep reading so obsessively that you completely ignore the a) pain in your neck, b) constant replaying of something from the John Tesh school of audio torture and c) persistent child wailing a few feet away in the kids' section who's been demanding "a nuvva cwacka! A nuvva cwacka!" for at least 20 minutes. (Yes, I could have bought the book and taken it home to read in peace at any time, but I couldn't even face taking my eyes off its pages for as long as it would take to fish some cash out of my purse and hand it over. And then they probably would have had to take the book out of my hands to scan it! And I couldn't bear to let it go.)

Yes, there may be some stylistic flaws in Meyer's, er, style. Her language usage is unimaginative and unremarkable, and I definitely concede that she made some odd, odd choices when plotting out her would-be climactic scenes (if such she did). But I believe that Meyer's gift lies in transcending these mere details, in making something extraordinary out of her very ordinariness. Her writing isn't capital-letter-Good, but it is good at telling her story.

I think my love of *Twilight* can be explained thus: it's like the difference between a good movie and a FAVORITE movie. I mean, *Schindler's List* is probably the best movie I've ever seen, but I have no desire to ever watch it again. Whereas *Howard the Duck* really isn't very good at all, and I've seen it at least fifty times.

And the *Twilight* movie is definitely up for multiple repeats at my place. Although I will add that several of those viewings will be accompanied by the RiffTrax commentary. Ah, the RiffTrax commentary. So very worth the price of admission.

In case you're unaware, RiffTrax is the brainchild of Michael J. Nelson and his cohorts from *Mystery Science Theater 3000*, and the premise is largely the same. One need only download the RiffTrax mp3 to be played in conjunction with the movie of your choice, and then let the chuckling commence.

> **BELLA:** It doesn't make sense for you to love me.
> **RIFF:** *The Twilight Series*, summed up in nine words.

Yes, okay, I concede there is plenty to mock in these movies. But there's plenty to mock in almost anything (you should hear the RiffTrax guys give *Avatar* hell), and we laugh because we love. Or, I do, anyway.

I love these movies for many reasons. Lovely cinematography. Awesome soundtracks. Excellent casting. Jasper (Jackson Rathbone). Oh, and Michael Welch as Mike (from *Joan of Arcadia*, and that time he played the young O'Neill on *SG-1*). But mostly because these films are among the very few adaptations I have ever seen that really do justice to their source material, and that pleases my nitpicky soul. In the books, Bella *does* have a difficult time completing a sentence; Edward and Bella *do* spend a lot of time gazing at each other's Immortal Beloved faces; first movie villain James *does* have a ridiculous ponytail; Jacob *does* get ripped as hell in *New Moon*.

And Edward *is* just really, really, ridiculously good looking. Which Robert Pattinson carries off with ease. Now, it has been suggested by my formidable opponent that he cannot act and has no charisma: I take exception. Violent exception! The moment the music swelled and Edward walked through that cafeteria door in the first movie, hair immaculately upswept and skin seemingly infused with an inner glow, remains one of the few times I have actually been able to articulate the sound a Tribble makes. (And it wasn't just me!) I will concede there are times when Kristen Stewart's Bella is a little inscrutable, but when you've read the books you know what's going on in her head, and therefore her occasional lapses into stuttering incoherence (okay, her perpetual lapses into such) make all kinds of thematic sense.

Is this a man/woman thing, this *Twilight* disconnect, the kind of eternal misunderstanding between the sexes that provides such endless fodder for stand-up comedians of a certain observationalist school?

No, I really don't think it is. I mean, I know women who hated the *Twilight* movie profoundly, and I know men – yes, grown up, rational, even heterosexual men – who actually enjoyed it. They saw it on a plane or were dragged along by their partners and later confessed to me, in confidence, that they didn't mind it at all. I will grant that those same men found *New Moon* far less acceptable, especially all the stuff before the werewolves show up, and, believe me, I get it. The whole thing where Bella is whiny, mopey, lost-without-him Miss Havisham-crazy probably came across as a little maudlin and histrionic. But believe me, in this case the movie actually bettered the book (which, when does *that* happen?); if you think Edward-less Bella was annoying in Kristen Stewart-form, imagine if you were privileged to experience every lovelorn thought that crossed her near-suicidal mind in drippy first person prose? Exhausting.

Now, it has been often suggested that Stephenie Meyer's Mormonism has influenced her story in a negative and insidious manner; there is certainly a big groundswell of resentment against Bella essentially going into a decline in *New Moon*. And I understand it, I do. It's definitely not the best message to be sending to the young women of the world. But for all that it's tragically pathetic, it's not that far off: no one takes a First and

234

Only Love more seriously than a teenage girl, and when the breakup comes (as it almost inevitably will), it can seem as though life is not worth living. As a veteran of more than one crying jag listening to endless replays of "The End of the World" by Brenda Lee after a particularly bitter breakup, I can kind of relate to Bella's pain — even if I do want to stab her in the neck with a fork and tell her to Get Over It. But what I love about the *New Moon* movie is that it manages to take what seems like hundreds of pages of dispirited woe-is-me-ing and turns them into a clever season-changey montage. ('Cause everybody needs a montage. Even Rocky had a montage.)

And this whole evil-Mormon-indoctrination issue is what drives me most crazy about the people who, on the one hand, scoff at the lack of depth in this series and then, on the other hand, exclaim aghast at the wrongs being done unto our daughters and daughters' daughters by Meyer's patriarchal religion infecting her books. If Meyer, in *Twilight*, is indeed successfully pushing her Mormon women-are-chattels agenda, then clearly the story must transcend mere paranormal teen romance and have deeper meaning, in defiance of the many critics who consider it superficial and inane — it's just that the deeper meaning is not one with which many enlightened, allegedly "liberal" souls happen to agree. As it happens, I'm not a big one for the God stuff either, but plenty of people are, and I don't think there is anything wrong with anyone cleaving to their own beliefs. Why is it we accuse religious folks of being fundamentalist and bigoted, and yet don't for a moment hesitate to call into question their sanity and intelligence, and cavil at their attempts at indoctrination? Don't they have the right to sell their world view in genre as much as scientists and evolutionists? I am secure enough in my beliefs that I don't find them threatened or challenged by the clear articulation (or even subtle insinuation) of someone else's. I even managed to get through *Battlefield Earth* without once feeling the desire to read *Dianetics*.

Besides, Orson Scott Card is a card-carrying Latter-day Saint, as are *Dragonlance* mastermind Tracy Hickman, *The Clone Republic's* Steven L. Kent and *Runelords* architect David Farland, yet there is way less of this "What of the Children?" hysteria bemoaning their unholy influence on impressionable young minds. Is it 'cause they write Science Fiction and High Fantasy, and are therefore considered the province of men? How sexist.

But this debate is not about the merit of the books. This debate is about the movies made of those books, and I just really love them. I do. And you can too!

People, it's easy. Just stop expecting *The Twilight Saga* films to be something they're not. These are not proper vampire films, so stop searching therein for metaphor and meaning (lest it be something Joseph Smith might endorse, apparently). I mean, if you go into a movie that is advertised with impossibly beautiful teens on the poster posed in dramatic clinches and staring soulfully out at you, are you really thinking you'll end up with *Near Dark* or *30 Days of Night*, or, hell, even *Daybreakers*? These are teenage vampire romance films. They're basically *She's All That* with more violence; *A Walk to Remember* with more mythology; *The Sisterhood of the Traveling Pants* with better laundry hygiene. (Do you know those girls never wash those jeans? Gross.)

I happen to like *She's All That* and its ilk, and I really like vampires; combine the two, and it's gold, baby! Diamond, even. And I know that, to some, it's dross at best, or maybe cubic zirconia—at worst, that imitation plating that turns your skin green, or something having to do with a Bedazzler. But that's okay. Y'know what? I don't really like *True Blood*. It takes all kinds, folks.

And some of us like our vampires Bedazzled.

© *Rachel Hyland, 2010*

VAMPIRE MYTHOLOGY
IT TAKES ALL KINDS
by Rachel Hyland

When sharing her thoughts on Laurie London's 2012 novel *Seduced by Blood* a while back, our paranormal romance expert, Amy Sharma, said this:

> *"... vampire lore needs some sort of IEEE standard. Aside from the ridiculous Twilight sparkling, there are some things out there that need to be standardized. Can vamps go outside? (And let's nix the special "vamp sunscreen", that's just lame.) Can they drink any blood, or must it be human? And what about garlic and personal invites into your home and crosses and mirrors? Can they breed? How does one become a vampire? Every time I pick up a vamp book, (which is a lot lately) I have to decipher a new set of vamp rules."*

While this, of course, made me chuckle – Amy's funny – I also disagreed most strongly with its central thesis. Standardizing vampire lore? Making every storybook vampire the same? No! No, no, no, no, no. The very idea was anathema to me, as much as sunlight is to a vampire. Or, at least, as it is to some vampires.

And I like that it that way.

Let's take a look back at the origin of the vampire myth, to that one single point in history about which we can definitively say: "That, right there! That is where the legend of the vampire began!" Oh, wait, sorry, we can't do that, can we? Because humanity's concept of the undead, blood-drinking nightwalker doesn't date back to any particular source, cannot be ascribed to a single story, or historical detail, or even country; the theories behind our belief and/or fear and/or worship of such creatures are as plentiful as are the types of vampire themselves. Was it a Mesopotamian lie conjured to terrify the masses? Was it born out of Slavic religious practice? Was it Vlad the Impaler and his documented cannibalism? Was it people with rabies, or with some other medical condition, perhaps one that necessitated blood transfusions? Did it have something to do with patriarchal societies fearful of female sexuality? None of us knows. Nor will we, most likely, ever.

And it's not like these historically legendary vampires – the lamia (Greek), or mullo (Romany), or Aluka (Hebrew), or mandurugo (Filipino), or ramanga (Madagascan), or Tunda (Colombian), so very etc. – all share the same characteristics, the same powers or even the same dietary requirements as each other. Throughout the millennia, and across the globe, their various appetites and activities have become increasingly multifarious; even in purely Western tradition, vampires (or, to be more ye olde about it, vampyres) don't hold to one single template. So why shouldn't fictional vampires – well, *more* fictional, as in those created by an author as opposed to a cultural tradition – get to be just as diverse and interesting? Here in this very publication, *Geek Speak*'s Editor at Large Kate Nagy and I once offered up Dead and Doing It, a handy-dandy primer to vampire-laden Paranormal Romance and/or Urban Fantasy series, specifying such details as the Mythology, Powers and Weaknesses of their immortal denizens. Varying from the demonic to the magical to the mystically scientific – Lynsay Sands's Argeneau clan are the result of nanobots from Atlantis! – the types of vampire therein mentioned are myriad, and their abilities range from the usual longevity, super-strength and speed to mind-control, flight and assorted telekenetic talents. Catch the gaze of one of Laurell K. Hamilton's Anita Blake-universe vampires, and they'll make you their slave. Startle vampire librarian Jane Jameson, from her eponymous series by friend of *Geek Speak* Molly Harper, and you could find her clinging to the ceiling by only her fingernails. P. N. Elrod's vampire P. I., the noir-cool Jack Fleming, can walk through walls!

Of course, this was only scratching the surface of the vamp-lit then available, and in the two years that have passed since we compiled that (even then) only relatively comprehensive guide, many more versions of vampiric lore have been added to the paranormal landscape, across almost as many subgenres; not to mention all the onscreen incarnations. But no matter what the manner of their making or the degree of their supernatural coolness, there is one thing that pretty much all vampires have in common: the one certain way they can be killed. Oh, they don't all care about garlic, holy water or crosses, and even a stake through the heart isn't necessarily fatal – like with L. J Smith's creations from *The Vampire Diaries*, where it takes a stake made out of only a certain type of wood to affect them – but cut the head off any vampire and/or burn them up, and hey presto, you generally have one even *more* dead vampire. (As you would of pretty much anything, it has to be said.) And it's worth mentioning here that the vampires in Terry Pratchett's Discworld books can actually be reconstituted from ashes with a single drop of blood, so decapitating them and burning them up probably wouldn't help you much.

I love that. I love that there are as many varieties of vampire, and potential vampire slaying, as there are writers' imaginations. Probably the only part of this inherently changeable mythos I don't love is that sometimes the ways in which the vampires are created seem just plain wrong. Oh, I don't mind the blood-exchange concept, or the virus-transmission concept, or even the soul-suppressing demonic possession concept, cf. *Buffy*. Some newborn vampires need to lie in dirt for three days before they rise, others writhe in agony for three days until their humanity leaves them entirely, and still others simply lie unconscious in a deep sleep for three days before awakening with a ravenous thirst—I'm cool with all of that. (Though, why is it always three days? Is it 'cause of Jesus?) But I am less enamored of the vampires who have kids, and not just in a Renesmee-is-the-worst-name-ever way. And do you know that that child's middle name is? Carlie! As in, a hybrid of Carlisle and Charlie. If ever there was an argument against teen pregnancy…

Anyway.

Sympathetic vampires as ancient, lonely, tortured creatures seeking redemption and believing themselves unworthy of love – occasionally while also protecting their species from ruthless enemies, or humans from their ruthless kindred – I can totally get behind. Reluctant, newly-turned recruits into the species, often female who then go on to become private detectives of some kind: oh, yes, absolutely. But related families full of vampires, born and raised – like in Kimberley Raye's Dead End Dating series, for example, where "pureblood" born vampires are the aristocrats of their society, and "turn" when they lose their virginity – I simply don't find as appealing. (With apologies to the wall of "transitioning" vampire hotness that is the Black Dagger Brotherhood.)

Nevertheless, it just makes sense to me that, in the absence of hard truth, in the absence of incontrovertible evidence that This is the Way it Must Be – and even then, Science Fiction novels often mess with established science fact, and they manage to make it work – vampires should come to us in every possible permutation, be they born or made, vicious or pattern cards of every virtue, of extra-terrestrial origin like comic book heroine Vampirella or merely a monstrous parasite like the creeptastic Nosferatu.

Or even, and I cannot stress this enough: sparkly.

© *Rachel Hyland, 2012*

VAMPIRE MYTHOLOGY
ONE LORE TO RULE THEM ALL
by Amy Sharma

First, I must thank my colleague Rachel Hyland for her thoughts on the other side of this debate. I mean, she called me funny, and flattery will get you a lot of places. Based on that, and her persuasive arguments, I was close to just packing it in and giving up entirely on the whole "standardization" thing. (Man, I have less self-confidence then the doe-eyed virgins in these paranormal romance books I keep reading.) Because I agree, creativity is a good thing. If everyone were the same, the world would be a boring place. (Although, if everyone were as perfect as me the world would be a better place, obviously.) But then I got to thinking and a) "You can't be creative if you can't read" and b) "This isn't Nam. There are rules."

It's time to lay some down.

If authors and screenwriters just had a few different takes on vampire mythology, perhaps I wouldn't feel so strongly about this. But, there have been some egregious offenses. Sparkling in the sunlight? Really? And vampire sunscreen? Cheating! Long ago you used to be able to buy a bottle of medicine and easily open it, but then some idiot come along and poisoned the Tylenol, and now it's impossible to get into the packaging without a jackhammer. Just like that, some teen-angst vampire story became a world-wide phenomenon and has ruined the whole subgenre for everyone. There's creative license and then there's stupidity. Thank you, Stephenie Meyer, for your stupidity.

And due to the whole *Twilight*-craziness, now, less than ten years later, we must deal with a plethora of middling quality vampire literature that insists upon just jerking the rules around willy-nilly. For example, I recently read a book were vamps can walk around in the sunlight. Not only is this a pretty outlandish shunning of standard lore, but there wasn't even an explanation. No sparkling, no sunscreen, no anything. There they were, just walking around in sunlight without a care in the world. It pissed me off. I spent the rest of the book waiting for an explanation and I was pretty peeved when none was provided. That, and a few other things about the book, made it pretty un-enjoyable.

Because, in the end, we need rules. We need standards. Have you seen Somalia lately? Aside from the fact that they have modern-day pirates (which is awesome… at least, in theory) it pretty much sucks to live there. Sure, they don't have to pay taxes, but that's about the only bonus to living in an anarchist state. You don't see people lining up to visit.

And books, I like books. They should be nice, pleasant places to visit. Which means when I open one up I shouldn't be in for a world of hurt when just trying to figure out what the back story is. Now, I am not saying books should only contain sunshine and roses and puppies and unicorns. They can have darkness and sorrow and angst and mystery and intrigue. But I would rather focus on getting to know the characters, solving the mystery and connecting with the theme than trying to wrap my head around yet another bit of confusing lore. Getting to know the fictional world can and should be part of the fun journey of the book, but it shouldn't be the main mental task-master.

Rules can be good and bad. But, we live by them every day. For example: physics. Physics is constantly in the driver's seat. It's a pretty strict thing, that physics. And it basically says what we can and cannot do at all times. But has it stifled our creativity? Has anyone besides a frustrated science student been overly constrained by physics? Do you wake up each day and lament: "Curse you, gravity, for keeping the earth revolving around the sun!"? No. In general, we live and die by the rules of physics and life is still pretty awesome.

I am not recommending we go so far and as to be as rigid and unyielding as physics. I am suggesting merely a set of standards that everyone can live and work with. The IEEE Standards Association webpage says:

> *"We are a leading consensus building organization that nurtures, develops & advances global technologies. Our work drives the functionality, capabilities and interoperability of a wide range of products and services that transform the way people live, work and communicate."*

That sounds pretty nice. *[Is "interoperability" even a word? – Ed.]* They are helping the wheels turn more efficiently by easing communication. Things are a lot more understandable when everyone speaks the same language. Let's make a set of vampire standards that we can all live with. It gives every author and every reader equality of opportunity but not equality of outcome. With standards, when a reader opens a vamp-related book he or she has something to lean on and hold onto in this topsy-turvy world. But a good author will still be able bend these standards to his/her will. And a bad author will still be a bad author, even when gifted with a well-defined mythos.

But where does one start? I will concede a point to my opponent in this debate: there is no true "origin" story for vampire lore. Making it hard to trace what is "true" and what is "false" among all the many stories and legends. Who is going to make the standard? Who is going to draw the line in the sand? Where do we draw it? Well, if a bunch of scientists can finally have the courage to declare Pluto not a planet (it isn't – get over it, you whiners), then I think a bunch of geeks can band together and provide some vampire operating standards for people to maneuver in.

So let's get cracking on those standards. Plus, life isn't very interesting if there aren't rules to break.

© *Amy Sharma, 2012*

ABOUT THE AUTHORS

David Baldwin (Film Columnist) was raised on an unhealthy amount of 80s and 90s cinema, and somehow equally admires bloody action sagas and seminal teenage coming-of-age dramadies. If he is not talking about movies or TV shows, he's probably sleeping. He lives in Toronto, mostly so he can conveniently stalk the red carpet of TIFF each year.

In between devising nefarious schemes for world domination, **K. Burtt** (Associate Editor) spends his time reading, gaming, and pretending to be a 14-year-old teenager pretending to be an adult online, because he feels that is an underrepresented group. He lives in Washington, D. C., for good or for ill.

Geonn Cannon (Senior Writer) is a lazy do-nothing who somehow conned people into paying him to write things he would've written anyway, such as four official *Stargate SG-1* stories (two of them, novels), a mystery series about a lesbian werewolf private eye, and the acclaimed, star-studded webseries *Riley Parra*, along with more than thirty other novels. He lives in Oklahoma – and also on Twitter.

William Cashin (Contributing Writer) refuses to participate in any of this.

Rachel Day (Senior Writer) is the pseudonym of a secret spy masquerading as a writer of essays and plentiful fanfic. She may believe (or hope) that she is an alien who accidentally ended up on Earth after a transporter accident. She lives in the UK, where she rereads *Imzadi* on a regular basis and plots to get Jack and Sam together, possibly with the help of the Doctor.

Rachel Hyland (Editor-in-Chief) is, she is pretty sure, the one true queen of Fantastica, raised in obscurity to protect her from the dark lord Sinisterium. If you see her magic sword, get in touch. The fate of the many worlds just may depend upon it. She lives in Melbourne, Australia with too many Pop Vinyls and a fish named Beetroot.

Matt Layden (Contributing Writer) is a film school graduate working in the industry in Toronto, Canada. His love of *Buffy* thrust him into the geek culture world and he's never looked back.

Gabrielle Lissauer (Contributing Writer) is the author of *The Tropes of Fantasy Fiction*. She is a lifelong Los Angeles native.

Jason Luna (Contributing Writer) is a reserve member of the Avengers, so he might get called into action at any moment. Beware his sharp wit and collection of yo-yos. Plus, he knows of kung fu. He lives in Los Angeles, where he befriends dogs.

Malcolm Matthews (Contributing Writer) is a published author, an award-winning poet, a blogger, and a professional freelance editor who would like to be a Predator in his next life. He lives near Niagara Falls – on the Canadian side.

Seanan McGuire (Guest Contributor) writes books. It is extremely difficult to make her stop. When not writing, she can be found watching horror movies, going to Disney Parks, or walking in the corn. Oh, the corn. It remembers you. Come home.

Jason Murdoch (Contributing Writer) is a writer, ninja, wargamer, lover of breakfast, co-creator of the *Unfauxcast Malifaux* podcast and master of his own underwear. He lives in Geelong, Australia with a dog, a wife and *Warhammer* figures.

Chris Nagy (Contributing Writer) was a geek before it was cool and a *Star Trek* fan before he could walk. He can expound for hours on his theory that *Rollerball* predicted the modern NFL. Chris lives in Minnesota, where he entertains his family and plots world domination.

Kate Nagy (Editor at Large) likes: home repair, thunderstorms, 80s references, and the *Lost* finale. Dislikes: home repair, big crowds, bad music, and the Joker in any incarnation. Yeah, she's a little weird. She lives in Falls Church, Virginia; not to be mistaken for Fell's Church, Virginia, where those *Vampire Diaries* people live.

Sara Paige (Columnist) is happy to put her enormous and completely unprofitable knowledge of random pop culture to work. She has lots of unpopular opinions on all sorts of large movie franchises and loves to share them all. She lives in New York, where she harbors a deep and abiding love of all things Anakin Skywalker.

Mark Ritchie (Staff Writer) enjoys long walks to the shop to buy ice-cream. Anime, horror and sci-fi are also main staples of his geeky diet. He lives in Dublin, Ireland, from whence he ignores the existence of those CW superhero shows completely.

Disfigured in a factory accident that warped his brain but expanded his mind, **B. C. Roberts** (Staff Writer) has chosen to use his talents to dissect the high and lows of popular culture. Never short of an opinion or a cranium-splitting headache, he can always be relied upon to fight the twin evils of stupidity and ignorance wherever they arise. He lives in your darkest fears.

Amy Sharma (Contributing Writer) loves giving unsolicited advice, waxing poetical on anything or nothing, and has a weakness for BBQ and romance novels. She lives in Texas, where she hopes to never read about vampires having babies ever again.

Kellie Sheridan (Contributing Writer) is an author of YA and adult books, a vlogger and a dog-addict. Her life is basically all books, all the time. She currently lives outside of Toronto, Ontario, with her husband and their labradoodle.

Kim Sorensen (Comics Editor) has been an avid comic fan since she stole her older brothers' *X-Men* comics in childhood. While currently residing in Georgia, USA, she is on a quest to discover the island of Themyscira – and develop psychic powers. If you can help with either of these pursuits, please let her know.

Regina Thorne (Guest Contributor) is an avid reader of just about everything, an aspiring writer, a lover of old movies and current TV shows, and a hopeless romantic.